CRANKS AND SHADOWS

THE MARIO BALZIC NOVELS

CRANKS AND SHADOWS
BOTTOM LINER BLUES
SUNSHINE ENEMIES
JOEY'S CASE
UPON SOME MIDNIGHTS CLEAR
ALWAYS A BODY TO TRADE
THE MAN WHO LIKED SLOW TOMATOES
A FIX LIKE THIS
THE BLANK PAGE
THE MAN WHO LIKED TO LOOK AT HIMSELF
THE ROCKSBURG RAILROAD MURDERS

K.C. CONSTANTINE

CRANKS AND SHADOWS

THE MYSTERIOUS PRESS

Published by Warner Books

A Time Warner Company

Excerpts from *Zen in the Art of Archery* by Eugen Herrigel, copyright © 1953 by Pantheon, reprinted by permission of publisher.

 Mysterious Press books are published by Warner Books, Inc., 1271 Avenue of the Americas, New York, NY 10020.

 A Time Warner Company

The Mysterious Press name and logo are registered trademarks of Warner Books, Inc.

Printed in the United States of America

First printing: February 1995

10 9 8 7 6 5 4 3 2 1

Library of Congress Cataloging-in-Publication Data

Constantine, K. C.
    Cranks and shadows / K.C. Constantine.
        p.   cm.
    ISBN 0-89296-543-6
    1. Balzic, Mario (Fictitious character)—Fiction.   2. Police
—Pennsylvania—Fiction.   I. Title.
PS3553.0524C73   1995
813\.54—dc20   94-34981
                                                                                        CIP

CRANKS AND SHADOWS

Rumors of layoffs at election time were hardly a novelty in Rocksburg's City Hall. Every election seemed to litter the halls and offices with grungy bits of bad news for public employees, as though every would-be politician believed the surest way to win a cushy public job was to serenade the voters about all the shiftless spongers who already had cushy public jobs. But when President Reagan's economic policies started to trickle down to Rocksburg in the early 1980s, the usual rumors that had warmed up that election turned into something cold with a speed that jolted even the most cynical city employees. City Council took four meetings over four months to dismantle the Sanitation Department. Police Chief Mario Balzic had stood in the city garage, in the shadows near the rear exit, while the city auctioned its two garbage packers to the company that one month earlier had submitted the lowest bid to collect Rocksburg's garbage.

The two men who had driven the packers were transferred to the Street Department, but the four men who had actually emptied the garbage cans and heaved the plastic bags into the packers had started to collect unemployment insurance two weeks later, and the day they received their first checks from the workers' compensation fund, the collection of garbage in Rocksburg had been completely privatized. Balzic found himself wondering if anybody was ever going to completely privatize the workers' compensation fund or the Bureau of Unemployment Security or the Department of Public Welfare.

Next to go had been the city's truck mechanic, followed by the city's auto mechanic, its plumber, and two carpenters, all having been replaced by private contractors as needed, as Mayor Kenny Strohn had said each time he'd called the *Rocksburg Gazette* to announce that he was laying off still more city employees.

Over the months that followed the end of federal revenue sharing, Rocksburg's workforce had been reduced to the Electrical Department, the Street Department, the Police Department, and a secretary and two clerks staffing the mayor's office, and one of the clerks had retired in 1982 and the other one quit when her first child turned out to be twins. By default, the mayor's secretary had become the city's manager, administrator, payroll clerk, and complaint department. Her name was Yolanda Sabo and she used to weigh 180 pounds, and what she was herself complaining most about was she was working so hard she'd lost forty pounds and she wasn't even on a diet.

So when Balzic got a note from her saying that the mayor wanted to see him, the last thing Balzic was thinking about was police layoffs. The note arrived around noon Thursday and said the mayor wanted to see him in the mayor's office at 7 A.M. Friday.

Balzic had long since slipped into complacency as the months waiting for the bad news had turned into years and he'd received no word from the mayor about layoffs in the Police Department. Even though the PD and the electricians and the street workers were all that was left on the public payroll in Rocksburg—aside from Yolanda Sabo—the fact was that years had gone by since the first layoffs shook up city employees. So when Balzic wandered into Yolanda Sabo's office Thursday right before she went home for the night to ask her what was up, he was not even remotely prepared for what she had to say.

"So, Yolanda," Balzic said. "What's the good word?"

"Um, good word, good word, lemme think. Oh. How about, I win the Lotto. I think those would be wonderful words. Yeppie, I win the Lotto and move to L.A. and buy a house next door to Sylvester Stallone. Those would be really good words."

"It's only a manner of speakin', Yolanda. I don't actually need some specific good words, you know?"

"Well, then how about some bad words? You wanna hear any of them?"

"Like what kinda bad words?"

"Oh, how about some of the worst words there ever were." Yolanda was not looking at Balzic as she spoke. She was continuing to work in a pair of ledgers, and then every few moments she would swivel around and type something onto the screen of her computer terminal. "How about layoffs? How about unemployment? How about food stamps? Those words bad enough for you?"

"Layoffs? Unemployment? Hey, Yolanda. You wanna stop what you're doin' and tell me what—is this what the mayor wants to see me about?"

"How about some really bad words, Mario? How about the city's broke? How you like those words?"

"Hey, Yolanda, yo! You wanna stop what you're doin' and look at me, huh? So I can see whether you're pullin' my chain or what?"

She swiveled away from the computer and looked up at him over the rims of her glasses. "You think if I look at you you would be able to tell whether I was makin' this all up? Mario, where have you been for the last ten years—in a coma? This place has been hangin' on by its fingernails ever since Reagan said no more revenue sharin'. What? You think Rocksburg has a sugar daddy someplace maybe? Honey buns, we is out of money. As in b-r-o-k-e. Busted. You know?"

"And the mayor wants to see me?"

"Not just you, honey buns. Everybody. You and the electricians and the street guys, everybody."

Balzic tried to tell himself on the way out to his cruiser that the only surprise was that it had taken this long. If he was being honest about it, he would've had to admit that he had never imagined it possible that the department would have survived Reagan's administration and lasted into Bush's. Over the last nine years, Balzic had often tried to figure out why the mayor hadn't cut the police budget more than he had. Except for putting a freeze on hiring and promotions—which as far as Balzic was concerned was more than enough of a budget cut— the mayor hadn't done anything to destroy the PD, to just wipe it out the way he'd done with Sanitation. When Balzic was feeling charitable about the mayor, the best he could think was that the major had just done nothing, had just let things take their course.

On Friday morning, Balzic got there ahead of everybody else. He'd been up all night wrestling with the numbers in his department, the table of organization, the pay scales, the benefits, trying to make reality look different, trying to turn what was into what he thought it ought to be. Even while he was doing it, he knew he wasn't going to sell his idea of reality to anybody.

He followed Mayor Kenny Strohn into his office and went on the attack. He was full of caffeine convictions and he didn't even say good morning. He just started to ramble. "Mister Mayor, before you say anything I'd like to say something."

"Mario," the mayor said, startled. He'd turned around and spotted Balzic and became flustered. "Mario, good mornin', good mornin'. You're early—"

"Mister Mayor, I have some things that need to be said and I need to say them. Before anybody else gets here."

"Mario, sit down, sit down. Would you like some coffee?"

"No, thanks. I've been up most of the night and I've had enough coffee to float a boat." He continued to stand.

"Up all night? What for?"

Balzic splayed his hands upward. "This."

"Oh." The mayor looked at his shoes and sniffed twice and

let out a noisy sigh. "Mario, is it all right if I make some coffee?"

"No no, go 'head."

The mayor busied himself with the automatic coffeemaker on the table behind his desk. After he'd got it bubbling, he turned back to Balzic and said, "Mario, if you don't mind my saying so, you don't look very well—"

"Uh, Mister Mayor, I don't feel very well. I know what you're gonna do here this mornin', I mean I got it from Yolanda yesterday before I went home, when she sent me this note you wanted to see me—"

"I don't want to just see you, Mario. This isn't about just you. Or me. This isn't—"

"Mister Mayor, you can get carpenters anywhere. Or plumbers. And I'm not puttin' plumbers down, or carpenters, or electricians, or truck drivers. Or for crissake I'm not puttin' down the guys who fix the potholes. But my point is you can get people to do that, you know, private people, and that's okay, but you cannot get private police, it's just out—"

"Mario, my god, what do you think I'm getting ready to do here?"

"Well, see, I don't know what you're gettin' ready to do, but I could not in good conscience let you do anything without tryin' to tell you what I have to tell you."

"Mario, I understand that you are a—"

"Mister Mayor, lemme finish, please."

"Go on. I'm sorry."

"Mister Mayor, we're—the department—we're way short of where we're supposed to be. I have no training officer, I have no juvenile officer, I have one detective. I should have a training officer, I should have a juvenile officer, I should have a PR officer goin' around to all the schools, I should have three detectives. On top of that—"

"Mario—"

"On top of that, I have *no* captains, *no* lieutenants, and three sergeants. I have three sergeants who passed the civil service tests for lieutenant *and* captain. I have six patrolmen who passed the sergeant's test. And not one of these people has been promoted." Balzic leaned forward and stabbed the air with his left index finger. "Mister Mayor, we've discussed this many times—so many times I don't discuss it with my people because they don't want to hear it anymore—but the fact is, Mister Mayor, nobody in my department has been promoted in five years! And—and! Four years ago, the Fraternal Order of Police signed a contract that called for wage increases of thirty cents in the first year, twenty cents in the second, and ten cents in the last year, and that year was up—that contract was history ten months ago. In other words, for ten months they been workin' without a contract, and Mister Mayor, from where I sit, morale in my department is—to put it bluntly—lower than snakeshit."

"Mario—"

"I'm not finished, Mister Mayor."

The mayor canted his head and shrugged slightly. "Go on."

"Thank you, sir." Balzic poked his glasses up the bridge of his nose. "Mister Mayor, we cannot have private police. It just flies in the face of everything we know about what the police are for. What we're about. Rocksburg isn't a goddamn shopping center. We're not a goddamn mall. This is a city. This is everything that a city means. This is . . ."

"Mario, I know full well what it means—or I used to think I knew what it meant." He'd been standing near the coffeemaker, leaning on the bookcase, the fingers of his right hand just touching it. When the coffeemaker stopped bubbling, he fussed nervously with it and finally filled a plain white mug with the coffee and added powdered imitation cream and a full package of sugar substitute.

"I know you do, sir, I know you do, but I'm very worried about this. I mean I've never been as worried about anything as much in my life. I mean, other than personal things."

"I understand, Mario."

"No, sir, I don't think you do. I mean, what you're proposin' is for me to tell people they don't have jobs anymore. And, Mister Mayor, I just—I just don't know how I'm gonna be able to do that."

"I haven't proposed anything yet, Mario."

"Yeah, well that's just 'cause I'm doin' my damnedest to not let you get a word in sideways here." Balzic took a deep breath and with the exhalation felt his shoulders sink lower than he thought they could.

"Mario, some things can't be avoided, they can't be postponed. They—"

"Mister Mayor, you're not—I don't mean to patronize you, but there are some things that can't be shared. I mean, they either are or they aren't. You can try to talk to people about 'em, but it's not the same. It's like a woman tryin' to tell a man what it's like to have a baby. I mean, she can talk till she turns blue, but a man ain't gonna understand, not because the woman can't explain it, but 'cause it's not somethin' the guy is ever going to be able to comprehend. Like I heard some woman try to tell a guy once, you know, just think of the worst constipation you ever had and you'll get just the beginning of it, and the guy looked at her and said, 'Yeah, but I've never been constipated for nine days, never mind nine months,' and she had no comeback, if you know what I mean. You know what I mean?"

"I think so—"

"Well, see, that's the way it is with cops. I mean, I've shared some things with my men—and women—that other people only see in the movies or on TV or maybe they read about it. But I have this feeling with my people that I don't have with anybody else—"

"I'm sure you do, Mario—"

"No, I don't think you are, 'cause as sure as I'm standin' here I know it, you're gettin' ready to tell me I have to lay people off, and I can't do that, I mean, that's just not somethin' I'm capable of doin'. You know, callin' 'em together in the duty room and sayin', you know, uh, you're laid off, I mean, you're— you don't work here, for the city anymore, turn in your shield and your piece. Jesus, how the fuck am I supposed to say that to these guys? Huh? Christ, I could never look at 'em again."

"Well, Mario, I'm truly sorry, I am, but that's exactly what you're going to have to do. I wish I could tell you something else, but I've been over this and over this with our auditor and the solicitor and the other members of the Safety Committee, and there's just no other way for it to come out. We do not have the money. That's the bottom line. That's it. I wish it were otherwise, but it isn't. You have got to eliminate—you have to . . . you have got to—"

"You can't even say it, can you?"

"Yes I can. I can say it. Five officers."

"Five!"

"I'm sorry. Five is the absolute minimum."

"Five!" Balzic fell into a chair. His shoulders started to ache. His neck was tightening up.

"Jesus," Balzic said. "Five . . . Mister Mayor, do you know how long it's been since we've hired anybody?"

"Uh, no, I don't, not offhand."

"That's 'cause we haven't hired anybody since you've been mayor."

"That's eight years in November."

"That's right, sir. Eight years. No. More. Longer. The last group we hired was at least a year before you got elected. And do you know what that means? Huh?"

The mayor swallowed. "It probably means you're going to lose some very experienced people."

Balzic looked at the floor and then at his shoes and then at his thumbnails. "Yes, sir. That's one way to put it."

"Mario, I'm sorry, but there isn't any good way to put this."

"Oh, oh," Balzic said, thrusting his right index finger upward several times. "Mister Mayor, I will not—I repeat—I will not do this at all unless I have your word—in writing—that we are going to do everything humanly possible to get these people other jobs. And not crumb-bum jobs either. I mean jobs as good as they're losin'—am I makin' myself clear, sir? Otherwise, I'm not gonna do it, sir. I mean, I want your blood oath on this, your honest-to-god blood oath that this city is going to provide every possible service to assist these people to find equal employment. And if you're not prepared to do that for them, Mister Mayor, then, goddammit, I will not be the truck carryin' the bad news. I will not. I'll quit first."

"Mario, you won't have to do that."

"I'm tellin' you what I will do and what I will not do."

"I understand that you have a tremendous loyalty to these people—"

"And I'm tellin' you you don't understand!" Balzic jumped up and began to pace. "I tried to tell you it was like my wife tryin' to tell me about havin' our girls! And no matter what she said, it's somethin' I'll never know. That's what it is between cops. It's somethin' *you'll* never know. And you—*you're* tellin' me I gotta tell these people, hey, good-bye, get lost, drop fucking dead. Well, I'll tell 'em, goddammit. But only if you put it in writin' that we're gonna put every available service at their disposal."

"I said we would."

"In writing."

"I will."

"Okay. Then, sir, do it. Now. Please."

"Mario, I think it would be better if I had the solicitor do that. I think he should be the one to write that."

"Mister Mayor, I disagree. I absolutely disagree. I can't think of a worse person to put that in writing. That's exactly what I don't want is a bunch of legal bullshit. And it doesn't make any difference that I personally think our solicitor is a scumball and that we oughta hang the front end of a car around his neck and toss him in the river. I mean, I think that would be a socially beneficial act, but that's not why I don't want him writin' that up. I just want it in plain language. And I'm gonna insist that you do it, sir, or I'm not gonna do what you want me to do."

"Mario, you're making this harder than it needs to be," the mayor said, rummaging through his desk for paper and pen. Having found both, he sat down and said, "Okay okay okay, what do you want me to say?"

"Okay, here it is. You solemnly swear and affirm that you will do everything humanly possible to aid and assist any member of the Rocksburg PD who has become unemployed through no fault of his or her own."

"Okay," the mayor said, writing hard to keep up. "Go on."

"Yes, sir. You swear and affirm that you will put every department and every employee—"

"Every employee? That's me. And Yolanda."

"Yessir. Every employee of the city to work on behalf of the police officers who've been terminated. You have that?"

". . . who have been terminated. Yes, I have it," the mayor said, shaking his head and licking and chewing his lips.

"Okay. Every effort will be made to find employment for said officers."

The mayor nodded. "I have that."

"Okay. This part's very important. You swear and affirm that the city will maintain the health and life insurance for each officer until the officer finds employment or—"

The mayor stopped writing and shook his head. "Mario, that's out of the question. There are federal laws governing that, what insurance protection we have to offer—"

"Wrong, sir. Wrong. That is absolutely *in* the question. I will not participate in turnin' these people loose without minimum protection for them and their families. That's just crap."

"Mario, the idea here is to reduce our expenses. That's first. Second, all we have to provide by federal law is two months' health coverage—and we can't afford more than that—"

"Mister Mayor, we can't afford *not* to afford this. For either a year or until they find employment, whichever comes first."

"Mario, you're not listening to me. Federal law says we have to cover these people for two months, and then all we have to do is offer to let them join our group coverage—"

"For either a year or until they find employment, whichever comes first, so help you God. And sign it. And put your seal on it, too, if you would please."

"Mario, listen to me! If they want to join our group policy we are obliged by federal law to let them, but we are not obliged to pay their premiums, am I getting through to you?"

"Mister Mayor, I'm not gonna tell five officers, that's it, tough shit, the city used you and now the city doesn't need you anymore, go find the unemployment office. And if you get sick or have an accident, hey, fuck you, you figure it out. Nothin'

doin', I'm not gonna say that to these people. I refuse. I'd be totally fucking humiliated to say that to these people."

"Mario, we're not the federal government. By law we have
to balance our budget. We don't have the luxury of deficit
spending, of borrowing money to pay our day-to-day bills—"

"I understand all that—"

"No, Mario, I don't think you do. To use your own anal-
ogy, this is like pregnancy and uh, and uh constipation. I can't
issue a couple of million dollars' worth of bonds on the assump-
tion that a bunch of Arab shieks are going to come in and scoop
them up over lunch. We don't have that kind of indulgence
here. Those guys in Washington, hell, they can do that. The
White House, it doesn't matter who's there if you ask me.
These presidents all talk a great game, Reagan and Bush and I
have to include Carter in this too, because he came waltzing in
there—just like Reagan did, just the same way—talking about
how it's all Washington's fault and you just have to cut out
waste and deregulate this and deregulate that and my god, who
can't see where all that deregulation Carter started got us. You
can lay the S&L mess right on Carter's doorstep, I mean it took
the thieves a couple years to figure out what to do and they just
had a picnic under Reagan, but it was Carter who started it.
But if it weren't for the Japanese and the Dutch and the English and the Arabs and the Germans and god knows who else,
there's no way Reagan could've financed the defense buildup he
got. My god, six hundred ships for the Navy, hell's bells if you
don't have to balance the budget who couldn't buy six hundred
ships? Or anything else for that matter. It's like the fire chief
around here. Everywhere I go, sooner or later somebody says to
me, Eddie Sitko ought to be mayor. He gets things done. And I
have to sit here with my mouth shut and take it. I can't say to
them what I know. Who couldn't get things done—if you do
them the way Sitko does. Anytime he wants to do something,
he just does it. No advertising of bids, no contracts, no trying
to figure out who's trying to screw you, who's trying to work a
kickback. Where does he get the money? Do you know? Huh?
I'll bet there aren't a hundred people in this town who know. I
sure as hell didn't know until I became mayor. But I'm not

Reagan or Sitko. I can't do what they do. When we're out of money, when the city's out of money, we're out of money and that's that."

"Mister Mayor, what I'm gonna say next is not said without serious thought. I gave it a lotta thought last night. If the city does not cover the insurance for these officers, I give you my word, I'll turn this department into a bookmaking operation. We'll book everything, from dog racin' to bingo, the works. I'll put every man I have on every intersection with strip tickets and tickets off the state lottery. I'll have these five officers you wanna lay off, I'll have them hustlin' door-to-door. I'll have auxiliary officers out with canisters just shakin' 'em at every goddamn intersection."

"Mario," the mayor said, sighing and shaking his head, "you can't do that and you know you can't do that, so why even talk like that?"

Balzic leaned forward. "Mister Mayor, who's gonna stop us? The state police? Not without orders from the governor, and the governor isn't that politically stupid. He's runnin' for everything he's worth right now. He's not gonna alienate every goddamn cop in the state, any more than you'd alienate every cop in this city."

"Mario, you're really overreacting here. This is wild."

Balzic spread his hands palms-up. "All I want is health and life insurance for these people until they find another job. What's wild about that?"

"Mario, I've already explained about that. But this stuff about making book and canisters at every intersection and bingo and so on, this is wild. Really."

"Mister Mayor, when this city was a borough, what I'm talkin' about wasn't wild. That was the rule. The burgess used to walk into the duty room when the watches changed and he'd have big envelopes full of raffle tickets and every cop on a walking beat had to take fifty or a hundred. And by god, you better have 'em sold the next day. And I lost count of the times I stood in the middle of Main and Market with a canister, shakin' it at every car that came by, sayin', 'Hey, how 'bout a hand for the Police Pension Fund?' Or the Police Athletic League. Pen-

sion fund my ass. Brought those canisters in, turned 'em over to
the burgess or one of his cronies and never even got a thank-you
for it, never mind a receipt. There wasn't any pension fund.
There wasn't any Police Athletic League. It all went straight
into his pocket and he had the whole goddamn department
moochin' for him. Hell, we made *Time* magazine. We were a
goddamn national embarrassment. A joke.

"And," Balzic stopped pacing and dropped into the chair
across the desk from Strohn and said, "if you don't put it in
writing that these people are gonna be covered for at least a
year or until they find a job, then by god that's what I'll do
again. 'Cause the lesson I learned from that time was nobody
stopped us. The goddamn burgess stopped it himself. Nobody
went to jail. Nobody even got indicted. Everybody may've been
laughin' at us, but nobody busted us. But this time, I'll do it in
front of newspaper and TV cameras."

"Mario," the mayor said, shaking his head slowly, "it's
been said all kinds of ways but it doesn't matter how you say it
it comes out the same: you can't get blood out of a stone. I
know you know what I'm talking about. All you have to do is
step out onto Main Street and look at the stores that used to be
here. Two department stores, a five-and-ten, at least two clothing stores, and two shoe stores and what do we have instead?
Empty buildings. Landlords exonerated from real estate taxes
'cause they have no income. Hell, the Tessmeyer family has
been trying to give us their building for five years and we won't
take it because that'll mean we have to maintain it until we
find a buyer. *They* haven't found a buyer. *We* sure as hell aren't
going to find a buyer. And the building sits there. Doesn't generate any income for them, doesn't generate any taxes for us.

"Do you know what really disturbs me, Mario? There is
not one food market within ten blocks of Rocksburg Manor.
All those old people have to wait on the vans in order to buy
food. Every one of the retail food chains has abandoned this
town as a market. And according to the last census, we have
nineteen thousand people living here! Of course we don't have
that many anymore—probably more like seventeen thousand—"

"Last census said it was closer to fifteen," Balzic interrupted him.

"Yeah, well, you're right, of course. But what kind of food markets do we have? Aside from that little place down the block from the courthouse, and Brunelli's down there near the railroad arch, I mean, what do we have? That's it. All we've got are those damn mini-marts with the self-serve gas stations. And the prices they charge are outrageous. They're not grocery stores anyway. All they sell is junk food."

The mayor put his pen down and pushed the paper around this way and that. Then he picked up the pen and flipped it end over end slowly. It was some moments before he spoke. "Mario, there are times when I—well, let me start again.

"I've known you for almost eight years now, and I have to say that, in all honesty, I've learned a lot from you. A lot of it was, to be perfectly honest, well, it wasn't things I necessarily wanted to learn. And I—quite frankly, I resented you for that. Winston Churchill said a good thing one time. He said, I'm always willing to learn, but I'm not always willing to be taught. I don't know if those were his words exactly, but I'm sure that's what he was trying to get at. Anyway, I didn't always like you teaching me. Sometimes . . . many times I resented it. And I resented you.

"Sometimes I asked myself why I ever wanted this job in the first place. Especially with you hollerin' at me. And I'm used to being hollered at. I mean, if you're mayor in a city of seventeen thousand people—"

"More like fifteen."

"—yeah, fifteen, whatever, I keep forgetting the census. But what I was saying, if you're mayor long enough, you're going to get hollered at by every darn person in this city, but, boy, it used to gall me when you did it. I used to say to my wife, 'Who does he think he is?' And she'd say, 'He's the chief of police. Fire him! And get one who'll do what he's told.' And I'd say, yessir, that's exactly what I should do. Fire him. He's an opinionated, profane, arrogant, insolent, insubordinate, uh, uh, generally crazy person. And a little bit dangerous. And and and you scare me and I guess that's why I never fired you."

The mayor leaned back in his chair and nodded several times quickly. "There. There it is. I said it. You scare me."

Balzic looked at his shoes and then at the mayor. "Mister Mayor, what scares you isn't me exactly. It's the thing I was tryin' to tell you about before, about what's between me and my people. Every day, every night, every watch, every time we come in we know some shitty thing could happen. All my life, I've heard people make fun of traffic cops, but, Mister Mayor, nobody who hasn't done it will ever know how scary it is to stand in the middle of an intersection during rush-hour traffic. You do that long enough and one day you'll realize there was a split second there when you were within an inch of your life, or where, if you didn't die, you were within an inch of spendin' the rest of your life havin' somebody roll you over to keep your sores from gettin' infected. Mister Mayor, thinkin' about things like that does somethin' to you that people who don't have to think about those things just don't understand.

"Mister Mayor, I know you heard what happened to Kellner last week."

"Yes I did."

"Well he was writing parkin' citations like he's been doin' for about fifteen years. He's had every problem you could ever have over a goddamn piece of paper worth seven bucks and costs—or so he thought. So he's writin' one up and here comes this guy in his best Sears and Roebuck polyester suit and he stands there until Kellner finishes and never says a word and Kellner asks him if that's his vehicle and the guy nods, yeah, it's his, and so Kellner shows the guy where the grace box is and hands him the citation and off he goes. He doesn't get two steps away and he hears that sound, that unmistakable click click, there is no other sound like it, it's a revolver bein' cocked, and so he turns around and there it is, on the other end of the polyester suit, a .38-caliber Smith and Wesson. About two yards from Kellner's face. The guy hasn't said a word yet. He's shakin' so bad he pulls the trigger and there's no tellin' how far he missed Kellner, probably half a foot."

"I already said I know about this," the mayor interrupted Balzic.

"I'm sure you do, sir." Balzic examined his fingernails. "I won't belabor the point then."

"Well, Mario, uh, you haven't even made your point."

"Huh? Oh. Yeah. My point is that what Kellner did is what scares you. About me, I mean. Because Kellner just went nuts. Instant insanity. The guy's still in intensive care up in Conemaugh, and when he gets out of there, he's gonna spend a long time in some rehab center learnin' how to walk and use his hands again. Kellner never even drew his piece and never used his baton, he just went nuts. It was all fury and fear. But neither one—fury or fear—kept him from functioning. Which was the difference between him and the shooter. The shooter was more irrational than Kellner—until he fired. Then it's anybody's guess who was more irrational. But after that, after the shot was fired, Kellner did what he did in spite of his emotion. And the shooter didn't. So that's my point. I know exactly what kept Kellner goin'. And I think that's what scares you about me. But, really, Mister Mayor, it's true of all cops—all the ones I've ever known anyway."

Neither of them said anything for what seemed a long time. It wasn't even a minute. Then Balzic said, "Mister Mayor, that's why you can't just dump these people. That's why I won't let you."

"Mario, what you just said about not letting your emotions affect what you do applies to me too. No matter how much I personally value those five officers, no matter what I feel about them, that doesn't change what I have to do. The finances of this city says as clear as anybody can say it that five members of your department have to be furloughed, I mean indefinitely, and that's all there is to it. I regret it, I feel terrible about it, but it's going to be done no matter how terrible I feel.

"And it's going to be done," the mayor went on, "no matter how much you scare me. It's going to be done for the very simple reason that we can't meet the payroll. And I'll tell you quite truthfully: I'm more afraid of that than I am of you."

Sgt. Vic Stramsky brought the five personnel folders in and put them on the desk in front of Balzic.

"Uh, Mario, you got a minute?"

Balzic snorted and laughed. "I got hours and hours. That's what it's gonna feel like tellin' these guys."

"Well that's what I wanna talk to you about."

"Hey, sit down. Talk to me."

Stramsky eased onto a straight-backed chair, his Slavic face looking to Balzic more jowly than usual, his eyelids puffier, his sideburns grayer, his fingers thicker.

"You wearin' trifocals, Vic?"

"Yeah. Just got 'em last week. Five years ago I never even wore glasses. Now I'm wearin' fuckin' trifocals. This stuff do creep up on ya."

"How are they? God, it took me years to get used to bifocals. They still piss me off sometimes."

"Yeah yeah, me too. 'Specially in the grocery store, you know, you're tryin' to check out the price on either the top shelf or the bottom shelf, the top shelf your head's back, your mouth's hangin' open, you're thinkin' any second now you're gonna start droolin', or—hey, or or, the only way you can read the prices on the bottom shelf is get down on your goddamn hands and knees and throw your head back, right? Am I right?"

Balzic nodded, laughing.

"Yeah, and then you wonder about those advertisin' guys, you know, the ones that measure your eye blinks and all that and they put in those goddamn scanners, right? So they wouldn't have to put a price tag on each thing, right? They're savin' money, right? Meanwhile since I got bifocals, I don't buy nothin' off the top shelf or the bottom shelf ever since they put those fuckin' scanners in the checkouts. I wonder if those fuckin' advertisin' guys ever thought about that, huh?"

"Yeah, right right," Balzic said. "I remember, my wife got bifocals long after I did and I told her, I said, hey, you gotta practice the posture, you know, throw the head back, the mouth drops open, and after you get that right you realize you just moved on to a new stage of life. You just went from a regular human being to a geezer. In her case, a geezerette."

"Right, right," Stramsky said, rocking with laughter. He

nodded many times and then grew pensive. "Which brings me up to what I wanna talk to you about."

"What's that?"

"Hey, face it. I'm a geezer."

"C'mon."

"Nah, it's true. Royer and Rascoli came over the house Sunday, we grilled up some kolbassi, drank a case of beer, sat around tellin' war stories, and what we decided was, we were three geezers and it was . . . it was time to get out."

"Come on."

"No, seriously, Mario."

"Christ, you're a young guy, Vic."

"Maybe as far as civilians go I'm a young guy, but, hey, face it, I been in the department twenty-seven years. I went from high school to the Air Force to here. Been here for twenty-seven years. Royer started six months before I did. Rascoli started two months after me. We should've retired two years ago. All of us. And if we go now, three of those guys won't have to." Stramsky nodded toward the files in front of Balzic.

Balzic shook his head. "Christ, Vic, I can't remember a time when you weren't in the department."

"Hey, you better recheck your memory banks, buddy boy. You were here when I started. You can't remember when *you* weren't in the department."

Balzic nodded and shrugged as though to say, yeah, right, me and the department, when *wasn't* I in the department? After that wave of nostalgia passed, he focused on Stramsky and said, "So, uh, this is serious, this retirement stuff?"

"Mario, face it. It's time for me to be a rent-a-cop. It's time I plunked my ass down in front of a bunch of TV screens somewhere, who knows, some goddamn college somewhere. What the hell am I now? I ain't a cop. I ain't been a cop for ten years. I'm a goddamn dispatcher, a fuckin' switchboard operator. And if this town was run right, a civilian would be doin' my job."

"Royer feel this way too?"

"Hell yeah. Sure he does. I don't know how many times he

told me, hey, I'm gettin' paid under false pretenses, I ain't a cop. Meantime, both of us should've made captain . . . long time ago. Rascoli too."

"There's nothin' I can say about that—"

"Hey, you don't have to say nothin'. I didn't tell you this to get stroked. I know where you stand. I know where the city stands. It ain't your fault. None of us holds anything against you. It's just, you know, this shit's gettin' old. I mean, if you ain't movin' up, you know, it's time to move on—especially if you're lookin' at a decent pension. And we are. Christ, we got no kick there. I know I can walk outta here tomorrow and I ain't gonna be pushin' everything I own around in a shoppin' cart. I'll live good, good as anybody like me deserves to live."

"So, uh, you really want me to start the paperwork?"

Stramsky nodded. "Yes, sir, I do."

"Royer and Rascoli? You speakin' for them?"

"Yes, sir, I am. They have authorized me to speak for them in this matter."

"Jesus, Vic . . . ," Balzic said, his voice breaking.

"I know," Stramsky said. "Sunday we—we bawled like babies . . . it was probably the beer. Drank a whole fuckin' case."

It was an hour after Stramsky's watch had gone. Balzic had found the applications for retirement and filled out a sample and then attached it to the personnel files for Stramsky, Royer, and Rascoli, and then had dropped them all into Yolanda Sabo's incoming basket. Now here he was, back at his desk, looking at the five personnel folders Stramsky had delivered earlier.

It didn't matter to Balzic that with the retirements of Stramsky, Royer, and Rascoli—no matter how bureaucratically long that might take—only two officers would have to be furloughed of the five whose files lay on his desk. What mattered to Balzic was that he was going to lose three sergeants, three intelligent, unflappable deskmen and dispatchers. It might be true, as Stramsky thought, that civilians ought to be doing the dispatching. But Stramsky didn't recognize his own value. He handled things over the phone that would have sent a civilian in search of the city solicitor. So did Royer and Rascoli. The city could switch over to the countywide 911 dispatching system and there would be no technological loss. All that switchover would require was a decision by City Council to join the system and to figure out how to collect the taxes to pay the bill, which would cause a howl among the citizens, but, hell, Balzic thought, that's the politicians' problem.

What was going to be lost when Stramsky, Royer, and Rascoli went was their craftiness, shrewdness, guile, that combination of the knowledge of the law and the sense to ask the right questions to determine whether what a caller needed was a sympathetic ear or a court order or two officers in a black-and-white ready to put a piece against somebody's head. What else was going to be lost mattered even more to Balzic. No matter who left the department, it was going to be understaffed by even five more bodies. He had thirty members now. There should have been thirty-five. And now, no matter which names were removed from the roster, what was left would add up to twenty-five, and there was no way in heaven or hell that twenty-five officers could adequately police a city of 15,000 population—13,000 was what the number was going to be when the 1990 census numbers came in—not as long as there were 168 hours in a week. You could divide seven days into twenty-five patrolmen until you wore out a pencil, but there was no pencil magical enough to change the fact that there were 18.5 shifts in the week and twenty-five officers to cover them, which meant, furthermore, that for 9.5 of those shifts you were going to have two officers on duty, and for the rest of the time, you were going to have one officer on duty. And if the City Council decided not to go with 911 dispatching? Balzic could not make the pencil he was holding do *that* kind of arithmetic. He threw the pencil against the wall and took off his glasses and rubbed his eyes with the backs of his index fingers. Jesus Christ, he thought, Jesus Christ himself couldn't police this town under these circumstances, and here I am and not only can't I walk on water, I can't even swim.

Who the hell am I going to lay off? And how am I going to tell them? How the hell am I going to get the words out without throwing up?

A knocking at his door startled him out of his moral doldrums. He had been unable to move for more than five minutes. He felt his head come up slowly, as though he were underwater, and then his mouth open and form the words "Come in," but it was all slow motion and the sound was wavily distorted. He half expected to see bubbles come out of his mouth.

"Chief? Got a minute?" It was Mary Margaret Duda, a meter maid who for eight years had been bugging him to make her a "real" cop, a patrolman—woman—with a piece and a baton and handcuffs and an honest-to-god beat instead of the parking meters of the Rocksburg business district.

"I got lotsa minutes," Balzic said, the sound of his voice returning to normal in his own ears. He wasn't underwater anymore. "Come on in. Sit down. What's on your mind?"

"A couple of things," she said, drawing up a chair beside Balzic's desk. Her physical presence—no matter how many times he'd been aware of it—always surprised him. She had powerful arms and shoulders from years of lifting weights. She could bench-press 250 pounds, she'd won the Rocksburg Police and Fire Departments' annual ten-kilometer run for the last six years in a row, and was the third best pistol shot in the department. At last year's Hose Company Number One's carnival, she'd flattened a fireman who'd questioned her gender and her gender preferences. She'd put him on the ground and subsequently in the emergency room with one foot and one fist. In addition to that, she was just a few courses shy of a bachelor's degree in criminal justice, all earned at night over the eight years she'd been a member of the department.

Balzic tried to casually move the personnel folders to a corner of his desk. Duda's eyes followed his hands. Her folder was among them. He cleared his throat and asked again what was on her mind.

"Is one of those folders mine by any chance?"

"Ummm, yes."

"Then it's true."

"What's true?"

"C'mon, Chief. I don't want stardust pumped up my dupa. We're history, right?"

"Who's *we?*"

"Oh come on!" she said.

"Okay, okay, your folder's there. It's there, it's there."

"So we're all gone? Riccardulli, Lawrence, Yesho, Metikosh, and me, right?"

"No. That's not right. It would've been right. But Stramsky and Royer and Rascoli have put in for retirement. So, unless something changes, only two, uh, only two of you will have to, uh, you know . . ."

"Which two?" she said, her gaze piercing.

"Jesus Christ, Duda, I don't know," Balzic said, his voice cracking. "I don't know how the hell I'm supposed to do this. I've never had to do it before. I don't know how to do it, I don't want to do it, it makes me sick just thinkin' about doin' it. Besides, who the hell told you? I just found out about it a couple of hours ago myself and I didn't tell anybody but—"

"Nobody told me. But it might as well have been on the bulletin board. Jeez, that's all anybody's been talking about for months."

"Yeah, yeah," Balzic grumbled. "Everybody might've been talkin' about it, but I didn't get the word officially until a couple of hours ago. The mayor said I got to—I got to let five of you go. Then Stramsky says he wants me to move the retirement papers for him and Royer and Rascoli, so that means only two of you gotta go."

Duda shrugged and nodded her head several times nervously. "So, uh, throw our names in a hat, right? The first two you pull out have to go, the rest stay."

"Oh no. I'm not puttin' anybody's names in any hat and I'm sure as hell not pullin' any names out. I don't want that on my head. Besides, I don't know if that's the fairest way."

"Whatta you mean not the fairest? We were all sworn in together. Lawrence, Riccardulli, Yesho, Metikosh, and me."

"I know who you are, Duda. I got your folders right here."

"Well then all you have to do is look at the date when we took the oath."

"I don't have to look at it. I remember it. We haven't sworn anybody else in since."

"So what fairer way is there?"

"I don't know, Duda, okay? I just think I ought to think about it for a while first, you know?"

"Well why prolong it? The sooner you do it, the sooner the ones that are out can start looking for something else."

Balzic rubbed his temples. "Duda, I appreciate where you're comin' from on this, but this is gonna be a real pain to decide, you know? And if you don't mind, I'll decide when I'm ready. After I've given it plenty of thought. Okay?"

Duda shook her head and said, "Hey, I'm just telling you what I think, that's all. I know it's your decision. I'm just thinking that if I'm one of the ones to go, I'd want to know about it as soon as I could. Can't blame me for that."

"Duda, aren't you supposed to be out writin' citations or somethin'?"

"Ha-ha. Very funny. My watch was over before I came in here. Jeez, I almost forgot the reason I came in."

"Which is what?"

"My cousin lives out in the township, you know, pretty far out in the boonies and he's been bugging me to talk to you about something."

"Me? About somethin' happenin' in Westfield Township?"

"Yeah. He called the state police and the National Guard and nobody there knows anything about it. Or if they know, they're not talkin'. So he told me to ask around."

"About what?"

"Well, I'm not real sure about this. If I hadn't checked with a couple of his neighbors I wouldn't even be asking. My cousin's been known to hit the brewskis pretty hard. So when he first called me, I thought, you know, yeah, right, he's starting to hallucinate behind all that beer. But the neighbors back him up. So I have to ask you."

"So ask."

"Well, seems there was this helicopter flying around out there for the past two weekends, guys with camouflage clothes, rifles, you know, M-16s, grease on their face and stuff like that, they're coming down ropes? Rappelling? You know what I mean?"

"I know what you mean. They always show guys doin' that in those recruiting commercials for the Army. On TV."

"Yeah, yeah, that's exactly what my cousin said. But what he can't figure is, they're not doing it out of an Army chopper, 'cause it's blue and white like the state police chopper, but he says that on the blue body, plain as day, in white letters is 'Mercy 2.' And his neighbors back him up exactly. No variations. Down to the same number of guys. Eight. You know anything about this?"

Balzic frowned. "Nothing."

"Well neither do the state police or the National Guard. I called them both."

"And it says 'Mercy 2' on it?"

"That's what they say."

"Well 'Mercy 1' is a medevac chopper outta one of the Pittsburgh hospitals. They've had that for five or six years, maybe longer. D'you call them?"

"Yes. I did. And that's the part I don't like. Nobody there wanted to give me a straight answer. They kept putting me on hold, dancing me around. I got a very uncomfortable feeling."

"Did you think of callin' Mutual Aid?"

Duda shook her head no. "I don't know why, I never thought of that. I guess I should've, huh?"

"You might give 'em a call. You never know what those people are up to. You know, they're like the goddamn firemen. They never tell anybody anything unless they absolutely have to. It's like with this thing's been goin' on now for months with the firemen and the mayor and the councilwoman, you know what I'm talkin' about?"

Duda nodded.

"See, that woman, the councilwoman. I gotta tell you, I feel for her. She makes a simple request: she wants to see their books. She's tryin' to prepare a budget, here they are, the city pays all the utilities and maintenance on all those hose company buildings, and she says, hey, open up the books. You guys have all these social clubs, you rent these halls out for weddings and bingos and you never tell anybody how much money you make and the city keeps payin' the utilities and the upkeep on the buildings and the city doesn't know—the city has *never* known—how much money these guys have got. So I've heard rumors that Hose Company Number One, the one out by the high school, I've heard that one alone has a hundred thousand invested in mutual funds. And they don't even pay their own goddamn electric bill. And you know their social club's jumpin' every weekend. Bingo every Friday, Saturday, and Sunday until ten o'clock, and then they start dancin', polkas on Fridays and Saturdays and then they get those, uh, disc jockeys on Sunday nights. Christ, they pack 'em in out there. And meanwhile, the city pays their water, electric, sewage, garbage—hell, the city pays a guy to cut their goddamn grass. And they been stonewallin' that woman and the mayor for like eighteen months now. And now I get the joyful noise I got to lay off five people—well, two, after those guys retire. I'll tell you what, Duda, that's bullshit. But I don't know anything about this helicopter, this 'Mercy 2.' This is news to me."

Balzic walked into Muscotti's just as three students from the secretarial school next door were leaving. He slid his rump onto a stool next to Panagios Valcanas, a stool that had moments ago been occupied by one of the secretarial students.

Valcanas pushed his straw hat back as he stood up to gaze wistfully at the departing future secretaries. He loosened his tie, stretched his neck, gave his crotch a tug, then hoisted himself back on his stool.

"Mario," he said, "a man reaches a certain age, he finds himself staring after women as they walk away from him. There's a certain hunger there—aw shit, I think I'd probably get more satisfaction if I started smokin' again."

"What the hell's this—women walkin' away from you and you wanna start smokin' again? Is that what you're talkin' about?"

"It's more complicated than that. It's just that I'm so goddamn sick of watching women walk away from me, and yet, there is no more pleasant sight than watching feminine hips swaying to life's hormonal rhythms . . . ah, Vincent! Service here, please!"

"Hormonal rhythms?"

"What's it gonna be for you?" said Vinnie, the bartender.

"What kind of wine the old man open today?"

"The old man," Vinnie said disgustedly, "didn't open no wine today. The old man ain't opened no wine in two days. The old man is drinkin' Canadian Club. And at the rate he's drinkin' it, he's gonna need the second team in here about five minutes after he starts his game and if he thinks I'm gonna play second team again tonight, he's fulla shit. So what were you sayin'?"

"What kind of wine you got reasonably cold?"

"Hey, my cousin told me—you know Louie, my cousin?"

Balzic nodded and said, "I busted him about six times, why wouldn't I know him?"

Vinnie held up his hands. "Hey, we all know about Louie and his firecrackers. So forget about that. Louie just come back from Abruzzi. And he told me—and you know me, I don't even like wine—but, no shit, you gotta try this. Louie told me, and I'm tellin' ya, this montepulciano is the greatest. For the price? Biggest fuckin' bargain in the state store. Three-eighty-six. Meanwhile, what makes you sick is Louie was payin' ninety fuckin' cents a bottle over there. He went over for two weeks, he stayed a fuckin' month, you believe that? Huh? Here, lemme get this for you."

Balzic turned to Valcanas. "Hormonal rhythms?"

"It's just the hips. What can I tell you? When you know they're always walkin' away from you, you just find yourself trying to search for the significance of their departure. But then, you can't always see things in terms of rejection, you know? If you do, pretty soon, walkin' away's a curse. So, uh, you know, you see what you see and you hunger for it and it's like you're on a generational diet, you know, so you find some polysyllabic words to hang on the reality."

"Here," Vinnie said, putting a glass full of red wine in front of Balzic, "try this."

Balzic did. "You're shittin' me. Three-eight-six a bottle? For this?"

"Ninety cents in Italy," Vinnie said. "How sick does that make you?"

"Pretty sick," Balzic said. "Jesus, we need to get our asses on a boat or somethin'. This is wonderful."

"I told ya, see? Louie's a fuckup, but he knows his grape juice."

Balzic turned back to Valcanas. "What the hell are you talkin' about—generational diet? What the hell is that?"

"It's not worth a moment of your time to worry about," Valcanas said ponderously.

"How long you been here today, Greek?"

"Hours. Hours and hours and hours. Why?"

" 'Cause you're not makin' a whole lotta sense."

"Well that's because it's a goddamn nonsensical world, and I just don't really enjoy being part of it."

"What happened?"

"What happened. Ha. I'll tell you what happened. My good friend the president judge called me yesterday morning at nine o'clock and said the public defender's office was all jammed up and this accused felon was indigent and I had to take his case. So I go read the papers and what do we have? Huh? We have a guy who rapes his wife who's filed for divorce and while he's raping her he's carving her up with a tile knife, one of those ones with the little hook on the end? Put fifty-two little love cuts in her arms, shoulders, chest, and face. And in answer to your next question, 'cause there are fifty-two cards in a deck, why else? Naturally, that's why you cut your wife fifty-two times. While you're raping her. 'Cause she's divorcing you."

Balzic scowled quizzically and waited.

"So you wanna know how come I'm drunk out of my mind, right?"

Balzic shrugged.

"So I'll tell ya. So the two state cops who partner this thing, both of them think the other one filed the affidavit of probable cause and got the search warrant. So when no one an-

swers their knock at this guy's trailer, neither one of them has any need to flash any paper, right? So they just go boppin' on in, find him, find the bloody clothes and the bloody tile knife and they take him to jail, take the rest all back to the lab and— ta-da! They look at each other and right about that time I guess was then they figured out how they screwed their case. Meanwhile, I've just come from a very brief conversation with the victim, 'cause I had this bright idea I might learn something from talking to her."

Valcanas tossed down half his gin.

"So I called the president judge and I said no thank you very much, I'm not doin' this one. And he said you know better than that, ta-da, ta-da, and I told him that there was no case and I was goddamned if I was gonna be the one responsible for seeing to it that this scum walked. So what do you think Vrbanic says to me, huh? He tells me a lecture. Yeah. A goddamn lecture he tells me about the rights of the accused to counsel. About five fucking minutes of his best judicial wisdom he gives me. And I gotta listen to it. And when he's done, I say to him, 'Your Honor, you owe it to me, you owe it to yourself, and you owe it to the victim to spend about ten minutes with her. And then you need to spend about one minute with those two yo-yos who're tryin' to impersonate police officers. And when you've done that, then—and only then—do you have the right to tell me I have to defend this scum. Anybody can walk the sonofabitch, but it's not gonna be me.'"

"Well," Balzic said, his head nodding and his shoulders rocking, "you're to be commended for your, uh, for your outstanding and exemplary and really first-class moral outrage. It's some of the best I've seen all day."

Valcanas snorted. He emptied his glass and set it down with a bang. "Innkeeper! More inebriation!"

"How many fuckin' times I gotta tell you," Vinnie said. "This ain't no inn, and I ain't no keeper."

"Just pour, all right?"

"See? Now that's orders I can understand. How 'bout you? More magic from Abruzzi?"

"Absolutely," Balzic said.

Valcanas groaned and slumped onto his stool.

"What's the matter with you?"

"See for yourself."

"Well well well," came the thin, raspy voice of Joe Radosich, the man nicknamed Joe Radio. He was nearly as wide as a door, barely five feet five, and so bowlegged from a childhood encounter with rickets that if his legs had been straight he probably would have stood six feet tall or more. "The chief of police himself." Radosich gave Balzic a backhand punch in the arm. "This seat taken?"

"Why you askin' me?"

"Just bein' polite, Chief. I don't care if it's taken or not. It's taken now. Hey, Vinnie! Remember me?"

"Who the hell could forget you?" Vinnie said. "What the hell you doin' in here? You runnin' for somethin'?"

"Nah, whatta you talkin' about?"

"Hey, the only time I ever see your face in here is when you're campaignin', don't give me that shit. So is there an election comin' or what?"

"I'm not runnin' for anything, listen to him, Balzic. Guy can't come around and see his old friends, what the hell."

"You know what?" Vinnie said. "Last time you came around here was four years ago, 'cause after you got your ass waxed in that one, you went bye-byes, pal. So you're here now, so you ain't gonna try to tell me you ain't runnin' for somethin'!"

"Vinnie Vinnie Vinnie, in the immortal words of the boss himself, it ain't whether you win or lose, it's how often you get to Vegas, or Miami, or in the old days, Havana. Whatta you say, Greek, remember Havana, huh? Before those commie bastards ruined everything? Huh? Should've been there, Balzic. That was city government the way city government's supposed to work, know what I mean?"

"I'll bet."

"You drinkin' somethin' or you just gonna make a speech?"

"Hey, hey, give me a vodka and orange juice. Give these fellas what they're havin' too."

"I'm fine," Balzic said.

"Me too," said Valcanas.

"Well, next time, next time," Radosich said, rubbing his stomach with both hands and sniffing. "No place in Rocksburg smells like Muscotti's. They try, they try, but they just don't make it. Ah well, you either got it or you don't, huh, Balzic?"

"Got what?"

"The atmosphere, the whattayoucallit, the atmosphere. When you stop in a place, you know you're in the right place or you don't. Smells right, looks right, sounds right, but mostly it smells right. Ever since I was a kid I used to love to stand outside saloons and smell 'em. Beer and smoke and onions on the grill, hey, if somebody put that stuff in a bottle I'd wake up every morning and rub it all over me. I love it. Love it!"

"One vodka and orange juice. That'll be two bucks."

"How much?"

"Two bucks. One deuce."

"Two bucks! You got some kind of face. I can get a bottle of Stolichnaya for less than eleven bucks. You're gonna sell me an ounce and a half of bar vodka for two bucks?"

"What can I tell ya," Vinnie said. "Vodka's cheap. It's the fuckin' OJ that's tough. Lotsa frost down there in Florida."

"It's August for crissake."

"Joe, I'm just a dumb bartender, I don't understand all this high finance. Maybe there ain't no frost, maybe it was a train got derailed or somethin'. All I know is price of orange juice is tough now."

"You little pisser you, huh? You always were a pisser. Two bucks, huh? Cheesus."

"So, uh, hey, Joe, what *are* you doin' here?" Balzic said, sipping his wine and searching Radosich's face.

"Hey, Mario, why you lookin' at me like that? Huh? I just came around to see how old Muscotti's was doin', that's all. But I'll tell ya what, the needle on the old paranoia meter's just creepin' right up there in this place. Christ, you three guys look like a grand jury waitin' to get sworn in, I'll tell ya."

"Radio, I'll be honest with you," Balzic said, "things *are* a lot duller since you aren't on Council anymore."

"See there, Vince? Huh? You got it straight from the chief himself—things're duller since I ain't around. I'll tell you, that's the nicest thing anybody said to me since I don't know when. I'll tell you when. That's the nicest thing anybody said to me since old Judge McClintock said, 'Divorce granted.' "

"Which wife was that?" Vinnie said.

"That was number three—I think. Maybe it was number four." Radosich howled and smacked Balzic on the shoulder. "Hey, you still married to Ruthie?"

Balzic nodded.

"Well by god you tell her Joe Radio said hello and good luck and long life. I always liked Ruthie. Course I never saw what the hell she saw in you, but, hey, there's no accountin' for taste, huh?" Radosich jabbed Balzic on the arm. "You know I'm kiddin', 'cause, you know? I always envied you, Mario. I could tell you had a great marriage, yeah, a really great marriage, and I always envied that and I respected you because of that. Yessir. Now me, see, I like marriage, I like it a lot. I must. I keep doin' it! But, ha! See, my problem is I keep gettin' the wrong women to do it with." Radosich was laughing and drinking at every pause throughout this speech. "One of these days I'm gonna run into that nympho mute with a beer distributorship and then I'm gonna have it made, I'm tellin' ya, huh?"

"So, Joe, uh, what the hell are you doin' here, I mean, other than givin' a speech about what a great thing marriage is—I mean, one of the things about you, Radio, was you were always hustlin' somebody. So, uh, who ya hustlin' now?"

"Funny you should bring that up, Mario. I mean I gotta admit what you say is true, that's right. I mean, I do sorta have that reputation. But, uh, in this case, really, old friend, all I'm doin' here is just sorta renewin' old acquaintances, keepin' my ear close to the barstools, you know, tryin' to listen to who's tryin' to shit who, if you know what I mean, huh?"

"Yeah? So who is?"

"Who's what?"

"Who's tryin' to shit who?"

"Oh, yeah, I get ya now." Radosich finished his drink and waved to Vinnie, who was at the end of the bar near the kitchen, to fill them up, all around.

Balzic and Valcanas both put their hands over their glasses.

After Vinnie had refilled Radio's drink, Radio said, "You know, I was on Council for sixteen years and I've been in politics and union work all my goddamn life, and I've never seen anything as uh, as uh, as uh, what do I wanna say here? Oh. Yeah. Divisive, that's the word. I never seen anything as divisive in this city like this thing between the volunteer firemen and the mayor and that councilwoman—what the hell's her name?"

Balzic snorted and smiled. "You can't remember her name? You're slippin', Joe. You would've never tried anything that lame—"

"Okay okay, so it was pretty lame. Pathetic, I guess. I might not remember her name exactly, but I know exactly how many votes she beat me by. Does that satisfy ya?"

Balzic shrugged. "I don't need any satisfaction."

"Well, the point is, she's tearin' this town apart with all this crap she's been puttin' out. Her and this goddamn clown calls himself a mayor. If they'd quit bitchin' long enough to do their homework, hell, all they have to do is read Third Class City Code. If they did that, if they spent twenty minutes with that book, they'd know they don't have a leg to stand on."

"Uh, exactly why is that?" Valcanas said, peering around Balzic.

"Well what're they askin' for? Huh? They keep hollerin' about wantin' to see the books, they wanna see the books they wanna see the books. Hey! They got no right to see those books. Each volunteer fire company was chartered by the city, and it says in every one of those charters that the fire company can raise money any way it sees fit—as long as it isn't illegal—and it can use that money to buy trucks, hoses, uniforms, masks, whatever."

"So what's that have to do with the Third Class Code?"

"Huh? Well it says right in there, in that section about settin' up a capital equipment fund—"

"Well if what you're referring to is Section 2403, paragraph one-point-one, what you're talking about is what's called 'Creation of Capital Reserve Fund for Anticipated Capital Expenditures.' If that's what you're talkin' about, there is nothing in that section that says any volunteer fireman or any volunteer anybody has anything to say about how those funds are administered except Council."

"Bullshit!" said Radosich.

"Bullshit nothin'," Valcanas said. "The reason the firemen and all their groupies think nobody can fuck with their precious social clubs is 'cause of guys like you—"

"Aw now wait a minute—"

"Wait a minute my ass," Valcanas said. "Guys like you and our previous mayor and the burgess before him let the firemen get away with any goddamn thing 'cause the firemen could deliver twelve to fifteen hundred votes—"

"Aw bull—"

"Let the man speak," Balzic said.

"Sheesh—yeah, go 'head go 'head."

"I've made my point," Valcanas said.

"What point? That there was some magic there, some ipso presto abracadabra that automatically turned out twelve to fifteen hundred votes? That's a joke. There's never been more than four hundred firemen in this town—ever! Never more than three-seventy-five. So you throw in all the auxiliaries, all the social members in all those hose companies, throw in all their old ladies for crissake, and you still wouldn't have twelve hundred. And half of them never voted. Don't tell me, I tried to get 'em to vote. You had to put dynamite under their ass, some of 'em, to get 'em to go across one goddamn street to vote."

"Just because they didn't vote on your command doesn't mean they didn't vote," Valcanas said.

"Greek, the difference between you and me is you're a thinker and I'm a counter. You get the ideas, and I go out and count votes and match 'em up against voter registration. In plain English, you talk a good game, but I paid people to tell me who voted and who didn't and who got voted for. And so I'm tellin' you there was never twelve hundred votes outta firemen votin' in no block at no time for nobody. Four hundred was tops and that was only during presidential elections when you got sixty percent turnout if you was lucky and it didn't rain."

"If you count votes so well," Valcanas said, "you mind tellin' me again how many votes you lost by to old what's-her-name?"

"No, I don't mind tellin' ya. Thirty-one. I was so busy countin' votes I forgot to pay attention to what the lady was talkin' about. I coulda used you then, Greek. I needed somebody to tell me what was happening instead of how many. Course I think it rained that day too." Radosich whacked Balzic across the arm. "What the hell, win a lot, lose one. I only lost one election in my whole life."

Balzic squinted at Radosich. "So you lost one and now you're gettin' ready to make your comeback, is that it?"

"Nossir, not me. I'm just waddlin' around, keepin' my ear close to the barstools, you know."

"So what'd you hear today?"

"I heard there's a least one Greek thinks the firemen are not altogether in the right. But I didn't hear what you think, huh, Mario?"

"My opinion doesn't matter. It's gonna wind up in court is what I think. The firemen's solicitor's been hangin' around City Hall for weeks now. Every time I turn around I see him talkin' to the city solicitor. And both of 'em are talkin' to the mayor— or tryin' to. And short of civil war, how else is anybody gonna settle it?"

"And when they get to court," Valcanas grumbled, "you can bet your ass Section 2403 paragraph one-point-one will be the center of attention. And the firemen, including his royal pain in the assness Saint Eddie the Great, are gonna find out that what they think they had a right to do was based on nothin' more than a cozy little arrangement between Saint Eddie and Angelo Bellotti when he was mayor and guys like you when you were on Council."

"Greek," Radosich said, "what're you so pissed off about? You act like this is somethin' personal here, like I'm tryin' to waltz you outta somethin'. *Me*. So what is it?"

"What it is, is I am not a member of the committee that is tryin' to get the fire chief canonized. I am not one of his fans, in other words."

"So what's that have to do with *me*, Greek? *Me?*"

"Radio, you're runnin' for Council again. Old Saint Eddie, the Great White Fire Chief, can't get this councilwoman off his back and so you're gonna do it for him. And you'll need all twelve hundred votes to do it. And you'll get 'em."

Radosich shook his head. "You can't count, Greek. You can't. Hey, Valcanas, give us another one. It's your turn, right, Greek?"

"I didn't order anything before."

"Me either," Balzic said.

"Hey, I got the last one, fellas."

"I didn't get one."

"Me either."

"Okay, Radio," Vinnie said. "Whatta you gonna play now?"

Radio made a great show of looking at his watch and giving himself a gentle slap in the forehead. "Geez, is it five o'-clock already? I'll tell ya, time really does fly when you're havin' fun. I gotta go."

Radosich left without a backward glance, finishing his vodka and orange juice while he walked and setting the glass on the bar before he reached the door.

"What is it," Vinnie said, "is there a rule someplace, you gonna be a politician the first thing you gotta do is sew all your pockets shut?"

"That ain't a rule," Balzic said. "It's a state law."

"I'm tellin' you," Vinnie said, "I'll bet I seen fifty politicians come in this bar and I ain't seen one of 'em pay—hey, the next one pays for somethin'll be the first."

"Politicians never carry cash," Valcanas said somberly. "It's the pols' divine right. Only taxpayers carry cash, don't you know that?"

Vinnie's services were called for and he hustled away to wait on other patrons.

Balzic peered sideways at Valcanas. "Divine right?"

"What better way to tell the world you derive your power from the gods, huh? Make everybody else pay your freight. How much sweeter could it be?"

"I guess," Balzic said, nodding many times. After a moment, he said, "How come you knew, uh, what section of the city code—how come you could come up with that off the top of your head?"

"It's not off the top of anything. Some guy's been buggin' me about these firemen."

"Who's that?"

"I'm not gonna tell you." Valcanas pulled himself up to his full height. "Hey! Non-keeper of the non-inn. Un-keeper of the un-inn. Bring un-sobriety! I want fuzz! I want vagueness! I want vacuity! I want stuuuuuporrrrr!"

"Greek, honest to Christ, you're gettin' worse and worse."

"Dear Chief of Police, I am gettin' better'n better. It's the world that's gettin' worse'n worse. Un-keep-er!"

Balzic was driving through the alleys, going barely fifteen miles an hour, looking every which way, trying to notice everything, watching out for kids and animals, trying to see whether the city was as clean as it used to be before its garbage collection had been privatized. He couldn't really say that it was any dirtier. He couldn't say it was any cleaner either.

"Hey! Hey, Mario."

He stomped on the brake pedal and turned from side to side and checked all his mirrors to see who had called him.

Then he heard the dog barking and little by little recognized that he'd stopped behind Paul Gmitter's house. The dog was a tan and white mongrel that came bounding out from between the hedges, its stubby tail wagging mightily, followed closely by the woman, Paul's widow.

"There, see, didn't I tell you?" she said to the dog. "Didn't I tell you it was Mario? Huh?"

Balzic put the cruiser into park gear and stepped on the parking brake and got out.

The dog barked and got on its hind legs and began to jump straight up and down.

"See? You never listen to me when I tell you it's one of your friends," she said to the dog. She'd been bending over, then she straightened and held out her hands to Balzic and he took them and pumped them up and down.

"How ya doin', Ann?"

"Oh, so-so, Mario. How're you doin'?"

"Hangin' in. I see you still got this goddamn mutt. Shithead."

"Poo, Mario. Poo. Poo-Poo."

"That's what I said, Shithead. The only guy in the whole world names a dog Poo-Poo was your old man."

She put her head down and gave his hands a squeeze and then had to let go to cover her face.

"Jesus, Ann, you cryin'? I didn't mean anything by that. I thought that'd make you laugh. It was a joke."

"I know, I know," she said, struggling to regain her composure and doing so after a moment. "Don't say you're sorry, please, okay? It was funny. It just brought back too much, you know . . ."

Balzic bent down quickly and scratched the dog's rump. It curled into a half-moon and walked in a staggery circle, pushing its rump into Balzic's fingers as he scratched.

"This is the only dog I ever liked," Balzic said.

"She still . . . every day she still runs through the whole house lookin' for him. . . . Runs and gets her Frisbee two, three times a day. Takes it to the front door and sits there with it in her mouth. And then she looks at me and . . . oh, god, Mario, do you think you ever get sick of cryin'?"

"Hell, Ann, I don't know. Sooner or later. I don't know. How old's this dog?"

"Poo? Poo's gonna be eleven."

"Uh, I don't know how to put this, but, uh, how long you think Poo's gonna live?"

"God, Mario, what kind of question's that?"

"Hey it's a crummy question. I don't know how else to ask it. But the real question is, what're you gonna do when Poo dies?"

"Oh, Mario, my god."

"Hey, Ann. So it's not a real delicate question and I'm not a real delicate guy. But the fact is, nobody's seen you in months. Nobody's seen you at the Moose, in church, at the bingos, nobody's seen you up at the hospital, nobody's seen you anywhere. And nobody's heard from you either. Poo's a neat dog. Only dog I ever liked. But he's a dog."

"Poo's a she."

"Okay, he she whatever. Doesn't change anything. He, she, Poo's a dog. And you ain't."

"That's right. I ain't."

"C'mon, Ann, you know what I mean."

"Uh, Poo's the best kind of company for me now, Mario. She's a good friend. And we both miss him. And nobody understands that better than she does. And I don't feel like talkin' about . . . about other things. And when I do, and I'm sure I will, well, then I will. And until I do I won't. Okay?"

"Okay," Balzic said grudgingly. "I didn't mean to, you know, get you all outta joint."

"I know, I know."

Balzic gave the dog another scratch and got back into the cruiser. "Hey, I know it's no consolation, but I miss him too, you know?"

"Mario," she said, nodding several times, her chin quivering, "it's not the same. I met him in the first grade and I never went out with anybody else in my whole life. I never kissed another man on the lips except him. Not even my father . . . And we couldn't . . . we had dogs. And Poo's our last one. And I just really don't need to spend any time with anybody except Poo if you don't mind."

"Oh, Ann, Jesus, I'm really sorry."

"No, don't be sorry. Just stop around every once in a while. And tell some of the other guys too, okay? I'd really like to see some of them. And tell Ruth too, okay? I'd really like to see Ruth. She's the only one I'd really like to see. I gotta go in now, Mario. I'm gonna start cryin' again, and I'm just really startin' to hate that. Come on, Poo, let's go in now. C'mon, let's go."

Balzic drove off but stopped as soon as he was out of sight of Ann Gmitter's house to make a note to remind himself to post a notice on the bulletin board that *Ann Gmitter, widow of Officer Paul Gmitter, would like some conversation. No consolation, no come-ons, just conversation.*

He was starting to pull out of the alley when he heard the roar and whop of a helicopter. He hit the brakes and got out and hustled to a break between the houses to get a vantage point. There it was, mostly blue on the body with a white tail and with big white letters, "MERCY 2," on the side behind the doors. It was very low, two hundred feet or so, and seemed to be getting lower and heading in the general direction of the Mutual Aid Ambulance garage on State Street.

He got back in the cruiser and decided to go there to see if that was indeed where it was going.

Mutual Aid's garage was a cinder-block building with six bays for ambulances and rescue vehicles, and a dispatcher's office, a kitchen, lavatories, showers, and a bunkroom. It was a one-story building and took up half a block; the other half was taken up by the Red Cross office and blood bank and a one-bay garage for the Red Cross bloodmobile.

As Balzic pulled into a visitor's space in the parking lot across the street from the Red Cross building, he could hear the helicopter and he knew it was on the ground, but he couldn't see it and didn't have a clue where it was. Behind the Mutual Aid garage, abutting it, was the perimeter of the Zukovsky Metal Reclamation Company. There wasn't anything else in either direction for two or three blocks but Abe Zukovsky's metal junkyard. Still, the sound of the copter seemed to be coming from there. Then it stopped, the blades whopping down to silence in a matter of seconds.

Balzic got out and walked to the Mutual Aid office, where he found a dispatcher, a young woman with wispy blond hair and a pale complexion, looking intense and somber as though expecting a calamity at any second. She frowned when Balzic approached her.

"Hi ya doin'?" Balzic said.

"Okay." She squinted quizzically at Balzic. "Do you need some help?"

"Me? No. What—"

"Does someone need help?"

"Huh? No, no. All I want to find out is where is that helicopter parked. Can you tell me that?"

"No."

"That's it? No? Just no."

"Yes, sir, that's correct. Just no."

Balzic chewed the inside of his cheek and drummed his fingers on the counter separating them. "Is this, uh, this *no* business, is this a decision you reached by yourself, or did you have a little help gettin' to that?"

"The helicopter is not for me to talk about. As far as I'm concerned, it might as well not even exist. It doesn't exist."

"Well maybe as far as you're concerned that may be true. But that thing came down around here a couple of minutes ago, 'cause I followed it up here and I heard the motor goin' when I got out of my car. I just thought you'd be nice and save me from goin' off in the wrong direction—"

"If you want to know about that, the only person who's authorized to talk about that is Chief Sitko."

"Uh-huh. That's Fire Chief Edward J. Sitko, right?"

"That's right," she sang, making two syllables out of the word *right*.

"Can I borrow your phone book, please?"

"There's one by the pay phone in the corner."

Balzic turned in the direction she nodded, went to the phone book, and looked up the Zukovsky Metal Reclamation Company. When he found the number, he dialed it and a woman answered.

"This is Mario Balzic. Is Abe around? I want to talk to him please, okay?"

After about fifteen seconds, the phone on the other end changed hands and a breathless, phlegmy voice shouted, "Muddio, Mudeeeoooo! How you do? Where you at, you never come around no more."

"Hey, Abe, I'm doin' okay, but my social calendar's all booked up. Besides, you're no fun anymore since you quit drinkin'."

"Drinkeeen! Hell. Dat ain't the worst. I don't eat no beef, no pork, no sauseeege, no cheese, cripesakes, I'm turnin' into a—I'll tell you what. I might as well be a monk. Huh? A Jew monk. How you like that? I should go over St. Malachy's and turn myself in. Put me on bread and water and give me one of them little cat-o'-nine-tails so I can beat myself up with it."

"What's the problem? Your heart actin' up again?"

"Actin'? My heart don't act. My heart's for real. When it goes on the attack, there ain't no actin' about it. Yeah, yeah, yeah, so let's don't talk hearts, huh? It makes me sick to talk hearts. I'm tellin' you I get a little heart attack every time I gotta talk hearts. So what's on your mind?"

"I'm tryin' to track down a helicopter, Abe. I know it landed around here someplace—"

"Where you at now?"

"I'm in the Mutual Aid dispatcher's office."

"Well, you're about seventy-five, eighty yards from it, give or take a couple yards."

"Is it on your property, Abe?"

"Just for a little while, Muddio. Be gone tomorrow."

"Since when you start runnin' an airport? Huh?"

"Nah, nah, don't get no ideas. I ain't runnin' no airport. This is just a little temporary thing, believe me. I'm still a junk man. That's the only business I'm ever gonna be in."

"Then what're you doin' with a chopper in your junk-yard?"

"Muddio, don't put me on a spot here, okay?"

"Hey, Abe, I'm drivin' around, I see this helicopter goin' down. I don't know whether it's landin' or it's crashin', you know, except whatever it's doin', it's doin' it right here in Rocksburg. So I gotta check it out. And I find out it lands in your place. And then I find out you're providin' temporary quarters for this thing. And then, I find out you're turnin' coy in your old age. Now this other stuff, maybe somebody'll explain it to me. But you? Turnin' coy? What's goin' on, Abe? Huh?"

"Hey, Muddio, talk to Eddie Sitko, okay? I'm just doin' him a favor, that's all. I'm lettin' him park it here till he gets this pad finished—which he promised me was gonna be tomorrow. So for one night he can park his helicopter here."

"I see. You mind tellin' where he *was* parkin' it?"

"Muddio, please. Okay? Please ask him. Okay?"

"Okay, Abe. I'll do that. Thanks. Take care of yourself."

Balzic hung up, turned around, and froze. Not three steps away stood a figure in full camouflage gear, hat, jacket, pants, boots—everything on him was green and brown except for the rifle he was carrying. Balzic was immobilized by the sight of this human being prepared for combat in, of all places, the office of the dispatcher of the Mutual Aid Ambulance Service.

The figure started to turn away, to go back whence he had come.

Balzic shouted, "Ho! Hey! Hold it! I wanna talk to you." He lurched forward and through the door into the first ambulance bay, where he stopped dead again. There were two others like the first, head to toe in camouflage clothes and carrying rifles.

"Uh, you guys mind tellin' me who you are?"

"Who wants to know?"

"Who wants to know is me, Mario Balzic, chief of Rocksburg Police Department." Balzic fumbled for his ID case, then produced it for all three camo men to see.

"What's the problem?" said the first camo man.

"The problem is, you three are carryin' what I hope is a civilian version of a military weapon—"

The camo man shook his head. "This is a military model—"

"Then by Christ I want to know exactly who you are because if that's an M-16 then that's an automatic weapon and if you three ain't in the military then you damn well better have a federal stamp 'cause that's a machine gun."

"We're in the military. These weapons were issued to us."

"Say what? What military? Issued by who?"

"Uh, I'm not at liberty to discuss that," said the first camo man. So far he was the only one doing any talking.

Balzic stepped to within arm's length of the first camo man and said, "Mister, I want to see ID and I want to see it now."

"That's not possible. We never carry ID—when we're on a field problem, and we just came off a field problem."

"Field problem! What the hell kind of field problem you talkin' about? Who the fuck are you?"

"Sir, it's not going to help to shout. All I will tell you is that we are duly authorized, and at the proper time, you will learn who we are and what our legal authority is. Right now, we have to go. So we'll be saying adios." The first camo man nodded to the others and turned away to leave.

"Freeze goddammit!"

"You two go on," the first camo man said. "I'll handle this."

"Nobody goes anywhere," Balzic said.

"Go ahead. Move out. I'll cover this."

"You deaf or what? I said nobody leaves."

"Move!" the first camo man said curtly to the others, who turned and broke into a run. They disappeared in seconds.

"Chief, your reputation is that you do not carry a weapon. As you can see, I'm carrying an M-16, fully loaded and locked. I also have a 9mm Beretta pistol, also fully loaded and locked, and a Ka-bar knife. I spent twenty-four years in U.S. Special Forces. I've told you all that I'm going to tell you, all that I'm allowed to tell you. If you persist in trying to detain me, I will defend myself. I think you're smart enough to know how that would end. So if you don't mind, I'll be on my way."

"Hey, yeah, sure. Right. If you guys are in such a big goddamn hurry, you're on such a goddamn secret mission then just tell me what the fuck you came into this building for? Why? Why're you in Mutual Aid?"

"I have to go now, sir."

"Hey, camo man. If you know that I don't carry a weapon, if you know that much about me, then you also gotta know that this ain't gonna stop when you walk out that door. By this time tomorrow I'll know what size shoes you wear."

"I'm sure you will, sir. But you won't learn it from me. Good night."

That said, he disappeared in less time than it had taken the other two.

Balzic looked around the garage. There was not another human in sight. He walked back into the dispatcher's room. The dispatcher with the wispy blond hair eyed him coolly.

"How do I get into the bunkroom?"

"Uh, that's off-limits. Only Mutual Aid personnel."

"Girlie, I can be back here in fifteen minutes with a warrant—"

"Go ahead."

"For your arrest—"

"For what?"

"How about obstructing administration of the law, hindering apprehension or prosecution, failure to report a criminal act, aiding a crime—that enough for you?"

"What crime is that—that last one—what crime is that?"

"That's the crime of carrying a prohibited offensive weapon. Those three guys were carryin' machine guns. And they saw me and they took off. And I ask you where the bunkroom is and you start to play games with me. So I ask you, Miss Dispatcher, exactly why would those guys be here if it wasn't to pick up their personal gear, or change clothes, and where would they be doin' that? Huh?"

"You could really arrest me?"

"And prosecute you and get a conviction and get your little buns thrown in the joint—how'd you like that?"

"Well . . . well, how can you just go in there if you don't have a search warrant? How can you do that?"

"I just saw three guys carryin' prohibited weapons. I asked one of 'em—I said to one of 'em—words to the effect that I *hoped* what they had were civilian models of those weapons. And he said they weren't. And he claimed to have authority to carry those weapons and he claimed to be in the military, but when I asked for ID he not only refused to show it, he ordered his buddies to flee and then he did. By any stretch of the law, I have probable cause to conduct a search. I don't need a goddamn warrant to do that.

"Look," Balzic went on, "I don't need your goddamn cooperation either. The bunkroom's gotta be behind one of these doors. So stay where you are and keep quiet—unless, of course, you have to talk to somebody wants an ambulance. Then you go right ahead and do your job."

Balzic stepped through an opening in the counter and opened the first door he came to. It led into a kitchen. At the rear of the kitchen was another door. Balzic went through that and found himself in the bunkroom. There were six double bunks against one wall. On the opposite wall were full-length lockers. Balzic went to these and started opening them. The ones he could open, the ones with no locks, had only a change of clothes in them and a bag lunch or a lunch box and a vacuum bottle. Eight of the lockers had very large padlocks.

Balzic looked at those, looked at the bunks, walked over to the bunk at the end of the room farthest from the kitchen door, and stretched out on it. In five seconds, he sat up, muttering, "This is stupid. She'll tell 'em I'm back here. Shit."

He stood and walked quickly out through the kitchen and past the dispatcher without a word. Out in the street he looked up and down for a good surveillance point. He hustled to his cruiser, got in, and drove to as near the back of the Mutual Aid garage as he could, searching for an entrance back there. He thought he spotted one, but he wasn't sure. He drove back out to State Street and parked in a block where he could see the front of the garage bays and the corner of the rear of the building. He couldn't see the door he thought he'd seen back there, but until he got somebody to help him, the spot he was in would have to do.

He called his station and got Sergeant Rascoli.

"Who's out?"

"Yesho and Metikosh."

"They loose?"

"Yesho's got a domestic dispute, Metikosh has a car wrapped around a utility pole."

"Well the first one gets loose, send him up here to me, okay?"

"It's gonna be a while, Mario. Metikosh has wires down, and I haven't heard from him in twenty minutes. And Yesho, poor bastard, he's got the superintendent of buildings and grounds."

"Oh no, not him again. Well tell Yesho to forget that clown and get his ass up here."

"Uh, Chief, I don't know what's goin' on with the superintendent, but it must not be the usual stuff, 'cause Yesho said it was something else and he'd call me back, but that was, uh, lemme see, that was twenty-eight minutes ago and he hasn't called back."

"Call him!"

"I tried that twice. He's not answerin'."

"Then call a neighbor and find out what the fuck's goin' on."

"I've called three of 'em already. Next door and the two houses across the street. Nobody's answerin'."

"Hey don't quit there."

"I can't call anybody while I'm talkin' to you, paisan."

"Call 'em! I'm out."

Balzic hung up his speaker, got out, and went around to the trunk and opened it. Hanging by two straps from the roof of the trunk in a vinyl boot was his Springfield .30-06. He looked at it for a long moment, his lips tight, his jaw taut, his breathing rapid and shallow. He reached into the trunk and flipped the dial on the combination lock on his ammo box. He opened the metal box and took out a clip, five rounds of 180-grain, copper-jacketed, hollow-point bullets in brass cartridges filled with enough powder to send those bullets out of the muzzle at 2,800 feet a second. He tossed the clip from one hand to the other and looked at it, and looked at it, and looked at it . . . and then he put the clip back into the box, closed the lid, set the lock, and pushed the trunk shut with both hands.

The sons of bitches were probably a mile away—or else they were all around him, laughing their asses off. What did it matter? What mattered was he was acting like an adolescent, all groin and gut, with not two coherent thoughts to hang together about why he was reaching for a rifle when he had no idea about who he might shoot or where they might be.

He rubbed his fingers and thumbs together to get rid of the dust from the trunk lid. To his right, between two houses, movement caught his eye. A black kid, eight or nine years old, his fingers drumming on his lower lip, his right shoe halfway up his left calf, peered curiously, suspiciously, at Balzic.

"Hey, you," Balzic called out. "Come here."

The kid advanced warily, looking all around.

"C'mon, c'mon, get over here."

The kid moved at the same speed and continued to look around. "What you want?"

"You live here?"

"Right there," the kid said, jerking his thumb at the house on his right. It was a boxy two-story covered in imitation brick with a tiny front porch covered by a grungy aluminum awning.

"What's your name?"

"Sidney."

"Sidney what?"

"Sidney Maples."

"You live in Rocksburg all the time, Sidney, or you just move here?"

"We jus' move here."

"How long ago d'you just move here?"

"I don' know."

"You know how many weeks are in a month?"

"Four."

"Then how long you lived here?"

"Mmmmm, 'bout two month."

"You a pretty good watcher, Sidney? You watch good, huh?"

Sidney nodded. "I don' know."

Balzic believed the nod and not the words. "You know what camouflage clothes are?"

"Yeah. They all brown and green. All mixed up."

"You been watchin' that building over there?"

"Where they keep the ambulance?"

Balzic nodded.

"I watch it all the time."

"Ever see guys go in there wearin' camouflage clothes, carryin' rifles? Ever see that?"

"Uh-ha."

"When do they go in there?"

" 'Bout the time cartoons go off."

"Cartoons?"

"On TV."

"I see. Five-thirty, six o'clock, huh?"

"I don' know."

"Whenever the news comes on, right? After the cartoons go off, right?"

"Uh-ha."

"Is that when you come out to watch?"

"Uh-ha."

"That's when the men wearin' the camouflage clothes, is that when they go in the building over there?"

"Uh-ha."

"How long they been doin' that? You tell me that?"

"Don' do it all the time."

"When do they do it?"

"All the time, 'cept they don' do it sometime. Oh-oh, here come my momma. I gots to go."

"Hold it, hold it. It's okay. I'll talk to your momma. You know who I am?"

"Uh-uh."

"I'm the chief of police here. I'm a cop. You know what a cop is, a police officer?"

"My momma goin' whip my ass."

Sidney's momma wore all white, blouse, pants, shoes. She carried a white jacket over her arm. She was scowling at Sidney and then at Balzic as she approached and her pace had gotten quicker the closer she'd come.

"Boy, whachu doin' out the house? And whachu doin'

talkin' to my boy? You some kind of freak? You funny? Boy, you better get inside!"

Balzic held up both hands. "Take it easy, ma'am, take it easy. I'm the chief of police." He got out his ID case and extended it for her to see.

"You the what? The chief of po-lice? Whachu doin' talkin' to Sidney? What he do?"

"Slow down, ma'am, take it easy. Your son's been helpin' me here. There's no problem, he's not in any trouble, I've just been askin' him questions about what he's been watchin'. Your boy is a very good watcher."

"Whachu been watchin'? You 'posed to be watchin' TV. Inside the house. You ain't 'posed to be watchin' nothin' out the house."

"I didn't come out on no sidewalk, Momma, not till he call me out. I jus' be stayin' between the houses, Momma, like you say it was awright. I didn't come out till he tol' me. Honest, Momma."

"That's right, ma'am. He's tellin' the truth. And if you don't mind, I'd like to finish talkin' to him."

"Finish talkin' to him 'bout what? The chil' already got an excitable mind, make me all nervous all the things he be seein'. Now you goin' come on and fire him up, tell him he be a good watcher? I'll never get the boy calm down."

"The boy's calm, he looks calm to me, he's answered everything in a calm way."

"The boy got an excitable mind. Ever since we been here, all he be talkin' 'bout is those damn ambulances, and people comin' and goin' with funny clothes and guns. And now you goin' tell him he be good at it?"

"How long you lived here, Mrs. Maples?"

"Six weeks. Why?"

"He's been talkin' about ambulances and guys in funny clothes all that time?"

"Huh? No. First it was the ambulances. That was okay. I mean I could see them myself. But then he be seein' these guys in funny clothes and—"

"How long's he been talkin' about them?"

" 'Bout three weeks. What's this all about?"

"Uh, your boy may have an excitable mind, Mrs. Maples, but he's not seein' things that aren't there. What he says he's seein', he's seein', believe me."

She put her hands on her hips and drew herself up very tall. "Guys with funny clothes and guns comin' out the ambulance garage, that what chu goin' tell me now? Huh?"

"Yes, ma'am, that's exactly what I'm goin' to tell you. I saw three of 'em myself tonight. And for a while there, I thought *I* was havin' an excitable mind. But I wasn't. And neither is Sidney here.

"So, uh, Sidney, I have to go now. But you keep watchin', okay? Don't do anything. Don't go any closer than you were tonight. But you keep watchin', and I'll be back to talk to you, okay?"

" 'Kay."

Mrs. Maples closed her eyes and shook her head. "Shoulda stayed where I was. All you be seein' there is sailors."

"It's all right, ma'am. Your boy's all right."

"Uh-ha, uh-ha. Sidney, I don't care what he say. Get yo ass in the house. Now!"

"Easy, ma'am, easy. Just take it easy."

"Easy my ass. If I find out you funny? If I find out you ain't the chief? I'm goin' put a hurtin' on you. I'm goin' do you some pain."

"I ain't funny, and I am the chief. Good night."

"Uh-ha. Yeah," she said, and took Sidney by the hand and pulled him between the houses, out of sight.

Balzic got into his cruiser and drove off. He had not gone a block before a sinking, queasy feeling got him. It got so bad he had to pull over to the curb and park for a minute or so. He had to lean against the steering wheel and he swallowed many, many times to dispel the nausea. He opened the glove box and rooted around in all the envelopes, Band-Aids, maps, notebooks, manuals for the cruiser, radio, and shotgun, and sundry junk trying to find a bottle of antacid tablets. He found the small plastic bottle, but it had only one tablet in it. He tossed that into his mouth and put the empty bottle in his coat pocket, and then he drove off looking for a pharmacy that was still open.

The pharmacies still doing business in town—the ones that hadn't packed up and moved to the malls—had years ago come to an agreement about taking turns staying open at night and on weekends. They took two-week shifts: the one that stayed open at night did so for two weeks and two weekends at a stretch. Then it wouldn't have to open at night again for two months. Balzic's only complaint about their scheduling was that they would tell the doctors and the hospital and the Mutual Aid Ambulance Service, but they wouldn't tell the police. They had to be asked. Balzic had long ago resigned himself to accept that some people loved to upstage cops, to exert whatever power they could over them no matter how trivial. It was a lot like a guy driving 25 miles per hour in a 45-mph zone on a two-lane road so that everybody behind him had to wait on him; it was a meager triumph, but a triumph nonetheless.

Balzic drove past three pharmacies before he found Paul's Drugs open on North Main. He also found one of the department's black-and-whites parked in front of it. He parked behind that and got out just as Patrolman Thomas Yesho was trotting out of Paul's front door.

"Hey, Chief. What're you doin' here?" Yesho said.

"I'm tryin' to find some Titralac," Balzic said. "What're you doin' here?"

"What I'm doin' here, uh, is the superintendent of buildings and grounds is tryin' real hard to go nuts."

"He's been a little nuts for years, so what?"

"No, nah, this time he's nuts nuts. As in crazy. He's in his boat, he's rowin' hard, only it ain't in the water."

"C'mon, Thomas, you gotta do better'n that. Specifics. What's he doin'?"

Yesho sucked in a deep breath and blew it out real hard, letting his powerful shoulders drop. When his shoulders dropped, they almost made a noise. He was the most dedicated weight lifter in the department among the male officers. He weighed 220 pounds, stood just slightly over five feet nine inches without shoes, and spent at least three hours every day in the weight room in the basement of City Hall. Balzic worried long and often about the emotional stability of police officers who seemed to believe they were never strong enough to do what they had to do. He knew that most of them would say they were only trying to stay in shape and they were only trying to gain an edge in any physical emergency, but he never felt comfortable with the illusion of physical strength. Maybe it was because he was older and wasn't as strong as he once was; more likely it was because he had taken some of the worst beatings in his life from women who didn't look capable of lifting more than a basket of wet clothes or a pot of soup.

"C'mon, Thomas, what's he doin?"

"Okay. Specifics. He got his wife tied up, wrists and ankles, with clothesline. He let me see her once for about three seconds, then he hauled her off somewhere. He also got her gagged. Why's he got her tied up? 'Cause she rented one of his apartments to a white chick who's livin' with a black dude and they're on welfare—he *says* they are. I thought for a while that that was the capper, but later on what I finally got out of him was he's pissed at his doctors and his drugstore 'cause they were all on vacation—spendin' *his* money naturally—and now that he needed these prescriptions refilled they didn't give a fart about him and he was gonna die if he didn't get his pills. Meantime, it took me almost a half hour to get all that outta him."

"Is that what's in the bag?"

"Yeah."

"So, uh, did he let you inside?"

"Hell no. Never got off the porch."

"How'd he keep you out?"

"Uh, good question. This is gonna sound stupid, but it looked like he had a piece. He never showed it to me, understand, but he kept walkin' around with his right arm stiff by his side, you know? And then once he turned on a light for a couple seconds, I got a look at it, but I got the feeling it was an air pistol, you know, something he got at Kmart. They got five or six of those things that look like the real thing. But it just looked like, the way he was holdin' it, it didn't have any weight to it—am I makin' any sense?"

"Yeah, sure."

"Well I didn't feel like bettin' anybody's life on what it was, you know? Least of all mine."

"So you told him you'd get his medicine for him and you came down here and got it. So that's good. Nothin' wrong with that move. So, uh, what's the medicine for?"

"Beats the hell outta me. He just gave me these three bottles and I came down here and told what's-his-face to give me a couple days' worth of stuff. It never occurred to me to ask what it was."

"Well let's go inside. I wanna find out if he's gonna die. I never even knew he was sick."

They went inside and to the rear of the store, where Paulie Ligo, owner, pharmacist, and son of the original owner of Paul's Drugs was working. He looked up over the rims of his half-glasses and gave a quick wave. "Be right with you, Mario. How ya doin'?"

"Okay, Paulie, how you doin'?"

"Hey, you know, everybody I can. The ones with skin diseases I do forever." He smiled at his own joke, typed something on a manual typewriter, and a moment later came out from his work area and stood on the other side of the counter. "Now. What can I do for you?"

"Uh, these pills you gave Yesho—"

"Who?"

"The officer here."

"Oh! Yes. What about 'em?"

"What are they for?"

"You gotta let me see 'em, Mario. I'm smart, God knows, but I'm not that smart. I can't remember everything."

"Here they are." Balzic handed the bottles over.

"Uh, oh, yeah, sure. Hydrodiuril, Klotrix, and Lopressor."

"Uh-ha. What are they for?"

"Well, Hydrodiuril is primarily a diuretic used to control high blood pressure. Makes you pee a lot, in other words. And if you pee a lot, you're gonna lose potassium, which is why you take Klotrix because that's what that is, potassium chloride. And Lopressor is one of a class of drugs commonly called beta-blockers, which also lowers blood pressure among other things, but because of this combination of drugs, it's pretty safe to say the problem here is high blood pressure."

"Is this guy in any danger if he doesn't get these drugs?"

"Danger?" Paulie shrugged and screwed up his face. "That depends on how you define danger—"

"Would he die? If he didn't get 'em?"

Paulie smiled and shook his head. "You mean if he misses one day, or two? Highly unlikely. Now if he quit takin' them for say, a couple of months, six months, then, who knows. But for a day or two. No, no real harm done."

"Okay. So, uh, where's the Titralac?"

"He didn't ask me for any Titralac."

"No no, this is for me."

"Oh. Behind you. Third shelf. Little heartburn, huh?"

"Little? Christ, I could spit napalm. I'm tired, my mouth tastes like a gang of bikers rode through it, I'm hungry, people been pissin' me off all day. I found out I have to lay people off, I just come from makin' a big ass outta myself—"

"You have to lay people off?" Yesho said. "Since when?"

Balzic tried to wave Yesho's question away. "We'll talk about this later, okay?"

"Hey. Last ones hired, first ones fired, you know? That's me."

"Later, Thomas, okay?"

"You're gonna lay me off? I can't believe you're gonna lay me off."

"Thomas, I'm not the one who's gonna lay you off. It's not a personal thing. It was not my decision, understand?"

"Gettin' laid off is very personal, don't you think? I mean the only thing I can think of that's more personal than gettin' laid off is gettin' laid."

"Yesho, please. Not now. Hey, Paulie, I don't see it here."

"You're lookin' right at it, Mario."

Yesho reached down and snatched a bottle off the third

shelf and jammed it into Balzic's hand. "Here for crissake." He stomped out of the store.

Balzic closed his eyes and shook his head several times. He straightened up and stepped back to the counter. "How much?"

"For the Titralac? Nothin'. Be my guest."

Balzic chewed his teeth. "Hey, Paulie, don't take this wrong, okay, but when I start takin' freebies, I'm gonna start with municipal bonds, you know? I ain't gonna start with antacid tablets."

"Okay, okay, say no more. It's three-seventy-nine."

Balzic paid, thanked Paulie for his help, and said good night. Out on the sidewalk, Yesho was waiting for him.

"Am I gonna get laid off or not?"

"Yesho, for crissake, now is not the time to discuss this, okay?"

"Well, you know, whether I'm gonna get laid off or not will probably make a real big difference in how I act whenever we get to where we're goin'."

Balzic stared hard into Yesho's eyes. "You listen to me, Patrolman Yesho. If you got any questions about what you should do when you're on your watch, then my advice to you is to get the blue flu and go home, 'cause the last thing I need is a guy watchin' my back who doesn't wanna be watchin' my back."

Yesho stared back as hard as he was being stared at. "Okay," he said, after a long moment. "Okay, I've been askin' you for six months now whether I ought to be lookin' for another job and you been tellin' me it wasn't in your hands. So now you're tellin' me it *is* in your hands. And all of a sudden I got a real high temperature."

"Then what you oughta do is go home and stretch out and put some cold rags on your head—after you report off to your watch commander."

"That's exactly what I'm gonna do."

"Good. Fine. Then do it. But before you go, just think about this. When you go, that'll leave one officer on the streets and Rascoli in the duty room and me. One . . . peace officer . . . on the streets."

"Chief, uh, don't take this personally, okay, but you're not a nun and I'm not back in the third grade and that guilt shit isn't gonna work on me. I don't care how many guys are on the street. Right now I don't give a rat's ass if there's nobody on the streets. The goddamn city doesn't care if *I'm* gone—"

"I didn't say anything like that—"

"You said there was gonna be layoffs—"

"I said I found out I was gonna have to lay people off—"

"What the hell's the difference between what you said—"

"What I said is what I meant. What I didn't say was *who* I was gonna lay off—"

"Well shit, you haven't hired anybody since you hired us—"

"And you're jumpin' to a conclusion—shit, you're *divin'* at it—"

"What else am I supposed to do?"

"Yesho, goddammit, stop yakkin' at me. Just stop it. I haven't figured anything out yet about who's gonna go and who ain't, but I damn sure don't wanna argue with you about it out here on the sidewalk. You wanna get sick and go home, go home, I don't care, but I'll be goddamned if I'm gonna stand here and let you think I made a decision I haven't made yet."

"Well . . . how many you got to lay off?"

"Thomas, I don't wanna discuss it. I'm not *ready* to discuss it. Just go tell Rascoli you're sick and go home."

"Aw bullshit, I'm not sick. I'm not tellin' anybody anything."

Balzic shook his head and went to get in his cruiser. He opened the door and stood there for a few seconds debating with himself whether he should say what he was thinking. "Yesho," he said after some seconds had passed, "it's time you started to understand that being a hard-ass does not necessarily mean you're tough. Bein' a hard-ass, kid, all that means is you're, uh, you're easy. I tell you to go the way I don't want you to go and you go the way I want ya to go and you think it means you're not gonna take orders from anybody, especially not me. You might wanna think about that the next time you're throwin' all those barbells around."

Yesho tried to look cool but failed.

Balzic dropped onto the driver's seat in his cruiser and shut the door. "I'll take care of the superintendent of buildings and grounds. You go give Metikosh a hand, okay?"

Yesho didn't answer.

"Okay?"

"Yes, sir."

"Good. Then do it." Balzic started the car and pulled away from the curb. At the stoplight on Main at State Street, he glanced up at the clock above the entrance to Mellon Bank. It said 6:35. His own watch said 6:36. The light changed and he turned left onto State Street wondering whether he ought to go home first or call his wife or go straight to the residence of the superintendent of buildings and grounds.

He decided to do the latter. The superintendent's house was only three blocks from Balzic's, and, though this business about tying the wife up sounded a little extreme even for the superintendent, Balzic figured he could calm him down in fifteen minutes, twenty at the most, and be on his way. He couldn't wait to get home, kick his shoes off, sip some pinot noir or maybe . . . Hell, he thought, I finished that bottle last night. Maybe I ought to swing past the state store and get a couple bottles of that montepulciano . . . that was wonderful stuff. . . .

He pulled over to the curb across the street from the Christoloski house. He tried to think who it was who'd pinned the nickname on Pete Christoloski, but he'd forgotten—if he ever knew. Everybody in and around City Hall had been calling Christoloski "the superintendent of buildings and grounds" for so long that sometimes they were stuck if anyone asked to know his real name.

Balzic turned off the ignition and stared up at Christoloski's house, four floors, red brick, cut into a hill so that his back door opened from the second story onto a small terrace. Behind and above that was the three-story white frame house that Christoloski owned and had divided into apartments. Beside that was a three-story brick house, also owned by Christoloski. Christoloski owned another house, somewhere near the middle of the block, but Balzic's recollection of that was vague.

Balzic tried to recall his last encounter with Christoloski.

He couldn't remember whether it was over the snowblower or the tree. The snowblower incident involved a guy who lived next door to Christoloski and who paid Christoloski by the month to keep his sidewalk clear in the winter and then became angry because Christoloski blew all the snow in front of his car and he couldn't get out and Christoloski tried to blame it on the city's snowplow. Nah, that wasn't the last time, Balzic thought. The last time was over the goddamn tree. Christoloski got on one of his campaigns to improve the buildings and grounds because the streetlight across from his house was hidden by branches from a sycamore with a trunk almost two feet thick, and once he started one of his campaigns there was no stopping him: he kept dialing the number for City Hall and kept getting Yolanda Sabo and kept pestering her to get the city to remove the tree. But, in his typical fashion, Christoloski never thought to take it up with the family who lived in the house on the other side of the tree. And when, after Yolanda Sabo finally got sick of listening to Christoloski complain and got the mayor to fill out a work order for one of the private companies that removed trees for the city and cleared utility lines for the power and phone companies, the crew showed up and started to cut the tree down while the family who lived on the other side of it was grocery shopping. More than half the tree was down before that family returned home, and the wife, a young woman intensely involved with the tree because it was their source of shade, became hysterical. It was at that moment, of course, that Christoloski decided to explain how much more important it was for the whole neighborhood to have a streetlight at night than it was for her family to have shade in the summer. The more he explained, the more she protested otherwise. Her protests turned profane when it was hinted by one of the members of the crew that she might be billed by the city for the time the crew spent removing the tree. Her profanity was too much for Christoloski: he called the police to complain that he was being abused and harassed by the very people who stood to gain the most from the increase in safety and security that an unobscured streetlight would provide. Balzic straightened that one out—temporarily—by telling the woman to call a lawyer and by telling Christoloski if he didn't shut up and get back inside his house he was going to be arrested for disturbing the peace.

That was Christoloski, Balzic thought. If ever a man needed to be employed sixty hours a week, it was Christoloski. Unfortunately, he hadn't been employed for more than eight years, maybe longer; Balzic couldn't recall exactly when Christoloski had last been employed. Maybe it was ten years . . .

Balzic got out and went across the street and up the steps to the side door on the second story of Christoloski's house, which was the first floor of the living space. The street floor contained a garage and cellar. He knocked on the frame of the aluminum storm door and called out, "Hey, Pete! Ho, Pete! You in there?"

"I'm right here, where d'you think? Think I'm goin' somewhere?"

"I can't see ya, Pete. I can hear ya, but why don't you turn on some lights? Why you got all the blinds down?"

"Well I can see you. I got all the light I need. Whatta you want?"

"I got some medicine for you. You want it?"

"I'll bet you do. Who's gonna take it first—you or my wife?"

"I only could get two days' supply, Pete, so I don't think they'd do you any good if I took one or your wife took one. Where's Freda? She here?"

"She's here."

"Can I talk to her?"

"What for?"

"I just want to say hello, that's all. You gonna come get these pills or not?"

"She's not very talkative right now. What kind of pills are they, exactly?"

"They're your prescription, Pete. How come Freda's not talkin'?"

"If they're my prescription, read the names off."

"Aw come on, Pete. I can't read these labels, they're all smeary. Uh, one of 'em's potassium, one of 'em's a diuretic, hydro-somethin', and the other one's low pressure somethin', I forget. I don't know how to pronounce it."

"Lopressor?"

"Yeah. Right, that's it."

"What color is it?"

"What color is it," Balzic said under his breath. "Hey, Pete, you want 'em? You come see for yourself what color they are. First, I want to talk to Freda."

"You want to what?"

"You heard me. I want to talk to Freda. And raise some blinds, turn on some lights. You turn on some lights, I talk to Freda, then you get your medicine."

There was no answer for nearly fifteen seconds. Then, his voice much closer now—though Balzic still couldn't see anything except Christoloski's outline when he passed in front of one of the windows—Pete said, "Looks like we have a little problem here. I'm the master in this house and all of a sudden you're giving me orders."

"I'm not giving orders, Pete. I'm tryin' to trade what I have for what you need. There's not an order in the bunch."

"Sure sounds like orders to me."

There was something about Christoloski's tone that Balzic found disconcerting. Balzic tried to recall if he'd ever heard that tone before. It was abrupt, that's what it was, abrupt and self-righteous. Christoloski in the past tended to run on and on: he was filled with one plan or another about how the city of Rocksburg could better itself, about how progress was nothing but an ability to recognize problems and to put everything else aside until they were solved. That's what made America great, that's why communism had been such a farce. Communists didn't recognize problems in manufacturing; all they wanted to do was take over the administration of manufacturing. For Americans, manufacturing came first, the product had to be right, and making it right was a pleasure all its own; all the commies had ever wanted to do was shoot the owners so they could become the owners . . .

Balzic wondered how long it was going to be before Christoloski was going to climb onto his podium. Or was there really a difference in his tone? Was there really something different about him? Or was the difference in the way Balzic was listening?

"I said it sure sounds like orders to me."

"Listen, how many times you been down to City Hall, huh? How many times you seen me operate? Huh? You ever see me give you an order? I ever give you an order?"

"You give lots of orders, don't try to kid me. Told me to get inside my house or you were gonna arrest me. Bet you thought I forgot about that one, huh?"

There was that tone again: abrupt, self-righteous, even a little smug. This was new. This was not the usual superintendent of buildings and grounds. Balzic's breathing was starting to get shallower.

"Where's Freda, Pete? Huh? How 'bout turnin' on some lights and havin' her come out and say hello, whatta you say?"

"She's fine right where she is."

"Uh, Pete, what's the problem here? How come you're in the dark?"

"Ask the guys outside."

The guys outside? "What guys? Where outside?"

"You tell me. Didn't you send them?"

Oh Christ, Balzic thought, and now his heart was starting to pick up the beat. What the hell is this—paranoia city here? "Hey, Pete, I don't know what you're talkin' about, but I didn't send anybody here. The only officer who came here was Officer Yesho and I don't know how he got here but I did not send him. What other guys you talkin' about?"

"Okay. I'll play. You didn't send anybody? Go around the other side of the house. I can see them from where I'm standing."

"You can, huh?"

"Doggone right I can. Go on, go around. See for yourself."

"Uh, how many of 'em are there?"

"I can only see two, but I know there's another one. There was three of 'em when they first got here."

"Uh, when'd they get here, Pete?"

"About a half hour before you did."

"Uh-ha. I see. Okay. Hey, Pete?"

"I'm still here."

"I know you are. What I'm really startin' to worry about is Freda. You wanna get her?"

"I don't have to get her. I know where she is."

"Uh, is she all right?"

"She's all right."

"Uh, I don't doubt your word, Pete, but you mind helpin' me out? You wanna give me a little help on this? I'd really like to hear from Freda herself how she's doin', okay?"

"She's okay. You don't need any more help than that."

Ohhhhhh shit, Balzic thought. This guy is too contained, too abrupt, too goddamn final. This is not good. This is definitely not good.

" 'Smatter, Balzic? Stuck for something to say?"

"I'm not stuck. I've already said what I wanted to say. I just can't get over the feeling you don't wanna do anything for me, and I'm wonderin' how it got that way between you and me. I'm tryin' to think what I ever did to you that would make you wanna take somethin' out on me like this."

"I'm not taking anything out on you—though if I wanted to I'd be within my rights I can tell you that. Far as Freda's concerned, I'm just not gonna let her talk to you, that's all."

"Uh . . . why's that, Pete?"

"She knows."

"I'm sure she does. Hell, yes. But I don't. And I'd really like to know that, Pete."

No answer.

"Pete? Ho, Pete? You wanna talk to me?"

"I don't think so. I think you should leave. I think you should go talk to the guys you sent. I think you should tell them to go home."

Balzic sighed heavily. He tried to inhale and felt his right nostril taking in less air than the left. His neck was tightening, his sinuses were constricting, his hands were getting clammy, the corners of his mouth were starting to get gummy.

"Pete, we've never had a beef, you and me. I've known you for a long time—"

"You never knew who I was till I got let go," Pete interrupted him. "And don't tell me we never had a beef. You're forgettin' about that time that crazy woman across the street abused me for almost an hour. You're not forgettin' it. You just wanna pretend you don't remember, just like everybody else."

"Uh, Pete, look, you never had anything to do with the city till you got let go, am I right or not?"

"That's not the point."

"What is the point?"

"Until I got let go, I was nobody. Nothing."

"Uh," Balzic chuckled in spite of himself and said, "Uh, that's a hellofa way to put it. Makes it sound like what you did up until then was all a waste."

"Well?"

"Well what?"

"Well wasn't it?"

"Uh, how do you figure that?"

"Well until then the only people who knew who I was were Freda and the kids and some of the people I worked with. And then when I wasn't a worker anymore, when I wasn't a worker-bee, when I turned into a watcher-bee, when I started to watch what was going on around this town, all the waste and the favors and the behind-kissing, then all of a sudden I became *somebody*. Just 'cause I complained. Didn't have to run for any office, didn't have to kiss anybody's behind, all I had to do was complain and things got done. And I wasn't even a statistic. I was a nonperson when I discovered that. I ran through all my unemployment compensation, and when I was done with that, when I wasn't even a number anymore, all I had to do was complain and I became the superintendent of buildings and grounds. Nonelected office. You probably think I didn't even know I was it, but I knew it—and I know it. And the only one who doesn't think it's important is Freda. She thinks it's a joke."

Oh Christ, Balzic groaned to himself. "Hey, Pete, quit foolin' around, okay? Is Freda all right?"

"Why you so worried about Freda? Freda, Freda, Freda . . . Freda's got a job, Freda's a re-spect-ed mem-ber of the com-mun-i-ty." His tone had turned snide, singy-songy, snarly.

Balzic was breathing through his mouth.

"Is there somethin' wrong with me worryin' about Freda? What's wrong with that?"

"There's nothing wrong with worrying about Freda. It just isn't necessary 'cause there's nothin' to worry about. What you need to worry about is those guys with the rifles."

Rifles? "D'you say rifles? What kind of rifles?"

"Go ask them. How'm I supposed to know what kind? What difference does it make?"

"Is that why you have the blinds down? The lights out?"

"Whatta you think?"

"C'mon, Pete, quit messin' with me, I'm tryin' to help you out here."

"You want to help me? Give me those pills. And send those goons home."

"Here's the deal, Pete: I talk to Freda, you get the pills. I have to know she's okay. No Freda, no pills."

"What about the goons?"

"Freda first. Then the pills. We'll deal with the goons later." Goons, Balzic thought, Jesus Christ. Paranoia on parade.

"And I keep telling you, Freda's okay. Open the door and put the pills on the counter."

"Pete! Listen to me. You will not get the pills. I will not open this door and put the pills anywhere, is that clear? Nowhere. No pills. The pills stay in my pocket till I see Freda, till she tells me herself she's okay. You got five seconds. If she's not out here talkin' to me five seconds from when I start countin' backwards, I'm gone and the pills are gone with me. You ready? Here we go. Five . . . four . . . three . . . two . . ."

"Okay okay okay okay, I'll get her."

Balzic heard scuffling, shuffling, sliding, grunting, and a burst of air exhaled in a fury. "God-DAMN you! PUT ME DOWN!" Balzic sagged with relief. No matter what else Christoloski had done, he hadn't done anything physically irreversible to his wife.

Heavy footsteps came toward him, the walk of someone

struggling with much weight. Then, with much huffing and puffing, Freda was set down on the floor.

"I can't walk like this," she snapped. "Untie my feet!"

"You wanted to talk to her, here she is."

"I can't move! Untie me!"

"Quit bossin' me around. You don't have to move. All you got to do is talk. And you already done that."

"*Did* that. Or, you *have* already *done* that. Is that so impossible to learn?"

"Freda, you all right?"

"Yes I'm all right."

"I can't see you, Freda, so I have to take your word for that."

"And stop telling me how to talk like a teacher, Freda. You're not in any position. It's my room, my school. I'm the one giving the test this time."

"You wouldn't have the first idea how to give a test. You never knew how to take one—never mind *pass* one."

"Uh, Freda, would you hold it off for a while? Huh? Would you just tell me what kind of shape you're in—specifically? Okay?"

"I'm tied up, that's what kind of shape I'm in. I'm hungry, I have to go to the bathroom, my teeth are floating, but other than these minor inconveniences, I'm fine, thank you—and no thanks to my husband, the ersatz rebel without a cause."

"Without a cause? Without a cause?"

"Uh, Freda, what's ersatz mean?"

"Phony," she said, accentuating the first sound of that word.

"I got no cause? No cause! Put you in charge of leasing the property and you lease it to who you leased it to and I got no cause!"

"*Have* no cause, Peter. I know it's difficult, given your deficiencies, but please try."

Balzic's chin sank and he sighed noisily. He'd heard this one before, more than once. This was when she ridiculed his lack of education and when he ridiculed all the educated people he knew who couldn't replace a lightbulb.

"My what?"

"You heard me."

"Deficiencies? Is that what you said?"

"I said it exactly. And while I'm at it, let's correct this impression you have that I was put in charge of anything around here, least of all leasing one of *your* properties."

"Well who leased it to those creeps if you didn't?"

"I didn't say I didn't lease *that* apartment to *those* people. What I said was I wanted to correct this erroneous—that means wrong—impression you have that *you* put *me* in charge of leasing. Or that *you* have ever put *me* in charge of anything! *You* have never *put me* in charge of anything. You left me no choice but to do something you would have done if you had been here. You *presume* that I will do what you would have done because the workings of your mind are so crystal clear that anyone would not only know what they are but would quite naturally follow them. Crystal Clear Christoloski, that's you. Only you never are!"

"You seen enough? Huh?"

"I haven't seen anything. All I can do is listen."

"You believe it's her?"

"Yes. I believe it's Freda."

"Then put the pills on the counter. Just open the door and reach around to your left there and put them down."

"Oh my god," Freda said. "You mean this was all to get your prescriptions refilled? Honest to god, Peter, you are the—"

"It was not just to get my prescriptions. It was what you did! It was that nigger bum! It was that whore!"

"My god my god, I did what you told me to do. I leased the apartment. She is not a whore. He is not a bum. And I will not use that other word and if you use it again I will scream—"

"You satisfied or not, Balzic? Is this Freda or ain't it?"

"I told you yes before."

"Then open the door and put my pills on the counter."

"All over your damn prescriptions. Just because *your* drugstore happens to be closed the day your prescriptions run out. Honest to god, Peter, you're getting worse by the week."

Balzic tried to open the aluminum door but it was locked.

"Hey, back away there, Balzic. Go on, step back. After I unlock it, then you can come close again. But not till I say so."

"Whatever you say," Balzic said, stepping back down two steps off the small, square porch. He heard a click and then Pete telling him to come on back. He stepped up, opened the door, and took the bottles out of his coat pocket and put them on the counter. Then he closed the door and backed one step away.

A night light snapped on and within two seconds snapped off. All Balzic could see in that time was Freda with her hands tied in front of her. She'd looked as though she was still in the clothes she'd been wearing when she'd come home from summer school, but Balzic knew he was assuming that. It didn't make any difference anyway except to give him a general idea how long she'd been putting up with her husband's shenanigans today.

"Hell these ain't the right pills. And there's only six of 'em. Whatta you tryin' to pull, Balzic?"

"Pull? What pull? I'm not pullin' anything."

"They're the wrong color."

"If you turned some lights on they might be the right color."

"I saw what color they was. They're not the right pills."

"Pete, right on the bottle there's the prescription—a copy of it. The pharmacist just—hell, you know what a pharmacist does. He gets pills out of a big bottle and puts 'em in a little bottle. He told me what they were 'cause I asked him to tell me what they were and what they were for. What's the big deal?"

"Oh he's just being willful. Just spiteful. If you want to know the truth, he's just being Polish."

"Don't you start on my parents, Freda. One more word about them and I shut your trap again for you."

"Ho, Pete. Whoa, whoa. No need to be shuttin' anybody's trap again."

"You're bossin' me in my own house again, Balzic. Same as she's tryin' to do. I'm not gonna put up with that."

"Pete, why don't you get yourself a glass of water and take

those pills, huh? Whatta you say? You wanted them, I brought them, now do yourself some good and take 'em."

"I'm not gonna take these things, Balzic. I don't know what the hell they are."

"You don't know what the other ones are either, but you take them," Freda said.

"You keep quiet."

"All of a sudden you have to have a chemical analysis of your prescription drugs? Had high blood pressure for ten years, Mario, and never once before did he want to know what's in his pills. Not until this moment."

"Never had a reason to think somebody might be tryin' to knock me out till this moment. D'ya ever think of that?"

"Why anybody would want to knock out somebody who's been unconscious for ten years is beyond me."

"Oh you're askin' for it now, you really are."

"Listen to him, Mario. Do you have any idea how many times his prescription was changed till his doctor found the right combination of drugs to get his blood pressure down finally? At least three different dosages of each pill. And never once until now did he ask if he was getting the right pill."

"Now's different goddammit!"

"Don't you dare curse at me in that tone of voice."

"Awwwwww. 'Don't you dare curse at me,' " he mimicked his wife. " 'Not in thaaaaat tone of voice.' Awwwww."

"Oh for crissake," Balzic growled. "Enough's enough. The both of ya, listen to me. I'm tired, I wanna go home, and this here, this—I don't know what to call this—this has gone on about five minutes too long. This is ridiculous. Stupid! You two got a beef with each other, it's time you took it up in front of a marriage counselor. You two been snipin' at each other for years. It's time you decided whether you still want to be married and if you do, to straighten this crap out. You both got an attitude problem, if you ask me—"

"Nobody asked you," Pete said. "And this isn't a marriage problem anyway."

"Oh yeah? Then exactly what kind of problem is it?"

"Yeah, really," Freda chirped up. "I'd love to hear what kind of problem this is."

"When you two both shut up, I'll tell you."

"Oh god," Freda said, sighing. "I can't wait."

"Yeah, right. You think it's some kinda joke," Pete said. "It's no joke. It's all fallin' down. The whole thing. And you think it's a marriage problem, both of you. And that ain't the half of it. That ain't one-fifth of it. America's goin' to hell and you think it's me not stayin' loyal in sickness and health and richer or poorer and that crap. That ain't it."

"So what *is* it, O great seer?" Freda said.

"Yeah, that's it. Call names. Make jokes. Treat me like a jerk. Why not? Everybody else does. Why should you be any different?"

"Mario," Freda said, "the U.S. government gives medals to men for valor and courage and heroism in war. It's about time those old fogies down there in Congress realized women deserve medals for having to live with men who have lost their sense of humor. Is there anything that requires greater heroism? My god, a Medal of Honor ought to be automatic if you live twenty years with a man who can't laugh at himself."

"If you don't shut up, I'm gonna tape your mouth up again."

"You're going to have to, Peter, because as long as I'm able to speak I will not be silent. Not in the face of your nonsense."

"Nonsense, huh? You think it's nonsense the state gives money to that nigger bum for doin' nothing? You think that's nonsense? And that whore? The state *pays* them to sit on their asses and do nothing! What does the state pay me?"

"You are a landlord. A property holder. A venture capitalist, my dear. The only mystery here is why you even consider the possibility that you deserve anything from the state."

"Why I deserve anything? Deeee-serve? 'Cause I been workin' since I was twelve years old, that's why! 'Cause I'm a veteran—a Purple Heart veteran, that's why! 'Cause I worked two jobs for years to buy my property."

"Nobody held a gun to your head, my dear. Nobody forced you to work two jobs—"

"And now I can't find one! Now I'm history! Now *I'm* the bum. I don't even rate food stamps—"

"Food stamps? My god, my god. What do *we* need with food stamps, Peter? Tell me. I make thirty-five thousand dollars a year before taxes. You averaged seventeen hundred dollars a month in rents last year. How in god's name do you believe we qualify for food stamps?"

"That's seventeen hundred before expenses and you know it."

"Peter, are you trying to tell me, in front of the chief of police of this city, that after all your expenses, mortgage, insurance, taxes, repairs, maintenance, whatever—that after all that, you did not net a thousand dollars a month last year?"

"Sheesh. A thousand a month. What the hell's that? That's nothin'!"

Freda groaned and shook her head wildly from side to side. "Peter! My god. In April—remember? In April we paid taxes on gross income of forty-nine-thousand-plus dollars! Peter. My god. There's only two of us. You and me. How much are we supposed to have? What am I missing here? Is somebody supposed to feel that we're deprived?"

"Nobody feels anything for you. You go out."

"Whaaaaat? What do I do?"

"You heard me. You go out."

"I go out? Out? What do you mean I go out?"

"Just what I said. Out. The opposite of in. *I* stay in. *You* go out."

Oh ho, thought Balzic. So now maybe we're getting someplace. So maybe soon I can go home, eat, drink some wine, shower, hug my wife . . .

"What are you talking about, out? What out?"

"Just what I said. Three, four nights a week you're out. You're on this committee, you got this class, you're down the YWCA, hell, you're never home anymore. Go 'head, tell Balzic where you go. Go 'head, see what he thinks."

"For crying out loud, will you listen to yourself? I go to the Y to take a cooking class one night a week for two hours. I go to—"

"And then you go out afterward."

"Another night I go to the White Eagles to help your sister with the bingo—"

"My sister's a jerk."

"Your sister is your sister and she's not my sister and I'm not Polish but I go to the Polish White Eagles to help your sister work the bingo and you don't speak to your sister but *I* go *out* and *you* stay *in*, my god. Believe me, Peter, it wouldn't break my heart at all if *I* stayed *in* those nights and *you* went *out* and helped your sister."

"My sister's a jerk I told ya."

"You've been telling me that for years, but if you went and talked to her once in a while like a normal person you'd find out she was a normal person too."

"You don't know nothin' about my sister, so just get onto somethin' else. Like where do you go every Tuesday, tell Balzic that, why don't ya?"

"That's my quilting night."

"Yeah? Take that to the bank all right. Know how long she's been quiltin', Balzic? Huh? Since before we was married."

"*Were* married. Godddddd. Your grammar's worse now than ever and it's purposely worse. You *want* to sound ignorant. You *want* to demean yourself. You *want* to be ridiculed. Why anyone would want to sound less intelligent is—"

"Less educated you mean. You know the only thing she ain't sewed into one of those damn quilts? Huh? She ain't sewed one full of diplomas. I been waitin' to see that for years now. Yeah. Any day now she's gonna bring one home and in every square there's gonna be somebody's diploma. She's the only person I know ever goes in a doctor's office and gets up and reads the guy's diplomas. Does it every time. What the hell you think, huh? You think you're gonna see somethin' new there, somethin' you didn't see before?"

"I want to make sure they have degrees from accredited universities, that's all I'm looking for."

"She never thinks anybody ever phonied one of them up."

"Of course—my god, I'm not a child. Of course there are

frauds. But when you put your health in a stranger's hands you want to start from somewhere."

"Uh, listen," Balzic broke in. "I know you two could keep this up all night, but I gotta go, so whatta ya say. Pete, huh? You wanna untie her so I can go home?"

"Nobody's gettin' untied until those goons leave."

"Oh for crissake," Balzic said. "Goons. What goons? What goons you talkin' about?"

"I told ya. How many times I got to tell ya? There's three of them out there."

"You said that. Several times. With rifles, right? Jeezus."

"Yeah, right. With rifles. In camouflage suits."

"In what? What kind of suits?" Nah, Balzic thought. Can't be.

"You heard me."

"Say it again." Camouflage suits? Balzic thought again. Impossible. No way.

"Camouflage suits," Freda said, shaking her head. "What next."

"Oh. Youse think it's a joke? A joke, right? Youse think it's such a joke, whyn't you go look, huh, Balzic? Go 'head. Whatta you waitin' on?"

Balzic closed his eyes and exhaled noisily. "Okay. So where are they, huh? Which side of the house? They ain't on this side. They in the back there, or where are they?"

"You'll find 'em. Just start walkin'. They're out there."

"Okay. Here's the deal. I walk, I search, I cover all four sides of the house, I don't find anybody in camouflage suits, I come back, you untie Freda, okay? Deal?"

"Deal," Pete said.

"Hallelujah," Freda said.

"Two minutes," Balzic said. "I'll be back." He bounded down the steps and started around the front of the house. He was almost to the corner and starting to turn up when he stumbled at the sight. Across the street there were not three men in camouflage clothes, but five. He closed his eyes and squeezed them shut.

When he opened them, the five men in camouflage suits

were still there. They had been having a conference, only now they had spotted him and, without a word, they dissolved their circle and opened up to form a rank to face him. Every one of them had a rifle.

"Jesus, Mary, and Joseph," Balzic said aloud. He sighed so loud he startled himself. He almost lost his balance. He inhaled deeply and exhaled, hollowing his diaphragm, and inhaling it out, and then he did it again. Then he started across the street toward them and was about four or five steps away when he stopped again.

"I'll be goddamned," he said, peering at the one in the middle. "Didn't I just see you up the Mutual Aid garage? What am I askin' for—damn right I did." He set off walking again and stopped when he was arm's length from the camo man he'd recognized from the Mutual Aid garage.

"Okay, let's try it again. Who the hell are you, and what do you think you're doin' here?"

"We're the Conemaugh County Special Weapons and Emergency Response Team. I'm Sgt. John Winkerburg commanding."

"You're the who?" Balzic was incredulous. His mouth was hanging open in spite of his effort to not look like an idiot.

The camo man reached into his jacket breast pocket and produced an ID case and extended it to Balzic.

Balzic took it and read it and felt his eyes go wide and his mouth slack.

"This says you're a deputy sheriff for crissake!"

"That's correct."

"Hey, Sergeant. Forgive me if I'm a little fucking baffled, but I've lived in this county all my life and I've never seen a deputy sheriff do anything but move people in and out of the courthouse and hustle raffle tickets. So what's with this special weapons and camo shit and automatic rifles?"

"Just what I said it is. Duly authorized and commissioned."

Balzic snorted and threw up his hands and let them fall. "Duly authorized how? By who? This card you give me, this is a deputy sheriff's card. That clown that calls himself a sheriff hands these things out the way people hand out combs or ball-point pens on election day. That card doesn't mean anything."

"Not true, sir. That card authorizes me to carry out all the duties of a deputy sheriff."

"Hey hey hey, wait a second. A deputy sheriff escorts prisoners, he serves court papers, he collects fines, he guards the courthouse. That's all he does. He doesn't go trampin' around with machine guns—not with machine guns."

"Sir, our commission was examined by the sheriff's solicitor. It was approved. It's legal, it's factual, it's authorized, whether you think so or not."

"What solicitor? The sheriff's got a solicitor? Since when? The sheriff takes his orders from the goddamn DA or from the goddamn judges. And you're gonna tell me the sheriff got his own solicitor now? Bullshit. And what in fucking hell are you doin' here anyway? Why are you here?"

"We're here because we're responding to a hostage situation."

"A what?" Balzic shook his head and laughed in spite of himself.

"My people monitored your radio transmissions. It's been understood for months that your department is undermanned. My people responded as they've been trained to do."

Balzic stuck his index finger in his right ear and wriggled it rapidly. Then he did the same with his left ear. Then he pinched his nostrils shut and exhaled until his ears popped. No matter what he did, the words he'd heard wouldn't go away, nor would their meaning.

"First," he said slowly, "there's no hos-tage sit-u-a-tion. There's no situation period. What there is is a guy havin' a beef with his wife, and I know the guy and I know the wife. Pete and Freda. Okay? They've gone round and round before. Not like this exactly—he's never tied her up before—but they've gone round and round before. Lotsa times. And I take care of it or one of my men takes care of it and we do it without machine guns and camo suits.

"D'you hear that part? Huh? We do it *with-out* machine

guns. So, if you don't mind, I'd appreciate it very much if you'd get the hell outta here."

"We might do that, sir, but one of my men has already taken fire."

"What? Will you quit talkin' like a goddamn TV movie, 'One of my men has already taken fire.' Shit, what're you talkin' about, one of your men has already—"

"That guy you know on a first-name basis, the one who isn't involved in a hostage situation, has fired at my men. That may be something you accept, but that is something my people are not prepared to accept."

"Uh, what did you say your name was?"

"Winkerburg. John A. Sergeant."

"Winkerburg, you talk funny. You don't talk like you're from here. You're from Virginia, North Carolina, someplace like that."

"Fayetteville, North Carolina, sir. And proud of it."

"Fayetteville, huh. Isn't that where they keep that airborne division? Which one is it?"

"That's the 82nd Airborne Division. And it is not *kept* there. It is *stationed* there."

"And Special Forces too, right? Green Berets?"

"You are correct, sir."

"And naturally you put twenty years in there, right?"

"Twenty-three years and six months. Not all of them there. Four tours in Vietnam."

"Lotta rules, right? Lotta regulations? Chain of command, Uniform Code of Military Justice, all that shit?"

"It's not shit, sir."

"I can see it's anything but, with you. So, uh, let me remind you about some of the rules we have around here—"

"I don't think that's necessary. We've been thoroughly briefed."

"Well then good. So, uh, you guys are so up on all the rules, so show me your Act Two-Thirty-Five Certification."

"Our what?"

"Your Two-Thirty-Five ID. C'mon, c'mon, you're supposed to have 'em on you at all times, let's see 'em."

"Sir, uh, I don't know what you're talking about."

"That's what I thought. What I'm talkin' about, Mr. Winkerburg, is the Lethal Weapons Training Act of 1974, Pennsylvania Law Seven-Zero-Five, Number Two-Three-Five, commonly known as Act Two-Thirty-Five. The fact that you do not know what I'm talkin' about plus the fact that you're standin' here holdin' these goddamn machine guns is all I need to know—"

"Just hold it a minute, Chief. Just one minute. We have been briefed by a solicitor—all of these people here plus the rest of the team—"

"Oh there are more of you, huh?"

"Yessir. And we've all been briefed and this is the first time I've ever heard anything about any Act Two-Thirty-what-ever."

"Well that doesn't surprise me, but, uh, just standin' here with those guns, you're all lookin' at one year and a thousand bucks fine plus costs, I don't give a shit what you were or were not told."

Winkerburg held up his right hand, index finger extended. "Give us a few minutes here, so we can talk about this."

Balzic shrugged. "You take however much time you want. The only thing I'm gonna give you is this: you are all gonna get a summons in the mail. It'll take me a while to find out who you all are and where you live, but believe me, don't ignore that summons. Failure to respond to that summons will be a big mistake. Now, you go 'head and have your conversation, but in five minutes I want those weapons unloaded, locked, and gone. I don't care where you take 'em as long as it's out of Rocksburg. Any questions?"

Winkerburg shook his head no.

"Good. I'm glad. And what I'm really glad about is that none of you got excited here. Thank you all for that. Uh, just one more thing, Winkerburg. Who's your next in command?"

"Since you're going to find out sooner or later, it's John Theodore."

"John Theodore, chief of county detectives?"

"I think that's his title, yessir."

"Oh for crissake." Balzic shook his head. "I hesitate to ask, but where's Sitko stand in all this?"

"He's in command."

"Fire Chief Eddie Sitko—we got the same guy?"

"Yessir."

"He's in charge of all of you?"

"Yessir."

"Jesus H. Christ," Balzic said. "I heard it twice before, and I kept sayin' nah, not him, not this time, can't be right. And it's right, it's right. Shoulda known . . . shoulda known."

Balzic turned away from Winkerburg and the other camo men and crossed the street. He looked back at them and then he looked up at Pete Christoloski's darkened house. Balzic bit down on his molars and exhaled and shook his head.

He tried to recall an incident more bizarre; he couldn't. This one topped everything in his memory. All domestic disturbances were bizarre in their own way. People got crazy over the damnedest things. But in all his years of trying to keep husbands and wives and parents and children from doing stupid things to one another, until this moment, he'd never been to a house where the paranoia factor was based on reality. Tens of dozens of husbands over the years had complained about somebody "out there" who was telling them to strangle the wife, shoot the dog, drown the sister-in-law, spill paint on the neighbor's cat, but this was the first time there was ever anybody actually *out there*. And the guys *out there* actually think they belong *out there*. Jesus, Balzic said, *they've* been *monitoring* our broadcasts—is that what he said? *They* know we're *undermanned*—is that what he said? Who the hell asked them, Balzic fumed. Sitko! The goddamn gall of that sonofabitch. He gets himself a goddamn helicopter, god knows how or why, and the next thing we know, he's got himself a squad of goons dressed up in camo suits who think they're legal 'cause they got a goddamn card from the sheriff, the sonofabitch passes 'em out like candy on Halloween.

"Ho! Winkerburg! What the hell are you gonna discuss over there? You got a chain of command or you got a committee? You in charge or not?"

"I am the ranking officer, if that's what you mean."

"Then tell those clowns to unload and lock those weapons and take a walk. There's nothin' for you to talk about."

"You said five minutes? I want five minutes."

Balzic chewed his lips, snorted, sucked his teeth, and cursed silently. He threw up his hands and then brought his fingers together against his thumbs and shook them palms-up at Winkerburg. "Ehhhhh," he growled. "Take your five minutes. But if you're still there five minutes from now, I'm callin' out my entire department including all the auxiliaries plus the goddamn meter maids and then I'm gonna call Troop A State Police."

Balzic spun around before Winkerburg could reply and went to his cruiser. He opened the door, slid behind the wheel, and snatched up the radio speaker.

"Hey, Rascoli, you there? This is Balzic."

"I'm here, Mario, I'm here."

"Okay, listen up. Find the mayor, tell him get his buns down to City Hall, we got a problem. Then get hold of the DA, the sheriff, the chief of county detectives, and Eddie Sitko."

"Okay, you want Strohn, Failan, Markle, Theodore, and Sitko. You want 'em *all* down here?"

"As fast as you can get 'em."

"Uh, what the hell's goin' on?"

"That's what I wanna ask them. 'Cause you're not gonna believe what I just found out. We got us a goddamn SWAT team. Right here in Rocksburg. Bet you didn't know that."

There was no answer.

"Rascoli? D'you hear me?"

"I heard."

"You sound funny."

"I sound funny, uh, I guess because I feel funny."

"What're you talkin' about?"

Again there was no answer.

"Hey, Rascoli? You know somethin' I don't know, you better tell me about it."

"Uh, I think I better wait till you get here. You are comin'
back here, right?"

"As soon as I straighten out this beef between Christoloski
and his wife. I thought I had it straightened out, then I found
out we got this SWAT bullshit. That set everything back.
Never mind. You try to round those people up and I'll try to
settle this."

"Roger, Mario. Out."

Balzic dropped the speaker on the seat, lurched out of the
cruiser, and hustled up the street toward the camo men. When
they saw him coming, they dispersed, two going one way, two
another, and Winkerburg yet another.

Balzic stopped and watched them until they got into three
cars and drove off. He hoped that what he saw was what was
happening, that their departure was genuine and not some stupid maneuver.

He shrugged and hurried back up the steps to the small
porch at the side of the Christoloskis' house.

He slapped the door frame twice. "Ho, Pete! You there?
You hear me?"

"I hear you," came the reply from somewhere deep in the
house.

"They're gone, Pete. D'you see 'em go?"

"I saw 'em."

"So that's two problems solved, Pete, right?"

"What two problems?"

"Hey, Pete, you wanna come a little closer? I can hardly
hear you and my throat's startin' to hurt shoutin' like this."

Balzic could hear him shuffling into the kitchen. He could
hear him breathing. Christoloski was medium height, five
eight or nine at the most, but his stomach hung over his belt
and it didn't take much exertion before his breathing got loud.

"What two problems?" he said again.

"Well, first you got your prescriptions and then I got the
camo men to take a ride."

"I'm not taking those pills."

Oh for crissake, Balzic thought. "Whatta you mean you're
not—hey, Pete, I thought we had that settled."

"*You* thought, not me."

"Pete, those are the right pills. I'm not gonna argue about it because I know they're right and so I'm not gonna waste my time arguin' about something I know is right. You don't wanna take 'em, fine. Don't. But we kept our part of that deal. The next part was the camo guys. I got rid of them. That's another part of the deal. I did that for you. Now I can't see Freda anymore. Where is she? I want to see her. Now."

"She's fine right where she—"

"I want to see her now. I brought you the pills, I got rid of the goons, I want to see Freda. Before I got rid of the goons she was out here. I want her back here. You owe me that."

"I owe you that? What about owin' me? What about anybody owin' me? I'm fifty-eight years old, I been payin' taxes since I was fourteen. I worked for two years underage, lied about my age to work in the foundry. I went to school all day, I worked second trick in the foundry all through high school. When I got out of high school I kept on the second trick in the foundry and then I sold Fuller brush, from then until the foundry went South, I never didn't have two jobs. I worked in the foundry from four to twelve and all day I sold everything. Jewelry, siding—I sold aluminum siding and awnings for ten years. How d'you think I bought these houses?"

"I know all about how you bought the houses."

"Oh sure, you don't wanna hear how hard I worked, right? Nobody does."

"Hey, Pete, I've heard it before. This is not the first time you and Freda been beefin', you know?"

"So what am I—boring I guess. Is that it?"

"Pete, listen to me. You are not gonna solve the problem by tellin' me all over again how you worked hard to buy these houses. That ain't gonna work. And just so you know—the problem here is you're involved in unlawful restraint and you're comin' real, real close to kidnapping, 'cause you've got your wife tied up and I could say you're close to terrorizin' her, which is one of the definitions, and they're both a first-degree felony. You know what that is? Huh?"

No answer.

"A first-degree felony means more than ten years—that's up to the judge. Hey, Pete, what you're doin' here could cost you four years before you ever had your first parole hearing. In the meantime, Freda winds up with everything, 'cause, believe me, a felony conviction? Guaranteed you'll come out of the joint with nothin'. Freda'll own all these houses."

"It ain't fair." Christoloski was close to tears.

"Fair! What the hell's fair have to do with it? Freda signs an information against you and your ass is gone, Pete. There's at least three witnesses against you: your wife, who's a teacher, and two cops. Never mind those nut cases that were across the street. Give it a break, Pete. Apologize to your wife and mean it. Hey, you been givin' her shit for a long time. I know it, your neighbors know it, there's lots of words on paper in our files about it.

"Then one of those goons told me you shot at one of them. I never knew you had a gun. You have a gun? Huh?"

"Maybe I do, maybe I—"

"Oh cut the shit. Yes or no."

"Yes."

"Hand it over. I want it now. This thing's gone far enough."

No answer. Worse, there was no movement.

"C'mon, Pete, goddammit. I'm tired, I've had a long day, and it's a long way from bein' over. You got a gun, give it to me."

"You want it?"

"Yes."

"You really want it?"

"Yes."

"I'll make you a deal."

"I'm listening."

"I'll give you the gun after I tell ya what's wrong."

"What's wrong? Is that what you said? What's wrong with what?"

"Yes or no, you gonna listen?"

Balzic sighed as quietly as he could. Oh shit, he thought. There's no telling how long this could take. "Tell you what,

Pete. I'll listen for five minutes. Then we got to move on. Agreed? Five minutes?"

"Cripes, I won't even get warmed up in five minutes."

"Five minutes, Pete. And if you leave the communists out of it, that'll eliminate a couple hours' worth, okay?"

"Can't leave them out. They're the reason for most of it."

"Well you gotta leave somethin' out, Pete, 'cause you get wound up you can talk for days, you know? And I'm only gonna give you five minutes. And then I'm gonna want the gun and I'm gonna want to see Freda walkin' around with no ropes on her, agreed?"

"Oh, god. Yeah, sure, what the hell. All right."

"You gonna turn on some lights? And can I come in? The bugs are startin' to get to me out here."

"Yah, sure. C'mon in."

Balzic could hear him shuffling toward the door and the lock being popped open.

Balzic opened the door and stepped inside as Pete turned on the night light near the sink.

Balzic didn't hesitate. He made for the sink, took a glass off the rubber drainboard, filled it from the faucet, and drank. He was parched; his throat was raw. As he drank the second glass he glanced at his watch. He put the empty glass in the sink and nodded at Pete. "Okay. Let 'er rip. But five minutes. I'm not jokin'—five, and that's it."

"Okay," Pete said, hitching up his pants and tucking his shirt in.

His stomach was bigger than Balzic remembered. More distressing to Balzic was the sight of the butt of a pistol waggling in the right rear pocket of his pants.

Christoloski leaned against the counter between the stove and the refrigerator, and his mouth started working as though warming up.

"Okay, okay, I'll tell you what's wrong. It started when those flight controllers went out on strike . . . and nobody went out with 'em. We used to have sympathy strikes in this country. When the carpenters went out, the plumbers went out, the electricians, the painters, the lathers, the plasterers, everybody went out. The Teamsters drove up to the picket line and that was it. Pow! That's where they stopped. Management wanted those trucks unloaded, brother, they unloaded them theirselves. Then somethin' happened. I don't know what it was. Maybe all them Teamsters goin' to jail, maybe all them steelworkers making thirty-five, forty thousand a year, coal miners making the same, I don't know what it was. But you know somethin' had to change when them flight controllers went out and not even the damn pilots went out in sympathy. That's when I knew somethin' was changed in America, and then when that TV cowboy fired all those controllers and nobody made a peep— nobody! All the rest of the unions kept workin' like there was nothin' to it, I mean, if the damn pilots don't go out when the controllers go out, and then they don't go out when the con- trollers get fired, I mean, when it's the pilots' dupas on the line, that's when I knew, brother, we're goin' back fifty years as far as the labor movement's concerned. We're goin' right to the days before unions were even recognized.

"So, hey, where these companies goin' in Pittsburgh? Huh? Where they goin' in western Pennsylvania? I'll tell you where. Those steel companies been doin' business with the Mexicans and the Brazilians and the Japs and the Koreans all along. Just like they done with the Germans after World War Two. Every chance they had to set up a mill in another country where they paid coolie wages, they done it. And they go on TV and they look you straight in the face and they try to tell you *they're* in com-pee-ti-tion with *us*. Yeah. Right.

"These are the same sonsabitches tell you kids don't want to work no more. I never played golf in my life but I know them damn golf carts just ruined the caddy job forever. You know how I know it? They done the same thing in the bowling alleys when they put them automatic pinsetters in. I mean when I was a kid, I needed some money, I went down the alleys and set pins every night. Many's the night I double-jumped 'em, boy. Two alleys. I always had money in my pockets. So did every other kid who wanted to work. Where these kids work now, huh? And the same fat farts that're always bitchin' about kids bein' lazy, they're the ones riding in golf carts."

Balzic thought that was as good a place as any to jump in. "If you don't play golf," he said, "how do you know who's ridin' around in those golf carts?"

"My brother-in-law belongs to two country clubs."

"I didn't know Freda had a brother."

"It's my sister's husband's brother. Well, maybe he's not my brother-in-law, but I talk to him a lot about this."

"Oh."

"You know what they talk about all the time? Huh?"

"Who?"

"Them guys riding around in golf carts."

"No. Whatta they talk about?"

"Communists. That's all—"

"Whoa. Just stop right there. You start talkin' about them I'll never get you stopped."

"Goddammit, Balzic, if you don't talk about the communists, you don't know nothin'. That's all they been thinkin' about ever since the Russian Revolution. 'What're the commies gonna do next?' 'Where they gonna do it?' 'How's it gonna screw us?' 'The politicians ain't got no guts, they won't let the Army win.' 'They send the Army in, but they won't let 'em win.'"

Balzic held up his hands. "Pete Pete Pete, whoa! What's the commies got to do with Freda? Just tell me that, huh? Please?"

Pete looked at the floor and shook his head glumly. After a long moment, he looked up and said, "What the commies got to do with Freda is just what you're doin' to me now."

"What I'm doin' to you now? You wanna run that by me again?"

"Jesus, Balzic, we used to talk, me and her. All the time. She used to tell me all the time I was the smartest person she ever met that never went to college. She used to brag about me to her teacher cronies, her friends, her relatives." Christoloski's face twisted in wistfulness and anger. "That was when I was workin' . . . when I was bringin' home steady checks . . . when I was buyin' houses." His voice dropped to just above a whisper. "Everything was fine. We used to have company every Saturday night and Sunday afternoon. She used to laugh, she'd just light up when I'd—when I'd outtalk one of her teacher cronies . . . now, hell, all she does is bitch about me not knowin' parts of speech. I talk better now that I used to.

"But that ain't the worst part. Now she acts like she don't ever wanna be seen with me. She don't ever tell me when she's goin' shoppin' anymore. We used to go everywhere together. Now she don't even want to be seen in the Foodland with me."

Pete pursed his lips and his voice turned to a low roar. "It wasn't the goddamn communists made Rocksburg practically a ghost town, Balzic. It wasn't ol' Stalin and Khrushchev and Brezhnev and the rest of those pinko bastards that shut everything down around here. It was those bastards in golf carts that sent those plants to Mexico and Brazil and Korea, just like they done with Germany and Japan after World War Two.

"You tell me I ain't allowed to talk about the communists? Yeah. Right. Those guys belong to all the fancy clubs around Pittsburgh, they're the sonsabitches declared bankruptcy and went south—South America, South Korea, South Carolina. Before that happened my wife used to talk to me. She used to look at me like I was a man. Now she don't look at me at all unless she can't help it. Now she goes out four five times a week. Half the time she don't even tell me when she's goin' or when she's comin' back." His words came in a rush, from deep in his throat, a guttural snapping and crackling.

"I don't know where to start with you," Balzic said. "Don't you watch TV or read the papers? Where the hell were you when the Berlin Wall came down? Did you see any of that? Huh? Didn't you read about any of that? The commies are history—"

"History my ass. My ass the commies are history. Not for the fat cats in the golf carts they're not—"

"Aw Christ, forget about the commies. Freda don't have nothin' to do with the commies. You think it's gonna solve somethin' to tie Freda up?"

"She can't go anywhere when she's tied up. And I can't forget the commies—I'm never gonna forget about the commies—"

"I asked you if tyin' up Freda was gonna solve anything."

"It solved it long enough that she had to stop and listen to me for a while."

"Okay, Pete, okay. I'm not gonna argue. Give me the gun and go untie her. Your time's up."

"No. No. Hell no, five minutes is not up."

"Yes it is. What're you gonna tell me that's different anyway? You're just gonna tell me the same stuff, just variations of it, and what's that gonna prove? Huh? Pete, give me the gun and go untie Freda. C'mon, I gotta go."

"Okay, just let me tell you one thing. You think the commies didn't influence everything we do, huh, you think—"

"Yo, Pete, hey, ho. Forget the commies, I'm tellin' ya. You been asleep for the last year or what? Huh? The fuckin' Berlin Wall came down, when? November for crissake. Remember? It ain't Stalin over there in Russia, it ain't Khrushchev. And what's-his-face, oh what the fuck's his name, the guy with the birthmark on his head—"

"Gorbachev."

"Yeah right, him. He's barely hangin' on, you know?"

"That don't make no difference. The same time that wall was comin' down over there, there was all this stuff goin' on here about the Constitution, two hundred years old and all that. Remember that? Huh? What'd we overthrow, huh? Not us, but them guys back in 1775, who'd they rebel against, huh? A monarchy, that's who. No more of some jerk rulin' 'cause he says he was appointed by god. So who'd the communists overthrow? Huh? Their own monarchy, the czar. So just tell me something, huh? How come in all those Arab countries, they're all run by a king or a shah or a sheik or something. They flog people for drinkin', they cut off people's hands for stealin', they stone people to death for makin' whoopee—"

"What's your point?"

"My point is, how come we got all these watchdogs yellin' at the Russkis for human rights violations and they overthrow a monarchy—which is what we done—and nobody says a goddamn word when those Arabs stone somebody to death for makin' whoopee. How come it ain't a human rights violation when the Arabs do it? How come we never said nothin' about human rights violations when the ol' shah of Iran had his secret police torturin' people by the thousands? But when one of those Arab countries went socialist or communist all of a sudden they're just loaded with human rights violations. You still don't get it why the commies were everything to the U.S? Huh? I'll tell you what it was, Balzic. What it still is. Those guys in the golf carts, they need the commies. Man, they have to have 'em. Those commies, they justify everything these rich bastards did—do. 'Cause they're still doin' it. Goddamn right. Build a steel mill in Korea, huh? That was to keep Korea safe from the commies. Piss on the three thousand guys they put on the streets in Pittsburgh. And then the sonsabitches tell ya we can't compete 'cause the Koreans only pay their labor about a buck an hour. So then they close another goddamn mill here. Oh, first they go through both the chapters of bankruptcy, you know, seven come eleven, and then they make four more thousand guys feel like shit."

"Pete Pete Pete, whoa whoa. Time's up. It's up. Hand over the gun and go get Freda."

Christoloski reached for his back pocket, brought the gun out, and pushed it into Balzic's chest. "Here's your goddamn gun."

Balzic caught it before it fell. Pete had already turned and was stomping off. In a second he was back. "Those guys, they used to call 'em steelmakers. You know what they make now? Huh? They don't make steel no more. Now they make bums."

"Will you get Freda, please? So I can go home?"

"Yeah yeah, sure." He stomped off again. In a minute he was back followed by Freda, who was rubbing her wrists and staring furiously at him, her mouth pinched so tightly no part of her lips showed.

"Okay," Balzic said, "I want you both to listen to me. This is the third time I've been here to settle something like this. Every other time you two both promised me you'd see a marriage counselor, and here we are again, same old noise. This time we get new wrinkles. This time we get rope and this thing—what is this? An air pistol?"

Pete nodded.

"You know those goons out there had automatic weapons? You know how close you come to—what the hell am I wastin' my breath for? You listen to me, both of you. No more promises. You make an appointment tomorrow morning to see a counselor. And then you call me by noon—"

"Tomorrow's Saturday," Freda said sourly. "We can't make an appointment tomorrow."

"Okay okay then Monday. First thing you do Monday morning you start callin' people. And then you call me and tell me who it's with and for when so I can verify it. And if I don't hear from you by noon Monday, I'm takin' all the paperwork we got on you and I'm goin' down Family Court and I'm gonna drop it on Judge Miller. And here's what I'm gonna tell him. I'm gonna say, 'I got no more time for this nonsense. Not another minute. So issue warrants for them so I can go arrest 'em and haul 'em in.' Both of 'em. But before I come arrest you, I'm gonna call the newspaper and tell 'em to send a reporter and a photographer to Family Court, I'm bringin' in two formerly respectable people who are now makin' asses of themselves. So those are your choices: either get with a marriage counselor or get in front of a judge, with your names in the paper and maybe your pictures."

Balzic held up the gun and shook it at Pete. "An air pistol? What the hell you think you were gonna do with this, Jesus."

He turned and stepped out of the kitchen, then bounded down the concrete steps to the sidewalk and across the street to his cruiser.

Five minutes later he was parked in his slot at City Hall.

Balzic hurried into the duty room to find Rascoli seated at the radio console, sipping something hot out of a mug.

"Where the hell is everybody? Anybody here yet? D'you call 'em?"

"Tried to, Mario. But nobody was answerin' at the mayor's house, the DA's out and so is Markle, probably at the same place, the Democrats are havin' a dinner I think. All I got from

Theodore was his answerin' machine. Sitko's wife thinks he's at the dinner."

Balzic scowled and slumped onto a desk. "Anybody say where this dinner is?"

Rascoli shrugged. "Hose Company One's where the Democrats usually do their things. Depends whether it's the city Democrats or the county. If it's just the city I'd say it's there for sure."

"Why would the DA and the sheriff be there?"

"Mario, I don't know they're there, I'm just assumin' they're there. But the mayor ain't there, I know that. I'm just sayin'—"

"Okay. Forget about that for a minute. I wanna ask you something else. When I told you over the radio about this SWAT, this goddamn SWAT team we suddenly developed, you said you didn't want to talk about it until I got back here. So here I am."

"Yeah, right." Rascoli cleared his throat—or tried to—several times. He pushed his chair away from the console and abruptly stood up, tugging up his trousers and thumping himself in the chest. After a moment, he said, "Guess something went down the wrong pipe."

Balzic canted his head and squinted at him. "Hey, Ras, what's goin' on here?"

"Uh, Mario, I don't know whether I oughta be tellin' you this."

"You haven't told me a thing yet, Ras. But you sure look like a guy with his hand in the wrong drawer."

"Yeah, well see, the thing is, I got absolutely nothin' to hide. My problem, uh . . ." Rascoli dropped into his chair and rolled it up to the console. He eased his head back and sighed, puffing his cheeks. Then he relaxed his shoulders and let his head come forward slowly. His eyes were closed.

"C'mon, Ras, what's the problem?"

"Problem is, I got big ears. Always have. My old lady, she gets pissed off at me. When I don't come home from someplace when I'm supposed to? She calls me Dumbo. 'Member? The cartoon elephant with the giant ears?"

"I remember. The one that couldn't walk 'cause his ears were so big they dragged on the ground and then he discovered he could fly and he turned into some kind of hero."

"Yeah, right, that's the one."

"Hey, Ras, your old lady didn't give you that name. I did."

"Huh? You?"

"Yeah, me. Your old lady was always callin' me to find out where you were and I told her you couldn't help it, you had to listen to everybody's story 'cause you had these big ears kept you from walkin' home. You kept trippin' over 'em, you couldn't help yourself, you just had to listen to everybody's goddamn problems."

Rascoli shook his head. "I'll be a sonofabitch. I always thought it was her."

"Well now that we got that straight, exactly what did you hear?"

Rascoli bopped his head from side to side four or five times. "Uh, I heard about this SWAT thing six, seven weeks ago."

"How long?"

"At least six weeks ago."

"You *heard* about it then? When'd you *confirm* it?"

"About a month ago."

"A month? A fuckin' month ago and you didn't say anything to me? Hey, Ras! We got people runnin' around this town in camouflage clothes carryin' M-16s and they never heard of Act Two-Thirty-Five. They're carryin' deputy sheriff's badges. That asshole Markle hands 'em out to every jerk who wants to carry a gun and doesn't wanna apply for a permit."

Rascoli held up his hands and turned away, squeezing his eyes shut. "I know, I know—"

"You know! If you know, why in the fuck didn't you say somethin'? Jesus Christ . . . a month?"

"Hey, Mario, it was a bad decision on my part. But the man had a decision to make and he came to me for advice. And I gave it to him. I listened to his problem and I told him what I'd do if I was him."

"Which was what, exactly—or is that confidential too?"

"Oh c'mon, Mario, don't make it any worse than it is, you know?"

"Worse! Me? I'm makin' it worse? I'll tell you how worse it is. There's a yahoo named Winkerburg runnin' around this town with an attitude from here to North fucking Carolina, which is where he comes from, a goddamn refugee from the Special Forces, you know? Green Berets? And he's the self-proclaimed commander of this bunch of goons, all dressed up like he is, and they're all carryin' automatic weapons, that's machine guns, Ras, paisan, and they all get this blank look when I say the words 'Lethal Weapons Training Act.' So now you tell me how much worse I can make that?"

"You already made it a lot worse, Mario. A lot worse."

"Really? Well, before you get all overcome by guilt here, I think maybe you better tell me who it was you advised. You wanna do that?"

"I don't want to, Mario, believe me I don't. On the other hand, I don't wanna not tell you." He squeezed his eyes shut again and rubbed his forehead hard.

Before he could say another word, the outside door was pulled open, and the Chief of County Detectives John Theodore stepped in. Theodore was a blocky man, balding, and barely tall enough to have met state police height requirements when he'd begun a long career with them. District Attorney Howard Failan had hired him to bring some respectability to a detectives bureau that up until Failan's election had been primarily a patronage job, filled by cronies who had campaigned for whoever had been running for DA. Theodore had done what Failan had asked: he'd hired good men, kept them sharp by rotating them through all the training programs the state police offered their own people, and absolutely refused to allow any of them to get near anything in the courthouse that smelled of politics.

What Balzic admired about Theodore was that he did his job despite the fact that his wife was diabetic, had had both feet amputated in the last two years, and was slowly going blind. Theodore never talked about his wife's health. He seemed to smile less frequently and he didn't seem to Balzic to want to talk about cooking much anymore. Theodore had once been famous for his sugarless desserts, almost as celebrated for them as for his patience in pursuing the smallest details in his investigations. More and more, he seemed intent on doing what he had to do and less and less convinced that making conversation had any part in it.

He came toward Balzic and leaned on the counter and laced his fingers together. "Mario. Sergeant. I got your message. What can I do for you?"

"Let's go back to my office, John, okay? Sorry to call you in like this, but I've got a real problem here. Straight back, John, last door on the left there, I'll be there in a minute." Balzic turned to Rascoli. "Okay. Gimme the name. No speech, no guilt, no nothin', just the name."

"Okay. Yesho."

Balzic felt his eyes go wide. "Yesho?"

"That's right."

"He came to you and asked you whether he should join up in this little foreign legion here, is that it?"

"Yessir."

"And you told him yes?"

"Not exactly, but, uh, yeah, more or less."

Balzic closed his eyes and let out a long breath through his nose. He turned and walked back toward his office, shaking his head and muttering all the way.

Before he even closed the door to his office, he said to Theodore, who was sitting in a straight-backed chair beside the desk, "Just confirm one name for me, John, okay?"

"If I can, sure."

"Yesho. He part of this SWAT we, uh, suddenly developed around here?"

"Yes. Uh, it's SWERT."

Balzic dropped into his chair, looking intently at Theodore. "Uh, SWERT SWAT, SWAT SWERT, whose fuckin' brainstorm was it, huh? You mind tellin' me that?"

"I'm not sure, Mario. Failan approached me about it. I don't know whose idea it was originally."

"How long ago was this?"

"You mean when Failan first approached me?"

Balzic nodded, rubbing his face.

"Three months. Maybe longer."

"Did you get the impression it was his idea?"

"No," Theodore said thoughtfully. "I got the impression then that it was Eddie Sitko's idea. As far as I understood it, the whole idea of the SWERT was wrapped up with the medevac chopper. That's the way it was presented to me. The one wasn't possible without the other. And Sitko was the force behind the chopper."

Balzic stared at his fingernails and shook his head. "Jesus Christ, John, I can't believe that somebody with your experience—what'd you have? Twenty-five years with the state?"

"Twenty-six. But before you start making connections here, I had nothing to do with this. Failan approached me about it when I said he did, but he did not seek my advice and I didn't give it. Not then anyway."

"You mean he didn't do anything more than just let you know what was goin' on."

"That's right."

"Did he ever ask your advice?"

"Never."

"D'you ever give him your advice?"

"No."

"Uh, you wanna expand on any of this, John? Huh? I'd really appreciate it."

Theodore took a long time to answer. "Mario, there's nothing I can say now that'll change what has already gone down, and I don't see much benefit to me saying anything that's going to remove the warm, dry blanket that's over my rear end."

"But, John, Jesus, this doesn't make any sense."

"Of course it doesn't. Do these concrete flower boxes in front of the courthouse annex make any sense? I'll bet ten dollars against a dime we have the only antiterrorist flowerpots in America in front of a county courthouse. Make that a hundred dollars against a dime. Whose idea was that? You know as well as I do it was Sitko's. The man's possessed. Obsessed. Hysterical. But *he* isn't what worries me. What worries me is, in order to get those concrete flowerpots in place, he had to get the permission of three county commissioners, the president judge, and the director of emergency management—and they all gave their permission. Without—as far as I know—one dissenting argument."

Theodore folded his hands in his lap and shook his head slowly, ruefully. "And why? When the White House said that goofball in Libya was sending over a team of assassins, we wound up with concrete flowerpots, four feet square, three feet high, and six inches thick. Two of 'em. I'll tell you, Mario, I would pay large money to have a tape recording of the conversation that led to the positioning of those flowerpots.

"I mean, think of it, Mario. The three county commissioners, the president judge, the director of emergency management, and the fire chief actually talking seriously about where to put those flowerpots to stop some nut from Libya, some 'holy warrior' in a Mercedes-Benz loaded down with three or four hundred pounds of plastic explosives.

"Imagine this. Seriously. Just try to imagine it. The four most powerful elected officials in a county of three hundred fifty, three hundred sixty thousand population, actually thinking there was anything they could do that was worthy of defending against some Libyan fanatic. Just imagine: you're a suicide bomber and you want to make it to Moslem heaven, so what do you do? What else? You bypass every U.S. strategic and tactical target in the world—I mean we do have a few military bases, computer intelligence centers, things like that—and you ignore all of them because your target of choice—are you ready for this?—your target of choice is the Conemaugh County Courthouse in Rocksburg, Pennsylvania.

"And you want me to expand on this airborne SWERT unit," Theodore said, as deadpanned as he had spoken throughout.

Balzic was shaking with laughter.

"I wish I, uh, I wish I could share your amusement in this."

"Oh, hell, c'mon, John. I was laughin' at the way you put it. I wasn't laughin' at it, for crissake."

Theodore nodded quickly several times. "I suppose whenever you encounter idiocy like this, you have to take your humor where you can find it. Personally, I'm not laughing too much these days. The thought of three hundred and fifty volunteer firemen walkin' around with deputy sheriff's IDs and shields, I'm sad to say, Mario, that thought just does not stimulate my laugh control center."

Balzic stiffened and suddenly had trouble clearing his throat. "How many?"

"At least three-fifty. I'm sure that's conservative. Mario, I can't believe you don't know about this."

"Oh I know about it. But it's always, you know, it's always been some kind of goddamn bizarre rumor nobody ever checked out."

"It's no rumor," Theodore said. "Since he's been in office, Markle's handed out at least six hundred shields. One afternoon I had nothing to do, so I had a long look through his purchase orders over the years. And then I checked it out with the company that sold 'em to him. There's no discrepancy. The man's been sheriff for at least twenty-two years. He's in his fifth term. When you think about it, the only surprising thing is that he kept it down to six hundred. In twenty-two years, jeez, you know, he could have hit a thousand easy."

"Well, I guess that's some consolation."

"That's no consolation and you know it." Theodore's eyes glazed over. For ten seconds he drifted off. His jaw muscles rolled, his nostrils flared, he seemed to settle deeper into his chair though he barely moved. Then just as suddenly he was back, his gaze locked onto Balzic's. "Mario, there's a time when you have to get out. I'm very close to that now. There's something loose here that's not like anything I've ever seen before. Maybe the thing is—and I don't know that what I'm saying is true—but I just have this feeling. Maybe the state police are too removed from politics—not at the top of course, but down where I was, I mean, politics just didn't enter into it for me. I mean, I tried very hard to separate myself from all of that. But,

I had my suspicions about it, my private jokes, but I was never really part of it, so I didn't know, not in my bones the way you know something. I never knew it that way, you follow me? Then when I got to be part of it, when Failan hired me, for a long time I kept telling myself that, you know, that old chestnut about politics is the art of the possible and the only true synonym for democracy is compromise and all I needed to do was get acclimated and I'd be all right.

"But, Mario," Theodore went on, "I've been acclimated for three years now, and these people squeeze my bladder flat. They scare the pee right out of me . . ."

"Uh, John, you're gettin' a little fuzzy around the edges. You wanna come back to the SWAT thing?"

"SWERT," Theodore said more somberly than before. "No I don't. I think if you really want to know about it, I think you should talk to the district attorney and the sheriff and the president judge and the fire chief. I include the president judge because of his position on the board of Mutual Aid Ambulance Service."

"Hey, John, you're not under oath here, you know? I'm just lookin' for background. There's no reason for you to get uptight with me."

"Do I look uptight?"

"Now you do. Sure as hell do. Few minutes ago you had me laughin'. Now you look like you wish you were someplace else—real bad."

Theodore shrugged. "That's probably because I do." He stood abruptly and peered intently into Balzic's eyes. Even when he wasn't trying, Theodore could stare as well as anybody Balzic had ever known, and when he was trying to measure someone, as he was now, his gaze could be unnerving.

"Mario, I'm going to say two words to you and then I'm leaving. In a very short time, I'm also going to be leaving this area. That's not for discussion."

"I understand," Balzic said, nodding.

"The two words are: Conemaugh Foundation."

"What?"

"I said them clearly enough and loudly enough that I

know you heard me. I'm not going to repeat them." He held out his hand. "Good-bye, Mario. Good luck."

Balzic stood and shook Theodore's hand. "Same to you, John." He was puzzled. "This sounds like, uh, you know, something permanent."

"No, no. It's nothing like that. I haven't done anything. But that's really the problem. I think I should have and now, well, it's way past time for that. What I'm talkin about is moving on. That's all, nothing more, nothing less. Just trying to get with a . . . with a . . . different organization so I can get my perspective back. Gotta go, Mario. Again, I wish you luck."

Balzic watched him leave and then tried to comprehend what had been said. Theodore hadn't done anything? He thought he should have? And now it's way past time? And now he's moving on? Conemaugh Foundation? What the hell is that?

Balzic picked up the phone and punched the numbers for Det. Sgt. Ruggiero Carlucci's home phone.

In the second ring, Mrs. Carlucci answered. Balzic rolled his eyes and swallowed hard. "Uh, Mrs. Carlucci, this is Mario Balzic. How are you?"

"Whatta you care? How am I. You wanna know how am I? Huh? I'll tell ya. I can't put shoes on no more, that's how all swoll up my toes are. And you want me to tell ya 'bout my ankles? Huh? Or my knees?"

Too bad your tongue ain't all swoll up, Balzic thought. "Uh, Mrs. Carlucci, I'm sorry to hear that."

"Yeah, me too. So whatta you want—as if I didn't know. Jesus Christ, can't youns do nothin' without botherin' my boy?"

"Uh, he's a valuable member of the department, ma'am. I'd be lost without him."

"Then why the hell don't you give him a raise, you cheap bastard—"

"Ma, who is that?" came Carlucci's voice. "Ma, is that for me?"

"It's that cheap bastard you work for, that's who it is."

"Ah Ma, come on, jeez oh man . . . Gimme the phone, Ma . . ."

"He's on vacation, you bozo, Balzic. Can't you let him have some time to himself, huh?"

"Oh Ma, for god's sake . . ."

"Ow! That hurt."

"I'm sorry, Ma, but let go of the phone, please? C'mon, Ma."

"Here, take the goddamn phone. Kiss his ass all over the place, go 'head. What's it get ya? Won't even let ya alone on vacation . . ."

"Mario? Sorry about that."

"Forget about it, I know your mother. So, listen, Rugs, I got a problem. You know anything about a Conemaugh Foundation?"

"A who?"

"Conemaugh Foundation. That make any noise in your head?"

"No. Pertaining to what?"

"I don't know. I just heard about it. And I thought I'd try you first."

"Uh, Mario, where are ya?"

"The station, why?"

"I'm gonna have to call you back. I gotta go. Bye."

Two minutes later, while Balzic was stewing again over what John Theodore had said, Carlucci called back.

"Sorry, Mario. Uh, where were we—foundation, what was that again? The what foundation?"

"Hey, Rugs, you know, sooner or later you're gonna have to do something about your mother."

"Mario," Carlucci said with a catch in his throat, "I've checked out every nursing home within fifteen miles. The cheapest one wants a thousand a month and they all want title to the house. How far you think I've gotten tryin' to get her to put the house in my name? Huh? So she won't have to give it up? Every time I even mention it, she gets crazy. Meantime, the waiting list to get in the county home is like ten months, you know? Not like I wanna put her down there. But if she has to give up the house, then where exactly am I supposed to live? But if I can't turn over the house, the cheapest one I can get her into—I mean the only one I wouldn't be afraid of puttin' her in—that one wants sixteen hundred a month. Hey, Mario, you know how much I make. I mean, I know your heart's in the right place, but, uh, I'd appreciate it if unless you got a solution for me you wouldn't tell me sooner or later I gotta make a decision about my mother, you know? I mean that doesn't help me out—"

"I'm sorry, Rugs—"

"And don't say you're—don't say that, okay? Please?"

Balzic cleared his throat.

"Uh, so where were we? This foundation, what is that?"

"I don't know. I was hopin' you'd know. Conemaugh Foundation. I never heard of it. Don't know what it is. This is a whole new thing for me."

"Me, too. Well, listen, I'll get out my little book of numbers and I'll start callin' around. But tomorrow, okay? Not now—oh shit, I gotta go."

The phone clicked off, and Balzic dropped it into its cradle. He started to get up and sat back down just as quickly because the door opened and District Attorney Howard Failan stepped in.

Failan's full name was Howard Ian Failan and he looked like a cherub. His favorite food was ice cream and his favorite beverage was Irish whiskey and his face and belly reflected both. For the last three Christmases he'd managed to get his picture in each of the county newspapers at least once, playing Santa Claus to retarded kids or orphaned kids or delinquent kids. He loved playing Santa Claus almost as much as he loved shaking hands and slapping backs and toasting all the sainted mothers of the world while running for office, and he was always running for office. Underneath all his Irish malarkey beat the heart of a vote-counter: his knowledge of where the votes were and weren't in every precinct rattled even the best county poll-watchers. In one sense, he was a walking cliché of every corny Irish gimmick that had been worked in every election in the twentieth century in local American politics. But in an-

other sense, he was utterly different: in addition to his law degree, he'd earned a master's degree in computer science. If
sweepstakes offers run by magazine sales companies could be
sent to every household with a specific salutation, then, by all
that was holy to an Irishman, so could voter appeals. Which is
exactly what Howard Failan had done. He'd combined mailing
lists and malarkey in a computer program that put him into office with the largest winning vote margin among all countywide offices in his first attempt at elected office.

And after he'd gotten into office, he'd computerized as
many facets of his work as he could. He entered the docket,
the calendar, and the status and disposition of every case into
his computer. If knowledge was power, Failan's idea seemed to
be that instantaneous knowledge was power distilled. He
knew who was being investigated by whom and for what, and
he knew it in a matter of seconds. In his office, with his computer terminal by his side, he tended to look a lot more smug
than he looked at this moment, when Balzic invited him to
have a seat.

Of course, Failan rarely drank in the daytime, and he'd
just now come from a Democratic fund-raiser where the
whiskey had doubtless flowed often—in his direction.

"Mario, me boy," Failan said, blowing out his ruddy
cheeks and patting his belly, "what calamity summons me
here?"

Oh shit, Balzic thought. He thinks he's one of those Barry
what's-his-names in all those hokey movies. All he's missing is
a goddamn derby.

Balzic spelled it out for him, from the helicopter to the
men in camouflage clothing to the Mutual Aid garage to Act
235, and throughout his recitation he watched Failan's reaction. He purposely said nothing about the incident involving
the Christoloskis.

Failan's reaction was to lace his fingers together on his
belly and peer intently at Balzic. Every so often Failan would
cant his head to first one side and then the other, but he said
nothing until Balzic was finished.

After a long moment passed, Failan thrust his tongue between his teeth and his upper lip and grunted softly several times. Then he sniffed twice, cleared his throat, and settled himself more upright on his chair.

"I can't quibble with the general outline of your facts," Failan began finally. "It's certainly true that a Special Weapons and Emergency Response Team has been formed at the county level. And it's certainly true that I was apprised of its formation very soon after the idea was first brought forward. Lots of people were apprised of this. Certainly the director of emergency management was directly involved. Certainly the chief of county detectives was apprised. The sheriff, no doubt in my mind the sheriff was apprised. I'm trying to think who else—"

"Excuse me, Mr. Failan, but you're missing my point here."

"Which point is that, Chief?"

"Uh, the point is that the people I'm talking about are runnin' around in my jurisdiction playing cops and robbers only they never heard of Act Two-Thirty-Five."

"You've mentioned Act Two-Thirty-Five several times now and you've just mentioned it again. What's your problem with that?"

"Uh, my problem is these people are carrying deputy sheriff's IDs and they're carrying prohibited offensive weapons and they've never heard of Act Two-Thirty-Five."

Failan cleared his throat and sniffed again. "Chief, it's been some time since I read Act Two-Thirty-Five, and my memory's a bit vague, but as I recall, that act had to do with private cops—"

"It does. You're absolutely right."

"—rent-a-cops."

"Right."

"Well how's that apply to these people you seem to be so upset about?"

"Well whatta you mean how's it apply? They're untrained. They admit they're untrained. When I asked them about Two-Thirty-Five, their head honcho gives me this dull, blank, stupid stare."

Failan held up his hand. "Again I ask, how's it apply to these people—"

"And again I tell you that they're carryin' machine guns in my jurisdiction and they're doin' it on the authority of the god-damn sheriff—uninvited. There's only two guys in this juris-diction who can invite outside help—the mayor and me, and I sure as hell haven't invited anybody's help and I don't know what the mayor knows 'cause I haven't talked to him about this but I do know that he sure as hell hasn't said anything to me about this."

"Well I don't know why he would," Failan said, chuckling softly. "This isn't a city issue here. This is a county matter. The county commissioners—all three of them—resolved to have the director of emergency management form a Special Weapons and Emergency Response Team to respond to certain prescribed situations. And he did so. That hardly falls under the mandate regarding private police in Act Two-Thirty-Five. This is a county police agency. This is—"

"This is a bunch of uninvited goons in camo clothes carryin' prohibited offensive weapons in my jurisdiction."

"There's no need for you to raise your voice, Chief. You've made your point. But you seem to have forgotten that the city of Rocksburg, while it is surely your jurisdiction, is also the county seat of Conemaugh County, of which I am the chief law enforcement officer."

"So?"

"So? Ahhhhh." Failan wiped the corners of his mouth. "You got any coffee around here? I would very much appreciate a cup of coffee."

"How do you want it?" Balzic said, standing abruptly.

"Just black. Black will be fine."

Balzic hurried out to the coffee urn in the duty room. He found a stack of Styrofoam cups, pulled one free, and filled it with coffee. He started back to his office, but stopped beside the radio console and squinted at Rascoli.

"A month ago you knew about this? A fucking month? And you didn't say anything to me? I don't understand how you can know about somethin' like this for a month and not say a word to me. Did I ever do anything to you that I can't remember? Did anything I do ever screw you? I mean you personally, huh?"

Rascoli swallowed and shook his head no.

"Then how the fuck could you not tell me about this?"

Rascoli hunched his shoulders, splayed his hands palms-upward, canted his head to the right, and thrust down the corners of his mouth, as though to say, "So? So I did it. So whatta you want from me?"

Balzic stuck out his chin, brought the fingers of his right hand against his thumb, and shook his head at Rascoli twice, as though to say, "Plenty. I want plenty from you. Most of all, what I want from you is a sense of priority about where your loyalties are."

Balzic growled something unintelligible finally and spun away, trying to walk evenly so as not to spill the coffee.

Back inside his office, he set the cup in front of Failan and resumed his own seat. "So where were we?"

"Where we were was in the middle of a jurisdictional dispute that, uh, qualifies as a tiff, I think. Thanks for the coffee. Tastes every bit as bad as I thought it would."

"You're welcome. I enjoyed pourin' it 'cause I knew how lousy it was gonna taste."

Failan put on his campaign face, his smile as warm as any Irish politicians who had ever kissed a baby or worn a fireman's helmet or eaten a pirogi off a fork held by a babushka. "Chief, we're better than this. I see no need for us to lose our perspective—"

"My perspective isn't in doubt here," Balzic interrupted him. "We—you and me—got a bunch of guys runnin' around on shaky authority carryin' illegal weapons. You may be the chief law enforcement officer in this county, but you can't fuckin' declare the laws of the Commonwealth null and void just 'cause they happen to conflict with your desire to have a goddamn SWAT team. A machine gun is any firearm that continues to fire as long as the trigger is depressed, and a machine gun is a prohibited offensive weapon. That's in Section 908,

Title 18, Crimes and Offenses, Pennsylvania Consolidated Statutes—which you know a hellofa lot better'n I do."

Failan took another swallow of coffee, set the cup on Balzic's desk, and stood, suppressing a yawn. "I think it's time for me to go home and get some sleep, so I'll be saying good night, Chief."

"Uh, that's all you're gonna say?"

"Well, what do you want me to say?"

"What I want you to say is you're gonna put a stop to this nonsense, that's what—"

"Well of course you would want that. But that's because you see this as a problem that needs a solution. And that's where we differ. I don't see it as a problem; therefore, I don't see it as requiring a solution—which is a long way of sayin', I'm goin' home. Good night."

"It's gonna be a problem for you when I bust these guys and confiscate their weapons. The guys can be bailed out, but their weapons can't. What do they cost—eight, nine hundred bucks apiece? I'll hold 'em forever if I have to. Which means you'll have to buy new ones and as soon as I find out about it, I'll do the whole razzmatazz again. So how many times you think you can buy six, seven thousand dollars' worth of weapons before people start laughin' at you?"

"Nobody's laughing at me. Good night." Failan lurched out of his chair and was gone before Balzic could get out another word.

Yeah, right, Balzic grumbled to himself. Nobody's laughing at anybody except me. I'm the schnook here. I got people in my own department playing commando and I'm stumbling around for a month, can't find my ass in the dark with either hand and don't even know enough to know my ass is missing. Right under my nose and I can't smell nothing. It might be time to get out, time to take a quick fade into the sunset. Sell the house, move to Florida, learn how to fish, learn how to barbecue, get myself a red-hot job patrolling a mall, wear one of those real ugly brown and tan uniforms, carry a big flashlight and a can of Mace and roust teenyboppers out of the pinball rooms. Couldn't be a punishment more fit to the crime than to have to deal with a bunch of pubescent wise-asses who laugh in your face. Serve me right. If you're too goddamn dense to know what's happening in your own department, you ought to be doing guard duty in a goddamn mall, nothin' but business, everything's for sale, that's the whole, sole reason they put those goddamn things out in the middle of nowhere, nobody lives there, nobody even thinks about living there, it ain't for living, it's just for buying and selling, and in bad weather, big fucking deal, they let the cardiac rehab patients in an hour early so they can exercise.

Balzic heaved himself out of his chair and lumbered into the duty room. He couldn't believe what he saw when he looked at the clock: 10:30 P.M. His body was telling him it was 2 A.M.

"Hey, Ras, I'm goin' to Muscotti's. When Yesho gets off his watch, you tell him to come find me. I wanna talk to him. You tell him he doesn't find me within fifteen minutes after his watch is over, he can consider himself suspended without pay."

"Yes, sir."

"Anything else you wanna tell me, Ras? Anything at all?"

"No, sir."

"Anybody else in this goddamn department playin' commando?"

"No, sir."

"Does that mean you know that nobody is, or does that mean you don't know?"

"That means I know that nobody else besides Yesho is."

Balzic nodded several times. "You tell him come find me. His ass is on the line here. His professional ass."

"I will tell him. It will be done."

Balzic walked out of the duty room, and each step felt like he was slogging through a swamp. He dropped into his cruiser and drove the three blocks to Muscotti's as though disconnected to his body: he watched himself go through the motions of driving, watched his hands on the wheel and had to tell himself that those hands were his, were connected to him and could do nothing without a message from his brain. It made no difference what he told himself; he felt disconnected.

He found a parking space near Muscotti's side door. He parked, opened the door and tried to ease out of the cruiser and heard himself grunting and felt stuck. Feeling disconnected was one thing. Feeling like he was walking through a swamp was another. But feeling so bogged down that he couldn't move? Then he realized he'd forgotten to pop the latch on the seat belt. Oh man, he thought, man-oh-man. When he finally got himself out of the car, he stopped on the sidewalk and peered up at the sky: it was dark, heavily overcast, not a star to be seen.

"What the hell you lookin' for?" he said aloud. "Somethin' up there gonna send you a message?"

He shrugged, sighed, shook his head at his lack of focus, and slouched through Muscotti's side door. He paused on the landing inside, letting his eyes adjust to the bar light, before going down the four steps to bar level. There were four persons at the bar, only one of whom Balzic recognized. Iron City Steve was slumped over the bar with his chin resting on his hands, one fist set upon the other. He was humming a melody he alone knew. The other three men seemed to be together and were arguing about some football player. Dom Muscotti was mixing himself a whiskey and water and scowling at his glass as though he'd just found unquestionable proof the water supply had been poisoned.

Muscotti paused in midswallow and eyed Balzic warily. "Don't you ever go home?"

"Just gimme a beer."

"One beer, comin' up. Fifty-eight bucks."

"It's gonna be one of those nights, huh?"

"You could pay cash, or you could listen to my story, the choice is yours." Muscotti poured a draft and set it in front of Balzic.

"This better be a good story."

Muscotti snorted and laughed, his stomach rising and falling, his eyes dancing. "You're gonna like it." He stood in front of Balzic and put his elbows on the bar.

"So this guy comes in, see? He's pushin' the paper around, give him a drink, give them a drink, blah blah blah. He's wearin' his best green collar, see, green shirt, green pants, hard-toe shoes, he got this pinky ring on, flashin' the sparkles, he got about four gold chains on his neck, he's smokin' this cigar big as a horse's dick, and I'm sayin' to myself, who *is* this friggin' guy, I know I know him from somewhere only I ain't seen him for a long time. So finally it comes to me, after I watch him in action for about a half hour, I says to him, uh, hey, didn't you use to be in the floor business? He says, 'I'm still in the floor business. I never left.'

"So I'm thinkin' right away, hey, yeah, this is him. This is the clown use to be up on the hill, got busted for not with-holdin' taxes for his employees, plus he never bought work-men's comp insurance, plus he kicked back on every job he did, he did all those nursing home jobs, remember?"

"Sort of," Balzic said.

"Well, it was him. Federales busted him on the tax thing, and he copped a plea there, but then the state got him on the fraud, the conspiracy, with those guys from the old people's home, remember now? The one over in Westfield Township?"

"Yeah, it's sort of comin' back to me."

"So whatta you think he's doin', huh? That friggin' weasel? He's in here puttin' the hustle on me. Yeah. Listen to this. *He's*—him—he's gonna cut *me* in for five percent of every-thing I throw his way. You talk about face. I thought I heard it all. I listened to him for about twenty minutes. Finally, I looked at him, I said, 'Hey, my mother works, she gives me ten percent. I don't tell you where to buy a money order for five percent.' He gets this hurt look on his face, that's the part I wanted to tell you, I'm not kiddin' you. He actually looked hurt! I said, 'Hey, don't let it get you down, you know? Life's fulla little setbacks.' "

Muscotti left to refill the glasses of the three sports fans who were still arguing about football. When he returned he said, "You know, I got curious about this guy, so I called some guys, and I had a little talk with a guy who was in the joint with him. What d'you think he told me, huh? You're gonna love this."

Balzic shrugged.

"He told me the only guy who ever came to visit this hot dog was a guy who used to be a gofer for the county Democratic Committee, only for the last four years or so, he's some kind of hot flunky in the state auditor general's office. So I had some other guy do some lookin', and whatta you think, huh? The auditor general and this floor guy? They used to play football together. And guess who used to be the head manager on that football team, huh? The head water boy?"

"I give up. Who?"

"The guy that took Tom Murray's job. Down at the newspaper. Whatta you think of that? Huh?"

"I know there's supposed to be some connection I'm supposed to be makin', but I'm not makin' it. So what're you tryin' to tell me?"

"Hey, Mario, you quit readin' the paper or what?"

"I read the paper every day. So?"

"So do you read what's there or do you also read what ain't there?"

"I try to do both. One you can do, the other all you can do is guess about."

"So you also read the Pittsburgh papers?"

"I try to, yeah. So what?"

"So you remember the job scam in the auditor general's office, right?"

"Well that isn't the one that's in there now. That was the one before. So what is your point anyway?"

"My point, my point, Christ, your head turnin' to cement or what?"

"Well obviously you got a point. Make it."

"I don't got no point. I just thought you'd be interested in the connections."

Balzic peered at Muscotti and then sighed and shook his head. "Sometimes, Dom, your stories are just a little bit too subtle for me, you know what I mean? Like right now. I got no idea what these connections are you're talkin' about."

Muscotti straightened up, put his hands behind his back, and started to rock from heels to toes and back. "So forget it."

Balzic studied Muscotti's face for a long moment, but then

gave up. No amount of face studying was going to lead to a sensible conclusion about Muscotti's "connections." Balzic shifted around on his stool and looked at the front door. He thought if he continued to look at the front door as though he was expecting somebody, Muscotti would give up this puzzling conversation and go away. As seemed to be usual lately, Balzic was wrong.

Muscotti shuffled close to the bar again and leaned forward. "So how come these connections don't interest you? Huh?"

"What connections? What the fuck're you talkin' about? Hey, Dom, I'm feelin' like my bulb's about to burn out. So if you want me to know something, just pretend you're talkin' to a real stonehead, okay? Spell it out for me."

"I don't have to spell nothin' out. You just have to think a little bit, like who's connected to who."

"A guy who installs carpets, a guy in the auditor general's office, and the guy who took Tom Murray's job at the newspaper—this is all supposed to mean somethin' to me?"

Dom nodded several times.

"Like what for crissake?"

"You know that lady on City Council?"

"The one who's givin' the firemen a bad time about their books?"

Dom nodded. "You know the Conemaugh Tax Bureau?"

"The one that collects all the nuisance taxes for the city—who doesn't?"

"You know what number they give you if you call 'em and you got a bitch?"

"The tax bureau?"

"Yeah. You oughta call 'em and tell 'em you got a problem and you wanna talk to the boss, see who you talk to."

Balzic's mouth was slack. He squinted at Muscotti and tried to fit all these "connections" into something approaching sense. After a long moment, he said, "I don't have the first goddamn idea what you're talkin' about."

"I know you don't," Dom said. "What I'm tryin' to tell you is, same thing happened to me is happenin' to you. It passed you up. Just like it passed me up. It was right under my chin and I never looked down. And the next thing I knew I was history. And that's happenin' to you right now. All this crapola's goin' on right in front of you and you don't see none of it."

Balzic drained the last of his beer and slid the glass toward Muscotti. "Just give me another beer, okay? And spare me your predictions about my, uh, my . . ."

"Your what? You can't even say it, can ya?"

"Aw fuck you, okay? Just gimme the beer."

When Muscotti returned from the tap with the beer, he leaned close over the bar and said, "Mario, they took the town right out from under ya. After this election you're gone. You and that councilwoman. You two are the last ones in the road. When they beat her, the only thing left is your badge."

Balzic snorted. "And this is all connected to some guy who installs rugs and some guy in Harrisburg and the guy who took Murray's job—is that it?"

"More or less, yeah."

"Well I don't know who all these lovelies are who want my shield, but a couple more days like today and they can have it and they'll be doin' me the biggest favor in the world. You wanna know why? Huh? 'Cause I don't have the brains to quit."

"You think, huh?" Muscotti said, smiling. At first it was genuine, warm almost. Then it began to sour around the edges. He snorted. "You don't have the brains to quit. Cut it out. You wouldn't know what to do with yourself you quit. You'll drive your wife nuts. Then you'll drive yourself nuts."

Balzic sipped his beer and looked over his glasses at Muscotti. He sighed in disgust. "You want me to know something, huh? Then tell me. I'm listenin'. I'm ignorant. I wanna learn. But stop talkin' fuckin' riddles and just tell me!"

Muscotti rocked on his heels and toes. " 'Member Mussolini?"

"What? Mussolini! Now what the fuck're you talkin' about now?"

"Mussolini would've loved it here."

"Mussolini would've loved it here," Balzic muttered, rubbing his sinuses. "Lemme see if I got this right. A guy who installs rugs, somebody in the auditor general's office, somebody in the newspaper, and somebody in the tax collector's office. And Mussolini. Who would've loved it here."

"Right right right," Muscotti said, sipping his whiskey and water.

Balzic drank more beer and peered across the bar at Muscotti. "I'm real sorry now I told somebody to come find me here, 'cause that means I'm gonna be sittin' here for a while lookin' at you lookin' real happy with yourself."

Muscotti rubbed his nose with the back of his hand and made sputtering noises. "You remember the fascists? Huh?"

"Of course I remember the fascists. So what?"

"What were they all about, tell me."

"Whatta you mean what were they about? They were a bunch of goons."

"Nah nah nah. Skip the propaganda. Think a little bit here. What were they—they weren't all goons. They had some very smart people with them. So what were they for—think. They were *for* somethin'."

"I give up. What. Tell me."

"Mario, you better start givin' this some thought. I'm tryin' to tell you what's happenin' here and you think I'm just jerkin' you around. I ain't. This is happenin' right under your chin and you won't even look down. Pay attention here."

"I'll pay attention. Give me some information. So far all I heard is a buncha crap about connections."

"Okay. Lemme tell you about the fascists. His mouthpieces—Mussolini's?—all they talked about was old Rome. The Roman Empire. The glory days when the world was ruled by dags. And they told everybody the way to do that, to get it back again, was to start pullin' the same way. One for all, all for one, that's all it was. Three-musketeers shit. Only Mussolini made it work. He got 'em all to buy it. The banks, the insurance guys, the guys that ran all the corporations, the ones that made the movies—everybody bought in. Anybody complained, the wagon came up, the Blackshirts got out, into the wagon he goes, and three o'clock in the morning he gets a serious headache. Pretty soon nobody's complainin'. Pretty soon no-body's even askin' questions. You know, not even, 'Hey, what-ever happened to Ignatz?' 'Cause Ignatz was in the dirt with no name on top. 'Cause enough Iggys go down, even the dumbest dag's gonna get the message."

"And this is all happenin' right under my chin, right here, and all I gotta do is look down, is that it?"

"You got it."

"Uh-ha." Balzic rubbed his neck and face. "These fascists, they had some real smart people with 'em, huh? And they be-lieved in something, right? What was that, exactly? Their dream was to make the trains run on time, right? That's what I always heard was Mussolini's greatest achievement."

"Why you sneerin' at this? Mario, you surprise me some-times. A guy like you, bein' in power long as you have and you act like there's no such thing as power."

"Power?" Balzic snorted. "I got power to enforce the law—the laws I can understand—in about eight square miles. Which is practically no power at all, in other words."

"Think about this. You know how many dialects there are in Italy, huh?"

"No."

"Hundreds. Hundreds, you hear me? People live fifty miles apart, closer, can't understand each other. And durin' Mussolini's time, half of 'em was illiterate. So he schemed 'em, everybody, he got 'em all to start believin' that what *he* wanted was what *they* should want, you follow me? And he got 'em to do it. That was no small thing, even though the look on your face is, what's the big friggin' deal? I'll tell you what's the big deal. Whether you think the trains runnin' on time is bullcrap or was bullcrap doesn't make any difference. That bald fart conned people who never set foot on a train into thinkin' it was their *job* to make the trains get to where they were goin'. He told 'em they were marchin' to glory. To the glory days of the fascists, when the dags ruled the world. And while all those il-literate peasants were gettin' in step, Mussolini and his paisans was turnin' everything they touched into lira. How do you like that?"

"That's what fascism was about—gettin' rich?"

"Of course! Whatta you think? They were actually gonna turn into the Roman Empire? In 1920? 1930? 1940? Who knows what Mussolini believed. All that ridiculous crap he was talkin' about—who knows? Maybe he actually believed it. But the ones hangin' on? The ones had ahold of his coat? They hung with him 'cause they could see how rich they was gonna get. All they had to do was put their lira in the right business, uniforms, flags, shoes, packs, bullets, bombs, airplanes, what the hell, everything the Army needs, the Navy, the banks are buyin' the bonds, and the bonds are payin' for the bullets. Hey, for a long time there, they thought they died and went to heaven—everybody was makin' money on the bullets and it looked like nobody was ever gonna get shot."

"Uh, let me interrupt here," Balzic said, motioning for another refill. "This is interesting as hell, but exactly what does it have to do with me?"

Muscotti took Balzic's glass, refilled it, and brought it back. "You know, for almost thirty years I been watchin' a guy operate here. He's a smooth one, he is."

"Who?"

"I ain't gonna tell you—"

"Oh shit."

"—nah, nah, I wanna see how long it takes you to figure this out."

"More riddles," Balzic growled.

"No. Listen to me. I mean I been waitin' for thirty years to see when you were gonna wise up, and I'm still waitin', that's what I mean. I mean I'm not tellin' you something you don't know. It's just somethin' you haven't figured out."

Balzic drummed his fingers on the bar. He ran his tongue over his teeth and thought about making an appointment to get his teeth cleaned.

"Tryin' to turn me off, huh? It ain't gonna work. I'm kind of enjoying this, watchin' you in the middle of the end for you, and you tryin' to act like you're above it all."

"Well, have a good time."

"No, I mean it. It's like watchin' a guy, a young guy, find

out the woman he wants to marry has been around the block a couple times. He hates that, but he loves her, and he can't stand himself 'cause he can't leave her alone."

"What the fuck're you, you a, what? What are you—a peeper? Huh? You makin' comparisons between me and a young guy in love and you're what—you're kind of enjoyin' it—is that what you said?"

"Absolutely."

"You're gonna enjoy watchin' a guy get crapped on—is that it? How's this comparison work again? I'm the young dude and what's my girlfriend supposed to be—the town here? Rocksburg?"

"Nah, not quite."

"Not quite, huh. Tell me something, Dom. You startin' to watch a lot of soap operas on TV? Or you startin' to read those goofy romance books all the women read—those, uh, whatta they call 'em—those Harlequin romances?"

"Nah, nah. See, you remind me of Murray down the newspaper, down the *Gazette* there. He worked there so many friggin' years, and the family that had that paper for all those years before this jerk bought it, they never messed with Murray. It was their paper, see. They counted all the money, but Murray, he thought all the rest of it was his. Then when this rich prick bought it and started to tell Murray what to put in and what to not put in, Murray just about peed all over himself. And I told him the same thing I just told you, that he sorta reminded me of some young dude who just found out his girl ain't as pure as he thought and he can't stand it, and Murray acted the same way you're actin' right now. He tried to make a joke about it. Then he got all fulla contempt. For me. And I remember what he said. He repeated somethin' some Frenchman said. He said—I'll never forget the look on his face—he said, 'There is no fate that cannot be surmounted by scorn.' He was tryin' to bluff it out with me."

Dom got suddenly wistful. "But you know what? Three years later he was dead. Three years . . ."

"I don't work for the paper. I work for the city."

"Yeah? Murray didn't work for the paper either. He was

married to the friggin' paper. And you're married to the lady with the blindfold on, the one with her tits hanging out. I could never figure out why you gotta see her tits. I mean, the scales and the blindfold and the sword I can see, but why don't they cover up her tits? Doesn't matter whether you're in Rome or Rocksburg, her tits are hangin' out there. Why is that? What's that supposed to mean?"

"You're askin' the wrong guy."

"You never thought about that? Huh? Much as you think about goofy stuff? You never once thought about that?"

"Never."

Muscotti nodded many times. "Man, I'll tell ya. If I was married to a woman had her tits out all the time, I'd sure give it some thought."

"My wife does not go around with her chest uncovered. And I'm not a bigamist."

"Yeah?" Muscotti snorted. "I'd like to hear what Ruthie has to say about this."

Muscotti smiled that sour smile again. One of the sports fans called out some question about a score in some championship football game, and Muscotti wove his way down the bar to answer it.

Balzic had started to tell Muscotti it was none of his business what Ruth would have to say. Truth be known, Balzic thought, Muscotti would be surprised to know what Ruth thought about who Balzic was "married" to. Muscotti would be very surprised to know what Ruth had been saying ever since Balzic's mother had died. Within days after the funeral, Ruth had started to talk about how cold Rocksburg was, how much it had changed, how she couldn't believe how the streets had once been jammed with people when the mills changed shifts, and now all it was was empty and damp and cold. Ruth's arthritis in her fingers was getting worse. She seemed to talk about the dampness and the cold all the time. She couldn't shake free of the idea that winter seemed to last most of the year. It never got really cold, it just got dreary and slushy and she'd wince when she first stood up after she'd been sitting for a while. She'd wince and make the slightest flinching move to favor one hip joint or the other or else her knee and then she'd say something decidedly unpleasant about winter.

Then she'd ask Balzic why they had to keep on living here. "What's holding us here?"

"Marie. Emily. My job."

"Marie and Emily are doing fine as hell without us. And it's time for you to quit."

She wanted to find some sun. She wanted to go where the houses were pink and white and yellow and where every time you went outside your biggest worry was the sun. That's the kind of worries she wanted to have now: sunglasses and sun-dresses, sun hats and sunscreen. She was tired of thinking about wool coats and salt ruining her boots and her sinuses drying out from forced-air heat. She didn't give a damn what the derma-tologists said about what the sun did to your skin. She was scratching herself awake at night from winter itch, and given the choice, she would rather look like a raisin than a scab.

A woman friend she hadn't heard from in years had begun to write to her from Florida, and had sent dozens of snapshots about her life on the Gulf Coast.

The woman was on husband number three and had moved closer to the beach with each marriage. She'd started in Or-lando when she'd left Rocksburg and now she was only five miles from the Gulf of Mexico. So what if she had to wash sheets and towels in a motel—her husband owned the motel and she was doing the laundry 'cause she felt like it and why didn't Ruth want to come down?

Ruth *did* want to come down. She'd written to the Cham-bers of Commerce in some of the places the woman talked about and was starting to get brochures in the mail. But when she tried to talk to Balzic about the woman and what she was writing in her letters, he couldn't even remember the woman's name and couldn't put a face with the name every time Ruth brought it up. All he knew was this woman was starting to get on his nerves and he couldn't even remember whether he ever knew her.

Balzic could understand—or thought he did—Ruth's way of thinking. If she wanted a life in the sun, she should have it.

He had no problem with that. What he had a problem with was her unblinking honesty that it was time for him to quit. And when he thought more about that, he didn't know whether it was her honesty that unnerved him or the idea behind those itty-bitty words: *time to quit. Time? To quit?* . . .

Where the fuck was Yesho?

"D'you say something?" Muscotti was tilted forward, expectantly, from the hips. He was smiling that smile again.

"Your clocks right?"

Muscotti straightened up and shrugged. "So if they're off five minutes, who cares?"

Balzic looked at his watch again, compared it with Muscotti's clocks—in the beer signs, in the whiskey signs, on the walls, on the backbar—and complained aloud that Yesho must be coming by way of Pittsburgh.

The front door was thrust open and Yesho came bouncing through, springy on the balls of his feet. He was wearing civvies, a pair of jeans, a skintight T-shirt, the better to display his muscles, and running shoes. He came and stood so that Balzic had to twist around on his stool to talk to him, which only further irritated Balzic.

"I been waiting for you since eleven, Yesho. What the hell took you so long?"

"I been talking to Rascoli. So I'm here now. So whatta you want?"

"I want your shield and the piece the city gave you. You can keep any personal weapons you have, but don't carry 'em without a permit, is that clear?"

"Huh? Whoa wait a minute. What about my shield?"

"I want it—"

"You make me come to a fuckin' saloon to—to, to do what? What is this? Suspension—what?"

"Suspension with pay, that's what it is. You can request a civil service hearing tomorrow, whenever, that's up to you."

Balzic crooked his finger at Yesho and summoned him closer, until their faces were only a hand's width apart. "I'm doin' this in this saloon—this public place—because I know I can't put my hands on you in here without making a real pile of shit for myself, 'cause all I would've been sayin' to myself was how come in the eight years this, this—never mind what this is—'cause in the eight years you been in the department I never did anything to you that made it okay for you to do this SWAT bullshit on me—"

"On you!" Yesho snorted a laugh.

"On me! Yes, goddammit! On *me*!" Balzic peered into Yesho's eyes, searching for some spark of comprehension. "You don't have a clue, do you? Huh? Not one. You can't understand what I'm gettin' all personal about. But that's what this is, stonehead. This is personal!"

Yesho hung his head and muttered something, and when his head came up again, his gaze was squinty cold. "I'll tell you what's personal, man, you wanna know. I passed the sergeant's test two years ago. No promotion—"

"Nobody's been promoted for crissake, it ain't just you. Nobody."

"I got the highest score on that test—"

"What're you talkin' about this for? It wouldn't've made any difference if you'd've got a perfect score. Nobody got a promotion, how many ways you want me to say that?"

"You're not lettin' me finish. You keep interruptin' me."

"So finish already."

"Aggggh, what's the point. I'm history anyway. And you do it to me in a fucking saloon—"

"What're you, stupid? I already told you I did it in here 'cause it's a public place and I'm really pissed about this—"

"Yeah well what I'm hearin' is if we were in your office, you would've, uh, like what, what would you've done? Grabbed me or something, huh? Take a whack at me, huh?"

"That's exactly what I'm tellin' ya."

Yesho snorted and hung his head again and laughed. "Hey, Chief, I think maybe you had a little too much beer, you know? I think you're not thinkin' straight. I think maybe twenty years ago, you would've given me a problem. I think maybe you oughta go find a mirror and take a look at yourself."

Balzic swiveled around on his stool until he was facing Yesho. "You've been a member of my department—"

"See there's your first problem," Yesho snarled. "It ain't *your* fuckin' department. You just run it."

Balzic could hear Muscotti laughing behind him.

Balzic turned on Muscotti and said, "Why don't you go wait on somebody, huh?"

"And miss all this?"

"This is sorta private," Balzic snapped, and knew before the words were out how stupid they were.

Muscotti didn't say a word. He just made a face that said, yeah, right, private, in my place, in front of me.

Balzic swiveled back to Yesho. "You're right. It ain't my department. I don't own it, I just run it. But in all the time I been runnin' it, in all the time you been a member—eight years, nine, whatever—I have never done anything to you that called for you to do me this way—"

"Man-oh-man, Balzic," Yesho said, smiling crookedly, "you really are makin' this personal."

"I told you I was!"

"It's not a personal thing between you and me, goddammit! It's a personal thing with the city and the department and me. We been workin' without a goddamn contract for how long now? A year? Huh? That's personal with me. But it ain't personal with me and you!"

"And so what is it? Because you passed the sergeant's test two years ago and because what? Because you don't have a contract for—and it ain't a year it's ten months—"

"Ten months, a year, what the fuck's the difference?"

"Two months is the difference. A guy five-eight ain't five-ten, that's the difference. Two inches is two inches, two months is two months."

"Hey, ten months, have it your fuckin' way, the principle don't change. We still don't have a contract. And the way it looked to me, it won't make any difference when we do get one, 'cause you're gettin' ready to lay me off—I mean as if you didn't already fuckin' suspend me. In a goddamn saloon. That's fuckin' class, Balzic, really, man, that's fucking class, man, suspend me in a fucking saloon." Yesho seemed to notice Muscotti for the first time and snapped at him: "What the fuck you grinnin' at, huh? Go stand somewhere else."

Muscotti shuffled forward until his belly was against the bar. He crooked his finger at Yesho and motioned him to come close. When Yesho leaned forward, head canted suspiciously, eyes flashing professional paranoia, Muscotti whispered to him, "You're right. Before you came in here I was tellin' him the same things you were just sayin', you know, it ain't his department and all that. Same things you been tellin' him. But, uh, this is my place. I stand where I want." Muscotti reached up and patted Yesho twice on the face.

Yesho pulled back as though stung, his face twisted in contempt. "Fuck you too." He reached around in his back pocket and brought out his ID case and tossed it on the bar beside Balzic. "There's my fuckin' shield. And you better believe I'm gonna be talkin' to the FOP lawyer tomorrow. I'm gonna be in his office a half hour before he gets there, bet on it."

Balzic nodded many times. "Good, that's your prerogative. That's what I told ya. You got a right to a hearing in front of the civil service board—"

Yesho was already walking toward the front door, muttering and shaking his head. "It ain't gonna make any difference anyway," he said over his shoulder at the door. "If I beat you on the suspension, you're only gonna lay me off anyway, so what's the point?" He dismissed everything with a contemptuous wave and was gone. In a second, the door was pushed open far enough for Yesho to get his head inside and he called out, "The point is, I ain't gonna make it easy for ya. It's all stupid, I don't have a fuckin' chance, but you're all gonna have to work for it, that's the point." Then he was gone again.

Balzic swiveled around on his stool and faced Muscotti, who was smiling a silly smile of self-congratulation.

"What the fuck you grinnin' at?"

"Hey, so what is it now, bartenders ain't allowed to smile? They pass a law against that too?"

"Yeah yeah yeah," Balzic groused. He held his right hand out palm-up and made quarter-circles in the air with it. "So, uh, what? What is this, this, uh, this thing that's happenin' to me right under my nose that you all of a sudden can see and I can't. What is this?"

"Oh. So now you got your nose open, huh? So now maybe I ain't talkin' in circles, is that it?"

"Well you're startin' to talk in circles all over again. Just don't be so fuckin' smug and tell me what you wanna tell me so I can go home."

"Maybe you should do that anyway. It's late. I wanna go home myself." Muscotti continued to smile his silly smile of self-congratulation. "I'll tell you one thing though. This retirement, it's good, it's good. You'd be surprised how good it is. But you gotta want it. And I don't think you know how to want it."

Balzic canted his head. "Ohhhhhh what? You forget how you were the night you told me they told you you were a dinosaur, you forget that? Huh? I didn't forget. You were fucking numb, you were so far past shock you were practically fucking in a coma on your feet. I remember the words you said. You said, after they told you, you said, it was like tryin' to walk on a wood floor all covered with marbles, that's exactly what you said."

"Yeah, yeah," Muscotti said, nodding several times, "you're right, that's what I said. I remember that. That's what it felt like then. But now? Huh? Now, it's nice. Now it's like for the first time in my life I got my life back. My life belongs to me now. If I wanna stand in here and get drunk, I do it. And if I wanna put a yard on a number 'cause I feel like it, I do it. And if I don't feel like it, I don't do it." Muscotti put his elbows on the bar and rested his chin on his hands. "I used to think I loved power. I used to dream about it. When I was young, it used to give me a hard-on. Yeah, no joke. About what I had to do the next day and who I had to tell what to do and watchin' 'em do it. I used to eat that up with a big spoon. It used to taste so good. And when they took it away from me, I thought I was gonna die. I thought, you're gonna be dead, six months, maybe a year, you're gonna be dead. I remember thinkin' just like that. You lost your power, you lost your dick, you're gonna lose your heart. Hey, who's kiddin' who—I lost my dick about twenty years ago. But then one day, when I was drinkin' and thinkin' like that, I said to myself, hey, who's talkin' here? Who's gonna lose what? I was turnin' into an old man, an old, withered-up, friggin' prune face. And I was startin' to shuffle around. I was walkin' like some friggin' geezer on his way to the county home. Prison. County home, crap. Prison, that's what this is. Awaitin' friggin' execution. You ever go down the county home, Mario, huh?"

"Not for a long time, no."

"You oughta go down there, no kiddin', just go in and start walkin' through the halls, listenin', lookin' around, takin' a good whiff of all that dried-up piss. You know what I smelled in there? Huh? I didn't smell piss. It smelled like piss, don't get me wrong. But that ain't what I smelled. I smelled death row. That's what I smelled. I smelled all these people waitin' to die. And I thought, you jerk, what did they take from you? Huh? If they could take it from you that easy, you never had anything to begin with, that's what I thought. 'Cause that was the truth. All that power I thought I had, huh?" Muscotti straightened up and snapped his finger. "They took it from me like that. Bang. Poof. Gone. They took it from me in less time than it takes to tell you about it. And I said to myself, you jerk, they didn't take noth-ing. What they did was give you a gift. They gave you your friggin' life back. Handed it to me on a big platter. And there I was, mopin' around, gettin' ready to croak out. Remember when I quit drinkin' there for about six weeks? Huh, you 'member that? Everybody was thinkin' I flipped out, they was talkin' like I was gonna get religion, remember that?"

Balzic nodded. "I remember. That's what Vinnie thought. He told me one day he thought you were gettin' ready to go over to St. Vincent's, join the monastery."

"Yeah he did. That's what he thought. Just 'cause I quit drinkin'. He never knew me when I wasn't drinkin'. He always thought I was attached permanent to a bottle of Canadian Club." Muscotti leaned across the bar again and put his face close to Balzic's. "You know what I found out? Huh? I found out I didn't have to drink. Yeah, you're smilin', you think I'm bullskatin' now, but I ain't. That's what I learned. I didn't have to drink. You know what that told me? Huh? That told me that all those years I thought I wanted to drink, huh? That told me I drank all those years 'cause I had to. Not 'cause I wanted to. 'Cause when they retired me? I found out I didn't have to drink. 'Cause when I found out I didn't have the power, huh? I found out I didn't have to play the friggin' role either, how you like that, huh? All those years I drank it was nothin' but a friggin' act. Tough guy drinks whiskey, drinks everybody under the table, that was me. Tough guy treats money like it ain't nothin' but paper. Don't bet a yard on a game. Bet ten Gs. How friggin' stupid can you be? Huh?"

"So how come you're drinkin' now?" Balzic said.

Muscotti's shoulders started to shake up and down with laughter. The ice cubes in his glass were rattling he was shaking so much. "I drink now," he said, " 'cause I like the taste. And I like the buzz. I drink now 'cause it's fun. 'Cause it's me drinkin', get it? It ain't the friggin' goombah drinkin'. It's me. And when I don't feel like drinkin', huh? I don't. 'Cause I don't have to front for anybody anymore—least of all me."

The sports fans down the bar called for another round.

"Hey, I'm closed," Muscotti said, waving his arm for them to leave. "Go home. I shoulda closed up an hour ago. Get outta here, hit the bricks."

Without a word of protest, the sports fans collected their change, drained their glasses, and set off for the front door, waving and saying good night over their shoulders.

"See that, Mario? Huh? You see that? Those jerks think I still got power. They're friggin' brain-dead, you know? I say get out, they don't make a peep, they pick up their money and go. Gone. Good-bye. See you later. They still think I'm somebody. And I ain't nobody! For the first time in my life since I was a kid, a teenie-weenie, this is me. This is all I am. What you see here. And I love it. And you don't even know what the frig I'm talkin' about."

It was true, Balzic had to admit it. All the way home, he kept thinking about what Muscotti had been saying, and the truest thing was the last thing Muscotti had said: Balzic didn't know what Muscotti had been talking about. Balzic tried to tell himself that was because he'd never seen himself as having power, certainly not the kind Muscotti had had at one time. So if he'd never thought about having that kind of power, it only stood to reason that he would not know how to deal with not having it anymore. But wasn't that Muscotti's point? That when it was taken away from him, in the snap of a finger, that was when Muscotti recognized that he'd never really had it at all, it had all been some kind of organizational front, a role that had been thrust upon him, a role he'd had to learn, including the part about being the hard drinker, the heavy bettor.

Through all of Balzic's ruminations, there kept appearing the picture of Yesho's face when he'd said that Balzic's first problem was that the police department wasn't Balzic's department, and accompanying Yesho's face was Muscotti's laughter. And that would be followed by Muscotti's maddening commentary about what was supposedly happening right under Balzic's nose, about somebody getting ready to get rid of him and the councilwoman who had made herself such a pain in the volunteer firemen's collective butt.

As Balzic pulled into his driveway, he was thinking that all of this was a pain in his butt. People he'd never heard of, prowling around in Rocksburg in camo clothes, rappelling out of helicopters, and District Attorney Failan saying it was none of Balzic's business, it was county business, and Failan not showing the slightest concern with Balzic's threat to confiscate the camo men's automatic weapons. And then there was what John Theodore had said, how he was getting out, moving on, and saying finally that hokey, off-the-wall thing about how he was going to say two words, *Conemaugh Foundation,* and that was just one more thing Balzic didn't know anything about. Maybe Muscotti was right, maybe it was all passing by right under his nose and he was too dumb to have the sense to look down.

Balzic hauled himself into the house and tiptoed into the kitchen to get a glass of milk and some cookies, hoping that Ruth had made some of those chocolate chip and walnut ones she'd said in the morning she was going to make. She was true to her word: there was a pan of them under cellophane wrap on the counter beside the stove. There was also a note.

It said:

Mario, Here's the cookies I said I was going to make. They didn't turn out right for some reason. Too dry. But I'm sure you'll like them anyway.

I hate to keep asking you this, but did you think more about Florida? I really want to go, Mar. I don't want to turn into a nag about this, but I really need to see something different, you know? I've been looking at Rocksburg my whole life, Mar, and it, oh, never mind. Just tomorrow when you get up tell me you thought about it, okay? Even if you have to lie? A week away from here isn't (She'd scratched out the next couple of words.) I don't even know what to say, except I know I'm starting to sound like a broken record, and that's the last thing I want to do, turn you off about this I mean. Love, R.

Florida? A week in Florida? What do you do in Florida? Look at palm trees? Christ, he thought, stop thinking about it from your point of view, try to look at it from hers. It isn't what there is for you to do in Florida. It's that she wants to go, that's all. That's what's important not what you can think up to do while you're there. So, okay. So what's she gonna do there? Look at palm trees? Well? Why not? It wouldn't be Rocksburg, that's for sure. What do you care what she wants to look at while she's there? She wants to look at something that isn't Rocksburg. So let her. So help her. So forget Rocksburg for once. If Muscotti's right, it can't wait to forget you.

When Balzic awoke the next morning and went out to the kitchen, Ruth was already out on the deck watering the tomatoes and basil and petunias, marigolds and impatiens. He stood by the kitchen door, scratching his sides and rubbing his eyes, squinting in the sunlight, watching her pour water from the green plastic can into one of the clay pots of Sweet One Hundred tomatoes. When she emptied the can, she came toward the kitchen and saw him and waved for him to come out. "I want you to see what the finches are doing," she said.

He went out and kissed her on the cheek. She stood for a moment with her shoulder against his chest and pushing her face into his neck and shoulder and then pointed at the pots of sweet basil. "Look what those bastards've done."

"What bastards?"

"The finches. The purple finches, you know?"

"Yeah. The bird finches? They did somethin' to the basil?"

"Yes, yes, look. For the last couple weeks, look. All this time I thought it was bugs, and this morning when I got up, I put the water on the stove, and I was standing there, lookin' out the window, you know, thinkin', god, what a morning, and there they were, hanging all over the pots, five or six of them on each pot, just goin' to town, havin' a feast, eatin' the leaves. Honest to god, I just stood there, I said, you ungrateful little bitches—they were all females, I didn't see one male—I said, we feed you all year round and this is what you do? Mar, they've done this in just two weeks, two weeks ago it started."

"They never did this before. Did they?" Balzic bent over the pots and examined each one, touching the chewed-off leaves and stems. "Man, they're really puttin' a job on 'em, jeez."

"Never. I never remember them doin' it. One year we had the slugs, those gray ones, remember? The year we bought 'em in that place that went under? The plants, remember? And they were all chewed up. But I never saw the birds do this. Never."

"You sure it ain't the squirrels?"

"Mario, I'm telling you I stood in the kitchen and watched them. The squirrels eat a tomato once in a while, they take a bite out of one, but this was the damn finches. I know a purple finch when I see it."

"Maybe they're eatin' whatever's eatin' the leaves, d'ya ever think of that? Maybe some kinda bugs eatin' the leaves and they're tryin' to eat whatever's eatin' the leaves, whatta you think?"

Ruth pursed her lips and shook her head. "Yeah, well, you'd think that would sound reasonable, but I can't find any bugs. I've been looking ever since something started eating them. I didn't bring a magnifying glass out here, but usually you can see something moving, just with your own eyes. Look yourself. You see anything moving?"

"With *my* eyes you want me to look, huh? I gotta get a magnifyin' glass, you kiddin'? The finches, huh? Spend ten bucks a week feedin' the little pricks and they eat your basil. See, that's why everybody has shotguns in Italy. I used to wonder why they shoot the songbirds over there, but this is why." Balzic stopped at the door to the kitchen and said, "But why would they never do it before this year? Why now?"

Ruth shrugged. "I was talking to Mrs., oh god, what's her name, I swear I'm gettin' Alzheimer's. Remind me to tell you what Millie said, honest to god, that woman, she's so funny. If she ever finds out I'm laughing at the way she talks, I'll be so embarrassed—never mind her. Mrs. whatever-her-name-is told me her husband said it's all the mild winters we've had. Five years in a row, and the winters don't kill all the insect larvae and they don't kill all the baby birds and it's just got things all out of whack. She said he swears what we need is a really hard winter for a change. Maybe he's right, I don't know. All I know is, the finches never ate the basil before. You know what that means, Mar."

"Damn right I do. No pesto. The little pricks. I'm gonna go out Kmart and get a BB gun. Next one I see eatin' basil is a dead finch, the little prick."

He was already into the kitchen when she called and asked if he'd seen the paper yet.

"No. Why? Where'd we put the magnifyin' glass? Is it still in the china closet?"

"On top," she called back. "In that big dish up on top. There's a big story on the front page about your buddy Sitko. And you're not gonna start killin' finches."

Balzic felt around in the round platter on the top of the china cabinet in the dining room until his hands landed on the cross-hatched handle of the magnifier. He went back outside and bent over one of the basil plants. "Wha'd you say about the paper? Story about who?"

"There's a big story about your buddy Sitko and his new helicopter. You're not gonna get a BB gun either, Mar, right? You were just joking about that?"

Balzic straightened up so fast he got dizzy. "There's a story in the *Gazette* about Sitko and *his* helicopter? The *Rocksburg Gazette?* We talkin' the same paper?"

"Yes."

"The *Rocksburg Gazette,* not the *Pittsburgh Post-Gazette?*"

Ruth nodded. "Yeah, the *Rocksburg Gazette.* All across the top and it goes on inside, big story, written by some reporter, I never saw his name before. Steve something. Hus or Hussle or something. You ever hear of him?"

"No. Where's the paper? In the living room?"

"Never mind, I'll go get the paper, you just see if you can see any bugs. You're not answering me about killing the finches."

She disappeared into the house while he turned over the leaves—what was left of them—looking for some evidence that something other than purple finches was eating the basil. He found nothing but dirt, splashed up on the lower leaves from rain or from Ruth's watering.

She came back out carrying the paper and opened it out across her chest for him to read the headline. He said, "I'll be damned if I can find anything. Nothin' looks like it's moving to me. Y'think bugs sleep? Or loaf? What's 'at say? 'SWERT Causing Questions In Courthouse, City Hall,' what the hell . . . gimme that, lemme see that.

"I'll tell ya one thing right now. I didn't hear any damn questions in City Hall about any of this crap until yesterday, so I don't know who the hell they been talkin' to, but it sure wasn't me."

Balzic started to read the story aloud. " 'By Steve Hussler.' Whoever the hell he is.

"Police officers and volunteer firemen from Rocksburg and surrounding communities, armed with shotguns and automatic rifles and pistols, have been given the power to make arrests and to use deadly force by high-ranking officials in Conemaugh

County Courthouse including the district attorney and president judge.

"Yesterday, District Attorney Howard Failan admitted to the *Rocksburg Gazette* that a SWERT (Special Weapons and Emergency Response Team), created 'for hostage situations, jailbreaks, and rescue operations,' was in fact on duty, standing by, 'on my authority and authority given me by the president judge.'

"Failan admitted that even though members of the team have not received basic police training as mandated by a 1976 state law, he had sworn them in as assistant deputy sheriffs. He said the 24-member team had been selected from among candidates who volunteered from two police departments and five volunteer hose companies.

"Failan said the unit receives no government funding except for liability insurance provided by Conemaugh County. Failan would not respond to questions about where the unit had received its funding to cover operations.

"The district attorney said the team was formed to track escaped prisoners and criminal suspects, and to deal with hostage crises or terrorist situations." Balzic stopped reading and looked at Ruth. "Did you read this?"

She nodded, rolling her eyes. "You think we oughta call 'em up and tell 'em about how the purple finches been terrorizin' our basil?"

"These fuckin' guys've lost their fuckin' minds," Balzic said. "Excuse me, darlin'. I know you don't like to hear me swearin' this early in the morning."

Ruth rolled her eyes again. "You think you're swearing now, just wait till you read where they got some of their equipment."

"Huh? Where they got their equipment? Where'd they get it?"

"Just keep reading, you'll find out. But I'm gonna go inside first," she said, " 'cause I don't wanna be here when you do."

"I can't hear you," Balzic said. "Either you're mutterin' or I'm losin' my hearin'. Wha'd you say?"

"I said I have to go to the bathroom," Ruth said, and left him to finish reading. "And you have to promise me you're not gonna shoot any birds, okay?"

Balzic hunted for where he'd stopped reading and then started again. " 'Failan's Rangers'—as they've come to be called around the courthouse—have plans to become airborne when Mercy 2, a Rocksburg-based helicopter medic service sponsored by Conemaugh General Hospital, officially becomes operational this week. The addition of the medevac chopper, said Failan, will 'increase the SWERT's capabilities enormously.'

"The newly sworn deputy sheriffs, their qualifications, their training, and their wide-ranging powers have raised questions from law officers in and out of Conemaugh County when they were told about the SWERT by the *Gazette*.

"A high-ranking state police officer who requested that his name not be used said that 'Special Weapons and Tactics (SWAT) teams rely on careful psychological screening of veteran police officers. The last person you want in one of those organizations is somebody who hasn't been screened by somebody who knows what to look for.'

"Asked to elaborate, the state police officer said, 'The first thing you have to do is obey the . . . 1976 Municipal Police Officers Training Act, which requires that anybody serving as a policeman is required to successfully complete 16 weeks of basic law enforcement. Taking that one-week security guard course won't make it.'

"All that does, he said, is teach handgun familiarization and a quick look at the Crimes Code and the laws relating to search, seizure, and arrest. 'Mostly,' he said, 'that course is designed to tell rent-a-cops about how really restricted their roles are.'

"In contrast, he said, the 16-week police training provides the fundamentals of law enforcement. After taking the 480-hour course, police candidates must pass a test in criminal law, both federal and state constitutions, criminology, the vehicle code, physical fitness, firearms, self-defense, pursuit driving, principles of investigation, surveillance, patrol, and communications.

"The training statute also requires 40 hours of in-service classroom instruction annually for every police officer." Balzic winced when he read that; he hadn't had a training officer in five years at least, and arranging for members of his department to attend classes run by the state police was a continuing hassle all around.

He went back to his reading.

"Given the arsenal the county's new SWERT has been authorized by the DA to carry—short-barreled shotguns, 9mm semiautomatic handguns, M-16 rifles, tear-gas guns, and a launcher used to throw ropes with grappling hooks—there seems to be a discrepancy between what is mandated by state statutes and county officials' understanding of those statutes.

"Furthermore, some of the SWERT's ancillary gear is also raising questions among police professionals about the role of the SWERT. Ancillary gear includes electronic devices capable of photographing or videotaping without light, tools for removing doors from hinges, sophisticated listening devices that do not require interruption or interference in telephone wiring (bugging), and voice-activated radios on headsets that allow wearers unimpaired movement of their hands.

"Although the district attorney would not comment on the funding for this equipment, members of the team who talked to the *Gazette* said they contributed personal money, supplemented by funds from certain fire department hose companies, to acquire most of the equipment. The rest was already in the property departments of the district attorney and the Rocksburg Police Department."

Balzic felt his eyes bugging. He read that part again. Then he read it out loud, snarling and shouting: " 'The rest was already in the property departments of the district attorney and the Rocksburg Police Department'! You sonsabitches! You fuck-ing two-bit fuck-ing Rambo bastards!"

He went storming into the kitchen, growling and snarling, and jerked the phone off its cradle and punched the buttons for the station.

The instant the call was answered with the words "Rocksburg Police" Balzic started roaring into the phone: "This is

Balzic. Call a locksmith, call Jimmy Buffaletti first and if you can't get him, get the guy from up on Norwood—Angelo, Angelo, what the fuck's his name—"

"Mario? Is that you?" came Sgt. Joe Royer's voice.

"Of course it's me! Who the fuck you think it is? I want the locks in the whole goddamn department—every fucking one of them—you hear me? Every fucking one of them, I want 'em changed—"

There was no response. Then, very hesitantly, Royer said, "Mario, you, uh, you can't do that, you know? Not without a requisition through the mayor—"

"You listen to me, Sergeant. You have a locksmith there by the time I get there. I'm goin' to get dressed. This ain't a city thing, this is a department thing. I don't wanna hear nothin' about any fucking requisitions. You get a locksmith there by the time I get there. The city ain't gonna pay for this, I am. This'll be comin' outta my own pocket so I don't wanna hear about no goddamn requisitions, is that clear?"

Except for a clearing of the throat, there came no response.

"Sergeant? You hear what I said?"

"Uh, yes, I did. I heard." There came more clearing of the throat, after which Royer said, "Listen, uh, Mario, this isn't gonna happen the way you want it to happen, you know?"

"And just why the hell not?"

"Well because, you just can't get a goddamn locksmith to come poppin' in like that, you know? I mean, I hate to be the guy to tell you this right now, 'cause I can hear you're really pissed off about somethin', but, uh, Jimmy Buffaletti's been dead, hey, almost a year now."

"Get outta here."

"I'm serious, Mario. And Angelo what's-his-name, hell, man, he's retired a long time now. You want me to call a locksmith I will, but, uh, I'm gonna have to call around. Last time we needed one, the only one was available was a guy from Uniontown. Hell, it took him like forty-five minutes just to get to where he was lost enough so he had to call, you know? So, uh, I'll do what I can, but you're gonna have to cool it a little bit, you know?"

"Aw shit," Balzic said, shifting his weight from foot to foot and tapping the newspaper against his thigh. "Yeah, yeah, okay, see what you can do. I'll be down there shortly. Oh wait a minute. I want you to put the word out: I want all the keys to the property room. Anybody has a key and doesn't turn it in? Suspended without pay till further notice. You got that?"

Royer suppressed a laugh with coughing.

"What?" Balzic said. "You laughin'? What? What're you laughin' about?"

Royer cleared his throat again. "Uh, Mario, I mean, you know, keys to the property room, that's, I mean, turnin' 'em in, that's, uh, you're jokin', right? I mean, hell, there's more keys to the property room than, uh, than I don't know what, you know? There gotta be like a hundred of them floatin' around—"

"How many?"

"Well so maybe I'm exaggeratin' a little bit, but, jeez, you know, everybody's got at least one of them, you know?"

"No I don't know. What I do know is, I want 'em all—every goddamn one of 'em—I want 'em all turned in. And we'll start all over again, see if we can't get it right this time, okay?"

Again Royer cleared his throat. "Uh, Mario, don't get mad, okay? I mean, I can hear you're really pissed about somethin', but don't get mad at me, okay? But I got to tell you, collectin' every key to the property room, well, that's sorta like tryin' to collect everybody's gun, you know? It might sound like a real good idea at the time, you might get a lotta guns, but pretty soon you're gonna notice that everybody's only turnin' in one or two bullets with each gun, so, I mean, sooner or later you're gonna have to ask yourself, you know, like, what're they doin' with all the rest of the bullets?"

Balzic canted his head and held the phone away from his ear and looked at it. When he pressed it to his ear again, he said, "Is there a message in there somewhere for me? Huh?"

"Well, you know, it's a fact. You wanna round up all the guns someplace, pay a bounty or whatever, like, for example, say the government says they wanna collect all the guns. So in the places where they try that, what they eventually figure out is, hey, you know, people are turnin' the guns in, but they're only turnin' in one or two bullets with each gun. Pretty soon everybody figures out they ain't turnin' all the guns in, is what I'm sayin'. I mean, there's always lots more ammunition than there is guns is what I'm sayin'."

"And the message for me is what, exactly?"

"Hey, you know, you get the locks changed, I mean, so what's that gonna do? So everybody who wants a key, they're gonna get one. You're the one always told me about how long it takes for people to find out your unlisted phone number, you know? Am I right? So I'm just thinkin' the same thing's gonna apply with new locks. I'm just tryin' to save you some money, 'cause, really, Mario, it ain't worth it. You'd have to change the locks every day, you know?" Royer cleared his throat again, and after a moment said, "Uh, the only reason you maybe forgot that, is, uh, you know, it's been a long time since you weren't the chief, you know? You maybe forgot how there ain't a cop alive who doesn't have a key to the property room, you know what I'm sayin', Mario? Huh? Help me out here, I'm havin' a hard time here."

"Nah," Balzic said somberly. "You're not havin' a hard time. I'll be down there shortly. Thanks, Joe."

"For what?"

"For savin' me from makin' an ass outta myself." Balzic hung up and turned around as Ruth was coming into the kitchen.

"So you read where they got some of their equipment?"

"You know, I must be . . . I don't even know how to say this. I mean, first it was the glasses, gettin' glasses, you know, first you're holdin' the phone book out to there. Then you get the bifocals. Then before you know, it's trifocals. And you start havin' all these close calls when you're drivin' and you're never really really sure whether they're close calls or whether they just look close because of the goddamn glasses. 'Cause everything you see when you turn around in the seat and you're tryin' to look at that place between the mirror and what you can see by lookin' out the window is like three pictures. Four with the trifocals. And you know from right then, right at that moment, you know there's a part of you you can't really ever completely trust anymore. The eyes. You say, hey, you can't really trust what you see."

"Mar." Ruth tried to interrupt him, but he held up his hand and went to the door to the deck and leaned against the jamb.

"Then you start not hearin' things. People are talkin' to you and pretty soon it gets to be real obvious that you're startin' to ask people, 'Huh? What did you say?' And you're doin' it all the time. 'Huh? Did you say something?' And you get used to that, just like you got used to the glasses. But every time you gotta get used to this stuff, each new thing you gotta get used to, you say, hey, there's one less thing I can depend on, one less thing I'm absolutely positively sure about. I can't be absolutely . . . positively . . . sure I'm seein' what I think I'm seein' and I can't be sure I'm hearin' what I think I'm hearin'."

"Mar, you're making too big a deal out of this—"

"No I'm not. Uh-uh, no way am I making too big a deal, Ruthie. The eyes and the ears, that's one thing. Two things. But this thing?" He held up the paper and pointed at it. "This? This SWERT thing? This's been goin' on for months. Probably a lot longer, they didn't put this thing together in a couple of months. John Theodore told me he knew about it three months ago. Who knows how long? The one guy who *doesn't* know how long it's been goin' on is me. 'Cause I didn't see nothin' and I didn't hear nothin'. And, Ruthie, this wasn't just because of tri-focals and me maybe needin' a hearin' aid, baby cakes. This is because I ain't payin' attention anymore. I'm in dreamland someplace. I'm practically in a goddamn coma for crissake."

"You're getting carried away, Mar," Ruth said.

He looked at the deck, the tomatoes, the basil, the flowers, the grackle washing itself in the clay saucer they set on the floor of the deck for a birdbath. "I'm not gettin' carried away," he said after a long moment. "If I don't start payin' closer atten-tion, I *am* gonna get carried away. I have never been this asleep in my whole life. Dom Muscotti was tryin' to tell me this last night. He said it's happenin' right under my nose and I'm too dumb to look down."

"You're still making too much out of it, Mar," Ruth said.

"I know how you can get about things like this, and you're doing it."

"Doin' what? Seein' things for how they are? That ain't gettin' carried away. That's wisin' up. That's wakin' up. That's *not* gettin' carried away. That's puttin' my feet back on the ground and not lettin' other people carry me away."

"Well it might have something to do with the fact that you're out there driving around in a black-and-white all day instead of being where you ought to be." Ruth bent over from the waist and looked at the floor and said, "I'm sorry, Mar. That's not any of my business. I shouldn't have said that."

"It's not the first time you said it, that's for sure."

"I know, I know. But it's not any of my business."

"Yes it is," he said. "Everything I do is your business. I didn't used to know that. I used to think there was what I did, and there was what you did, and I didn't tell you about what you did, and you didn't tell me about what I did. But that's bullshit. And we both know it. You've always known it. It's just taken me about forty years longer to learn it than you did. I don't know. Maybe you were born with it, I don't know."

"Oh I wasn't born with anything you weren't born with—"

"Hey, Ruthie, just stop right there, okay? Don't start bull-shittin' me now, okay? I'm not at the point in my life where I need to be humored, you know? The last thing I need is for you to start pattin' me on the head. I've been a real asshole here. And you're right. The last place I need to be is out in a black-and-white. Maybe where we both need to be is in Florida—though I cannot imagine what the hell I'd do there."

"Oh Mar, you've been thinkin' about it?" She couldn't help herself. She blinked and suppressed a giggle and did a sort of a dance to get where he was and slipped her arm under his arm and around his middle. She was beaming when she looked up at him.

"Hey, you asked me to think about it, I've been thinkin' about it. But I still don't know what the hell I'd do down there. What in the hell do you do there?"

"Well the first thing you do is you stop thinking it's for-ever. 'Cause it's not forever, Mar. We go there for a week, that's all I want to do, just go there for a week, and we don't make it any bigger deal than that. Just a week, I just want to look around, that's all, see something."

"Well we can't go until all the tomatoes are gone, right?"

"The tomatoes are gone after the first real hard frost, buddy boy. Remember? That's when I pick all the green ones and spread 'em out on newspaper in the dining room?"

"Yeah, yeah. So we still have to wait until they all get ripe. You ain't plannin' to leave and then come home and find a pile of red mush stinkin' up the whole house, right?"

"Right, of course right. But I hate it when I have to cut them down. That means all winter, in the house, no windows open, no doors. God, Mar, I'm startin' to really hate that. Really really really hate it."

"I know," he said. "I know you are. But, Ruthie, it's a bad sign, a bad bad sign, when you always wanna be someplace else. 'Cause that oughta tell ya you're not doin' a whole lotta livin' where you are."

"Mar? This may come as a surprise to you, but I don't need any more signs and I don't need any more interpretations of what those signs mean. I know what they mean. I've been trying to tell you what they mean, god almighty, Mar, I've been trying to give you the sign for about two years now. Ever since I found out how totally unsuited I am to be employed right here in the good ol' U.S. of A."

"Ruthie, don't take this wrong, okay? But please don't start in with that again, okay, please?"

"I'm not going to 'start in' with anything. Really, I'm not. I'm just glad you've thought about Florida, that's all. So, uh, if I get your message here, does it mean it's all right with you if I call a couple of travel agencies? Start checkin' things out?"

Balzic gave a half-nod, half-shrug. "Sure, why not? I figure, maybe, you know, right around the week after election day, right in there's when you should start askin' for prices."

She frowned up at him. "After election day? Why you saying it like that?"

"Well," he said, tilting his head and pursing his lips, "I

think maybe right about then is where I ride off into the sunset."

"Well," she said, rubbing his back. "Well, if that's what you want. Is that what you want?"

"You'd be real pissed off if I quit, wouldn't you?" he said, giving her a squeeze. "Go 'head, tell me how pissed off you'd be, huh?"

She looked at him, her face suddenly full of questions.

"Yeah, right, I know," he said. "That gives you so much to think about you don't know where to start. Well me too, cakes. Me too. Like what am I gonna do all day, for one thing. Huh? I can only play my harp for about twenty-five, thirty minutes before my whole mouth starts gettin' a charley horse. So that leaves like twenty-three and a half hours in the rest of the day I gotta figure out somethin' to do. I'm not real good at that, you know? Course you know—what am I askin' you for? You know as well as I do about all the guys who retired, especially the ones the company forced it on 'em? How many stories you heard about couples bein' married forty, fifty years gettin' divorced 'cause the ol' man retires and they don't have enough money to buy her her own TV? I don't want nothin' stupid like that to happen to us, but if we don't give this a whole lotta thought, Ruthie, god, look at how small this kitchen is, babes. Most of the time, shit, I forget how small this kitchen is. We're gonna be trippin' over each other in this kitchen, you know?"

"We do that now, Mar."

"You know what I mean," he said, almost whining.

"Yes, Mar, I do know what you mean. But the kitchen's not going to get any bigger—"

"Maybe we oughta be writin' country songs, like, uh, like how about this?" He cleared his throat and growled, "I neeeeeeeev-er knew how small the kit-chen was, till I lost my baby afffffffffffffff-ter I lost my jobbbbbbbbbbbbbbbbbbbbb."

"Oh god, Mar, please please, anytime you want to write songs, god, please promise me you'll try to find somebody else to sing them, okay?"

"Well, on that unqualified vote of confidence, my darlin' wife, I will take this ol' body into the bathroom and get it prepared to face my fate. Yes, ma'am, the chief of po-lice who couldn't keep his property room locked, that's me. The chief of po-lice who couldn't stay awake long enough to see enemy guerrillas operatin' behind his lines. Some goddamn reporter I never heard of knows more about this town than I do."

"Mar, you're makin' too big a deal out of this."

"I am, huh? Well what you better be doin'—after you start shoppin' around for the price of life in Florida? After that you better start callin' some contractors and find out which walls we can knock out here. 'Cause this kitchen's gettin' smaller by the minute."

Balzic pulled into the City Hall parking lot from the alley that ran in front of the animal shelter. Something in bright red caught his eye as he passed the shelter, but he didn't pay attention to it until after he'd parked in his slot. When he got out of the cruiser, he could hear his name being called and he could see that the thing in red was a woman waving to him. She was standing by the corner of the animal shelter, and she continued to call to him and wave. She was wearing a bright red satiny blouse and he saw as he approached her that it was Council-woman Julie Richards. He wondered if he would've noticed her if she had not been wearing that blouse.

As he walked toward her, he loosened his tie and removed his coat because it was already in the mid-eighties even though it wasn't yet eight o'clock. Ruthie wants to go to Florida? God, how hot does it get down there? Hot as this? No sooner had he asked the question than he put it out of his mind because he knew he was going to get heat of a different kind from the councilwoman.

As he continued to walk toward her, feeling the heat in the concrete through his shoes, he thought about her name and how she'd come by it, Julie Richards. She'd been christened Giulietta by her parents, Armand and Nicoletta Mastrangelo, and very soon after starting school her mother had died—of what Balzic couldn't remember—and her father had sunk into a depression that lasted until the end of his life. Neither father nor mother had relatives in this country, so, as far as others could see, Giulietta had grown up without a family. She'd been forced to become her own mother, and though her father continued to work and care for her financially, he was almost no support for her in other ways. He'd died the year she graduated from high school, and when she was barely out of high school she'd married one of the Riccardullis, whose first name Balzic couldn't remember. Balzic just remembered that he was the one who'd shortened his name to Richards after he'd gotten into a thing with his brothers after their father had died over who wanted to stay in the family produce business and who wanted to sell out and move on. He was the one who'd wanted to sell and move.

Balzic knew parts of the story because his mother had persuaded many of the women of St. Malachy's parish to look out for Giulietta after her mother had died, to be her mother in everything but name. Until she was nine or ten, the girl had welcomed their kindness and interest, but it was around that age when she showed she was capable of taking care of not only herself but her father as well. Balzic's mother had joked often that the girl hadn't had a childhood because she didn't need one: she was thirteen years old when she was born. Still, whenever the girl had questions or problems, the one she willingly came to for advice was Mrs. Balzic.

And she'd especially come to ask his mother's advice when she found out her husband was fooling around, not only with other women, which his being a man she could understand, but with her money, which no matter what gender he was she could not forgive. She had inherited every cent her father had not spent on necessities, and one day she discovered—Balzic couldn't remember how—that it was being spent on women she'd never heard of in ways she'd never thought possible. Giulietta had come to see Balzic's mother in a murderous rage.

Balzic remembered that his mother advised Giulietta that divorce was better than prison, no matter what the Church or her relatives would say or think or do. "God will forgive you," his mother had told her, "even if the Church won't, because He'll be glad you obeyed one of His commandments. So don't you get a gun. You get a lawyer. You get Mo Valcanas and tell him to fix it so he can't touch anything with your name on it. And then divorce the sonofabitch."

Balzic was wiping his face with his hanky by the time he got close enough to her to speak. "Mornin', Councilperson," he said, smiling. He wanted to call her by the name he knew her by when she was growing up, but because everyone else called her Julie and because he thought Julie was a poor second to Giulietta, he'd taken to calling her the title the newspaper used. It was a feeble joke, but it helped him avoid having to call her Julie. "You don't look too good," he said when he got close to her. "You okay?"

"No," she said. She did not even try to smile. She was now in her middle forties and tall, taller than all the men on City Council. She was also a long way in every respect from the girl Balzic had watched grow up, especially since she started complaining publicly about how the volunteer firemen seemed to get anything they wanted in Rocksburg and didn't have to account to anybody. It seemed to Balzic, on those rare times when he attended council meetings, that she was growing old fast, so fast she was on the verge of stooping, as though this fight she'd taken on was getting heavier than she'd ever anticipated. Now, with no makeup on, not even lipstick, she seemed to have aged ten years since the last council meeting, less than a month ago.

"What's up?"

"They're throwing rocks through my windows now, Mr. Balzic." In public she called him by his official title, but in private whenever they talked she addressed him that way. He'd long ago given up trying to persuade her to call him by his first name.

He looked at the ground and shrugged, hoping he wouldn't be dumb enough to say any of the I-told-you-sos that were hovering in the back of his throat.

"I changed my phone number, I bought a different car, I get all my mail through a box, but I can't just up and move, Mr. Balzic. In six more years that house is going to be mine."

He looked at her and waited, struggling hard with his worst inclinations to tell her that she should never have picked a fight with the firemen in the first place.

When he said nothing, she went on: "I remember every-thing you told me about what I was getting into. I remember how you said I can't go messing around with these people, 'cause even if they were wrong I was going to be wrong just for saying so. But this is too much. Where do we live? Is this America? Am I an elected official? But even if I'm just a citi-zen, even if I wasn't on Council, is this America or not?"

Balzic let out a long sigh and swallowed and licked his lips. But he could think of nothing sensible to say.

"Mr. Balzic, this can't go on. They're breaking the law every day. They're making fools out of all of us. Nobody does anything to stop them."

Balzic looked at her and then looked away.

She reached out and caught hold of the sleeve of his shirt and shook it once. "Look at me! This isn't Sicily. This isn't Naples. This isn't Italy. This is Rocksburg. This is Pennsylva-nia. This is America. These firemen think they're the Mafia, the Camorra, all rolled into one. They think they can do anything and get away with it. Mr. Balzic, excuse my language, but that's bullshit. They're a bunch of goddamn firemen, and no matter how many fires they put out, no matter how many kitty cats they get out of the trees, no matter how many blood drives they run, they have to obey the laws just like the rest of us."

Balzic smiled wanly and said, "Hey, you got my vote."

She put her hands on her hips, and the skin on her jaw got tight. "That's not funny, Mr. Balzic. I'm sorry I have to talk to you like this, but that was not funny."

"Uh, you're right," he said. "It's not. I'm sorry. But there are—I don't know for sure how many—but there are at least four hundred of them. And there's only one of you and there's only one of me. All those guys ridin' on those trucks during all those parades on the Fourth of July, Memorial Day, you ever look at their faces? All of 'em, every damn one of 'em, when they were little kids? They were the ones who, you know, when somebody asked 'em what they wanted to be when they grew up, they said, 'I wanna be a fireman.' And there they are. They're on that truck and they are what they said they always wanted to be.

"And then along you come, a woman for crissake—you notice there ain't any women in any of these fire departments?"

She nodded her head, her lips pinching more tightly shut.

"Women have tried to get in, you know that as well as I do. Couple of 'em took it to court. But the Rocksburg Volunteer Fire Department is as male now as it's ever been. And you come along and start tellin' the world they're cookin' their books and they don't answer to anybody but themselves, and all those guys who get to ride on the trucks during the parades, all they know is, hey, some broad wants to take my fire truck away from me."

"That's baloney and you know it. I don't want to take—"

"Of course it's baloney. I know it, you know it. But they don't. How many firemen in this town you think've ever seen a copy of the Third Class Code? Huh? How many you think've ever read a copy of their own charter? Hell, never mind the firemen, how many of your fellow councilmen you think've ever read the Third Class Code? They don't give a crap about that. That's what the solicitor's for. He reads the code, he tells them what he thinks they can do or can't do. That's what the hell they pay him forty bucks an hour for—"

"Sixty bucks an hour."

"Sixty, forty, what's the difference? They're payin' him to read the laws for them, tell 'em what they can and can't do. And as far as the firemen are concerned, all they're thinkin' about is how they can get around it anyway. When was the last time you saw Eddie Sitko at a meeting doin' anything but puttin' his hand out for more money? The next time he comes in a council meeting and says, 'Hey, guys, I've been readin' up on the old Third Class Code here, and it says plain as hell we ain't allowed to do what we been doin', so I'm just gonna have to pay you guys back for all the maintenance you've done on our fire halls and social clubs for about the last fifty years'—the next time Sitko does that, you be sure you get it on tape, you hear?"

"Stop making fun of me, please?"

"I'm not makin' fun of you, Councilperson. I'm just trying to give you the facts of life without being a smart-ass I-told-you-so. But I did tell ya. The first time you came to me and told me what you were gonna do, I said—did I not?—don't do this. Those guys have no idea what you're talkin' about. They think—didn't I tell you this?—they think the charter for their precious volunteer fire companies came down the mountain with Moses. They think it says on there, 'Thou shalt have fires, but thou shalt have volunteer firemen to put them out, and they shalt sit on the right hand of the Lord.' "

"Please stop making fun of me," she said.

"Hell, Councilperson, how could I be makin' fun of you? You see today's paper? Huh? If I'm makin' fun of anybody here, it's me. You might've picked a fight you can't win, but at least you had an idea who the enemy was. I'm in a fight I didn't even know I was in, and I've been so busy playin' cops and robbers, I've let the bastards get behind me. While I'm drivin' around tryin' to make it look like we still have a police department, hey, the DA, the president judge, the county commissioners, the goddamn sheriff, hell, people in my own department have been doin' a polka on me like I'm sawdust on the floor. They're stealin' out of my property room for crissake. You read the paper today?"

"Yes I read the paper today. And I know it's all Eddie Sitko's idea. But I don't care how much they want to play soldier, they can't throw rocks through my window. I'm not gonna put up with that. I'm not." She was in that queasy crossroads between fear and anger and her eyes were just beginning to fill with tears and her voice to quake. "I bought a gun. I want you to write me a, a whatever you write to get the sheriff to give me a permit."

Balzic looked at his shoes and shook his head. "That's not a good idea. You know anything—"

"No I don't know anything about guns. I didn't know how to drive a car either until I had to drive one. I didn't know anything about computers until I had to learn or I was gonna lose my shop. We don't know anything about anything until we have to learn. But we learn. If I can cook four things on a stove at one time and not get burned or set the kitchen on fire and people tell me it tastes good, then I can learn how to shoot a gun. If I learned how—oh forget it. Will you write what you have to or not?"

"Sure," he said. "On one condition. You get taught how to use it. You get signed up for a course real fast. Don't put it off. You go see a guy named Walker Johnson. He runs a pistol range out in Westfield Township. Used to be a lieutenant in the state police. Good man. Come on inside, I'll give you what you need to get the permit, and I'll tell you how to get to Johnson's place. But you gotta promise me you'll call this guy today and get signed up today, you hear me? I know it's more complicated to cook four things at once than it is to shoot a pistol. Shootin' a pistol's real simple, it doesn't take much brains or coordination at all. But, young lady, a pistol ain't a spatula. You get a gun in your hands, it's 'cause you're operatin' under a whole different set of emotions, and you better know what you're doin'."

"Excuse me, but I already have a whole different set of emotions ever since I heard the window break and I go into my living room and there's glass all over the couch and all over the rug."

He nodded many times. "Yes yes, I know. But it's because of those emotions you have to know what you're doin'. Why do you think this SWERT thing, or SWAT or whatever the hell they call it, scares me so much? 'Cause I don't know how these guys have been trained. I *do* know they haven't even done the lethal weapons training you have to do to be a rent-a-cop, and rent-a-cops ain't allowed to carry guns for crissake. And these guys're walkin' around with M-16s for crissake. I saw 'em myself, three of 'em, yesterday." Balzic shook his head again and made tsking noises. "Now *you* want a gun. Do you know that I don't wear one? You know that?"

"Yes. I know. Doesn't everybody?"

"You know why I don't?"

"No."

" 'Cause if I'd've been wearin' a gun all these years, Jeezus, all the years I was in uniform and I had to wear one? It scared me to death every day, every day I worried whether I'd have to shoot somebody. I have a gun. It's in the trunk of my car. It's a

rifle. But it ain't loaded. The ammo's in a box. Locked. So before I even think about shootin' somebody, I gotta get to my
car, get out my trunk keys, open the trunk, take the rifle outta
the rig I got it in so it don't get bounced around and wreck the
sights, I got to remember the combination on the lock for the
ammo box, get the ammo, load it, and then—hey, all that takes
time. And every step I'm thinkin', is this somethin' I really
wanna do? So, uh, other cops hear about that, hey, they thinks
it's real funny. They been laughin' at me for years and years. I
don't care. I have never shot anybody since I been a cop. And
believe me, if I'd've had a pistol on my belt? Since I been chief?
I would've shot some people. Oh yeah. 'Cause there are some
people I would've loved to've shot. Yeah. Right at that moment? Damn right. You sure you wanna do this thing?"

"Here. Read this. Then you tell me." She pulled a crumpled piece of paper out of her slacks pocket and handed it to
him.

He smoothed it out and read, in crude printing, "Fireman
need hose and bunker suits. Maybe you need firemans hose."
He cringed and screwed up his face because the words made
him feel instantly uncomfortable for himself and angry for her
and all he could do was screw up his face. "Well, this should
tell ya what you're dealin' with here. You want any evidence
these guys don't know what's in the Third Class Code, here it
is. And more important, they don't care what the law says.
You're messin' with their thing, that's all they know, that's all
they wanna know. I'm gonna add this to the file, okay? And if I
get a chance today I'll drop by your house, see if they left anything behind. One of these days, we might find somethin' so
we can bust somebody."

He turned away quickly because he wasn't sure he wanted
to see how she was reacting to that. Without looking back at
her, he gave a little nod and a wave for her to accompany him
into the station.

Once inside, he led her back to his office, nodding good
morning to Sergeant Royer, who was seated at the radio console, on the way.

Balzic tried to get her to sit down in his office, but she

was too agitated. She held her arms across her chest and paced around on the other side of his desk.

As he got out the form requesting a permit to carry a firearm, he said to her, "I got some questions maybe you can answer. Okay if I ask 'em?"

"Sure. Why not?"

"Well you just look real real nervous right now and I didn't wanna do that without askin' you, that's all."

"Go ahead and ask. I probably won't know the answers anyway."

"Uh, tell me again what it was got you started with the firemen. I know you told me all this before, but I'm tryin' to refresh my memory about a lot of things, you know? D'you mind?"

"No I don't mind. I was going with this guy, he was a stockbroker. One night we were having dinner in my shop and he just started talking about the firemen buying bonds from him, municipal bonds. Real big numbers. And it took a long time for it to sink in, you know, because at that time I was having a whole lot of trouble paying my rent. And my taxes. I was really, you know, really struggling to keep my head above water, and he was just talking, you know, just trying to impress me with how much he knew about Rocksburg, my town, you know? He was from Pittsburgh someplace, the South Side, I forget. Anyway, I go, 'Wait a minute. These firemen, they're from Rocksburg? And they have so much money they're investing in tax-free bonds? Municipal bonds? Where the hell do they get this kind of money?'

"And he goes, you know, 'Well what do you think they do with all that money they make from those bingos and those social clubs and renting out their halls for weddings?' And I go, 'Get outta town, I rented one of those halls when I got married. I've catered so many weddings in those fire halls, I go, no way. There's no money there. When I rented one, for my wedding, it was seventy-five bucks for the whole night. Even with inflation, they're not getting twice that much now. Nobody gets municipal bond money renting halls for weddings, that's crap.' And he goes—and I'll never forget this—he goes, 'Hey, my uncles run a bingo game. In a real small town in Butler County. For a real small volunteer fire department. And they make seventeen, eighteen thousand bucks a month running two games a week.' And I go—to myself, not to him—I go, 'Whoa, what am I missing here?' 'Cause at that time, I was in a constant hassle with the guys that ran Number Six Social Club, 'cause I was complaining about their customers always parking in my lot, 'cause my place used to be right across the street—listen to me, like you don't know where my place used to be—but when their parking lot would get full, they'd block me in, remember? How many times did I call you guys and say, 'Hey, get these guys out of here,' how many times did I do that?"

"Many times," Balzic said.

"And then when this guy told me they were buying these bonds, I said, wait a minute. They treat me like shit—excuse my language—especially the guy that used to be steward up there then, Charlie, uh, Joyce, you know, the one his brother's with the county emergency management? He was a real smart-ass, used to just come barging in, no matter what I was doing, I'd be talking to a customer, he'd come in and go, 'Hey, you got space for six cars in your lot, what're you complaining about? Half the time you don't have anybody here, so we park here sometimes, so stop callin' the cops,' ya-ta-ta, ya-ta-ta, boy, he was so loud and arrogant, god, he made me sick, 'You don't like where we park, just don't have a fire, you know?' God he used to give me the creeps. Then, after I started nosing around, I find out not only do these guys not pay any taxes on any of this money, those bastards in Number Six got an account with Prudential-Bache, two hundred thousand bucks in a mutual bond fund and, like, thirty-eight, thirty-nine thousand bucks in a money market account. This guy, the stockbroker? He let that little cat out of the bag one night. I almost had a stroke. I'm barely hanging on, I can barely make the rent every month and these guys are hassling me over my parking spaces and they're socking away hundreds of thousands of dollars and they don't even pay taxes?

"That's when I decided to run for Council. And then, after I get elected, I find out they been doing this for like forever, like since there was income taxes, seventy-five years or something and nobody ever said anything! I can't believe it! And when I go looking for all the people who voted for me, suddenly I can't find any of them. I'm getting hassled day and night, phone calls—they send me shoeboxes full of dog crap through UPS, letters with pictures of men's penises in them, Mr. Balzic, can you believe that? They write all over it, 'This is what you need,' and . . . and . . ." She fought back a sob, her shoulders shivering. "And these, these are the good guys? Please finish writing that, please, Mr. Balzic. And I'd appreciate it if you told everybody, you know, just sort of spread it around, okay? That I got a permit for a gun? And that I'm going to learn how to shoot it and I'm gonna have it with me everywhere I go? Would you do that for me?"

Balzic finished filling out the form and said, "As long as you go see Walker Johnson and listen to what he tells you, sure, I'll be glad to spread the word. Here." He handed over the paper and she took it and said thanks and started to leave.

"Hey, wait a minute. I got some other questions for you, okay? And I didn't tell you where Johnson's place was."

"I'll find it, Mr. Balzic. I promise. But I can't talk anymore right now. I'm so mad, I have to go to the courthouse and get this permit business started. I can't talk anymore. I'll be damned if I'm gonna cry and right now that's all I want to do. And I can't let myself. I'm not going to let myself. Thank you. Good-bye." Then she was gone.

Balzic took off his glasses and rubbed his eyes with his knuckles. "Jesus Christ," he said. "What the fuck is goin' on here? She's applyin' for a pistol permit 'cause the goddamn firemen are after her? The goddamn firemen?"

The phone rang. It was Royer. "There's a reporter here says he has an appointment with you. Should I let him back?"

"Huh? I don't have any appoint—" Balzic stopped himself in midword and tried to think if this was just another thing he'd forgotten. Or overlooked. Or stepped right over. "Who'd he say he was?"

Royer mumbled something, then somebody else mumbled something, and then Royer spoke clearly: "Says his name is

Steve Hussler. Says you told him last week you'd talk to him and he hasn't been able to catch up with you since."

"You ever seen him before?"

"Yeah, sure, lots of times."

"Lotsa times? He ever ask for me before?"

"Yeah. Pretty sure he did. I think."

"D'you tell me about it?"

"Oh, now, about that I'm not sure. I'm pretty positive I did, but, uh, so you want me to send him back or not?"

"Well shit, why not. Since he seems to know more about what's goin' on around here than I do, maybe he's exactly who I need to be talkin' to. Send him back, hell."

In a minute or so, the door opened and Steve Hussler came in. Balzic immediately studied Hussler's face and build as he did with every person he met, mostly out of habit but also out of professional necessity because he didn't want to forget people he was probably going to be dealing with and he didn't want to give the impression that he couldn't put names with faces. Hussler was in his early forties; medium height, five-ten or so; medium weight; one-seventy or one-eighty or so, stomach slightly protruding; a full head of straight brown hair, very fine, parted on the left; grayish-brown eyes; fair to dark complexion; no blemishes, acne, or scars on his face or neck; all his features fairly symmetrical; no scars or tattoos or jewelry on his hands; single-lens glasses with clear plastic frames. He wore a tan corduroy sport coat, faded blue jeans, white shirt with a plain reddish-brown knit necktie, collar and tie both starting to fray on the edges. Balzic couldn't see Hussler's shoes. The clothes were way too hot for this time of year, especially the jacket, but Hussler didn't seem uncomfortable in them, even with the collar of his shirt buttoned and the tie knotted tightly.

Balzic rose into a kind of half-crouch and extended his hand, limply, hoping that this Hussler wasn't a bone-crusher. To make sure of that, Balzic withdrew his hand just as Hussler reached for it and said, "Don't squeeze, okay? Got a little arthritis in my fingers."

"Hell, our flesh need not ever touch," Hussler said, withdrawing his hand and laughing, revealing at once two of his most distinguishing features. His teeth looked like he hadn't been in a dentist's chair since childhood, and his breath, swept along by his laughter, reeked of tobacco.

"Suits me," Balzic said, slumping back down in his chair. "What's on your mind? Have a seat. What's your name again?"

Hussler had started to sit, but then stopped. He eyed Balzic from a half-crouch and said, "Neither one of us has the time it would take for me to tell you even a very small part of what's on my mind." He then dropped with a thump onto the chair opposite Balzic and laughed again. He obviously liked to laugh and was quick to do it. "My name's Steve Hussler. You can call me Stefanino—which is my given name and was my father's also—or you can call me Steven, Steve, Steverino, or—and this is the one I prefer—Mr. Hussler. But you can never call me Stevie. I don't answer to Stevie. I spit on people when they call me Stevie. Not in their face necessarily but someplace on them. Usually I wait until they turn their backs and then I spit on their necks and tell 'em it was a bird." All the while he was talking he continued to grin impishly, wickedly.

While Balzic was wondering how much of what he'd just heard was an act and how much was the truth, he felt himself squinting at Hussler. Something kept trying to squeeze into Balzic's mind from somewhere about this guy. "You, uh, you always been a reporter, Mr. Hussler? You ever done anything else?"

"Oh I've been lots of things," Hussler said, the laughter never far from the surface. "In lots of places, doing lots of things."

"I don't wanna say I know somebody when I don't," Balzic said, "but there's somethin' about you, uh, d'you ever used to be a cop?"

"Oh absolutomento, ohmyyes Jesus a-god I used to was a-be a cop-a," Hussler said, suddenly talking in a very broad Italian accent.

Balzic started to nod. "Yeah. Would that be about, oh, ten, twelve years ago maybe? Huh? In Allegheny County?"

"At'sa-right, give-a dat-a man a big-a ceegar," Hussler said.

"You were, uh, with the county cops there, am I right?"

"At'sa right. County dicks to be more precise," Hussler said, losing the Italian accent. He was still smiling, his head slightly canted, his eyes bright with mischief. He put Balzic in mind of half a comedy team, Hussler being the half who spoke the punch lines, the half who had a lot of trouble not laughing because he knew what was coming and he couldn't wait to hear himself say it.

"You were with the Allegheny County Detectives, outta the DA's office?"

"The same."

"And you and I had some dealings? Your face is awful familiar."

"My face is what again—awful or familiar?"

"You know what I mean. So did we or did we? Didn't we I mean."

"Well if we did it must've been very casual because I don't have any real strong recollection of it. But possible. Oh wait. I remember now. Uh, yes, the pross that was offed in Pittsburgh, but the offer hauled her out here somewhere, dumped her. Behind a what? A garage, no. Body shop, yes. The offer, I remember now, his old man was a cop in the town where the body shop was, down the road here somewhere, down Route 30. Is that the one you're talking about?"

"Yeah yeah yeah right, that's it. That's the one. You were the one chasin' paper out here, in the courthouse."

"No, I mean yes I was but I wasn't. What I was tryin' to do when I ran into you was chase down somebody who'd give me a peek at his juvey records. That's how we nailed the freak. He had a history of tyin' critters up with a certain kind of twine, remember? First he got it out of his grandpappy's barn? He'd been tyin' critters up and offin' 'em for years and years. Animal Rescue League had paper on him in one of the Pittsburgh magistrate's offices. They had him and I think if I reco-member correctly, your dog officer here had paper on him when he was real young. The pross was a step up for him."

"You *nailed* him that way? You mean you didn't have a case until then?"

"Not that would satisfy the prosecutor who had the case, no. She was some dip who got the job because her old man was a big Democratic groupie, and she kept pissin' me off, you know, personally. Everything we had wasn't enough for her assertive little ass, so that's why I was chasing his juvey records. I'd already got the paper from the city magistrate in Pittsburgh from Animal Rescue and I'd also got it from the Air Force. He was Section Eighted out of the Air Force for the same thing, tyin' up critters and stranglin' 'em. Air Force had pictures of some calves and real good close-ups of the twine and the knots. That's how we got him. But I had to give the dip DA the pictures 'cause she wanted to slap each one down in front of him while my partner and I were doin' the talkin' 'cause she'd seen some goddamn thing like that in the movies once, or on TV. Imagine that, we were the one talkin' to him, but she had to be the one holdin' the pictures and slapping 'em down on the table in front of him, one at a time, like she was dealing cards. She wanted to be Perry Mason when she grew up. Or Raymond Burr, I forget which. Course that's the way it's done went most of the time with me." The last was said in the voice and tone of a mischievous boy, none too bright, and was followed by loud laughter, blasting another wave of tobacco breath across the desk at Balzic.

Balzic tried to refresh his memory about the father of that killer, the cop. Balzic was trying to imagine what it was like to discover one day that your son had certain preoccupations, certain tendencies, certain bends in his way of looking at the world.

"You still with me, Chief?" Hussler said. "You're startin' to look a little vague, if you don't mind my sayin' so."

"I don't think I could stop you from sayin' so even if I did mind," Balzic said. "I was just thinkin' about that kid's father."

"Well don't waste any sympathy on him. He was how and why junior grew up to be the fine lad he was."

"You know that for sure? Or you just speculatin'?"

"Oh I'm not speculating. Two of his wives told us that. The kid's mother and his stepmother. I'm not speculating at all. The first wife was scared to death of the both of them, senior and junior. The first time she left, senior hunted her down and beat the crap out of her, but the second time she left, it was junior who tracked her. He put her in the hospital for about four days. I think he was fourteen or fifteen at the time. This wasn't just disgruntled wives bitching about a husband. It's all on paper. The second wife, apparently she was into the wham-bam-thank-you-ma'am stuff. So she and the cop got along just fine. But by that time, of course, junior was already pursuing his life's dreams on his own."

"So, uh, how come you're not a cop anymore?"

"Fired."

"You were fired from the county cops? In Allegheny County? What the hell could you possibly have done that would get you fired from that bunch?"

Hussler crossed his legs and leaned back in his chair. He smiled and said, "I can honestly say—and with more than a little pride actually—that I've been fired from every job I've ever had. No. Only as an adult. I never got fired from any of the jobs I had when I was a kid. I was a good little boy. Solid little brownnoser."

"Yeah? So what'd you do with the cops there that got you fired."

"Nothing, I didn't do anything. New DA. Out with the old, in with the new. Political crap, nothing personal. I'm not suing them if that's what you're thinking."

"I was wondering about that. How come I have this feelin' you're not goin' to talk a whole lot about any job you got fired from?"

"Now let me get this straight, Officer. Are you suggesting that I may be under court orders or something not to discuss my previous employers with you, is that what you're trying to imply? Are you insinuating that you think I'm involved in some sort of litigation against *all* my ex-bosses?"

"Sort of."

"Well you'd be sort of right," Hussler said, roaring with laughter.

"So is that your job now?"

"What?"

"Work awhile, get fired, sue somebody, live off your winnings."

Hussler howled. "Who the hell said anything about winning? I just said I got fired. I didn't say nothin' about winning nothin'. Although I did win a turkey once when I was in junior high school. Besides which, this is Pennsylvania."

"So?"

"What do you mean, so? Pennsylvania's hire-and-fire. People don't have to have a reason to fire you. They don't even have to tell you anything except, you know, 'You're fired.' The shysters they hire to write their laws know what their job is, and they know what they have to do to keep it. And if the employers don't have to have a reason—which the best legislators money can buy have guaranteed—how exactly are you supposed to defend yourself against a charge that doesn't exist—legally or otherwise? If somebody says you're fired because you're incompetent, they might be required to present examples of your incompetence. But that gets real hard to do if you've been giving somebody raises and bonuses for their work for X number of years and all of sudden now they're incompetent. Easier to prove they're incontinent, you know? If they were peeing their pants, you could obtain photographic evidence of wet spots on their chairs."

"Wait a second. You get raises *and* bonuses workin' for the Allegheny County cops?"

"No no. Not them. With newspapers I'm talking about. And anyway, I told you: I got fired 'cause a new DA got elected. Didn't have anything to do with me personally. New DA, out with the old, in with the new, that's all that was."

"But you've been fired from places—newspapers?—that gave you raises and bonuses all along and then all of a sudden fired you?"

"Absolutomento, you kiddin'? Not me. But I know guys who were fired the day after the boss told them they were getting a raise. The next day. The next morning. Mister-a Boss-a-man, he is a-say. 'Ho boy, I'ma like ayou avery much. Yessiree Boob. There'sa gonna be alotsa extra moolah for-a you, you betcha. Gooda nighta.' Next day, Mister-a Boss-a-man, hisa secre-ta-ree-a, she is a-say, 'A-good morning, a-clean out-a you desk. You-a fee-neesh.'"

"So you don't get fired for the money, you get fired for love, is that it?" Balzic said, smiling crookedly.

"More or less," Hussler said, laughing. Then he attempted to grow serious. "I do it because I truly love the pain of humiliation and rejection. But enough about me. Let's talk about you. Your pain, your humiliation."

"Aw, smooth, real smooth."

"Well that's just because I've become expert in recognizing pain and humiliation. This is America. There's a whole lot of it going around now."

"So, uh, let me get something straight, just for my own, uh, peace of mind. Did I really agree to see you for some reason last week? Or is that just one of your bullshit lines to get in the door?"

Hussler threw out his hands and looked wounded. "Me? Use deception? To speak with a public official? About public issues? I'm deeply hurt. My journalistic honor, my professional integrity is in question. Gad-zooks."

"So is it bullshit or not? Did I make an appointment with you?"

"Not that I know of. But I made many appointments with you. You were just never here to confirm them, that's all. You were always out. Ridding the streets of deviation both in thought and deed—"

"You ever give anybody a straight answer?"

"Only when the electrodes are connected to my nuts and nipples and I see the finger on the switch."

"Yeah, right. Okay. So whatta you want now?"

"Does this mean the interview is about to begin, Mister Policeman?" Hussler said in mock wonderment. He leaned forward and touched something in his coat breast pocket and then settled back in his chair.

"That a tape recorder you just started?"

"No, my brassiere was pinching me. Of course it's a tape recorder. It's the working boy's best friend. If I play it back for you, you can't say you didn't say it after I say in print that you did."

"Tapes can be made to say all kinds of things."

Hussler pretended to look horrified. "You mean there are people who would distort another person's words? Electronically? Why, why on earth would they do that? And how? How do they do that? I mean do they just use a regular pencil eraser. Why, that's . . . that's un-eth-i-cal. That's un-scrup-u-lous. That's a violation of the sacred trust between interviewer and interviewee."

Balzic sighed and looked down at his fingernails. "Okay okay, I see that gettin' a straight answer outta you ain't worth my time, so whatta you wanna know?"

"Well, what I would like to do now is give you an opportunity to comment on some things before I put them in the paper for all the world to see, or at least those members of the world who buy the *Rocksburg Gazette* and who read something besides sports and the comics and the personals."

"About what exactly?"

"Why the Special Weapons and Emergency Response Team, exactly. Of Conemaugh County. And the assertion that certain members of your department are participants. In that team. And the assertion that certain weapons and equipment being used by said team have come out of your property room—among other things."

"Oh, what's the phrase I'm searching for?" Balzic said, rubbing his chin and looking at the ceiling. "It'll come to me in a second here, just let me think. Oh. I know what it is. Yeah. No comment. That's the phrase I was lookin' for. No comment."

Hussler leaned back in his chair and looked at his shoes. "Aw come on, man. You know this isn't gonna go away. And I'm not gonna go away. And every time you try to act like it's gonna go away and it doesn't? You're just gonna come off lookin' more and more like a guy who wasn't paying attention. And I know enough about you to know that's not the kind of message you wanna send."

Hussler had spoken softly and seemed to be doing his best to sound sincere. This immediately put Balzic on edge.

"Is that a fact. Now how exactly would you know what kind of message I wanna send?"

"Look, Chief," Hussler said, again talking softly and seriously. "I've been where you are. Not as an administrator, certainly not, but you have to know that I know what it's like to be a cop in a political beehive. That's all the detectives were in Allegheny County. The only time it wasn't political was when we were dealing with street stuff. Everything else? Gad-zooks, you couldn't make a move without bumpin' into some pol's behind, which had some bureaucrat's nose up it, you know? So I have a pretty good idea what you're going through here. A whole lot of people are trying to do an end run around you. I know a lot about it. I could help you out. But this is like every other thing in life, Chief. Quid pro quo. I scratch your back, but only when you agree to scratch mine. This is America. You gotta give me some words I can put on the page, you know? I got space to fill. That's how my boss knows it's okay for him to pay me."

Balzic nodded several times. "Uh, when you go back to wherever you go to type up this stuff, d'you also type that speech you just made? Or do you put that tape player on, whatta they call it? Fast forward? Do you fast-forward right over that speech of yours?"

"Ohmygod no. Certainly not. That's usually the best part of any interview, where I get to listen to me asking pertinent questions impertinently," Hussler said, shaking with laughter.

"Uh-ha. So. So whatta you wanna know again?"

"I just want you to comment on the fact that certain members of your department are participants in the Conemaugh County's brand-new counterinsurgency strike force or special weapons and response team or whatever name they're calling it. SWERT, Special Weapons and Emergency Response Team, that's it. Do you really think Eddie Sitko looks like Arnold Schwarzenegger?"

"What? Sitko looks like who?"

"That's what I heard some dip say in a restaurant yesterday

when I was having breakfast, the one where Isaly's used to be, across Main Street from the courthouse? Yeah. She said she thought Eddie Sitko looked just like the Terminator man. And she thought when they make a movie about him—Sitko—that Arnold Schwarzenegger should play him in the movie."

"Oh for crissake," Balzic said, putting both hands on his head and closing his eyes and sighing. "This is all gettin' too, uh, too, what the hell is this gettin' to be?"

"Surreal?" Hussler said.

"Sur-what?"

"Surreal. It's my favorite word to describe life here in America. Life characterized by an irrational arrangement of material and people and events, everything out of context. Some dip sitting in a restaurant talking about how a very real fire chief, who's behaving in his usual dictatorial way, suddenly causes this dip to see him as a movie actor who plays this creature that was dreamed up over lunch out in Hollywood. Reality keeps getting harder and harder to figure out because supposedly educated people start confusing actors for the roles they play and then confusing real people for the actors, you know what I'm saying?"

"I'm not sure," Balzic said. "But I don't have any trouble knowin' who Eddie Sitko is. He's looney-tunes. He's been looney-tunes as long as I've known him, which is ever since I got back from World War Two. His old man used to be fire chief, and he was loonier than his kid. His old man used to carry a long piece of rubber hose in his car and whenever he saw somebody doin' something he didn't like, he'd whack 'em with that hose, he didn't give a fuck where he was or who saw him. So Eddie's just carryin' on the family tradition. The difference is, you can't whack people with a rubber hose anymore and get away with it just because you're the fire chief—"

"Well of course," Hussler said, getting ready to laugh. "Now you have to be a part of a Special Weapons and Emergency Response Team, officially sanctioned by the president judge of the Court of Common Pleas and administered by the DA and the director of emergency management, among others—"

"Okay okay okay, you made your point."

Hussler gave an exaggerated shrug. "Gad-zooks I wasn't even trying to make a point—"

"Yeah right. Well I still got no comment. I mean, Jesus Christ, what comment you want me to make, exactly? Is that fuckin' tape recorder still on?"

"Oh. Don't worry about that," Hussler said. "I'll edit all this out. You can trust me." He waited a second, then howled with laughter.

Balzic leaned back and folded his arms across his chest and nodded several times. "Everything's a goddamn joke, right? Is that it? Everything's funny?"

Hussler composed himself and said, "Look, who am I talkin' to here? You know the game better than I do. Doncha? I mean, really? We all trust each other as long as it suits our purpose, right? Until we find out which one of us is the screwer and which one the screwee, right? In God We Trust, right? Says so all over the place, money, everywhere. Everybody else pays cash. Except for the ones with plastic, and the ones with so much money they don't even carry pens to sign anything with less than six figures on it. I personally haven't believed in Santy Claus since I was in kindergarten. I mean I measured our fireplace chimney, I knew nobody with a belt size bigger than thirty was comin' down *that* chimney. Now the Easter Bunny, that was a little tougher. A rabbit that laid eggs? The only thing I'd seen come out of a rabbit's behind was these little-bitty black things—my grandfather used to raise rabbits, but one time I did convince a neighbor kid to eat one of those because he believed me when I told him that the rabbit was just workin' out, exercising. I told him the Easter Bunny had to build up to the big colored eggs by practicin' with these little black ones. This kid said it didn't taste bad, except it smelled like shit—"

"Aw come on, Jeez-sus," Balzic said, groaning.

"Well what do you want me to say? Of course the recorder's on. And you know I can screw with anything you say. But I don't need a tape recorder to do it. But I also know you know that if I screw with you, I'm dead here, right? I never get anything from you, ever. So give me something I can use, something you can use. Really, just, uh, think of it as me giving you the opportunity to cover your behind a little bit, think of it that way. Hey, everybody else is running their mouths, speculating all over the place, why shouldn't you get a chance to get in the game?"

Balzic thought about that for almost a minute. Then he said, "Maybe 'cause I don't know enough and I don't wanna look like a bigger fool than I already am."

"Aw come on, Chief. They tricked you, man, it happens. They're gonna try to trick me real soon. Gad-zooks, you gotta have a little fun with 'em before they—"

"They're gonna trick you? Real soon? How's that?"

Hussler shrugged. "You know how many firemen work at the *Gazette*? Dozens and dozens. They work in the composing room, in the pressroom, they sell advertising, they're all over the place. The whole time I was writing the piece that was in today's paper, there was this guy from advertising sniffin' around every time I looked up. Turns out he's a lieutenant in Hose Company Number Six. How long you think it's gonna take before they put my name in the hat? What do you think they've got planned for me? They're givin' the councilwoman hell right now."

"She was just here," Balzic said, figuring he might as well start putting out the word as she'd asked. "She wanted me to write her up a chit for a gun permit."

"Did you?"

Balzic nodded. "You gonna write that?"

"You think maybe she would want me to?"

"I think maybe she would."

"See, now, that's the kind of stuff we can do to help each other out here, Chief," Hussler said, grinning broadly. "My boss'll just think this is the greatest scooperoo in the world. 'Councilperson Pursues Pistol Permit.' We got a night editor thinks alliteration's just the cutest little cup of cuddly concepts. I'll buy you lunch if that headline isn't on page one tomorrow."

"I try to eat lunch at home."

"So, uh, in your opinion, Chief, is the councilwoman justi-
fied in believing that she's in danger? And who does she think
threw the rock? Does she have any ideas? Who do you think
threw the rock?"

"You know about the rock? How'd you hear about that?"

"Oh hell, I told ya. Dozens and dozens of fireboys work at
the paper. That was the first thing I heard this morning. Hadn't
even got to the coffee machine. 'Hey, didya hear? Somebody
threw a rock through the councilwoman's window.' I got that
from one of the lifestyle ladies."

"One of the which ladies?"

Hussler looked genuinely surprised. He leaned forward
quizzically. "Not only don't you read the paper real real carefully, you don't read it very much at all, do you?"

"Try not to," Balzic said. "Not since Tom Murray died.
You couldn't really bullshit Tom. I sorta get the feeling, since
he died, you know, that the *Gazette* really, well, maybe I oughta
just stop talkin' right here."

"Hey, it's okay. I wouldn't do you that way."

"Yeah, right. As long as you got that little hickeydo in
your chest pocket runnin' I'm not sayin' another word about
your paper. So don't ask. It so happens I do know how many
firemen work there. Not exactly, but close enough. I also know
who owns the joint. And I also know that he doesn't have Murray around anymore to put up even a little bit of opposition to
him. So you just forget I said anything about the paper, and I
damn sure better not ever find out you let that tape recorder
layin' around where you work so somebody else with big ears
can push the play button, you take my meaning?"

Hussler splayed his hands and made a "who, me?" face.

They looked at each other crookedly for a long moment.

"So, you gonna give me anything else?" Hussler said finally.

Balzic sighed. "I have suspended one officer with pay until
he has a hearing before the civil service board. I have not filed a
formal charge against him yet, because mostly what I want to
have happen is for the civil service hearing to be a sort of, hell,
I don't know, a kind of imitation grand jury. Look, I don't

know what the hell the procedure is. I've never had to deal with anything like this before, I really don't know what the hell to do. I haven't talked to the mayor yet or the city solicitor, I don't even know if I was out of line for suspending the officer for crissake. I mean, when it comes right down to it, I may be way outta line thinkin' it's any of my business that he's part of another law enforcement operation. I mean if he's been led to believe that it's a duly authorized organization and I can't prove otherwise, what fucking grounds do I have for suspending him, is what I'm sayin'."

"So you want me to write this or not? That you suspended him, I mean."

"Well that's what I'm tellin' ya, I don't know. For crissake, whatever you do, don't print his name."

"So I can write that you suspended him, you just don't want me to say it was Yesho."

"Well now how the fuck'd you know it was him?" Balzic exploded.

Hussler grinned lopsidedly. "Well, Chief, you did sort of suspend him in a—how do I want to put this—in a saloon? That ring any bells?"

"Oh gawd," Balzic groaned, cringing and hanging his head.

"Well wait a second," Hussler said. "How about I say you are looking into all the legal questions, uh, you have suspended one officer, you don't want anyone to misinterpret your motives about your actions regarding that officer, he's a fine officer with an exemplary record, but some equipment has been missing from the property room and—"

"No no Jesus Christ no, you can't put it down like that. I mean you put those two things together one right after the other like that and what the hell's everybody supposed to think about my motives? 'He's a fine officer but some property's missing'? What the hell else would anybody think I suspended him for? Come on, you can't put it together like that, Jesus."

"Well I wouldn't put it down one two like that. I would separate those two things, really, I'd give them some space. Trust me."

"Why do—every time you say 'trust me'—why do I get these real sharp needles in the middle of my chest, huh?"

"Maybe you should see a doctor," Hussler said, grinning wickedly once again.

The phone rang. It was Royer again. "Carlucci's here. He said he gotta talk to you now 'cause he gotta be someplace in about half an hour and he don't know how long before he can see you again."

"Yeah yeah, tell him come on in." Balzic hung up and said, "Look, Mr. Hussler, I gotta talk to my man here, so, uh—"

"So this interview is over," Hussler said, standing and stretching. "Was it as good for you as it was for me?"

"Huh?"

"Nothing, nothing. You sure didn't give me a whole lot, Chief. My boss is gonna be real disappointed if all I have to justify my wages today is what you told me here."

"Well why don't you go interview Eddie Sitko? I'll bet he'll give you lots to write to justify your pay."

"Oh I don't think so, no. Mr. Fire Chief Sitko has already let it be known that he doesn't want to wish me any bad luck but he hopes an act of God like two bolts of lightning hit my neighborhood, one to set my house on fire and one to destroy communications so nobody can call the firemen, so when they finally do show up, my house will be a total loss, insurancely speaking of course. He doesn't wish that my eyebrows should be singed off or anything. He wants to do that himself—with a butane lighter."

There came a knock and Carlucci opened the door without waiting for Balzic to invite him in. Carlucci gave Hussler a quick once-over and screwed up his face in thought. "Huss, right?"

"I was just leaving," Hussler said. "It's Hussler. But don't worry your pretty head about it."

"Yeah, right," Carlucci said. "Hussler? Not Huss?"

"Ciao," Hussler said, giving a little salute to Balzic as Balzic looked first from Carlucci to Hussler and back. It was obvious to Balzic that this was not their first meeting.

After Hussler had gone, Balzic waited until Carlucci had taken a seat and then asked him, "You know that guy from somewhere?"

"Yeah. I'll think of it in a second here. What's his name? Huss?"

"Hussler."

"Nah. Huss. No that isn't it either. When I first ran into him, he had a real long dago name. Started with Huss something. Oh. I remember now. Husbandini. Yeah. He was a postal cop. I was workin' a construction scam the Leone brothers were doin', remember? That shit they used to pull on the geezers, you know, one of the brothers would show up in a suit with a clipboard and say he was a zoning enforcement officer and write up all those wiring violations? Then the younger one would show up in a truck in about an hour and start fuckin' around in the geezer's fuse box and blow all the lights and the refrigerator and scare the shit outta the geezer—"

"Yeah yeah, I remember. The geezer'd get a bill for about twelve hundred bucks," Balzic said. "So that's when you met this Hussler? What was his name again?"

"Husbandini. That's what it was when he was a postal inspector. The Leones were also workin' a vacation scam outta some resort in, uh, oh crap I don't remember where it was. Up in Erie maybe. They were sellin' time in a bunch of cabins that didn't exist. And they were usin' a post office box here and that's when I ran into him. What'd he tell you his name was?"

"Hussler."

"Oh I know now. He's the one's been writin' for the *Gazette* about the SWERT thing. Man, what is *wrong* with these people?" Carlucci shook his head and let out a low whistle. "I'm startin' to think maybe everybody's goin' fuckin' buggy, really, Mario. And this Conemaugh Foundation? Jesus Christ. No wonder this country's fucked-up."

"How's that?"

"Listen, I gotta tell ya, I been talkin' to my cousin Vince, the CPA? To get him to explain this stuff to me? And he starts laughin', shakin' his head, he says whatta piece of work I am. I want him to explain something that takes up about three hundred and fifty pages of real small print in the IRS Code, and he says, how much time am I gonna give him, and I says, hey, you know, how's twenty minutes sound? He goes in another room and comes back with the stack of pages and says, 'Here, you figure it out.' So what I'm sayin', Mario, this stuff is so fuckin' complicated, you gotta be a tax attorney to figure it out. And that's no guarantee. 'Cause in half those three hundred and fifty pages all they are is appeals about what's tax-exempt and what isn't. 'Cause I swear nobody knows, not even the CPAs or the tax attorneys, none of 'em knows what the fuck the IRS is talkin' about. Man, it's got loophole and bribe and kickback written all over it. This is allowed, that ain't allowed. This is exempt, that ain't exempt. If you get a certain percentage of your income from the wrong kind of organization, it don't matter what kinda charity you're runnin', you're not exempt."

Carlucci reached in his coat pocket and brought out his notebook. "Listen to this. This is right at the beginning of Section 501 of the IRS Code. This is called period zero one scope of exemption. Tax-exempt status, that most prized of all tax concessions sanctioned by Congress, is available to various classes of nonprofit organizations parenthesis corporations, trusts, community funds, social clubs, civic groups parenthesis by way of Code Section 501 parenthesis A parenthesis, which sets the range of tax exemptions. The most common basis for invoking tax-exempt status falls under Code Section 501 parenthesis C parenthesis another parenthesis the number three another parenthesis—"

"Hey, Rugs, what's the word for two parenthesis?"

"Huh? For parenthesis? Parentheses. I think."

"Parentheses. Good. Don't read those. Stick with the fucking words."

"Huh? Oh yeah, sure. Uh, where was I? Oh here, 'the most common basis falls under'—no here—'the broad category of exemptions for religious, charitable, scientific, literary and educational organizations. Nonprofit organizations survive largely on contributions and might avoid taxation altogether by excluding the donations received from their income computations as nontaxable gifts. But with membership fees, rents, interest, dividends, etc., as lucrative—and taxable—sources of revenue, organizations must rely on the provisions of Code Section 501 to ensure exemptions.' Then it goes on for like another three hundred and thirty-forty pages to tell you what you can and can't get away with."

"So, uh, Rugs, I don't mean to rush you, but what about the Conemaugh Foundation?"

"This whole thing's a scam, Mario, really. I mean, you got to have a whole different way of thinkin' to understand this stuff."

Balzic could see he wasn't going to get any satisfaction about what he wanted to know until Carlucci told what he knew. Sometimes Carlucci was like that. It wasn't arrogance; it was just his rhythm.

"A different way of thinkin' how?"

Carlucci shook his head. "I don't know how to say it exactly. I just know, uh, it's like there's a whole different class of people in this country. I never knew this before. I mean, I knew there were people with money, you know. But before? When I used to think about people with money? Hey, I was thinkin', you know, 'cause a guy was drivin' a Cadillac, wearin' a spiffy suit, livin' in a house with four bedrooms and three bathrooms and it was all paid for, and the guy carried like two grand cash on him all the time, I mean, I used to think that guy had money. It sounds so stupid now when I'm hearin' it come outta my own mouth, but that's the truth, that's what I used to think."

"Yeah? So now whatta you think?"

"So now I think there are people, hey, the last two things in the world they wanna see are cash or a title to anything. A car, a house, the stuff I used to think was property, you know? Like the more stuff you owned the richer you were? Like that kind of property?"

"I'm followin' you. So go 'head," Balzic said.

"The ones that own these foundations, Mario, they don't own anything. Well I'm sure they own somethin', but I don't know what. Some of 'em don't even own the clothes they wear.

They get their goddamn clothes for free just for sayin' who made 'em, you know?"

Balzic shook his head no. "The only people I know get their clothes for free are the ones get 'em from St. Vincent de Paul."

"Well it's true, man. Some of these people get their clothes to wear for one night and then the next day they take 'em back, but it ain't like you or me rentin' a tux for a wedding, you know? They don't pay for 'em. They just wear 'em. And if some gossip columnist mentions their name in the paper and says they were wearin' such and such's dress or gown, hey, that's how they pay for it, they get free advertisin' for whoever made it.

"Like my cousin was tryin' to explain to me how you could be rich if you didn't own anything. I mean I really had— have—I really have a hard time understandin' this. 'Cause all my life, I been livin' like the whole thing's about gettin' your own place to live in, gettin' clothes, furniture, a car, and in order to do that you gotta have a steady paycheck, and the taxes come outta your check before you even see it. That's my life. Food, clothing, shelter, transportation, and insurance for you and yours and for all your stuff. And a square job to pay for it. But these guys, well, like I said to Vince, how can you be rich if you don't have a fuckin' checkin' account somewhere? So okay, so you don't carry cash, so how do you pay your bills? You can't tell me these rich fucks go to the post office every day and buy money orders.

"Man, he was laughin' and shakin' his head so hard like I'm the biggest chump in America, and he's sayin', 'No no, you gotta stop thinkin' like that. These people don't pay bills the way you do. They arrange it so everything's an expense for the exempt foundation they're runnin'.' I said get outta here. He goes, 'No no, these people, every day their whole life is connected with some exempt hustle—only in the papers and magazines and on TV, you know, it's always this disease or that hospital or that medical research. The last thing in the world anybody ever calls it is a business—or a hustle god forbid. But every time they go to lunch in some fancy restaurant, they're doin' exempt business, tryin' to raise money, puttin' the arm on whoever they're eatin' with, so when they're done eatin', the foundation guy's gonna pick up the check and sign it in the name of the exempt foundation and then he's gonna turn it over to his tax guys and it gets written off as a tax-deductible expense.' "

"Hey, Rugs, it works like that for everybody," Balzic interrupted him.

"Yeah yeah I know. But these guys, you know, they're never payin' for a meal in a restaurant the way you and me think about payin' for a meal or the way some salesguy pays for it. That's just out of the question. Same goes for a car. You buy a car. These people don't buy cars. They don't lease cars. The foundation leases the car. They just drive it. If their tax attorneys can convince the IRS the car was used primarily for foundation business and was leased, you know? Not bought. But leased with money set aside by the foundation as part of its normal business expenses, what the hell difference does it make whose name is on the title? It's not their car, but they got the only set of keys.

"Mario," Carlucci said, eyes wide, shrugging, "honest to god, it took me I can't tell you how long to figure out what was the difference between buyin' a car the way I buy one and buyin' one the way these guys buy one. I mean, they don't even think about ownin' the car. I mean, ownin' the car to them is stupid the way I think about ownin' the car. I mean all my life, since I was a kid, I've been takin' pride in what kinda car I own. I'm drivin' a fuckin' Chevy, I paid for it, I take all kinds of stupid-ass pride because I do this, and they're drivin' around in a fuckin' Mercedes and their fuckin' name is not on the fuckin' lease. But anybody looks at 'em, they figure, hey, it's their car. This is a really hard thing for me to understand, Mario, I don't know about you. Do you understand it? Seriously, am I just stupid? Or did I let myself get bullshitted all my life, like about what ownin' property means?"

Balzic splayed his hands and shrugged. "How do you expect me to answer that? What do I know. I wanna know about the Conemaugh Foundation. I wanna know what the fuck John

Theodore was talkin' about when he told me, 'Two words: Conemaugh Foundation.' That's what he said, that's what I wanna know."

"Mario, I don't have that for you. I'm sorry, but I haven't had time. You just told me about this yesterday, you know? I haven't been to the IRS office. It's Saturday. You wanna find out whether somebody applied for exemption from taxes, you gotta go to the IRS. You gotta see who filed the application for exemption and whether it was approved and whose name is on it. Then you gotta call Harrisburg, see whose names are on the incorporation papers. And if some bureaucrat wants to play their game, you know, 'I-know-something-you-don't-know-and-you-have-to-kiss-my-ass-to-find-out,' if they want to jag me around it could take weeks."

"So you don't know anything about the Conemaugh Foundation is what you're tellin' me."

"No, I'm tellin' ya I'm tryin' to figure this, uh, this whole new way of lookin' at ownin' stuff. This isn't the same as when I found out there wasn't any Santa Claus, you know? I mean, I remember when that hospital down the road went nonprofit— just to show you what an asshole I was then, I remember thinkin', what the hell they doin' that for? I mean, they were all doctors—you know the one I'm talkin' about?"

Balzic nodded. "Yeah yeah, I know. So?"

"So doctors make a lotta money, I mean that's why everybody's old lady wants their kids to be a doctor, right? Or to marry one? So I'm sayin' to myself, how you gonna make money ownin' a hospital if you're a doctor if you don't wanna make a profit anymore? I mean what the fuck's the point?"

"Yeah. So?"

"So, it's simple," Carlucci said, with a little shrug. "It's so simple you think it can't be. But it is. If you can do what you want, whenever you wanna do it, what do you want with money? Only schnooks think you need money. And I was a schnook. And so are most of the people in this country. Believe me. Listen to this, I copied this too, right outta Section 501 'cause it's, man—never mind, just listen.

"'The chief difference between a private foundation and a

nonprivate foundation (better known as a public charity) is that a private foundation relies on a narrow group of contributors, while public charities receive a substantial portion of their revenue from a broad base of the public or from a governmental unit.' You hear that part? Huh? 'Or from a governmental unit'? Where the fuck you think that governmental unit gets the money? Huh? From us assholes, that's where. So where was I? Oh. 'Private foundations may exist due to the largess of a handful of benefactors, and therefore become suspect of serving the private needs of these "substantial contributors." That private foundations do not become vehicles for private gain and unjustified charitable contributions deductions is the imperative behind the special rules.'"

Carlucci looked at Balzic and shrugged deeply. "You hear that last sentence? Here's the fuckin' IRS tryin' to tell us the reason they make all these special rules is so nobody can say you use private foundations to be, uh, here, 'vehicles for private gain.' Mario, nobody can accuse you of 'private gain' if you don't have your name on any paper that schnooks think is a title to somethin'." Carlucci stood up and sighed deeply again. "I gotta go. My mother's out in the car. She's gonna rip my ears off if I don't get out there."

Balzic squinted up at him. "You okay? You don't look so good."

"Course I don't look good, what've I been tellin' ya? You don't get it, do you?"

"Get what?"

"Mario, I've been collarin' thieves since I was twenty-one. A thief is somebody who takes something that belongs to somebody else. That's supposed to be behind all our laws. And not only do we, us, you and me, and all cops, not only do we get it from the law, but I had that pounded into me by the nuns. And the nuns got it from the Vatican. And the Vatican got it from Moses. Thou shalt not steal. Section 501 of the IRS Code changes the whole idea of what stealin' is. Maybe not anybody else's idea of what stealin' is. But I won't ever be able to think of stealin' in the same way I used to, not ever again. You can't be accused of stealin' something if you use it but you don't claim it's yours but nobody else claims it either. It's yours, but it ain't yours, you know what I'm sayin'? How many kids we put the slam 'cause we caught 'em drivin' around in a car that wasn't theirs, huh?"

"Aw come on—"

"No no, I'm serious. We see a kid drivin' a car we think he couldn't possibly have paid for, we pull him over. It's automatic. And why? 'Cause we assume we think we know what somebody can or cannot pay for. Neither one of us, never in our whole lives—and you gotta admit this, Mario—never did either one of us ever pull a guy over in a Mercedes with that thought in mind—unless it's a spade. Then we pull him over 'cause we automatically assume he's dealin' drugs. But if it's a white guy in a suit? Never in a thousand years would we think about pullin' him over and askin' to see his registration."

Balzic leaned back and folded his arms. "So exactly what're you gonna say when this happens—whatever the odds are on it happenin' here—so when you pull this suit over and he shows you a registration and it happens to be one of these foundations, what're you gonna say? Huh? You gonna charge him with bein' a thief without bein' a thief? I don't think that's in the Crimes Code, you know?"

"I'm not gonna charge him with anything, Mario. Course it ain't in there. Ain't gonna happen anyway 'cause the only time I ever see a Mercedes in this town is in the doctors' parkin' lot up the hospital. But if it happens? And I hope it does, 'cause what I'm gonna say is this. 'I know what you're doin', Foundation Man. It's legal 'cause the IRS says so. But it's a scam as sure as I'm a cop. And I just want you to know that I know it.' That's all I'm gonna say."

Carlucci had his hand on the doorknob and was starting to open the door when he stopped and leaned back. "Know what else, Mario? The words 'charitable deduction' have taken on a whole new meaning for me. I gotta go."

"Yeah, right." Balzic took off his glasses and rubbed his eyes with the heels of his palms. "'Charitable deduction' has taken on a whole new meaning for him, but the fucking Conemaugh Foundation is still a deep dark fucking secret. Swell."

Balzic slumped against the back of his chair and sighed, baffled yet again by what was happening around him. Councilperson Julie Richards was getting boxes of dog crap through United Parcel Service and pictures of penises through the Postal Service and her windows are now getting broken because she had this simple idea that if volunteer firemen made enough money from selling bingo cards, raffle tickets, beer, and potato chips to buy municipal bonds, then they certainly had enough money to maintain their own buildings instead of expecting the city to do it—and to pay for it.

That looked like a sane, sensible idea. There was only one thing wrong with it. Every time Richards sat at the council table and said for the record that the least the firemen could do was open their books to let the public see if her suspicions about how much money they had were true or not, it just made firemen fans mad. Trying to say that volunteer firemen were scamming a city and all its taxpayers was like standing up in the middle of Mass and accusing the priest of molesting altar boys. The priest might in fact be molesting altar boys, but nobody in the pews during that Mass was going to have much sympathy for the accuser. Making the right accusation in the wrong place at the wrong time was almost as bad as making a wrong accusation, and as far as Julie Richards was concerned, taking on the firemen didn't have a right time or place. Every time she said the firemen were stonewalling her by refusing to open their books, she lost points on the sympathy meter because if the rest of Council didn't want to go along with her— and she'd never had even one second to any of her motions to that effect—and if the firemen didn't voluntarily open their books, there was no way she could prove her accusation. She'd gotten elected on the promise of lowering everybody's taxes by making the firemen pay their own way, but ever since then, she couldn't find one ally to make her quit looking and sounding like a crazy woman who should stick to her catering business.

Still, Julie Richards was trying; Balzic had to give her that. But she had about as much chance of getting the firemen to open their books as she had of getting reelected in November. Which was none. Mo Valcanas and Joe Radio might both be wrong about how many volunteer firemen there were in all nine of the hose companies in Rocksburg, but there wasn't any question the number was considerable and there was even less question that they decided who ran the city. There wasn't anything new in that. The volunteer firemen had always decided who ran the city.

The wise guys who had retired Dom Muscotti might run the numbers and the sports gambling, and the politicians might sit in the mayor's office and on City Council, but nobody bucked the firemen for long and got away with it. The wise guys had their gambling and the firemen had theirs and there wasn't any question about which was which. If you wanted to bet on a football game you talked to one of the wise guys' bookies. If you wanted to play bingo, you went to one of the churches or the Moose or the Sons of Italy, but the games with the biggest cash prizes were in the hose company garages. And while the wise guys' bookies took all the daily numbers bets and practically all the sports bets, each hose company ran its own monthly lottery, where they sold a thousand tickets for two bucks apiece and paid $1,400 to the winner and used the rest for whatever. More and more lately, the numbers were getting bigger: five bucks each for a thousand tickets to win $3,000 with the hose house keeping the rest.

Dom Muscotti, forced into retirement though he had been, still made it a point to let the hose company nearest his saloon drop off fifty or so of their monthly lottery tickets as a way of making sure that if he had a fire, there wouldn't be any hesitation when the call went in. It was just another tax to him.

So if Muscotti was still doing things like that, Balzic thought, then what was all his conversation about last night that he'd been watching somebody for thirty years? What was all that about? What were all those connections supposed to mean? Muscotti loved connections. For as long as Balzic had known him—which was practically all his life—Muscotti was always trying to find out who was talking, who was getting married, who was getting unmarried, who was fooling around, who was betting big, who was working, who wasn't. It was Muscotti's table of organization, his social crossword puzzle.

Muscotti knew what was going on in Rocksburg not only because it had been his business to know but because he truly liked knowing about who was related to whom and how and why. It was work and hobby both, and that's why he was good at it. Still, in Muscotti's own words, sometimes things escape you because you refuse to look down, you refuse to look at what's right under your nose.

Balzic had to smile: nobody had more in common with Muscotti than his own mother. She'd loved knowing what was going on every bit as much as Muscotti did. She'd just put her information to a different use. But if she knew that her one and only son was now comparing her with Dom Muscotti, even in this one aspect, she'd be screaming from the grave.

Saturday, Saturday, Balzic sighed. What can you do on Saturday? Nothing. No offices open, no way to check records, no way to get information. Then what the hell am I doing here? Trying to figure out what the hell Dom Muscotti's connections are about? Is that what I think I'm doing here? I need to go home and think about something else, I'm never going to figure out what the hell he was talking about, not with what I know now. I got to wait for Monday.

So he did. Or he tried. But every time he tried to do something to distract himself—like grilling some yellow zucchini and eggplant to put under Ruth's marinara sauce—it was a struggle. He burned one batch of eggplant because he couldn't take his mind off all the connections. And when Ruth told him to forget about it, the yellow squash was plenty and if he wanted to grill something he could cut a couple of slices of polenta and grill that, he started snapping at her that he knew how to grill eggplant, thank you, if she'd just let him alone he would bread another batch and she wouldn't have to worry about it.

"I see it's going to be another rollicking Saturday night."

"What's that supposed to mean?"

"Just what it says, Mar, just what it says."

"Hey, Ruthie, if you don't mind, I got a lotta things on my mind right now and I don't need you—"

"I don't need you snapping at me either and I don't care what's on your mind."

Balzic hung his head and sighed. "Look, I'm sorry, okay? I just—"

"No, Mario, it's not okay. Sayin' you're sorry does not make it okay. What would make it okay . . . what would make it okay . . ."

"What would make it okay, yeah, I heard ya, so go 'head, I'm listenin'."

"What would make it okay . . ."

"C'mon, c'mon. We're friends here—I think. What would make it okay?"

"What would make it okay is if you quit."

"Quit? Quit what? Quit the department? Is that the quit you're talkin' about?"

She nodded several times, looking out over the railing of the deck. She was standing in the doorway to the kitchen, a wooden spoon in her right hand, her left hand cupped under to catch the drips, the wooden screen door propped open against her left shoulder. She looked to Balzic sadder than he'd ever seen her.

"Yes," she said, her eyes filling with tears. "Honest to god, that's all you talk about, the goddamn department, the goddamn firemen, the goddamn Council, the goddamn this, the goddamn that."

"I haven't said a goddamn word about the department today."

"No, not today, you haven't. But the other night, two nights ago, you were sound asleep and you were swearing at the goddamn chairman of the goddamn Safety Committee. You were so sound asleep I couldn't wake you up, you wouldn't even budge, and there you were goddamning Egidio Figulli, the goddamn chairman of the goddamn Safety Committee. I wanted to scream. Mario, for god's sake, enough is enough. You're sixty-five years old! Quit! My god, with your pension and with Social Security, we'll live like kings."

Balzic came toward her, his shoulders hunched forward,

his face pinched, lips tight, jaw tight. "And do what? Huh? And do what? Exactly."

"Do nothing, Mar. Retire. You know? My god, you've earned it, you've earned a vacation, a—"

"To do what, I said. What do I do on this vacation? What do I do on this retirement? Come on, I wanna hear. What do I do?"

She shook her head and said, "My god, what do other people do when they retire after they've worked all their lives. They loaf. They do nothing. They do whatever the hell they want. Whatever they want that they can afford, that's what they do." She turned away from him and let the screen door slam.

He pulled it open and followed her into the kitchen.

"I don't know how to loaf. I don't know how to do nothin'!"

"What about all the time you spend in Muscotti's?" she said, stirring the sauce with her back to him. "Don't you ever think of that as loafing? Hangin' out? Just goofin' off?"

Balzic started to speak and then stopped abruptly. He didn't know how to answer that. Him? Loafing when he was in Muscotti's? Hangin' out? Goofin' off? In Muscotti's?

He sputtered something and tried to speak several times but nothing would come out but blusters of protest. Finally, he shook his head hard and said, "No. Hell no. That's not what I'm doin' when I'm in there."

She turned around and said, "Then what *are* you doin' when you're in there?"

"I'm talkin' to people. I'm workin'. I'm talkin' to people. I'm findin' out what's goin' on." He was saying the words and he heard himself saying them and the words were words he was familiar with, but he couldn't believe what he was saying. He sounded pathetic. He *was* pathetic. These words were the lamest excuses for doing something he'd ever heard.

Ruth turned her face toward the screen door and sniffed. "I think the zucchini's burning."

"Oh shit," he said, barging through the screen door and rushing to the grill to try to save the zucchini. Too late. The side nearest the coals was black and brittle. "Aw shit," he said. "Shit."

Balzic spent the rest of Saturday and most of Sunday alone. Ruth was avoiding him. She generally avoided him—or tried to—whenever she thought he'd said something that was clearly nonsense. The thing was, she could hide out in their house better than he could because she seemed to have no end of things to do and could do them calmly and quietly and didn't seem to allow her mental or emotional state to interfere with what she was doing. He could be sitting reading the paper or watching TV and she would be past him with an armload of clothes out of the cellar and halfway into the bedroom before he'd sense that she'd just come and gone.

This was unsettling to him even when he felt everything was fine between them; when he was nursing his guilt over having said something really stupidly self-serving, as he had about the reasons he went into Muscotti's, then her moving around the house with her quiet and quick assurance made him feel like a guest.

He tried to patch things up Sunday morning when he came into the kitchen for breakfast. Ruth listened to everything he had to say, but she didn't volunteer anything except answers to his questions, so unless he asked something specific she didn't say anything back.

After a long moment after she hadn't replied to his comment that it looked like it was going to be another scorcher, he finally threw down the towel he'd been drying his favorite mug with and said, "Look. So maybe when I'm in Muscotti's maybe what I do is, uh, maybe what I do in there could be called loafin'. Maybe. Hangin' out. But . . ."

She canted her head up at him as she passed him on her way out to the porch to water the tomatoes and basil and flowers. She said nothing, but the "but?" in her glance was as big as a house. He hustled around to hold the screen door for her. Her next glance told him that she could hold the door for herself, thank you, and why didn't he just go sit down somewhere.

He chewed his teeth and stepped back inside the kitchen

and spooned instant coffee into his mug and then filled it with boiling water. He opened the fridge and discovered that they were out of milk. He reported this to her.

"Make some," she said. "You know where the Sanalac is."

"The what?"

"Sanalac. Powdered milk. It's on the bottom shelf."

"The milk we use is powdered milk?"

"We've only been usin' it since the first time you had your cholesterol checked."

My god, Balzic thought. We've been usin' powdered milk since the first time I had my cholesterol checked? That's fifteen years ago! "Fifteen years we been usin' powdered milk? We don't use real milk?"

The glance she shot him said "real milk?" She was filling the watering bucket in the sink again. She turned to look at the level of water in the bucket and then shot him another glance that said "that milk's as real as any you're gonna find, big boy."

"No wait. I'm serious. This is powdered milk and we been usin' it for . . . and I never knew this?"

She apparently couldn't resist any longer. "Maybe it's like you hangin' out in Muscotti's . . . only you call it working. There's milk you make mixing water and powder and then there's milk that comes already mixed. And then there's sittin' in Muscotti's talking to your buddies and then there's sittin' in Muscotti's talking to your, uh, fellow investigators . . . I guess."

He cringed. He could feel himself blushing. "Okay, okay, so I had that comin'. So I deserved that. Can we please move on to the next phase of our lives, or what?"

"Well the next phase of my life is finishin' waterin' the tomatoes and the basil. I guess the next phase of yours is makin' some milk."

He sighed and said, "Where'd you say it was?"

"On the bottom shelf behind the chair. If you can't remember, don't use as much water as they say. It says three and a half cups for each package. Just use three cups."

"Uh, did I ever do this? Don't BS me now."

"What, make milk?"

"Yeah."

"Sure. Lotsa times."

"Then right now how's come I can't remember it?"

"Oh, Mar, I don't know! Don't make a big deal outta this, just do it. It's not anything, really. Just do it and don't think about it. Okay?"

"Okay," he said. But they both knew that was something he could not do, not unless he could force himself to think about something else.

"So listen," he said quickly. "How 'bout I cook tonight? You up for that? Huh? I was thinkin' maybe some tuna on the grill, some potatoes, little salad, whatta ya say?"

"Fine with me. You want any help or you want me to stay out of the kitchen?"

He shrugged and shook his head up and down and side to side. "Hey, I'll be okay, uh, by myself. Do what you want, you know. I was figurin' I'd be givin', uh, just givin' you a break, okay?"

"I have plenty of things to do," she said, her glance telling him that she needed a break all right, only it wasn't from cooking.

After he made the milk, all the while belaboring himself about whether he had made it before or not—he couldn't decide—it turned into a very long morning. Balzic prowled the house searching for something to do that would hold his attention. Nothing worked. He tried to remember if it had always been this way, if there wasn't a time in his life when he could focus his attention on whatever was at hand. He was sure there was, but he could not remember when that was or what it was or how he did it. He remembered that at various times he'd tried to study how different people in different cultures had trained themselves to focus on the moment, to concentrate on the here and the now, but he'd never had more than fleeting success with any of their methods. His infrequent successes made his many failures all the more frustrating.

Years ago, Mo Valcanas had given him a paperback book called *Zen in the Art of Archery* by some German professor whose name now eluded Balzic. No, wait. Harry something. No. Herry something. No. Herrigan. Shit, that's Irish. Herrigel.

That's it. Herrigel. Yeah, went to Japan to study Zen Buddhism by learning how to shoot an arrow the way the Zen monks did.

Balzic hurried to the bedroom and got down on his knees and started scouring the small bookcase on his side of the king-sized bed in search of that book.

Ruth was sitting at her desk, writing.

He knew it was a very skinny book and he knew it had to be there, but on his first search through the three shelves he didn't spot it. He was going to ask Ruth if she'd seen the book, but he thought better of that and continued to search. He could feel her glancing at him, but he was too flustered to say what he was doing.

On his second run through the shelves, he found the book on the bottom shelf, partially hidden by his collection of Berke Breathed cartoon books, which had curled out around the Herrigel book. He heaved himself up with a grunt and hurried back into the living room and plopped down in his recliner and started thumbing through the book.

On page two, he found that he'd underlined a passage. "By archery in the traditional sense, which he esteems as an art and honors as a national heritage, the Japanese does not understand a sport but, strange as this may sound at first, a religious ritual. And consequently, by the 'art' of archery he does not mean the ability of the sportsman, which can be controlled, more or less, by bodily exercises, but an ability whose origin is to be sought in spiritual exercises and whose aim consists in hitting a spiritual goal, so that fundamentally the marksman aims at himself and may even succeed in hitting himself."

On page three, he'd underlined another passage. "It is not true to say that the traditional technique of archery, since it is no longer of importance in fighting, has turned into a pleasant pastime and thereby been rendered innocuous. The 'Great Doctrine' of archery tells us something very different. According to it, archery is still a matter of life and death to the extent that it is a contest of the archer with himself; and this kind of contest is not a paltry substitute, but the foundation of all contests outwardly directed—for instance with a bodily opponent."

Balzic closed the book. There it was, in two pages—parts of two pages. Everything that was gnawing at him, everything that had snapped down on his arm like a well-trained guard dog and was pinning him to the ground until its master showed up and took over. Only there wasn't any guard dog "out there." The guard dog was right there, inside himself. He had pinned himself to the ground with his own jaws and was waiting to be taken into custody on a charge of being an inattentive jerk.

Balzic didn't know how the Zen archers achieved a religious experience; understanding what they understood was something that had always seemed tantalizingly beyond his comprehension—except for rare moments. But just when those moments came, just when he thought he might be on the verge of understanding, they would slip away and he'd be left with an infuriating sense of inadequacy.

On the other hand, he understood very clearly how you became a jerk because it was easier to become a jerk and to stay one than it was to not be a jerk any longer. All you had to do was stop paying attention to the details of the here and the now, and one day you'd wake up and newspaper reporters were telling your world, small as it was, that that was exactly what had happened to you.

He put the book down on the lamp table beside the couch and went into the kitchen and started rummaging through the fridge to see what he needed to make dinner tonight. He found nothing for a salad but two rock-hard Bosc pears. There was no lettuce of any kind, no onions, no tomatoes, though all he had to do to get a bowlful was step out onto the deck and pick all the Sweet One Hundreds that had ripened since yesterday.

He closed the fridge and went to the cellar to see how the supply of potatoes looked. The red ones were all spongy and sprouting. He pitched them into the garbage can as soon as he went back upstairs. The five solid Idahos that he'd bought Wednesday were for potato pancakes and he didn't want pancakes. He wanted potatoes and onions marinated in tarragon vinegar and extra-virgin olive oil, halved and grilled. He had to go to the market.

He made his list and then stuck his head into the bedroom to ask Ruth if there was anything that she could think of that they needed and if she wanted to go along.

She said no to both, which, given the earlier tone of the day, relieved him. Before he left the house, he took the tuna out of the freezer and thawed it in the microwave. After he came back from the market, where he'd bought a couple of heads of Bibb lettuce, a five-pound bag of red potatoes, two sweet onions, and a loaf of sourdough bread, he started on his marinade for the tuna.

It was his usual marinade for seafood: white wine, extra-virgin olive oil, lemon juice—more wine than oil, and more oil than juice—and fresh basil leaves chopped, along with minced dried garlic out of a bottle, all into a plastic bag with the tuna. This time he added some chopped sun-dried tomatoes somebody had given him for his birthday, he couldn't remember who.

He was starting out onto the deck with a bag of mesquite charcoal when he caught sight of the clock in the stove. Good god, he thought, I'm getting ready to start a charcoal fire for dinner and it isn't even noon. Talk about paying attention to the here and the now. Well, what the hell, so what can it hurt to get the fire ready to go now? Have to do it later anyway. He filled the top of the starter-chimney with charcoal and the bottom with three sheets of newspaper, and put grill and starter-chimney under the porch roof to keep them dry in the unlikely event of rain.

Then he went back into the kitchen and cleaned one head of Bibb lettuce, separating the leaves and washing away the dirt. Bibb lettuce was such a pretty combination of whites and yellows and greens, and the colors brightened instantly when the cold water hit them. He put the wet leaves into a plastic bag and then put them into the fridge, reminding himself to be sure to dry them in the spinner before he put the salad together. He leaned his rump against the sink and thought that this was what paying attention to the here and the now was all about. Going about the daily business of living, putting your whole mind on it, doing each thing as fully as you were capable of doing it—this was exactly what it was about all right, but it was such a frustrating struggle for him because he couldn't get his ego out of the way.

Every second that he wasn't forcing himself to focus on what he was doing, his mind was wandering, scattering, sliding away. The theory was so goddamned simple, the practice so goddamned hard, and he knew it was because, in addition to his ever-present ego, he was invariably trying to do two things at once. That was really what the problem was: he had been conditioned over a lifetime to believe that ordinary everyday things were supposed to be done without thinking about them so that your mind was free to think about whatever else you wanted to think about, and he'd gone along with that conditioning because he'd been led to believe—or had led himself to believe—that the more things a person could do at once, the more intelligent and coordinated that person was. Plus there was the additional notion that a person somehow was saving time by thinking about one thing while doing another that seemed like it could be done without thinking about it.

And wasn't this the joke on America? The Japanese, the Koreans, the Chinese, the Taiwanese, the Orientals were whipping hell out of the U.S. of A. economically because the crudest, cruelest thing you could say about a person in America was that he was so dumb, so uncoordinated that he couldn't walk and chew gum at the same time. And the persistent joke about the Orientals was that they were "inscrutable." Whether Orientals were inscrutable or not was for somebody else to say, but Balzic knew his countrymen loved to talk while they were doing something. You couldn't shut Americans up. No matter what they were doing, they were constantly yapping about it. They were either predicting what they were going to do, or explaining while they were doing it, or they were analyzing what they'd done and how and why—unless, of course, what they'd done was a crime and they didn't have much prospect of selling their story to TV for a movie of the week.

It was like what had happened to sports: you couldn't watch a game on TV anymore without being assailed by jocks constantly bragging, constantly advertising for themselves, walking billboards of every piece of clothing or equipment they had a contract for every time a microphone and a camera were in their faces. But it wasn't just the interviews. It was baseball brats practically freezing in the batter's box to watch the flight of the ball if they hit what they thought should be a home run, and then if it was a home run, prancing around the bases waving their index fingers in the air in that contemptible gesture of arrogance of one who cannot enjoy his victory without gloating over his opponent's loss.

Balzic couldn't think about any of this without recalling the photograph of heavyweight boxer Cassius Clay standing over Sonny Liston, Clay shaking his fist at Liston, Clay's white mouthpiece exposed as he snarled in triumph. Oh, how Balzic wished for the days before Cassius Clay became Muhammad Ali and shouted into the world's face, "I am the greatest of all time!"

Then there was the night Balzic had come home and turned on ESPN, the sports channel on cable TV, in time to see Ricky Henderson of the baseball Oakland Athletics, videotaped immediately after he'd stolen a base to break the all-time base-stealing record, announce into a microphone—while the game was in progress—"I am a legend in my own time!" Balzic could not believe that somebody had actually thought it was a good idea to interview Henderson at that moment—it was apparently not enough of a ceremony to take the base out of its moorings and present it to Henderson on the spot and announce the new record to the spectators in the park—somebody had actually reached a decision beforehand to have a TV announcer run onto the field and give Henderson the chance to make his outrageous boast to people watching on TV. Balzic had nearly choked on his wine at the sound of Henderson's words and had spit red wine all over himself and the recliner. The recliner was easily cleaned, but his clothes were ruined.

What bothered him most of all about this was what it had done to the kids. Rocksburg's Recreation Department decades ago had built five baseball fields end-to-end in the Flats, alongside the Conemaugh River, and every year the city's Recreation Board sponsored baseball leagues for all the kids, starting at age seven. The seven-, eight-, and nine-year-olds played T-ball, where the ball was set on a rubber tee on home plate at the right height for each batter so the games could proceed without waiting for young pitchers to try to throw the ball over the plate. The batting tee saved endless walks and wild pitches and kept the game moving. At ages ten to twelve, the kids played by Little League rules, and then up to Pony League and American Legion and so on.

What bothered Balzic was that the city and the American Legion furnished all the equipment and uniforms—even the kids seven, eight, and nine played their T-ball games in full uniforms, complete with batting gloves—and the stands were full of mommies, and each team had at least one adult coach, sometimes two, and each game had at least one adult umpire, sometimes two. At the end of the season there were banquets and trophies and jackets. Nobody was left out; every kid collected some material reward.

What bothered Balzic was that if there were no adults supervising the games, if there were no uniforms, no coaches, no umpires, no mommies, there were no kids. Every single time Balzic had driven past those fields in the Flats in the summer, what he saw was either adult-supervised and -organized games, or the fields were empty. Balzic could not remember the last time he'd seen a bunch of kids having a pickup game of baseball, or one kid hitting ground balls to another, or two kids just playing catch, or one kid throwing a ball up in the air and racing under to catch it himself. Either the games were organized, with coaches, umpires, uniforms, spectators, or there was nothing. The game wasn't enough anymore. By itself, the game didn't seem to attract kids anymore. It made Balzic very sad, especially because the kids seemed to have no idea what they were missing or that they were missing anything. It was like every other goddamn thing in the country: it had been overrun with administrators, bureaucrats, organizers, cheerleaders, hypesters.

The only time Balzic had been in Three Rivers Stadium to see the Pirates play, he'd gone because somebody had bought tickets and couldn't go and offered them to him. He talked

Ruth into going. They found their reserved seats in the highest
tier of seats along the left-field foul line. Once they got over the
shock of how high they were above the field, he then discovered
in that so-called modern baseball park, built at the cost of
many tens of millions of dollars, that once the game began they
could not see the left fielder. He remembered turning to the
people on either side of them and saying, "Hey, does this
bother you? That we can't see the left fielder? These ain't the
cheap seats, you know? These ain't bleacher seats or general ad-
mission. This is supposed to be a major league ballpark! And
we can't see the left fielder for crissake. Doesn't that bother
you?" And those people had just shrugged. From then on, all
he remembered was constant music, between every pitch, between every batter, between every inning, music, music, music,
including cavalry charges, while the gigantic scoreboard in center field flashed one distracting electronic show after another,
leading cheers for the Pirates one moment and jeers against the
visitors the next.

He'd dragged Ruth out of the stadium in the sixth inning,
belaboring her all the way home with, "How come the game's
not enough?" She saw no need to answer the question, and he
couldn't answer it, but he'd never had any doubt after that
about why the kids couldn't play by themselves anymore. . . .

He stopped where he was in the kitchen and whispered,
"So what the hell was I just doin'? I just put the lettuce away. I
got the grill ready, I got the tuna marinatin', where the hell
was I? Oh yeah, the rest of the salad. Got to make something to
put on the salad, little oil, little vinegar, little mustard, lemme
see what we got here." He found a tarragon-flavored red vinegar somebody had given him last Christmas and then he got
the Dijon mustard out of the fridge. He put two tablespoons of
the vinegar in a measuring glass and two tablespoons of extra-
virgin olive oil and a big dollop of mustard and got a fork and
beat it together until it looked blended. When he tasted it, the
vinegar was so pungent he almost recoiled.

He got the two rock-hard Bosc pears out of the fridge,
quartered them and cored them and put them in a dish with a
little water and covered it with plastic wrap and stuck it in the

microwave on high for three minutes. He was guessing about the time, but as hard as the pears were, he figured there wasn't much of a chance he was going to overcook them. To be on the safe side, he took them out after two minutes, and tasted one, and guessed he'd been right in his first guess. After another minute in the microwave, they were the consistency he wanted and also sweeter.

He got the Bibb lettuce out and spread the larger leaves in a circle around two plates and heaped the smaller leaves in the middle and then diced the pears and spread them over the small leaves. He hunted in the fridge until he found the left-overs of a can of pitted black olives and put one olive atop the middle of each salad. To be sure, he dipped a piece of pear into the dressing and tasted it. It was exactly what he was after: the sweetness of the pear countered the sharpness of the dressing nicely. He covered the two salads with plastic wrap and put them in the fridge, reminding himself to take them out in plenty of time to get them to room temperature before they ate.

He looked at the clock in the stove. It was five till two. The only thing left was to scrub the potatoes and halve them and rub them with oil and vinegar and get them ready for the grill. Once he was done with that it wasn't even twenty after two—and he'd been working slowly, concentrating hard on every movement of his hands on the potatoes. Damn if this Zen concentration wasn't tougher than hell to do.

He thought about setting the table on the deck, but the sky was starting to cloud up and he didn't want to have to rescue everything in a rush if it rained. So that left him with hours until dinnertime. And that left him with baseball on television. TV baseball, the thing that made it so the game wasn't enough anymore. Maybe the Pirates were on, but if they weren't, it was a sure pop the Atlanta Braves were on. The guy who owned the Braves owned a TV station and broadcast his games everywhere there was a cable network. Balzic wondered how many lawyers had gotten rich arguing that owner's rights to broadcast into other teams' territories. "Territories?" Of course *territories*. What else would that have been about but a turf war?

Balzic went back into the living room and flopped into his recliner again. He reached for the remote control, started the TV, and flipped through the channels until he found a baseball game. Atlanta was playing the New York Mets. He tried to watch the game, but his mind kept going back to the Herrigel book. God, he thought, I can't think about one thing for five seconds without slipping onto something else. He picked up the book again and started flipping through the pages, and then looked at the TV and shook his head. "Cheezus. Either shut the goddamn TV off and read the book or else put the goddamn book down and watch the goddamn game, make up your mind for crissake."

Ruth happened to be passing through at that moment and said, "Did you say something to me just now?"

"Huh? No, uh-uh. I was just, uh, thinkin' out loud—I think." He felt himself blush, felt the heat go up his neck into his face, and turned quickly away from her, hoping that she hadn't noticed.

He wished he could go to sleep and wake up in time to start the charcoal and begin dinner. He tilted the recliner back until it was fully extended. In minutes, the book slipped out of his fingers and fell into his lap. The game on TV played on. Balzic had got his wish.

He awoke with a jolt. He'd been dreaming: an interminable meeting of Rocksburg City Council where he didn't recognize the mayor or any of the members of Council or anyone in the room except Yolanda Sabo, who was reading names from an endless sheet of computer paper. While she was doing that, the mayor Balzic didn't recognize was saying, "You say you're the chief of police? We don't need a chief of police. The firemen police us now. We don't even have to give them a uniform allowance. They wear civilian clothes under their bunker suits. We're all civilians here. You say you're the chief of police? We don't need a chief of police. The firemen police us now. We don't even have to give them a uniform allowance . . ."

He wriggled into a position where he could pull the lever of the recliner so that it became upright. The book fell off his lap to the floor. He rubbed his face and tried to focus on the

TV. The baseball game was still on, but it was the top of the ninth inning. The Mets were batting. Piss on the Mets, he thought. He reached down and picked up the book, stood up and stretched, and went into the kitchen. The clock in the stove was showing five minutes after four. "'We don't need a chief of police,'" he said under his breath. "'The firemen police us now. We don't even have to give them a uniform allowance.' Jesus, Mary, and Joseph."

He went onto the deck and glanced up at the sky. It was still slightly overcast, but there didn't seem to be much likelihood of rain, so he got the grill and set it on the floor of the deck equidistant from the potted tomato and basil plants and the picnic table. He patted himself down, looking for matches, but had to go back into the kitchen to get the box of wooden ones. Once back on the deck, he held the starter-chimney aloft and lit the crumpled newspaper in its bottom. It took four matches to get it going properly, and then he set it in the middle of the grill. He went back into the kitchen, got a jelly glass of cold Chablis, and went back out to sit and wait for the charcoal to turn grayish white, all the while forcing himself to focus on every move as though it were his last. That was too difficult, too intense, and he knew there was no way he could ever keep it up.

Did people who understood Zen really do that? Could they really focus that completely on whatever they were doing at the moment, on those everyday ordinary things, shopping, preparing food, lighting the charcoal like he was trying to do, so that they became so absorbed by what they were doing that they forgot about themselves? Wasn't that one of the aims of Zen? To do what you were doing so fully that you weren't doing it anymore, it was doing you, and you didn't have time to worry about your petty little ego and what was going to happen to it? Did Zen have aims? Didn't he read somewhere that its aim was to be aimless? How the hell did you do that? And if you were always focusing on the here and the now, how did you get ready for what you had to do in the here and the now tomorrow? Questions, questions, god, there was never any end to them.

But if I don't get some answers to how to do this, how the hell am I ever gonna think about retiring? Good god almighty, I'll have all day long to think about this!

He took a long drink of Chablis. Thank god for wine. If you didn't know how to be aimless, you could always be woozy from the boozy. As long as you didn't get shitface, what was wrong with being just a little bit woozy from the boozy? Maybe that's what I'm doing in Muscotti's all the time, sliding off the straight and narrow, wobblin' around the bent and wide, learnin' how to stagger and slouch. Maybe Ruthie's right. Maybe all the other stuff I've been tellin' myself is just a lot of hypocritical bullshit. Getting information. Talking to people. Finding out what's going on. Good god. It's a wonder I didn't choke on that crap. No wonder I had to run and hide. And then here we are, right back at the beginning. Trying to run and hide and getting pissed at Ruth 'cause she *knows* how to hide in her house. She just does stuff—all the time! Never hear her yakkin' about any Zen crap. She just does it. Everything! Everything she has to do every damn minute of every damn day. Cookin', washin', ironin', sweepin', waterin' the plants, takin' care of everything around here, never any bullshit theory about Zen or any other goddamn thing. She just does it. Only time she ever complains is about missin' Ma, though lately she really is on this Florida kick. Wants to see Florida, wants to look at something different. Well shit fire, if she isn't entitled, who is?

"You're whispering," Ruth said.

Balzic turned with a start and almost dropped his glass.

"I'm what?"

"You're whispering." She was standing just inside the screen door. She had not opened it.

"Whatta you mean?"

"Just what I said. Little while ago you were talking out loud. I could hear you clear back in the bedroom. Something about the firemen didn't need a uniform allowance. That's all I heard anyway."

"Oh."

"Oh? Just oh?"

"Yeah. Just oh." Balzic sighed and took another long sip of wine, draining his glass. "Uh, you gettin' hungry yet?"

"Yes. Are you?"

"I could eat a pound of potatoes myself. I been thinkin' about grilled potatoes all day."

"Except when you're thinkin' about the firemen."

Yeah, right, he thought. He stood and went past her into the kitchen and poured himself more jug Chablis, more woozy from the boozy, more bent and wide, more stagger and slouch. He went back onto the deck and peered into the top of the starter-chimney to see how the charcoal was progressing. The briquets on the bottom were starting to glow. "It'll be a little while yet," he said.

He turned to face her and canted his head and started several times to speak but wasn't sure of what he wanted to say. Finally he blurted it out. "How come you know all this stuff?"

She was looking at him through the screen door, but then came out. "How come I know all what stuff?"

"How come you . . . how come you know how to do all this stuff you do, everything . . . everything you do, you look like you got your mind right on it, how do you do that?"

It was her turn to cant her head. "This is a trick question, right?"

"No, nah, I'm serious. I wanna know. You walk around here doin' everything. The only time I see you ever doin' two things at once is when you're ironin' in the living room and you got the TV on. Most of the time you're not even lookin' at it. You're lookin' at what you're doin'."

"Yeah. So?"

"So how do you do that? How do you manage to look like, uh, like you're never flustered or, uh, excited or, uh—"

"You want me to be excited about ironing?"

"No no, flustered, excited, they're the wrong words, that's not what I mean."

She scrunched up her face at him.

"I mean, you never look out of joint because you're doin' somethin'. You look like, hell, I don't know, like you're doin' what you're supposed to be doin'—does that make any sense?"

"Uh-uh."

"Well, I mean, like when you're out here, waterin' the plants and takin' care of 'em, or when you're cookin' or ironin', whatever you're doin', you never look like you're doin' anything else—that's what I mean."

"Well if I'm ironing, what else do you think I'm supposed to be doing?"

"No no, I'm not sayin' you're supposed to be doin' anything. All I'm sayin' is you look like you're, uh, content! You know, satisfied! You don't look flustered, it ain't pissin' you off, you're not gettin' it done just to be gettin' done so you can move on to somethin' you like—am I makin' any sense here? Huh?"

She stuck her tongue out over her upper lip and tilted her head to the other side. "I look *content* when I'm ironing? I look *satisfied*? Believe me, buster, there are times I'd like to throw the iron through the TV 'cause what's on TV makes me as nuts as ironing is makin' me."

"Well that's what I'm askin', see? 'Cause whenever I look at you, you don't look like that."

"Mario, you are not here every time I'm ironing, believe me."

"Well sure, of course. But whenever I am, that's the way you look to me. Like you got everything under control and you're not pissed off about these jobs you have to do. I mean, you have these jobs and you do 'em."

"In the first place, Mar, I don't have everything under control. Most of the time I don't have *anything* under control. But havin' things under control is not that big a deal to me. You're the one always has to have everything under control, not me."

"No, see, control is not the right word. Control's the wrong word. Forget I said control—"

"Mario, I can't forget you said control because control is what your problem is."

"Control is what my problem is? How you figure that?"

"Oh god, Mar, why do you get so nuts every time I say you should quit? Why do you get so crazy when I say the word retire? Why do you hate Sundays so much?"

"I don't hate Sundays. Who said I hate Sundays? I never said that—"

"Mar, you don't have to say it, god, everything you do on Sundays says it. Every move you make on Sundays is practically screamin' it: I hate Sundays! Saturdays are almost as bad. But Sundays are definitely the worst. You can't wait for Sundays to be over so you can have your week back. Sundays, you're just puttin' in time. I never understood that about you, but I stopped talkin' about it years ago. Maybe I shouldn't have. Maybe if I had kept talking about it, maybe we wouldn't be in this fix we're in now—"

"We're in a fix now? A fix?"

"Well what would you call it? And it doesn't make any difference what anybody calls it anyway. It would still be here if we called it, oh god I don't know, Madeline."

"'Cause I can't wait to get through Sundays?"

"Not just Sundays, Mar. Sundays are always the worst for you, but it's not just Sundays, believe me. You were never very comfortable in this house. Not this house specifically. What I mean is you were never comfortable being here, home, by yourself."

"Somebody told me once a man alone was in bad company."

Ruth sighed and shook her head. "You weren't alone. You were with me. With Ma. With Emily and Marie. Now there's just us. But it's not just you being here alone. You're alone here with somebody. Me? Remember me?"

Balzic suddenly remembered the salads. He went into the kitchen and took them out of the fridge and took the plastic wrap off them. While he was there he thought he might just as well microwave the potatoes for five or six minutes before he put them on the grill. He hunted around in the cabinet over the sink for the right-size glassware pot with a lid, all the while thinking about what Ruth had been saying. It made him very uncomfortable, the more so because as much as he didn't want to admit it, he knew that what she was saying was true.

When he'd put the potatoes into the microwave, he turned

to look at her. She was standing just inside the screen door again, her arms folded, waiting for him.

"Do you?" she said.

"Do I what?"

"Oh god, Mar. Remember me? Do you remember me?"

"What kind of question is that? Sure I remember—shit, what kind of question is that?"

"Mar, it's part of the question you've been putting off since you were fifty-five years old, remember?"

"Fifty-five? What was so special about bein' fifty-five?"

"Fifty-five was the first year I thought you might seriously think about retiring. If you had twenty years in the department and you were fifty-five you could retire, that was the rule then, remember? I knew there was no way in hell you were gonna retire after twenty years, so I kept hoping that when you hit fifty-five you'd give it up. But you got so crazy every time I said even one word about it, you wouldn't even think about it."

"Wait a minute, wait a minute. Remember what kind of money bind we were in then? Huh? Both the kids were in college."

"God, Mar, you could've had any job you wanted then. You could've had—remember Westinghouse? That guy wanted you to be head of security, they wanted to pay you ten thousand bucks a year more than you were makin'."

"You never forgot that, did ya?"

"Mario, I'm not draggin' up old stuff just to be draggin' up old stuff. That's not what I'm talkin' about here, for god's sake. I'm talkin' about you not quittin' because you are just not comfortable doin' anything else. You can't see yourself doin' anything else, that's all I'm saying. Don't you dare try to say that I wanted more money. That's not what this is about."

"Then what is it about?"

"It's about you tryin' to hide from what to do with yourself when you're not a cop. When you're not *the* cop around here anymore. You've been runnin' from it for ten years now. And you can't run anymore, Mar. It's not gonna be up to you anyway. You've been sayin' it a hundred different ways. They want you out."

"They want me out. They. You're startin' to sound like Dom Muscotti for crissake, you know that? That's what he told me. After this election I'm gone. He said I was the only thing standin' in their way. No. Me and Julie Richards. The council-woman. Now you're sayin' it."

"Mar, I'm only sayin' what I hear you sayin'! That's all you've been talkin' about for months and months now. It's what Eddie Sitko and his firemen've been after for years, you, *you,* you've been sayin' that, not me. How would I know about it? I'm just repeating what I hear from you. So why is it all of a sudden a surprise to hear it from me? Or from Dom—if that's what he said, and knowin' Dom, I'm sure he did. *You* say the words, *you* tell me what's goin' on, but *you* don't want to believe it when I say the same thing back to you."

He got the carafe of jug Chablis out of the fridge and filled a glass from off the rubber drainboard. After he'd filled the glass, he said, "Did I leave a glass of wine out on the deck?"

Ruth took a look out the door and nodded.

He shook his head ruefully and said, "Man, more and more this stuff's happenin', more and more."

"Aw who cares? So you left some wine out there, so what? I forget stuff all the time. Everybody does. That's not what's important."

"Yeah it is. It's how I been not payin' attention around here. It's how I let Sitko and his gang get behind me. It's—"

"Mario, stop! That's just bullshit. You *have* been paying attention! You have so! You've been tellin' me for months and months that Sitko was up to something, you knew it, everything told you so, you just didn't know what it was, but you saw all this schemin' and connivin' comin' months ago, goddammit, I won't let you stand here and pretend the problem is you weren't payin' attention and now you're not payin' attention to how many glasses of wine you're drinkin' out of and that's what's wrong with you. That's not what's wrong! What's wrong is you don't wanna believe what you have been payin' attention to because you don't want to deal with what's gonna happen to you when they move you out.

"Goddammit, you have been payin' attention! You have, you have, you have! You pay attention, you know what's goin' on, but you refuse to deal with it! What I'm tellin' you is you cannot refuse to deal with it anymore, goddammit! They're gonna make up your mind for you now whether you like it or not."

The timer dinged on the microwave. He found a couple of hot pads and took the potatoes out, drained the excess water, and then put them in a round bowl with extra-virgin olive oil and vinegar and tossed them around until they were coated. He got the tuna out of its marinade and dried it with paper towels, and then he went out onto the deck and emptied the now ashy-gray and glowing briquets out of the starter-chimney into the center of the kettle grill. He went back into the kitchen and nosed around in the cabinets until he found a spray can of oil, which he took back out onto the deck and sprayed on the grill so the tuna and potatoes wouldn't stick.

All the while he was taking care of the tuna and potatoes and the grill, he kept chewing on what Ruth had been saying. He looked her in the eyes after he'd got the potatoes arranged on the grill and said, "I forgot to cut up some onions. We got any onions?"

"Right there," she said, nodding to the two sweet onions on the counter next to the sink, the two he'd just bought when he'd bought the potatoes.

He shook his head and sighed. "I'd forget my ass if it wasn't hooked up to my back."

"I keep tellin' you, Mar, your problem isn't rememberin' whether you have a behind. Your problem is findin' a comfortable place to put it, so I wish you'd stop playin' with me about this."

"I'm not playin'."

"You are too. You're playin' this game harder'n you ever played one in your life and I don't know why. I just wish you wouldn't. But we better stop talkin' about this, 'cause I can see you're gettin' ready to be real mad at me about this and I don't want that to happen, so could we please stop talkin' about this for right now, okay? And can we eat? I'm starvin'."

He looked at his shoes for a long moment. "It's gonna be a while before the, uh, the potatoes get crusty. The tuna'll cook up real fast, but the potatoes—I already said that."

She came up to him and put her hands on his arms and tried to nudge his chin up with her head. He resisted for a moment, then finally gave in.

"Mar, you can't put it off. September's coming, then October, then the first week of November. And after this election the whole damn City Council is either gonna be firemen or guys who chase fire trucks for fun. That's not me talkin', that's you. You said those exact words to me right after the primary. In April, remember? And now you're tryin' to act like it's all something new and you haven't been payin' attention. I don't know why you're thinkin' like you're thinkin' now, but you are. And it's just such a goddamn waste of time. There is nothing you're gonna do that's gonna change what's gonna happen. The only thing you can do anything about is how you're gonna react to it."

"You're right." He tugged away from her and said, "I gotta check the potatoes. If you wanna do something, how 'bout slicin' some of the sourdough and paintin' it with olive oil and fryin' it?"

"You want me to cut some garlic and rub it first, or you just want it with oil?"

"Either way," he said, going out to the grill and turning the potatoes over to see how they were coming. They were gold and brown and crusty and just starting to blacken. He pushed them out to the edge of the grill and then laid the tuna over the hottest coals. He checked his watch and figured that as thick as these steaks had been cut, three minutes on each side should do it. He put the lid on the grill and leaned against the deck railing. Sometimes life was so good, wine, tuna, potatoes, a smart, good-looking woman slicing sourdough—shit, he forgot about the onions. He lurched back into the kitchen and started to peel the onions and looked at Ruth and said, "It's too late for these onions, huh? By the time I get 'em on the grill the tuna's gonna be done, whatta you think?"

"Hey, I'm doin' bread in olive oil and makin' sure I don't

burn it. I can't think of two things at once. Some guy I know says that's how I stay satisfied and content." She grinned up at him, her eyes full of teasing mischief.

"Man-oh-man, a guy says somethin', he's marked for life, I'm tellin' ya."

"Oh put the onions on, we'll have 'em for dessert. And I hope you're timin' the tuna, big boy."

"I am, I am," he said as he lifted the lid on the grill and checked his watch. He flipped the tuna and it set the coals sizzling as some of the marinade oozed out. Sometimes life is so sweet, he thought, you wonder why you gotta be such a jerk about the rest of it. "Three more minutes," he said.

She barely said it, but he heard it nonetheless. "Three more months. Three more months."

On Monday morning when Balzic walked into the station, Royer asked him if he'd seen the *Gazette*. Balzic said he hadn't.

"Think you better," Royer said, handing over a copy.

"Why? More crap about the SWAT or SWERT or whatever?"

Royer nodded. "Lots about that. Lots about other stuff too."

"What other stuff?"

"Check out page one, top right. Eddie Sitko says he's gonna resign."

"What? Oh bullshit. What the hell's he up to now."

Balzic opened the paper and found the story where Royer said it was, under the headline "Fire Chief To Call It Quits." Balzic read it aloud: "By the Rocksburg Gazette.

"Edward J. Sitko, claiming he's fed up with city politics, announced yesterday that he intends to resign his post as chief of the city's volunteer fire department after nearly 45 years of service, thirty-seven as chief.

"Sitko said his resignation will be effective at the beginning of next year. He will continue to serve as a fireman, he said. 'I've been a fireman all my life. That ain't going to change. I just won't be chief anymore.'

"Sitko says he's sick of battling some members of the city

administration ever since the last election when they brought
pressure on him, first privately and then publicly, to turn over
fire department financial records to the city. Refusing to name
any single city official, he added, 'Everybody knows who's who
around here and what they been up to.'

"Mayor Kenneth Strohn and Councilwoman Julie
Richards, who led the move to audit the firemen's books, both
lauded the chief for his decades of service to the department
and the city. Strohn, however, was quick to add that the chief's
service, exemplary as it was, nevertheless included fiscal responsibility to the city.

"Councilman Egidio Figulli, chairman of the Safety Committee which oversees police and fire department activities, said
Sitko's resignation spells doom for the department. Figulli,
himself a fireman for more than 30 years, said that the 'volunteer firemen see Sitko as a legend, a powerful leader who's taken
the department to the heights of professionalism.'

"Figulli cited the time a Hollywood studio, in creating a
series for television about fire and emergency service departments, rated Rocksburg's 'fire department among the top 10
volunteer fire departments in the entire nation. That wouldn't
have been conceivable without Eddie's leadership.'"

Balzic exploded with laughter. "Did you read this shit?
What the fuck's Figulli talkin' about, 'a Hollywood studio,
blah blah blah, rated Rocksburg's department among the top
10 . . . in the entire nation,' what the fuck is that, huh? You
ever hear anything like that?"

Royer shook his head no.

"Even if it's true, for crissake, this is how we're supposed
to decide whether we got a good department now? 'Cause a
fuckin' Hollywood studio says so? Jesus Christ. Oh man, listen
to this.

"Figulli said Sitko's resignation 'frightens me. The men in
the department are not going to let him quit. They'll quit with
him. The city will have to start over. They'll probably wind up
with a paid department instead of volunteers.'

"Oh paid department my ass. Talk about cheesy threats.
And what's gonna happen to all the money they got, huh?

Figulli must think we're just gonna stand around while Sitko and his buddies disappear with the money they claim they don't have. Man, I'll call the U.S. attorney myself.

"Here's more threats, listen to this, no shit.

"'Figulli said the volunteer department is going down the tubes. And the people can point to (Mayor) Strohn and (Councilwoman) Richards for that and the people need to remember that come election day.'

"I can't read any more of this crap," Balzic said. "So is there somethin' else, or is this it?"

"Check the inside of page two, about the middle right, right above that chiropractor ad."

Balzic found the story under the headline: "Pistol-Packing Firemen Draw Fire Themselves.

"By The Rocksburg Gazette.

"Area law enforcement agencies expressed caution and surprise when they learned recently that the Conemaugh County District Attorney's Office had formed a Special Weapons and Emergency Response Team.

"After the news spread, words of reservations and concern came in a rush to this newspaper from representatives of state and local police departments, primarily because the SWERT contained volunteer firemen authorized to carry firearms.

"Most outspoken were members of the staff of the state police Regional Police Training Center in Westfield Township, who were vehement in their concerns about the liability implications of having untrained personnel operating with full police powers, including lethal force.

"Sgt. Michael Powell, firearms instructor at the training center, emphasized that a SWAT or SWERT required 'specialized training apart from basic law enforcement curriculum.'

"As examples, Powell produced the rosters of enrollees in two upcoming courses being offered by the center next week and again in September for municipal police officers to become familiar with initial-response procedures for hostage situations prior to the arrival on the scene of officers trained specifically to deal with that.

"The classes cover such topics as initial negotiations with

the hostage taker, taught by an FBI agent, and shooting under stress.

"Powell pointed out that no member of the Conemaugh County SWERT had signed up for either session of the course. He added that in his memory no member of the SWERT had taken any course at the regional training center in the four years since he had joined the staff."

Balzic started to put the paper down when Royer told him to keep reading. "There's more, don't stop now."

"Huh? In the same story you want me to read?"

"No, uh-uh. In that little gray box right next to it."

Balzic picked up the paper again and saw the shaded box Royer was talking about. The headline read, "Richards Pursues Pistol Permit."

Balzic snorted. "That Hussler guy—remember him? He told me this headline was gonna say this, almost word for word. Here we go again.

"By The Rocksburg Gazette.

"The Conemaugh County Sheriff's Office confirmed reports that Rocksburg Councilwoman Julie Richards applied for a permit to carry a handgun.

"A clerk in the sheriff's office, who did not wish to be identified, verified that Richards filled out application forms for the right to carry a pistol on her person at all times.

"The clerk also indicated that Richards brought with her a written endorsement of support for her application from Rocksburg Police Chief Mario Balzic. The clerk said such endorsement is customary and usually routine.

"Richards also provided two character references, but the clerk refused to say who they were.

"'She gave us a valid driver's license, she was photographed and fingerprinted, and she paid the fee,' the clerk said. 'She'll be treated like anybody else. Her application will go to the National Crime Information Center just like anybody else's.'

"When asked if Richards gave any reason for the need to carry a concealed weapon, the clerk said 'she sometimes carries money late at night from her catering business is what she told us.' "

"Well," Balzic said, shrugging at Royer, "she said she wanted me to put the word out, so I guess that puts the word out." He started to fold the paper to hand it back to Royer.

Royer said, "Hey, don't stop now. Check out the letters to the editors, on page six I think. Check out the first one there."

Balzic found the editorial page and the letters to the editor. The first one was an open letter to Mayor Kenneth Strohn.

Mayor Strohn:

Your asinine attacks on the honesty and integrity of Fire Chief Ed Sitko are a disgrace!

In public you talk about Sitko's years of dedicated and devoted community service out of one side of your mouth but in private you talk about his financial chicanery out the other side of your mouth.

What you and your cohort Councilfemale Julie Richards ought to be looking at is the bottom line of how much the city would have to pay for fire services if the volunteers follow their leader and resign as I know he is announcing in Monday's paper.

Instead of quibbling with the marvelous volunteers (all 400 of them) over the pennies they make renting out their halls for social events such as weddings, common sense ought to tell you that money doesn't come anywhere near covering the cost of equipment that is earned by the fire department through donations, fundraisers, etc.

It ought to be plain as the nose on your face that getting on with the business of fighting fires and rescue operations is a far greater use of the firemen's time and energy than trying to answer to the penny how they spend their donations.

I think the public is more interested in going to bed every night knowing that Chief Sitko and his selfless volunteers are standing guard over their property than they are worried about what the firemen are doing with the social funds.

You seem to fancy yourself an expert on whether the firemen need all their new equipment. I'd sooner trust Eddie Sitko when he says his equipment needs to be updated than I would trust you to tell me where City Hall is. The men who have to use that equipment, the fellows who put their lives on the line every day, are the best judges of whether it needs to be replaced or not.

Take a look around at their equipment, see how much it costs, and even you will have to admit what a fantastic deal the city is getting. Take an unbiased look, if you can, and remember your manners and say THANKS FOR AN OUTSTANDING JOB WELL DONE.

In the future, you ought to concern yourself with other areas of public service. The Rocksburg Volunteer Fire Department is doing just fine. Leave them alone!

Yours truly,

Orville Householder,

President, Householder Enterprises, Inc.

Copies to:

All members Chamber of Commerce

All 400 firemen

Julie Richards

Editor, Rocksburg Gazette

Balzic looked at Royer. "Orville Householder? I thought he was dead."

Royer shook his head no. "He's still kickin'—and still bitchin'. Must be close to ninety."

"Wonder if he still owns the dirt under both the malls, you think?"

"Oh he owns the dirt, no question. But he sold the buildings years ago, probably fifteen years at least. That's when he started that foundation—hell that was the next thing I was gonna tell you to read. It's right there on the next to the last page of that section. It's a real little story—Conemaugh Foundation, that's it."

"What'd you say about the Conemaugh Foundation? D'you say he started that?"

"Yeah. Him and the guy that owns the paper."

"The *Gazette*? This paper?"

"Yeah yeah yeah, that paper, the one you got in your hands there."

"How you know all about this? Christ, I've been buggin' Carlucci to chase this down. Why didn't you tell me this?"

"Tell you what? You didn't ask me nothin'. Tell you what?"

"This goddamn Conemaugh Foundation, uh, uh, John Theodore leaves here on Friday night, it's like some lousy spooky movie, he says, 'I'm gonna say two words. Conemaugh Foundation,' and then he leaves. Christ, all he needed was a cloud of phony smoke. And here you are talkin' like it's common knowledge or some goddamn thing."

"Well, Mario, Christ, it ain't exactly like they're the CIA. My wife's cousin's daughter is their secretary over there."

"Over where? Your who?"

"My wife's cousin's daughter, don't ask me what that makes her to me, I don't know. She's been workin' for them ever since she got outta business school, right when they started it, probably fifteen years now. I'm certain. At least fifteen years she's been workin' for them."

"Over where did you say?"

"On the second floor of the library. That's where they have their meetings. That's where she works anyway. She's there every day. They come in, I don't know, I guess whenever they have their meetings, who knows when they have their meetings, every coupla months, I don't know."

"I'll ask her," Balzic said. "What's her name?"

Royer started at once to shake his head no. "Save your breath, she's not gonna tell you anything except who their lawyers are and their phone numbers. Besides, I'm tryin' to tell ya. There's a story back there on page eight or nine, I forget, about who they give money to."

Balzic hunted through the paper again until he found the story buried near ads for Horne's department stores. There was a very small headline that said, "Area Foundation Distributes Funds." Under that the story, without a byline, said:

"The Conemaugh Foundation, at its last meeting, approved the distribution of funds to the following:

"American Cancer Society, American Red Cross, Boy Scouts, Community Nursing Service, Conemaugh County Arts and Heritage Festival Inc., Conemaugh County Assn. for the Blind, Conemaugh County Central Catholic High School, Conemaugh County Community College, Conemaugh County Historical Society, Conemaugh County Literacy Council, Conemaugh County Museum of Art, Conemaugh General Hospital Inc., Conemaugh Symphony Orchestra, Cooperative Extension Service, Girls Scouts, Go Rocksburg Inc.;

"Greater Rocksburg Area Cultural Council, Greater Rocksburg Area School District, Greater Rocksburg Garden and Civic Assn., Greater Rocksburg Health and Fitness Center Inc., Greater Rocksburg Senior Citizens Center, Greater Rocksburg Therapy Services Inc., Greater Rocksburg Women's Services Inc.;

"Mercy 2 Air Rescue Inc., Parents Anonymous Inc., Rocksburg Recreation Board, Rocksburg Mutual Aid Ambulance Inc., YMCA, and YWCA.

"Next meeting of the funds distribution committee will be announced. Requests for funding should be submitted no later than Sept. 30 to Conemaugh Foundation, P.O. Box 93, Rocksburg."

Balzic shrugged at Royer. "Who the hell are these outfits, I never heard of half of 'em."

"Well, one thing you can almost bet on. If it says Greater Rocksburg in the title somewhere, it's probably, like ninety percent, either Householder or the guy that owns the paper or Sitko's in on it. What the hell's the guy's name that owns the paper, I can never remember it. I don't know why, it's a real simple name."

"All you gotta remember is LSD. Lyman Stiles Dunne. Only he never uses his first name, just the initial. L. Stiles Dunne, if you please, the one, the only."

"I remember now. That's good, that LSD. I'll use that."

"Yeah, well never mind that, what about this, uh, him and Householder and Sitko, what was that you said?"

"Huh? Oh, if it's got Greater Rocksburg in the name somewhere, you could bet it's a sure pop those three guys are runnin' it someway, or somebody they picked is runnin' it."

Balzic pulled up a chair and turned it around and straddled it. "How do you know this? I mean, how come you know this and I don't?"

"Well I don't know how come you don't. But I'm sorta makin' some connections here, 'cause my wife belongs to the Garden and Civic Association, that's one of those with Greater Rocksburg in it, and that's Householder and Dunne, I've seen the stationery. Their names are all over it, you know, like in charter members and founders and founders committee and stuff like that. And Householder shows up at all the meetings. He's no officer, you know, he doesn't run the meetings, but he's there. And they don't make a move without talkin' to him first. Plus their meetings are in his building, he owns it, but they don't pay him any rent. He donates the building and all they do, you know, is pay the utilities."

"This is real interesting, Joe, keep talkin'."

"Well, hey, same thing with the Greater Rocksburg Health and Fitness Center. You go in there, take a look to your right and there's this brass plaque inside the door, and their names're all over it. Right above the names of all the people who were in City Council then and on the rec board, Dunne, Householder, and Sitko. You know how that place got started, doncha?"

"Refresh my memory."

"Hey, Sitko got tired waitin' to use the weights and the machines in the YMCA, he got tired bumpin' into people runnin' around that little track they have above the basketball court there, so, uh, next thing you know, there's a backhoe there, diggin' a hole in Householder's dirt."

"That was Householder's land? Where the fitness center is?"

"Oh absolutely. Sure. That was in his family, shit, his grandfather had that land. That used to be a polo field, you knew that, right? Up until I guess the Depression. I guess they figured it wouldn't look too good, those rich fucks playin' polo while all the hunkies and dagos were starvin'. So it just sat there. But it was his. I know that for a fact, 'cause when I first started thinkin' about gettin' my real estate license, I used to do title searches for a coupla lawyers, Chiangarullo and his brother, oh Christ, I can't think of either of their names now."

"Yeah yeah, I know who you're talkin' about. So go 'head, tell me what else you know about these chudrules."

"Hey look, I know they're behind these two things. I know they're on the board of the Mutual Aid Ambulance thing, I know they're behind that medevac chopper, the one they been usin' to play commando with—"

"Whatta you mean, behind that chopper? Behind it how?"

"Well who do you think paid for that thing? C'mon, you kiddin' me? I heard numbers like from a million two to a million five for that thing. Where you think that money came from? Who else has that kinda money, huh? Dunne and Householder, Mario, c'mon, you had to figure that out."

"Joe, I haven't even started to think about that from that end yet. But don't stop now, c'mon, my nose is wide open here. You're on a roll, keep goin'."

"Well what else is there to say?" Royer said, splaying his hands and shrugging. "Go look at the brass plaques all over this town. Go up the hospital, go check out the names on the board of directors, those guys' names'll be there. The community college, same thing. That new science building they're puttin' up right now, you know what the name's gonna be? Dunne Hall. Why you think there's a community college in the first place? You remember that? I know you remember that."

Balzic nodded. He did remember. "Remember what everybody used to say about that? Huh? Remember the joke? It started out as a school for firemen because Eddie Sitko wanted firemen from all over the county to have to sit and listen to him talk about how much he knew about puttin' out fires."

Royer laughed as hard as Balzic did. "Only it wasn't any joke, remember that? Huh? He got the county commissioners to pass a law makin' every volunteer fireman in the whole fuckin' county go to fire school every year, and he was the fire school. He was the only guy on the faculty. I know some guys still call him 'the Professor,' yeah, no shit. Meanwhile, Householder and Dunne, hey, they're honorary chiefs. Shit, it wasn't too many years ago, when he was still drivin', Householder used to drive one of the trucks in the firemen's parade every year, remember that?"

"They still sit in the front with Sitko, in the first truck. See, Rugs oughta be here now. He could be throwin' a whole lotta light on how these guys got their donations rigged so they don't have to pay taxes. What I can't figure out is how Sitko got in with these two guys—oh man!" Balzic slapped himself in the forehead.

"Cheezus Christ," Balzic said. "It just came to me now. Sitko's mother was Householder's sister! Householder's his god-damn uncle! I'm sittin' here goin', how'd these two WASPs let this hunky get in their clique? How the fuck did they let that happen? What, does he have pictures of them fuckin' goats or what? Jesus Christ I'm tellin' ya, Joe, I swear to god, I'm losin' my memory. No wonder things get done around here the way they do. And now, they got their own goddamn police force. All these years that shithead sheriff's been givin' out those deputy shields and IDs, and everybody's thinkin' it's a fuckin' joke, nobody's askin' any questions about it, including stupid-ass me, 'cause it's so stupid, we think it's got to be a joke. Only the joke's on us. On me. Dom Muscotti was right. It's been happenin' right under my nose and I been too dumb to look down."

"Uh, you lost me, Mario," Royer said after clearing his throat.

"No," Balzic said, standing and pushing the chair away. "I'm the one that's lost. I'm right here and it's Monday morning and the sun's shinin' and I can't find my ass with either hand."

He started to walk back to his office. He turned around and said to Royer, "You remember Joe Gregowicz?"

"I remember who he was, but I didn't know him. He was already retired by the time I got here."

"Yeah. Big, ugly Polack. Not many people took him serious, but he was a real good detective. He wasn't just naturally ugly, he also had kind of a stupid look, you know? His mouth was always a little bit open, he had real thick lips, and his eye-lids were always at half-mast, and he walked stooped over, you know? So people'd always be tryin' to jag him off. But there was a real mind behind that face. He told me somethin' once I thought I'd never forget. He said to me, 'Balzic, never overlook the obvious.' It turns out I forgot."

"What happened to him?"

Balzic shrugged. "He moved to New Jersey. Had a brother there. Then his brother died. Then he ate the pipe. That's what I heard anyway. So what else is new?"

Royer looked thoughtful for a moment and said, "I'll never eat the pipe. Never."

"Don't never say never."

"Nah. I wouldn't do that to another cop. That's the worst thing I ever had to deal with in my life. The day I found Joe Figgles. Right after his kids found him. His kids were like twelve and nine. I don't give a fuck what's wrong in your life, that's a really shitty thing to do to the people that gotta clean up the mess you made. I made up my mind right then, if I gotta go? I'm goin' out with a bottle of Valium, a bottle of Wild Turkey, a six-pack of Iron City, and my VCR full of the Three Stooges. I'm gonna go laughin' at stupid shit. 'Cause it's all stupid shit."

Balzic nodded a few times and said, "Maybe it is. Maybe that's all it is. All stupid shit." He went back to his office and closed the door and slumped into his chair.

Something Dom Muscotti had said Friday night started to nag at him. It had been almost the first thing Balzic had thought of when he'd rolled out of bed this morning. Muscotti had said something about calling the Conemaugh Tax Bureau, the business that back in the 1980s had convinced municipal governments and school districts all over the county that it could collect more taxes more efficiently and at less cost than any of the governments or school districts could on their own. The Tax Bureau—the name made it sound like it was a government agency even though it was strictly a private business—sold their collection service by subscription and had contracts with more than ninety percent of the local governments and schools in the county. All taxes for the city of Rocksburg—city, school, wage, and residence, all the so-called nuisance taxes—

were collected by the Tax Bureau in return for two and a half cents pay for every dollar collected. It didn't seem like much; every member of Rocksburg's City Council had said it was a good deal when they'd first agreed to it, and no one had complained about it since—not in Balzic's memory. But his memory of it was very sketchy.

He turned first in his phone book to the blue pages that listed all government offices in the county. The Conemaugh Tax Bureau was not listed there. He flipped next to the yellow pages. It was not listed there either. He found it in the white pages.

He called the number. When a woman answered and identified the bureau, Balzic said he had a complaint about how much taxes was being deducted from his paycheck. "This is the second time this happened this month and every time I try to talk to your boss out there I keep gettin' the runaround. I wanna talk to the president or the chairman or whoever runs that place. I'm sick of this crap."

"The president isn't in, sir. Maybe I can help you."

"Nah-uh, nothin' doin'. I talked to some other lady last time I called and nothin' happened. And now it happened again. I wanna talk to the president. Who's the president, what's his name? I wanna know his name and number."

"Well, sir, he's not here now. I can give you his name, but I can assure you that he won't talk to you about this. His secretary will refer you to our office manager."

"Yeah, well tell me who the big cheeses are out there anyway. That's a private business, right? I mean, youse ain't no government agency or nothin', am I right?"

"Yes, sir, you're right, you're absolutely correct. This is a private business. If you want to know who the officers of the corporation are, I can give you their names, but I promise you they will not be available to speak to you about your problem. You will be referred to the manager."

"Yeah, that's okay, just tell me who they are."

"Yes, sir. The president is Mr. Orville Householder—"

Balzic had to quickly cover the mouthpiece to mask the snorting, gagging noises he was making.

"The vice-president is Mr. Edward Sitko, and the secretary-treasurer is Mr. L. Stiles Dunne. But as I said, the person you want to speak to is our office manager, and you can reach him—do you have a pencil and paper, sir?"

"Yes, yes," Balzic managed to say without sounding like he was choking.

The woman gave Balzic the number and said, "Sometimes he can be pretty hard to find because he works, well, sort of irregular hours. The best time to get him is after eight o'clock at night."

After eight at night? Balzic thanked her and depressed the buttons and then dialed the number she'd given him.

During the fifth ring, a voice came on and shouted over a thunderous roar. "Pressroom. Latta speakin'."

Balzic could barely make out the words. "I'm callin' the office manager of the Conemaugh Tax Bureau."

"What? You gotta speak up, pal, the presses are runnin'."

Balzic shouted into the speaker as loud as he could, repeating himself.

"He ain't here now. He starts at eight. Call back tonight."

"What's his name?" Balzic bellowed.

"Figulli."

"Who?"

"Figulli, Figulli. Fa-goul-lee. Eg-gid-ee-oh Fa-goul-lee."

Balzic dropped the phone onto its cradle. It missed and in trying to grab it, he sent it clattering around his desk. He felt like Royer ought to be there, watching this stupid shit.

He captured the phone finally and went hustling out to the duty room.

"Hey, Joe, Joe. You know where Figulli works?"

"The councilman? Yeah. At the paper. What about it?"

"The paper. The Rocksburg paper. The *Gazette.* That paper?"

"Yeah."

"D'you know he is also the office manager for the Conemaugh Tax Bureau?"

"No. I mean yeah. I mean I knew he was somethin' out there, I didn't know what his title was exactly."

"Do you know who owns the Conemaugh Tax Bureau, the fucking private business that collects all the fucking nuisance taxes—well not all of 'em but practically all the fucking nuisance taxes in this whole fucking county?"

"Who?"

"Householder . . . Sitko . . . and Dunne." Balzic was nearly hyperventilating.

Royer cocked his head and chewed the inside of his right cheek. "Uh, Mario, I don't . . . I don't wanna say nothin' or nothin', but, uh, that's no secret either."

"You knew this?"

"Well, look, Mario, Jesus, you know, when they were makin' their move, uh, I remember you used to try to miss as many council meetings as possible, so you probably, uh, weren't there. But believe me, they were all over the building for a coupla months back then. If not them, then their shysters, you know. But believe me, it was no secret who was the tax collection business. And Figulli, I guess they hadda throw him a bone 'cause I guess at the time they needed his vote to pass it, you know? So it stands to reason they were gonna make him some kinda hot-shit flunky in there. I can see from the look on your face this is kinda, I don't know, like it's some sorta surprise or somethin', but, uh, hell, Mario, this happened back in, like, '84."

"Eighty-four?! What the fuck?! I musta been in a fuckin' coma."

Royer shrugged mightily. "Hey, Mario, I don't wanna say nothin', you know, but you have not made any big secret over the years about how much you did not wanna get mixed up in politics, you know? I mean, I've had many many conversations with you about this, and, uh, I don't know why you're actin' like this is such a revelation—is that the right word? But believe me, Mario, I mean, you're famous for it. Tell the truth now. Really. You ever voted?"

Balzic looked out the windows. "Never," he said.

"So? So I mean if that's the way you are, and, uh, if that's the way you've always been—at least as far as I know ya that's the way you've always been—so maybe I'm not too swift, but I don't see what's the mystery here."

Balzic thrust his hands deeply into his pockets and shook his head. "'Member what I just said about Joe Gregowicz? Huh? Never overlook the obvious? And Dom Muscotti. Him too. He said I don't understand nothin' about power, never have. It's right under my chin and I won't look down. They're both right. I tried to put myself above it all. I didn't say that. I never used those words. I never thought that thought exactly that way. But that's what I did. I thought I was above it all. This shit these people were doin'? Sitko and Figulli and all their kind? I thought I was better'n them. I thought they were doin' politics. And I was fucking determined that politics was never gonna get into my department, nossiree baby, fuck you very much. And now I'm in a jackpot. 'Cause it turns out I don't understand a goddamn thing that's goin' on around here. I'm walkin' around here thinkin' there's something wrong with my memory. There's nothin' wrong with my memory. My memory's fine. But you can't remember somethin' if you never observed it. And you can't observe somethin' if you never saw it. And you can't see somethin' if you never looked at it. I learned that from Joe Gregowicz too. He wanted to be an artist when he was a kid. Whoever his art teacher was told him, just drummed it into him, you know, look, see, observe, remember. Turns out he was a lousy artist, but it's what made him a great detective. I heard the fuckin' words, but I didn't pay attention. I didn't pay attention . . ."

"Hey, Mario, you okay? Huh? You look real white. You okay?"

"Yeah sure. I mean fuck no I'm not okay. But I'm okay, I'll be all right. I just gotta clear my head about this stuff. I gotta stop thinkin' like the asshole I've been . . . for about the last forty years. Right under my chin, Joe. Right under my goddamn chin and I wouldn't look down."

The phone rang. It was Royer telling him that suspended patrolman Thomas Yesho was waiting to see him and that the mayor had called and then hung up suddenly and wanted Balzic to call him back.

Crap, Balzic thought. He hung up and dialed the mayor's business phone. He got an answering machine message telling him to leave his name and number. He left his name and then depressed the buttons and called Royer to tell him to send Yesho back.

Yesho, muscles bulging under a black T-shirt, came in carrying a large envelope. He grumbled a good morning. Balzic motioned to a chair, and Yesho took a seat and pulled a manila folder out of the envelope. He cleared his throat several times.

"What's on your mind, Thomas?"

Yesho was having trouble looking at Balzic. He was also having trouble with something in his throat.

"You want some water or somethin'? Some coffee?"

Yesho shook his head and waved his hand no. He continued to cough and to avoid Balzic's gaze.

Balzic leaned back and waited.

"Gimme a second here," Yesho said between coughs. "I'll be okay."

Balzic shrugged. The phone rang again. Balzic picked it up and said, "Not now, Joe, I'm busy."

"Mario, this is Strohn."

"Mister Mayor, I have someone here right now. I'll have to call you back."

"Hey," Yesho croaked, "if that's the mayor I can come back." He jumped up and started for the door.

Balzic waved him back. "C'mere, c'mere, sit down. Mister Mayor, I'll call you back, I promise." Balzic hung up before the mayor could respond.

"Thomas, for crissake, you look like you're carryin' fifty pounds of guilt on one shoulder and fifty pounds of shame on the other one. Sit down. What's on your mind?"

Yesho eased onto the chair, still trying to clear his throat. "Chief, I, uh, I know I said some things, you know, Friday night, uh . . . I'd like to take 'em back, but I know I can't do that. I mean, once you say it, it's said, you know? Once it's out of your mouth, you can't reach in the other person's ear and pull it back out. Uh, no matter how much you want to."

Balzic nodded. "I'm familiar with the problem, Thomas. So what's on your mind? You wanna apologize to me, is that it?"

Yesho tried to shake his head yes, but it didn't work. Balzic couldn't tell whether he was shaking his head yes, no, or maybe.

"Listen, Thomas, you can forget the apology, okay? I think you really don't wanna do that. That's just a guess on my part, but I think it's a good guess, so why don't you just tell me what's goin' down, okay? Just start talkin'. Just say it."

"Uh, okay. I know a guy in Florida. I was in the Army with him. He works in the Tampa PD. He's a sergeant, another year in grade and he can take his lieutenant's test. He said no problem, c'mon down, you know, with my experience, service record, et cetera, I'm like a sure pop. Says his rabbi is now a captain in personnel and recruitment. All I need, uh, you know . . . all I need is like a, you know—"

"You need a recommendation from me, Thomas, is that what you want? And not just a recommendation, but a good recommendation, right?"

Yesho, eyes downcast, nodded.

"And you don't know how that can be possible since you are under suspension and since I'm the guy that suspended you?"

Yesho nodded again.

"And you can't see how I'm gonna erase all the words that have been put on paper since the suspension, am I right so far?"

Yesho heaved a large sigh. "Yes, sir. That's the problem."

"It's no problem, Thomas. It would be a problem if I was an efficient administrator. If I was right on top of things. But I ain't. I haven't written a word about your suspension, not even a memo to myself to do it."

"You're kiddin' me. You ain't kiddin' me?"

"Unofficially, the only people know you're suspended is you, me, Dom Muscotti, and a reporter. Don't ask me how the reporter heard about it, but he hasn't written anything about it yet. But it doesn't matter anyway if he does. Even if he gets somethin' into print, as far as you and me are concerned, there's still nothin' on paper around here. So officially, you're still a member of this department. In good standing."

Yesho blew out a sigh of relief.

"But I'm not gonna write any goddamn recommendation for you. Not a fucking chance. I got a better chance of flyin' by flappin' my arms than I got of writin' you a recommendation."

"Huh?"

"You write your own recommendation. You address the envelope, you bring it in here to me. You hand it to me personally, you hear? And if I don't gag readin' your letter, I'll sign it. Then I'll make a copy of your file, and I'll buy the postage for it and drop it in the box for ya. Understood?"

"Oh man I'm lousy at writin' letters. Why won't you write it?"

"You're lousy at writin' letters? Really. No shit. Well I'm lousy at recommendin' officers who think bein' in my department ain't enough for 'em. I'm lousy at recommendin' officers who think the everyday ordinary routine business of bein' a beat cop ain't enough so they gotta go behind their superior officer's back and join up in some fuckin' supercommando terminator bullshit outfit—without ever once lettin' their superior in on it. And if I ever find out that any equipment ever went out of this department's property room in your hands? Huh? You hear me? If I ever find out that you personally took so much as one fucking paper clip, I will blow the whistle on your ass no matter what department you're in, you hear that?"

"I hear you," Yesho said, eyes still downcast.

"So I'm gonna ask you one question, Thomas. Because I have to know your answer. Did you personally ever take any equipment out of the Rocksburg Police Department property room to be used in any way with this SWAT or SWERT or whatever the fuck it's called? Yes or no?"

Yesho's head came up slowly. His gaze met Balzic's and locked on it. "No, sir, I did not."

Balzic leaned across the desk and pointed his left index finger at Yesho. "There used to be a detective when I was a rookie. He was a big ugly stupid-lookin' Polack. His name was Joe Gregowicz. You wanna know what Joe Gregowicz would be sayin' if he was sittin' here right now? Huh? He'd be tellin' me, don't never believe anybody who looks you right in the eye without blinkin' like you just did, Thomas. You know why? 'Cause Gregowicz told me the first thing you gotta learn is there never was a con artist who didn't know how to look people in the eye and look sincere and honest and full of trust and all that other Boy Scout bullshit civilians believe about what people do when they're supposedly tellin' the truth. But I'm not gonna rely on your looks, Thomas. I'm gonna take you at your word.

"And that's why you're gonna write your own recommendation. You. Not me. *You* are gonna write the letter of recommendation. You're gonna have to figure out what to tell 'em about what kind of police officer you are. And if I can read it without gaggin'? You hear me? If I can read it without gaggin' I'll sign it. I promise you that. Then I'll make a copy of your personnel file, I'll put it in the envelope, I'll seal the envelope, I'll buy the postage, and I'll drop it down the slot myself. I'll do all that but I'll be goddamned if I'm gonna write the letter for you. That's on your head, buddy boy. You can tell 'em what a dependable, reliable, loyal police officer you are. If you can write it without gaggin' and I can read it without gaggin', I'll mail it without gaggin'. I already promised that and I keep my promises. Good luck and good-bye."

Yesho stood slowly, his face pinched in puzzlement. "I don't understand. Why are you takin' this so personally, Mario? It was a chance for me to do a coupla things. It was a chance to get involved in a whole lot of different kinds of training with lotsa different kinds of people. It was a chance to get involved in different kinds of police work. It was a chance to do some exciting things. It made me feel like I was doin' some good. Hell, it was even a chance to make some more money. It wasn't like I was sellin' dope for crissake."

Balzic stood and moved to within a hand's width of Yesho's chest. "If it was so good, Thomas, if it was so educational, if it was so exciting, if it was such a chance to get involved in so many different kinds of police work, if it filled your chest with so much feel-goody, then why was it so fucking necessary to not tell me about it? You wanna answer that for me?"

"Orders. We were under orders . . . not to tell you about it. We took an oath."

"Oh. You took an oath. What, this oath you took superseded the one you took here? In this fuckin' building? From the mayor? Huh? You remember that oath, Thomas? From who did you take this new oath, huh? And who gave you the orders not to tell me?"

"Eddie Sitko."

"Ed-die Sit-ko. He give you the orders or the oath or both?"

"The orders."

"Uh-ha. Who gave you the oath?"

"I can't tell you that." Yesho tried to back up.

Balzic moved with him, so that the distance between them stayed the same. "Thomas, bad move to lie to somebody who already knows the answer. It was Vrbanic. The president judge, remember him? Good luck, Thomas. I'm really lookin' forward to readin' the letter of recommendation I'm gonna sign for ya. Good-bye."

"You can be a real prick, Mario, you know that? A real prick."

Balzic went back around his desk and sat down. "Chief Balzic to you. Good luck and good-bye. I'm not gonna say it again."

Balzic picked up the phone and started to tap the buttons for the mayor's business phone number. He glanced up at Yesho, who looked like he had a bellyful more he wanted to say, and stopped dialing.

"Thomas, save yourself some grief, okay? Don't say anything. Just go. 'Cause you call me another name? Huh? I'm not gonna sign that letter. And it won't make any difference who your buddy is in Tampa or where his rabbi is. Nobody sneaks cops into anybody's department anymore. Those days are gone forever. You need a letter with my name and rank on it and you need it real bad, so get outta here before you piss me off worse than I am."

Yesho growled something unintelligible, jerked open the door, and stomped out. Balzic could hear him growling and cursing until he'd left the building.

Balzic tapped the buttons for the mayor's business phone again. "Strohn Insurance," came the receptionist's voice.

"This is Chief Balzic returning Mr. Strohn's call."

"One moment, sir."

After a couple of clicks, Strohn came on, his voice sounding like he had the beginnings of a cold or like he'd been yelling at someone. "Mario, have you seen today's *Gazette*?"

"Yes I have."

"Oh. Then you know."

"Know what, Mister Mayor?"

"Who they've found to run against me."

"Uh, nossir, I do not. I thought you were talkin' about Sitko blowin' smoke about resignin'."

"Well that too of course. But they've got Bellotti out of retirement. He's coming back from Florida for god's sake!"

"I didn't read that, Mister Mayor." Balzic did not know how else to respond.

"And they've got Joe Radosich to run against Julie Richards. Didn't you see it? You have to see it. It's on the bottom of the front page. They're going to do a write-in campaign. Starting today! They've got every fireman who isn't working daylight out handing out flyers house-to-house. And they're going to get the rest of them out after work, from here on until election day."

Balzic tried hard to think of something to say.

"Chief? Are you there?"

"Yessir. I'm here."

"Well don't you know what this means?"

"Well, Mister Mayor, I'm sure what you think it means and what I think it means would be two different things—"

"Oh god, Balzic, sometimes . . . never mind. The first thing it means to you and me is you can stop worrying about cutting back on your department. That would look like the pure desperation on my part that it is."

"You sayin' I don't have to lay anybody off?"

"Well what would be the point now? Really, Mario, sometimes you, uh, sometimes you astonish me with how you've managed to survive for as long as you have with how little you understand politics."

"I wonder about that myself, sometimes."

"Is that all you can say now?"

"Well, Mister Mayor, I mean, what do you expect me to say? I mean, right this minute? What'd you call me for?"

"Just to tell you . . . oh god I don't know what I called you for. To tell you you don't have to lay anybody off. I guess I thought you might have something to say . . . I'm babbling. I don't know why I called you."

"Well sir, I know this isn't gonna be any consolation to you, but as impartial as I tried to be about politics my whole life as a cop, even I know we're both gonna be out of a job come November. But, if you want me to be honest about it, I never could figure out why anybody would want a job that only paid a buck a year, like you did. That's nothin' personal against you, sir. It really isn't. But what're you gonna be givin' up but a bunch of headaches and hassles—for free. Whatta you think Julie Richards is gonna be givin' up? Huh? She can get rid of the gun she just bought for crissake."

"Oh god, Mario, you don't get it, do you? You really don't."

"Uh, apparently I don't."

"Mario, somebody said once, for evil to happen, all that is necessary is for good men to do nothing. I can't remember who said that right now and that's probably not exactly the way he said it, but I . . . you may find this hard to believe, but that's why I ran for mayor in the first place."

Balzic could not help sighing.

"Am I boring you, Chief Balzic?"

"No, sir. I just don't know what to say. Except it's probably time for me to get outta here anyway. No matter what. I'm sure you had all the best motives in the world for doin' what you've been doin', but I think what it comes down to, more than likely, is most people in this town don't think Eddie Sitko and his guys are doin' anything wrong. I mean, I haven't heard one complaint from anybody about that new medevac helicopter they got, have you?"

"No I have not."

"You heard any complaints from anybody but other cops about the SWAT or the SWERT or whatever the hell they call it? The only other guy who's out of joint about that is this reporter, this Hussler."

"Oh, Mario, come on. Police officials all over the state are up in arms about it."

"Yessir, that's true, that's right. Police officials. But I'm talkin' about people in this town. You had any single civilian or any group of civilians call you and complain about the dangers of havin' firemen carryin' automatic weapons or bein' sworn in by the goddamn president judge to use lethal force? You had any calls at all about that? I haven't. Not a goddamn one."

Strohn said nothing for a moment. He sighed heavily. "No," he said. "Neither have I."

"Well what kinda calls you been gettin' since you and Julie Richards started asking Sitko to open his books? Huh?"

"You know very well what kind of calls I've been getting."

"Well did you get like one in ten calls in your favor? Huh? D'you get *any* calls in your favor?"

"We got a few."

"A few."

"Yes a few," Strohn grumbled. "Excuse me, Mario, but it seems to me you've got an ant's-eye view of the world. For god's sake, the Berlin Wall came down, the Iron Curtain is coming down all across Europe, the Soviet Union, my god, the Soviet Union is on the verge of collapse. Totalitarian governments are just collapsing all over the world. It's on TV every night, and . . . and in the papers every day—"

"And the guy who manages the Conemaugh Tax Bureau runs it outta the pressroom of the *Rocksburg Gazette.*"

"What? Are you talkin' about Figulli?"

"Yes I am."

"Well, see, that's what I mean about you. Right now, from the tone of your voice, this cozy little arrangement the Tax Bureau has with the paper seems to strike you as wrong that, that Figulli's running that office out of the newspaper pressroom. But when I first heard about it, I screamed conflict-of-interest until my lungs gave out but nobody else paid any attention—least of all you. So where were you when that old bastard Householder was ramming that collection agency down our throats? I don't recall ever seeing you at any of our council meetings. I didn't hear you complain about that, never once. I called every municipality in the county, I tried to warn them what an outrage that was—is, I don't know how many meetings I went to, councils, commissions all over the county, I don't know how many phone calls I made—from my home phone! I didn't charge any of those calls to the city. Where were you all that time? Now all of sudden you're indignant about it."

"Mister Mayor, I must be gettin' old, really. 'Cause I'm fresh outta indignant. I don't have any left."

"Mario, not how many days ago did you come into my office—how recently was that?—that you were breathing fire down my neck because I told you you had to lay off some members of your department? You remember what you said? I do. Clearly. Vividly. You were telling me how private police just flew in the face of everything we know civilization to be. Rocksburg isn't a shopping mall, you said. Private garbage haulers, you said, that was one thing. Private electricians doing contract work for the city, that was one thing. Private carpenters, private street crews, private everything, you said, that was all one thing. But private police, oh boy, that . . . you were having a screamin' fit. It was just wrong, no two ways about it, you said. Just wrong, you said. And I said, yes, of course it's wrong, but, I said, I couldn't work the way Eddie Sitko and his gang works. Everybody around here loves the way they work, I said. They don't have to take the lowest bidder on anything they want done. Hell's bells, they don't have to take any bids at all! They want something done, those three, Householder and Sitko and that goofy publisher, that Dunne, they just reach down into their pockets in that damn tax-exempt foundation of theirs and they find somebody to be their front men for them and they build it! You think I don't know what a colossal swindle that all is? Huh? Hell, you don't want private police, you think the very idea of private police is an abomination, well what do you think those guys have? I'll tell you what they have. They have their own private government! And who complains about it? It's the very antithesis of representative democracy.

"Did I hear you say anything against it until I told you you had to lay off people in your precious department? No! Double no! Ten times no! You had a conniption just thinking—*just thinking*—about the possibility that private police were somehow in the future, but what the hell are you? You're a cop. But are you a citizen? No! You don't even vote. And you think that makes you impartial! Well it doesn't, Chief Balzic!

"It's very unlikely that anybody is ever going to write the history of, uh, Rocksburg. This is just another third-class city in western Pennsylvania. They're all over the place, and it's not very likely anybody's going to sit down and write about what's going on here, but if somebody did, your name and my name are going to be spoken in the same breath. People are going to say that I, me, Mayor Strohn, I *couldn't* do anything—and you, Chief Balzic, they're going to say you *wouldn't* do anything. We just fumbled and stumbled around while a bunch of wannabe fascists just took over this whole damn town! And everybody cheered. And there were parties all over the place. Hats and horns! Yippeeeeeeee! And they didn't have a clue what was going on. Because the people who did have a clue did nothing!"

Balzic cleared his throat loudly. He hoped it would be enough to bring the mayor back to a more normal tone.

"Yeah, right," Strohn groused. "What am I doing ranting at you? I've got nobody to blame but myself. I did a lousy job of selling the, uh, the absolute necessity of exposing Sitko. It's not your fault. I'm not blaming you. Or anyone but me. Course it might've helped if that Hussler fellow had showed up a little sooner. Maybe if he'd been here sooner, he could have put the word out, could've helped me put the word out. Us. Not just me. But now that I think about it, I can't imagine how he was allowed to write what he did write, can you?"

"I'm sure I don't know, sir."

"Oh what's the use. I'll let you go, Chief. Uh, thanks."

"Thanks? For what?"

"For listening. I really needed to get that out of my system. And there's nobody . . . god, not even Julie Richards wants to hear it anymore. She's almost as sick of listening to me as I am of listening to myself. Good-bye, Chief. I'll talk to you later. Maybe."

Balzic said good-bye and hung up. The phone rang immediately. It was Royer again. "Mario, Steve Hussler's here. That reporter from the *Gazette*? Says he wants to talk to you if you got five minutes."

"Hell, I got the rest of my life. Send him back."

Hussler, looking haggard, pale, raw-eyed, slouched into Balzic's office and slumped into a chair.

"What the hell's wrong with you?" Balzic said. "You look like death warmed over."

"I just been fired." Hussler hunched over and put his elbows on his knees and held his face in his hands.

"Fired?" He gets fired, Balzic thought, and he comes to see me?

"Yup. Fired," Hussler said through his hands.

"Uh, is there, uh, somethin' you want me to do for you, maybe?"

"I just need someplace to sit for a while."

Someplace to sit? Hell, you could sit in a park, Balzic thought. You could go out to one of the state parks and look at a lake. You could go to a saloon. That's what all the people I know get fired do. They go tie one on. "You need a place to sit? And you come here?"

"You busy? Am I interruptin' something?" Hussler didn't look like he was going to break down exactly; he looked like he was crying but his eyes were dry and he was not sobbing.

"No more than the usual Monday morning crap. Course everything you been writin'—and I assume you been writin' it, maybe I'm wrong—that certainly got some people's attention around here. I just hung up talkin' to the mayor. He's real upset about what the firemen are doin' today—and I guess they're gonna keep doin' it right up until the election. D'you write that?"

"Yeah."

"D'you also write the stuff about Sitko resignin'?"

"Yeah."

"So what'd you do? Forget to say Sitko was on the pope's short list for canonization?"

"No. I wrote a story about how the auditor general got his office redecorated."

"Yeah. So?"

"Well the guy who installed the carpet in his office is from here, from Rocksburg."

"So's the auditor general, so what?"

"Well so is the managing editor. They were all on the same football team. Well the managing editor wasn't. He was a manager. A water boy."

"Yeah. So?"

"So I got to wondering who installed the carpet in the *Gazette* building. They just had the whole place repainted and new carpeting installed in all the offices, like about six months ago, right before I came here. So I called the guy back who installed the carpet in the auditor general's office and asked him if he also happened to install the carpet in the *Gazette.* And he did. And since he's already done time and paid a whole lot of fines for not buyin' workers' comp insurance, I thought it might make an interesting story to find out if he was still operatin' that way. So I asked him who his insurer was. And he told me to do something anatomically impossible to myself and he hung up. So I figured he had to be still operatin' dirty, and I checked it out. I called every insurance company that writes workers' comp in this end of the state to see whether he'd bought insurance while he was doin' the *Gazette* job. And he hadn't. Now maybe I missed one, I'm not sayin' I called 'em all, but I don't think so. So then I did the same thing in Harrisburg for when he was doin' the auditor general's office. And he hadn't bought any there either. So I called him back and asked him how much he charged the *Gazette.* And he got real real upset and told me to stop botherin' him or I was gonna have something bad happen. So then I went to the guy at the *Gazette* who contracts all the construction and maintenance work on the building, and he tried to do a sales job on me, and then when that didn't work he told me he had a lunch date, and when I told him I'd still be there when he came back from lunch, he practically ran out of his office, so then I knew for sure what was goin' on except I didn't have any proof. I mean, you'd have to be deaf, dumb, and blind not to see the scam. He gets jobs—"

"He? The carpet guy?"

"Right. Yes. He gets jobs because he doesn't buy insurance or pay anything but about a buck an hour above minimum wage. Then to make sure, he includes a little baksheesh in the bid numbers—"

"Back what?"

"Baksheesh. You know, baksheesh."

"If I ever heard of it I can't remember what it is right now. What is it?"

"A bribe. I don't know where it comes from, the word. The Middle East I think. Maybe India, I don't know. You want something done over there, you got to grease the wheels or nothing moves. Over there, crap. Over here too. Least that's what I heard it means."

"Yeah, okay, so go 'head."

"Where was I? Oh. So he, the carpet guy, he includes a little grease in the bid numbers so whoever gives him the job can tell *his* boss what a great price *he* got, only *he* doesn't tell *his* boss what's in it for *him.* I just thought that would make an interesting story."

Balzic had had to lean forward to hear all this because Hussler had been talking through his hands. Now Balzic leaned even farther forward and said, "And so what? You gonna tell me now you wrote this story and then you showed it to the managing editor? The guy who used to be the water boy on the same football team the auditor general and the carpet guy were on? You wrote that story, is that what you're tellin' me? And you showed it to the managing editor? And now you're in here with your face in your hands? Is that what you're tellin' me?"

"Yup," Hussler said, sitting up and letting his hands fall into his lap.

"Lemme get this straight. You wrote a story about how at least one of your bosses—I'm assumin' the managing editor is not the same guy who made the contract with the carpet guy—am I correct?"

"They were both in on it."

"Uh-ha. So you wrote a story without documentation, is that it? On speculation? Am I right so far?"

"Yup. Well no. I mean I had documentation from the auditor general's office on who did that work and I had quotes from insurance companies that this vendor didn't buy workers' comp coverage."

"Yeah, but you were still speculatin' that your boss and another guy ripped off their boss when they hired an outlaw carpet installer, isn't that what you're tellin' me?"

"Yup."

"So where are we now? You're in here, lookin' like death warmed over, and so whatta you want from me exactly? Misery loves company? Commiseration? What's goin' on here?"

"It was a bad idea."

"What? Writin' the story? Or showin' it to your boss? Or comin' here?"

"Coming here. I guess."

"Well, from over here where I am, I can't remember ever hearin' three worse ideas. Ah well, comin' here, maybe that's not the worst idea I ever heard, but those other two? Christ, those are two of the worst ideas I ever heard."

Hussler said nothing for a long moment. "I need a cigar," he said. "Okay if I smoke in here?"

"No it ain't." Balzic peered at Hussler and said, "Listen, I'm in a bad place for me. My nose is open. Wide, wide open. Why would you—I mean, you used to be a cop, right?"

Hussler nodded.

"A county cop and a postal cop, am I right?"

"Yup."

"The part I don't get, I mean, I get the rest. I get you thinkin' that's a good story. I get you workin' on it, makin' all the calls. I get you writin' it. I get that. What I don't get is you takin' that story and handin' it to your boss, who is the guy you're accusin' in the story, right? In the story you're accusin' him of defrauding his boss—am I right so far?"

"Yup."

"I don't get that. I don't get how you can write a story accusin' your boss of committing conspiracy with the guy who does all the contracts at the paper and with the carpet guy—they're conspiring not only against the state workers' comp laws, but they're also workin' a kickback conspiracy fraud against their boss, the guy that owns the paper, am I right?"

"Yeppie. Right so far."

"And so when you turned this story over to your boss, what'd you expect him to do? I mean, did you think he was gonna say, 'Oh, wow, what a great story. What a great job of reporting. I'll just put this on page one. And by the way, for exposing fraud and corruption right here at your very own place of employment, for exposin' me for a crook, why I'm sure you'll be seein' a much bigger paycheck this next time. Because the big boss, *my* boss, he always gives raises to people who make him look like an asshole, like he don't know what's goin' on in his own business.' Did it go somethin' like that? In your mind?"

Hussler flushed a deep pink from his collar up. "Not exactly. But close. Pretty stupid, huh?"

"Buddy boy, there ain't a word for what that is. But I still don't get it. What're you doin' here?"

Hussler shrugged. "I don't know. I guess I had to tell somebody. And I didn't know who else to tell. There isn't anybody I know who'd give a crap. I can't tell my mother and father. I'm sure as hell not gonna tell my ex-wives. And I can't tell my kid. He doesn't want to talk to me as it is. Am I supposed to call him up and tell him I just got fired again?"

Balzic felt his face scrunching up in bafflement, and he shook himself. "And you think I will? Give a crap I mean? You think I'm goin' to? C'mon, you can do better'n this. No shit, what're you doin' here? Hey, you've gone this far, spit the rest of it out."

Hussler's face turned pinker. He rolled his head from side to side and grunted. Balzic could hear vertebrae cracking.

"Oh, wait a minute, wait a minute. I get it. You do your work, you show it to your boss, you expect a pat on the back for a job well done. And since he didn't give it to you, since there's no way in hell he's gonna give it to ya, you come down here looking for it. Am I right?"

Hussler closed his eyes and his head came forward until his chin was nearly on his chest.

Balzic ran his tongue over his teeth and nodded several times. "Uh-ha. Uh-ha. I remember Mo Valcanas told me once his theory about why people invented god. He said people sooner or later get tired of takin' their work and showin' it to the boss, their daddy who art at work, or who art out in the garage, or who art out drinkin', so they go to their daddy who art in heaven, hallowed be his name, only they're still not gettin' any answer. But somehow people can live with that, with the, with the daddy who art in heaven. Now this is according to my friend—do you know him by the way? Huh? Mo Valcanas? No?"

Hussler shook his head.

"Very smart man. You should make it your business to meet him. Now he says that not gettin' an answer from the daddy who art in heaven doesn't piss us off like not gettin' an answer from our daddy who art at work. Somehow people can live with that. But that's not what happened to you, is it? I mean, you got an answer this time, didn't ya? You did your work, faithfully, right? And you got fired. Hey, gettin' fired's better than nothin', right? Gettin' fired's a whole hellofa lot better than no answer at all, am I right?"

Hussler's face looked frozen.

"Gettin' fired, hey, he noticed ya, right? Couldn't ignore you anymore, right? Had to take time outta whatever he was doin' and pay attention to you for a change, right?" Balzic wondered where all this was coming from. He wondered, furthermore, who he was talking to. Himself or Hussler. And did he really hear this from Mo Valcanas? "Now you want *me* to make it all better, doncha? You want *me* to tell ya you're a good boy no matter what, right? You did your job, you did the work, you exposed the crooks, you exposed the corruption, the penny-ante, nickel-dimin' greed, and now you want me to tell you what a fine boy you are. Hell, I don't know, maybe you even want me to go down there and arrest 'em.

"There's only one problem, Hussler," Balzic went on. "I got problems of my own. And nobody to make 'em right. And I can't make yours right. I'm sorry you got problems. But so do I. As you well know. Since you're the guy who's been documentin' mine for all to see. Remember me? Huh? I'm the chief of police can't make his own property room secure from burglary. I'm the chief can't make the members of his own department not wanna steal from him. Or join another police force, legit or not. So I think maybe you came to the wrong guy."

"There isn't any right guy," Hussler said, standing and heading for the door.

"Yes there is," Balzic said. "You said you can't tell your parents, so I know yours is still alive. Mine died a long time ago."

"Yeah. Right." Hussler pulled open the door and left, closing it so gently Balzic didn't hear the latch click.

The phone rang again. When Balzic picked it up, Royer said it was Freda Christoloski calling as she said she'd been ordered.

"Yeah yeah, put her on," Balzic grumbled. "Yes? Hello, Freda. Yoo-hoo, you there?"

"Chief Balzic? This is Freda Christoloski."

"Yes I know. What's up?"

"Well I'm no longer in bondage, thank you. I'm calling to report—as you requested—that I have made an appointment with the Louis Cupps Counseling Service—"

"With who? D'you say Louis Cupps?"

"Yes I did."

"Aw why'd you pick him?"

"I beg your pardon? Did you say why did I pick him? You sound like something's wrong. What's wrong with him?"

"Well why'd you pick him?"

"Well because he said he could take us this week and you said—"

"Don't get him, Freda. He's a male, uh, oh, what the hell's the word—oh. Chauvinist. He'll be sidin' with Pete about everything. You gotta find you a woman."

"I *tried* to find a woman. There aren't that many women marriage counselors around here, believe me, I looked!"

"Call Lutheran Services in Pittsburgh, they'll find you one. You might have to go to Pittsburgh—"

"Oh, Mario, stop. My god, I'm not going to get Peter to go to Pittsburgh. To get marriage counseling? He hates this, absolutely hates the whole idea. I have to get him to someone we can get to in five minutes—"

"Then call Lutheran Services I'm tellin' ya. They have a coupla women around here they use. I know 'cause I've sent other people there. I don't know where the one is, uh, she used to be out by that nursing home out in Westfield Township, oh, man I can't think of the name of it. But you call 'em. Stay away from that Cupps guy, I'm tellin' ya. He'll have you tearin' your hair out in fifteen minutes. You listen to me, Freda, Pete's the one who needs to be talkin' to somebody here. So don't be puttin' yourself in a position where you're talkin' to some guy thinks you oughta be walkin' three steps behind your old man, you get what I'm sayin'? Huh?"

"Mario, there are some women who believe exactly the same thing, and if we happen to get one of them, the fact that she's wearing perfume and lipstick isn't going to make one bit of difference."

"No, no, you're absolutely right, you are. But I still think you're gonna have a better shot if you start out with a woman. That Cupps guy, I'll tell ya, I've had a coupla conversations with him. In fact, I talked to him 'cause a woman called me tryin' to get me to check him out 'cause she thought he was a fake. I told her that was not a police matter, but she insisted, you know, wouldn't let me go. So I wound up callin' the, uh, American Psychological Association I think it was—that's probably not the right name—but anyway I called them and they told me he had all the paper, you know, all the credentials, the diplomas he was supposed to have, but then they sorta let it slip they've had some complaints about him, pretty much all from women. Now they weren't about to tell me what kinda complaints they were—not over the phone anyway—and I don't wanna jump to any conclusions here, but my point is, for every complaint they got, I figure there musta been a bunch more who wish they did, you know what I'm sayin'? Freda?"

There came a long sigh. "Yes," she said. "Unfortunately, I do."

"And I gotta tell ya, Freda. After my conversations with him? Huh? I wouldn't send any female relative of mine to him." Balzic spun the wheel on his phone file until he found the number he was looking for. "Here, write this number down. You got a pencil, pen, huh?" He gave her the number of Lutheran Services in Pittsburgh and wished her luck and hung up.

He took off his glasses and closed his eyes and rested them on the heels of his hands. What the hell am I doing? As if I don't have enough problems, now I'm Dear Abby. Just call me up and tell me which brain-strainer you hired and I'll tell you whether you made the right choice. Yessir, Rocksburg's very own Dear Abby. Just dial the cops and talk to me. Ought to get a toll-free number. Hey, maybe this is the business I should've been in all along. Then, when some asshole cop like me calls up and tells me how his whole goddamn life is disappearing right before his eyes only he's too dumb to look around, I can explain how it all got started with sibling rivalry. Except I never had any sibles. Sibles? That ain't the right word.

He started rooting through his desk for a dictionary. He found a ragged paperback one in the bottom drawer under manuals for the walkie-talkies. He found *sib* and *sibling,* but no *sible.* He tossed the book back into the drawer atop the manuals and closed the drawer with his foot. He stretched and rubbed his eyes and wondered yet again if he had the brains to know what to do with himself when he wasn't doing this—whatever it was he was supposed to be doing. What the hell difference would it make, he thought. If I don't know what I'm doing, what the hell difference does it make if I don't do it anymore? Who could tell? Me? Sibles. Jesus . . .

Ten minutes later he was on Norwood Hill trying to find the house where a domestic disturbance had been reported. Officer Larry Fischetti was the only other officer available and he was already out working a domestic disturbance in the Flats. Balzic arrived on Harrington Avenue in Norwood and pulled up beside an elderly woman standing in the street waving both hands and pointing at a house.

"In there, in there," she said, covering her mouth with her bony right hand as though that could hide the fact she had no teeth, and pointing with her left to a three-story house covered with aluminum siding that used to be white and was now dingy gray, especially under the eaves. Balzic pulled against the curb, got out, and asked the woman if she knew the people and what their names were.

"Vittone. Frank. His wife is Ann Marie."

"You the person who called in?"

"Huh? Me? No. I didn't call nobody. Uh-uh."

Yeah, right, Balzic thought. He could hear the screaming and shouting coming from the dingy gray house as soon as he'd opened the door of his cruiser.

Balzic took the three steps up to the porch one at a time. He didn't like the sounds of this one. There was another voice in there. It wasn't just a husband and wife. There was another woman. Two women, one man. And now me, Balzic thought. He pounded on the aluminum storm door with the flat of his hand.

"Police! Open up!" He had his ID case open in his left hand at about chest level.

A man, short, with muscular arms and shoulders and ropey veins in his neck, wearing a T-shirt and blue shorts and scruffy black loafers came lurching around a corner after apparently jerking his arm free from whoever had been holding it. "Police? What, what police? Who called the friggin' police? Your sister called the police? Huh?"

"I think it was your neighbors," Balzic said. "Your name Vittone?"

"Yeah. So?"

"So I need to come inside and we need to have a talk."

The talk—the shouting—lasted for nearly ten minutes. As near as Balzic could make out, the man, Frank Vittone, was accused by his wife, Ann Marie, and her sister, Mary Theresa Vittone, of selling the sister's watch to buy beer, cigarettes, and state lottery tickets. It had taken Balzic at least eight of those minutes to learn that two sisters had married two brothers and that Mary Theresa Vittone had left her husband, George Vittone, and moved in with Frank and Ann Marie Vittone because she, Mary Theresa, didn't have any income and no place else to go and was scared of her husband but her husband was scared of his brother so she knew her husband wouldn't bother her there so that's why she moved in with them, only now her brother-in-law was sick of her mooching off them, so he took her watch and sold it, and what set Mary Theresa off this day was she found out that he only got about fifty bucks for the watch which *her* husband had told her was worth at least a thousand dollars.

"How could you be so dumb?" Mary Theresa screeched.

"In the first place, for about the nine-thousandth time, I'm tellin' ya, I didn't sell your goddamn watch. I took it to a pawnshop. Whatta you? You think a pawnshop's gonna give full value? You stupid or what? And that watch ain't worth no thousand simolees anyway, giddoutta here."

"You still shouldn'ta took her watch, Frank," Ann Marie kept repeating. "That wasn't right."

"And you shoulda never let her move in here without talkin' to me about it first, whattaya, kiddin' me? Three days you said. She been here three friggin' months, you kiddin' me? What the hell I look like? I ain't the friggin' welfare department, get her outta here I'm tellin' ya. She should go back with her husband where she belongs I'm tellin' ya."

"He's a sonofabitch!"

"You watch your mouth I'm tellin' ya. That's my mother you're talkin' now."

"I'm talkin' your brother now, I ain't talkin' your mother!"

"When you go sonofabitchin' him, you're talkin' my mother and I ain't gonna put up with that shit. You say it again I'm gonna bust you right in your mouth for ya."

"Don't you threaten me—"

"Don't you threaten her—"

"Yeah, right, Ann Marie, don't threaten her," he mimicked his wife. "I told ya twenty years ago quit treatin' your sister like she's a baby, she ain't never gonna grow up, didn't I say that or not? But did you listen? Huh? Did you listen? If you'da listened to me your sister'd be a grown-up person now 'stead of a friggin' crybaby every time somethin' don't go her way—"

"Oh yeah you're so smart you know everything, how's comes you sold that watch—which you stole! Which you stole! How's come you only got fifty bucks for it you're so smart, how's come? For Lotto tickets, man, you're so smart, you know everything—"

"I'm gonna smack you so hard, tell your sister to shut up, I'm tellin' ya, I'm gonna bust her right in her friggin' mouth, I'm tellin' ya, tell her to shuddup and get off my back about that watch. 'Cause that's one week's room and board, that's what that watch is. And that's a bargain! You ain't stayin' no place for no fifty bucks a week—"

By that time Balzic had had enough and pleaded and coaxed and cajoled and pushed the two women out of the living room onto the front porch while their screaming and screeching was setting off bells and crickets in his ears.

He wheeled around on Frank Vittone and held up his right hand and said, "Enough! Go sit down. Now! I know this is your house, I know you pay the bills, I know you're the man here, but enough! Sit down—now! Or it's gonna cost ya three hundred bucks plus costs plus you're gonna lose work and it's gonna be total aggravation for you, you understand me? You hear me? Yes or no?"

"Aw sheesh, yeah yeah yeah I hear ya. Tell them too. Tell them shuddup for crissake! My wife don't even talk to me anymore. She's all the time talkin' to her goddamn sister. Bad enough before they was always on the phone, now, man, I don't get a word in edgewise with my own wife for crissake! My wife asts me a question, bigmouth there answers it before I get a chance to open my mouth—"

"I hear ya, I hear ya, just go sit down and let me do my job. You do your job every day, you work hard, now let me do my job, okay? This is my job. Just sit down and let me do it, okay?"

All the while the sisters were continuing to squabble with each other and with Frank behind Balzic's back while he was trying to get Frank to take a seat and just when it looked like he was going to take a seat, just when his head turned away from Balzic and he took a step toward the couch, just when Balzic thought the sisters were still out on the porch, in that instant Balzic felt the press of someone behind him and heard the grunt and caught sight of the arm and hand and the ceramic ashtray coming around and over his right shoulder and saw it, felt it, crack Frank Vittone behind his left ear and send him tripping over the coffee table and sprawling face-first onto the couch.

Balzic instinctively grabbed the wrist and hand holding the ashtray with his left arm and reached back with his right hand and caught hold of the arm above the elbow and brought the arm down over his left knee, sending the ashtray crashing in pieces over the floor. Bone snapped at the same time as Mary Theresa's scream pierced the room, and Balzic blinked but he didn't let go, not until Ann Marie jumped him from behind and threw one arm around his neck and began to pummel him on the face and neck and shriek at him to let go of her sister.

It took all his strength and guile and training and experience to subdue Ann Marie after he let go of Mary Theresa's arm. He saw her collapse to her knees clutching her arm and wailing. She pounded the floor with her good arm and hand and then tried to punch Balzic's legs.

Ann Marie was a tiny woman, not more than a hundred and ten pounds, but she was wiry and her rage seemed to give her another hundred pounds of strength and Balzic had to stomp on her toes and whack her across her cheek with his elbow twice before she finally let go and slid off him to her knees. He cuffed her wrists around one leg of the oak coffee table that was in front of the couch just to the left of where her husband lay moaning and whimpering and holding his head and kicking his toes into the torquoise shag rug in time with his whimpers and curses.

Balzic hustled out to his cruiser and called for assistance and an ambulance and found another pair of cuffs in the glove compartment and went back in and cuffed Mary Theresa's good arm to another leg of the coffee table. Then he went into the kitchen and opened the freezer section of the fridge, looking for ice. But better than ice he found four bags of frozen vegetables, including one of frozen peas and one of mixed vegetables, and he took those two bags out and tossed the mixed vegetables on the couch beside Frank and told him to put it on his head and then he took the frozen peas and knelt down and put it on the reddening hump on Mary Theresa's forearm just below her elbow.

The sisters' groaning and crying and Frank's whimpering and cursing were more than Balzic could stand. "Aw shut the hell up, all of ya! You make me sick. Shuddup! Buncha spoiled brats. Look at ya. Fightin' like a buncha brats in junior high school for crissake. Shuddup! You hear me?"

They blubbered and wailed that they heard him but that didn't make the pain he caused go away and he was a rotten man and Mary Theresa was going to sue him for police brutality and he'd lose his job and have to pay them hundreds of thousands of dollars and Ann Marie hoped he got the clap from his wife, at which point Balzic walked out onto the front porch where he could watch the street and still keep an eye on them. He was convinced that the women were out of action but he wasn't at all sure about Frank. Frank was still rolling from side to side on the couch and kicking the rug with his toes and cursing and whimpering, but Balzic had nothing left to restrain him with and so he kept his eyes on him.

The Mutual Aid ambulance got there just moments behind Officer Larry Fischetti, who came out of his cruiser on a trot.

Balzic held up his hands to ward off Fischetti's questions. "Don't ask. Just keep your eye on that guy on the couch in there. I don't think the women are gonna move, but watch him, okay? The one woman, the one on the right, she's got a broken arm. I broke it. The other one, I don't know if anything's busted on her, but I had to whack her twice across the chops with my elbow to get her off me. Come to think of it I mighta busted her toes. I had to practically jump on 'em to get her off me." Balzic shook his head and blew out a long sigh. "Where were you? How come you didn't answer this one? Huh?"

"Hey, Mario, I had one of my own down the Flats. Wasn't as bad as this one, there was only two of 'em, but believe me, I was occupied. I was in the emergency room when I heard your call. I never heard the first call on this one, I must've already been down the Flats."

"Okay okay, I'm just a little testy here. I gotta go sit down, man, my heart's poundin' I'm tellin' ya. I'm too old for this shit."

"You okay?" one of the EMTs said to Balzic.

"No. But I'm better off than the ones inside. Check them out first, then you got time, check me out. I'm gonna be in my cruiser."

He went slowly, carefully down the steps, rubbing his face and neck and ears where Ann Marie had been punching and slapping him and he winced when he felt a stabbing pain in his left shin. She must have kicked him there, but he'd never felt that. He looked at his hand and there was blood on his fingers and he tried to find where he was bleeding from and then he became aware that he had no glasses on. He went hustling back up the steps and inside.

"Hey, hey, everybody watch where you're steppin'. My glasses are down here somewhere. Everybody stop what you're doin'. Don't move till I find my glasses."

"Here they are, Mario," Fischetti said, holding them up while he sat beside Frank Vittone on the couch. "They were on the couch. I thought they were his. They're all right, don't even look bent or nothin'."

"Good goddamn thing," Balzic said. "These things cost, the lenses alone, goddamn trifocals cost a hundred and forty bucks, just the lenses for crissake. Hey, Fish, if he's awake—is he awake? Huh?"

"I'm awake, I'm awake," Frank Vittone said.

"Then you better get off that couch if you can stand up, you're bleedin' all over it."

"What? Aw shit," Vittone said, lifting his head and looking at the cushion. "Aw man lookit here. Look at this friggin' couch. This is your sister, Ann Marie? You hear me? I'm gonna break her face—did she hit me? Huh? Ann Marie, you better tell me it was her, you better not tell me it was you I swear to god you'll never sleep in this house again . . ."

Balzic shook his head while he examined his glasses to make sure they hadn't been damaged. Apparently they'd flown off and landed on the couch when Ann Marie had jumped him. He couldn't detect anything wrong except a slight bend in the frame connecting the lenses, which he straightened easily. He went back out to the cruiser and slumped onto the seat and turned an air-conditioning vent on his face.

Monday. It ain't even noon. And already I'm bleeding and I don't know from where. This is what I think is the best thing I can do with my life? With what's left of it? And now I gotta go do the paperwork and go to the magistrate and deal with these three dipshits all day long? It's gonna take until five o'-clock to get this squared away. Up to the hospital, back to the magistrate, out to the jail, back to the typewriter. Man. And listen to 'em in there for crissake. All they're talkin' in there is how much they're gonna sue me for for crissake. This is what I live for? This is what I think I can't live without? I got a problem all right. I got no imagination. That's my problem. It ain't my memory I'm losing. I've lost my imagination. I can't see what else could be true. Jesus, Mary, and Joseph . . .

Balzic had been wrong. It had taken until six o'clock to get Frank and Ann Marie Vittone booked on various charges after their injuries had been attended to in the emergency room of Conemaugh General. Their booking in the county jail almost turned into another brawl when Frank Vittone refused to put up his house as property bond for his sister-in-law as well as for himself and his wife. He didn't hesitate about using the house for his wife's bond as well as his own, but he was telling everyone who would listen—and nobody listened for long—that his sister-in-law should stay in jail until their trial happened and he hoped the trial wouldn't happen for five years.

After his wife told him for about the tenth time to stop bad-mouthing her sister like that, and after he expressed his heartfelt wish that his sister-in-law get cancer of the vocal cords, Ann Marie Vittone had to be restrained by two male corrections officers and one female who finally had to put her in leg chains and then had to chain her wrists to her legs.

When it came time for her to get fingerprinted, she doubled her hands into fists and tried to spit on the CO who was trying to take her prints. He put up with her for about fifteen seconds. Then he made his own fist with his right hand, except he thrust out the large knuckle of his middle finger and drove it into the back of her left hand twice until she screamed and doubled over in pain. Then she opened her fist. "And everybody in here didn't see that, lady," the CO said, "so relax your fingers and close your mouth. And don't even think about spittin' on me again, you hear? 'Cause you do, I'll fix it so you wind up spittin' on yourself for about ten days, lady, 'cause that's how long it'll be before you see another human face. I can fix that, lady, don't think I can't, so don't even think about spittin' on me again, you hear?"

Ann Marie looked up at him and said, "I have to go to the bathroom. And if you don't let me go, I'm gonna do it in my pants."

"By my guest," the CO said. "I got allergies. My head's all stuffed up, I can't smell nothin'. And I got news for ya. You go to the bathroom here? Now? I'll fix it so you stay in those clothes till you get outta here. All I care is you relax your fingers, c'mon. Crap in your pants, pee if you want to, I don't care, just relax your hands and let me turn 'em."

Balzic kept shaking his head and asking himself if this was

what he could not live without. I gotta be the biggest schmuck
in the Northern Hemisphere.

After Frank and Ann Marie Vittone had finally been
booked, Balzic had to take the district justice to Conemaugh
General to try to book Mary Theresa Vittone, where they
learned that she was going to have to spend the night for obser-
vation. She had been so frantic and furious and hyperventilating so much before the surgery to repair her broken forearm
that the attending physician was concerned about her irregular
heartbeat. He was also concerned that she'd fainted twice. During her occasional moments of lucidity, she kept insisting that
she'd always had an irregular heartbeat, that she had mitral
valve prolapse. He finally gave her enough Demerol to put a
horse to sleep, he told Balzic, but he wanted to keep her for a
day just to be on the safe side anyway, he hoped Balzic didn't
mind.

Balzic didn't mind because he didn't have any choice. It
just meant he and District Justice Ralph Parma couldn't get
her to stay conscious long enough to answer questions about
her identity and place of residence, and neither Balzic nor
Parma had thought to bring along fingerprinting equipment.

"Look," Balzic said, "I don't wanna lose this 'cause we
can't book her right. You gotta give me your word this is gonna
fly, okay? She coulda killed her brother-in-law. And I was right
there. I mean I couldn't stop her from doin' what she did, I
don't wanna add embarrassment to that by losin' the case 'cause
we screw up the booking is what I'm sayin', you with me on
this?"

Parma shrugged and said, "Well I don't see what else you
can do that you haven't already done. What are you so worried
about?"

"Well I don't want some shyster claimin' that we delayed
her bookin' through incompetence or some crap like that, is all
I'm sayin'. I want you to make specific notes here on what time
I brought you here and what her condition was. And while
you're doin' that, I'm gonna be doin' the same thing with the
doctor and the nurses and the clerk out there, you know what
I'm sayin'?"

"Chief, stop worryin'. I keep very accurate records. It's my job. No attorney's gonna walk this woman because she's under sedation and can't respond to questions, if that's what you're worryin' about. And so what we forgot the fingerprinting stuff? How could we be expected to get her fingerprints anyway? She's got one arm in a cast down to her fingers and the other hand's got an IV needle in it. You worry too much. C'mon, c'mon, take me back to the jail."

I worry too much, Balzic thought. Me? I worry? God, if he only knew.

After Parma got out of Balzic's cruiser back at the county jail, Balzic headed for Muscotti's. Once inside, he called home and told Ruth he would be home in an hour or two. She asked him to stop for a box of raspberry tea and some bread. "Try not to get too drunk, Mar, okay? You sound terrible. Just watch yourself, okay?"

He admitted he sounded terrible because he felt terrible, but he didn't say why. His ear and right cheek were starting to throb. After he hung up, he went down the steps to the bar and took a stool beside Mo Valcanas, who was nodding his head in time to a recording of "Satin Doll" by the Duke Ellington band.

Balzic started to speak to Valcanas but he held his index finger to his lips until the music stopped. Then he turned to Balzic and said, "You can't interrupt me when I'm listening to 'Satin Doll.' Some of my finest memories are stored up in those notes—Jesus, what happened to you?"

"Aw it's too goddamn depressing to talk about."

"Well what happened to your ear? God, you've got blood all over your shirt and suit."

"Aw I got in the middle of a family, husband, wife, sister-in-law. The sister-in-law brains the husband with an ashtray—he needs, like, about thirty stitches—I break her arm gettin' her to drop the ashtray, and his wife jumps me and bites my ear, and if I hadn't tromped on her toes so hard she had to scream, she'd've probably bit my goddamn ear off. Took a chunk out of it. I don't know how much. Not much, but I didn't wanna look. Startin' to hurt like hell I know that. Goofy thing is, when she was doin' it, I didn't even feel it. Didn't even know that's what she did 'til the doc told me in the emergency room. Who's tendin' bar here, anybody?"

Valcanas nodded. "Dom just went to the can. Should be back soon—'less his piles are in an uproar."

"We gotta talk," Balzic muttered, rubbing his temples and his face.

"We? We as in you and me? I didn't hear you. What did you say?"

"I said we got to talk, yeah, you and me."

"I thought that's what you said. What I really want to do is to find oblivion if you don't mind. I don't want to talk."

"I do mind. You said somethin' in here the other day, when Joe Radio came in, remember? You were talkin' about a section of the Third Class City Code, somethin' to do with the firemen usin' money, capital improvement or capital equipment reserve fund or somethin', you remember that?"

"Unfortunately I do."

"Well when I asked you how come you knew about that, how come you could quote that right off the top of your head like that, you give me the runaround. You came up with some lame thing about some guy buggin' you about the firemen, and when I asked you who it was, you give me this see-ya-later crap. So now I'm askin' you again. How come you knew about that? And who's the guy buggin' you about it? And no bullshit this time, okay?"

Dom Muscotti came around behind them and settled in behind the bar, nodding to Balzic and pointing quizzically in vague circles to Balzic's bandaged ear and bloodied clothes.

"You don't wanna know. It's too stupid to talk about. I'll just tell you this much. Some woman weighed about half what I weigh did it. Gimme a big glass of cold white wine, the bigger, the colder, the better. And if you got any aspirins, I'll take three of those too."

Muscotti rummaged around near the coffeemaker and found a small bottle of aspirins and slid it across the bar in front of Balzic, who shook three out into his palm and went around the bar and poured himself a tumbler full of water while Muscotti was filling a pilsener glass with jug Chablis and cracked ice.

"That big enough for you?"

"Perfecto." Balzic swallowed the aspirins with the water and then drank half the glass of the Chablis.

"You gotta watch them little ones. The littler they are, the more you gotta watch 'em. My wife don't weigh a hundred and five pounds. I took my eyes off her once, I let her get behind me. She let me have a shot behind my ear I thought a truck hit me. Yeah. She punched me. Knocked me right off my chair. Kitchen chair. And all I was doin' was not listenin' to her. Like as if I never done that before."

Balzic looked at Valcanas and Valcanas looked back and they both had to look at the floor to keep from bursting out laughing. Balzic's ear hurt when he started to laugh so it was easy to stop.

"It's okay, you can laugh. I laugh at it myself. Except when she's around. Then I always pretend like I'm still scared she's gonna belt me one."

Valcanas said he had to go to the john. Balzic could hear him chortling and giggling all the way down the steps.

"The Greek thinks that's real funny, don't he?"

Balzic shrugged. "He must. Wish I could say the same. 'Cept every time I start to laugh my ear hurts like hell. Maybe after the aspirins kick in. And the wine."

"Hey, like my grandson said. The other day—he's gonna be five next week—he said, 'Hey, Paw-Paw,' he says, 'whatever floats your boat.' I laughed like hell. Yeah. He ain't even five. Where you think he heard that? Television probably."

"Probably."

Valcanas returned from the john and nodded for Balzic to accompany him to a table against the far wall out of Muscotti's hearing.

"What's up?"

"What's up is I know you're not gonna get off my back about this so I may as well tell you."

"Yeah? Tell me what?"

"I wrote to the attorney general. And to the state bar. And

to the county bar. I suggested as strongly as I could that our esteemed president judge ought to be investigated for his participation in this SWERT thing."

"You what? You shittin' me? You? *You?*"

"Yeah I know. Apathetic cynic such as I am. Nearest thing I can figure is I must've had a severe attack of nobility, or else I just got tired waitin' for somebody around here to do somethin', lettin' that goddamn Sitko get away with whatever the hell he feels like doin' anymore. And he's not in it on his lonesome. They're all in on it. Sitko, Vrbanic, Failan, that publisher, that Dunne, that witless wonder, and that goddamn Householder. They've been gettin' away with their crap for twenty years now. Longer. And I know that most of what they do through that goddamn foundation of theirs is perfectly legal. I've got letters from the IRS that go back five years tellin' me how legal they are."

"You been writin' to the IRS? About Householder and Dunne and Sitko? For five years?" Balzic felt his mouth hanging open.

"Stop lookin' at me like that. I haven't accomplished a goddamn thing—or at least I hadn't 'til this morning."

"Yeah, yeah, so what happened this morning?"

"I got a letter from the state bar that said their committee on judiciary review—that's not the official name, I forget what it is at this moment. I'm half shitface. Whatever. They said they'd already looked into Vrbanic's involvement in this SWERT crap. They said they'd found it, uh, 'questionable' was the word they used, to say the least, that a president judge would allow himself to be party to any quasi-police organization that had so blatantly violated the rules of police training, especially weapons training, in violation of state Acts 120 and 235, et cetera, et cetera, but they were taking my allegations seriously and they wanted me to know an investigation had already begun. They also said they were gonna notify the state attorney general's office, ya-ta-ta ya-ta-ta, and they would get back to me. I haven't heard from the county bar yet, but I think that's because everybody around here is trying to figure out exactly how to cover their asses on this one. I think they wanna make sure they've got plenty of light between them and Vrbanic before they say anything." Valcanas shrugged and stood. "I just thought, you know, since you're askin' me about this . . . it was me. I was the guy who wanted to know about that section of the Third Class City Code. Wasn't anybody else. It was me. Satisfied now?"

"Yeah. I guess. Well no. I got a lot more questions."

"Yeah, well some other time. I need to get back to oblivion now."

Balzic squinted up at Valcanas. "Honest to god, Greek, sometimes you scare the shit outta me."

"I? Me? I scare the shit out of you? What's that supposed to mean?"

Balzic shook his head many times. "Hey, lots of people been talkin' about this for, uh, like years, and you come along and nobody says they were talkin' to you about anything, and the next thing I know you got people up and runnin' for crissake. That just scares me, don't ask me why. Just does."

"Finish your wine, you'll feel lots braver."

"So the fuckin' AG is in on this now? For sure?"

"No. I didn't say that. I said the state bar said they were gonna notify his office. That's all I said. They said *they* were gonna investigate Vrbanic's involvement on their own. They didn't say anything about what the AG was gonna do, so don't go gettin' out of joint about this. Don't read more into it than what I said is what I'm sayin'."

"Right right. I won't. I won't. But shit, that's, uh, that's . . . you fucking amaze me sometimes, Greek, no shit you do."

"My my. First fear. Now amazement. Maybe I oughta be on TV. Maybe I'm a star and don't know it." He was grinning crookedly and raising high his empty glass. "Innkeeper. Oblivion if you please."

"Two of them," Balzic said. "And I'm payin'."

"What're you talkin' about you're payin'? You ain't paid for the last one. C'mon, get somethin' up here, c'mon, c'mon, shoulda closed up already."

"Closed? Christ, it's not even seven-thirty."

"Hey, you want a saloon stays open all the time, go buy your own joint. I'm tired, I wanna go home. Last call."

"Last call?"

"Yeah, last call. What, I'm gonna stay open'n make eight hundred bucks on you two? You kiddin' me? You both get blasted I don't make ten bucks, not on the stuff you're drinkin'. I'd rather be home playin' with my grandson. Least he's funny. You two're about as funny as the big casino. Sheesh."

Balzic shrugged and he and Valcanas drank and listened to Duke Ellington on the jukebox. When they finished their second drink, the one that was served on the last call, Muscotti, true to his word, told them he was going home. Balzic said good night, picked up his change, and went out to his cruiser.

Driving to the Giant Eagle to pick up the tea and bread, he tried to think about what he'd done today and what he hadn't. Nothing that he'd done had felt like good work, and everything that he hadn't done felt like hunger; it rumbled around in his gut and gave his mouth a coppery taste. Inside the supermarket, he couldn't remember whether Ruth had said she wanted raspberry-flavored tea or raspberry herbal tea, so he bought a box of each. Then he got a loaf of sourdough bread and one of Jewish rye, and hurried to the express checkout line, feeling that people were staring and gawking at him like he was a traffic accident.

On the way home, he kept thinking about what he hadn't done. He hadn't talked to Rugs Carlucci to find out what progress, if any, Carlucci had made checking out the Conemaugh Foundation. Balzic's conversation about the foundation with Royer was fine and filled in a lot of little gaps and crannies in Balzic's ignorance, but it was still just a conversation between two cops speculating about what might be true. There was nothing like solid documentation to quiet the rumbling in Balzic's gut, and for that he needed to know what Carlucci had learned. Carlucci wasn't the fastest detective investigator Balzic had ever worked with, but he was persistent. "Talent," Joe Gregowicz used to say, "everybody talks talent. But give me tenacity. Tenacity beats talent every time." Balzic wondered why, after not thinking about Joe Gregowicz for many, many years he was suddenly remembering things Gregowicz used to say to him when he was a rookie. He could wonder all he wanted. This question, like all the other ones he'd been asking himself lately, would have to get in line. Besides, it didn't matter how tenacious Carlucci was if Balzic hadn't found time in the day to learn what Carlucci had learned.

And then there was Sgt. John Winkerburg, commander of the SWERT. Balzic had made several boasts about finding out who Winkerburg was. What had he said to him in the Mutual Aid garage? That he'd know Winkerburg's shoe size by Monday? Well, here it was nearly 8 P.M. Monday and he didn't know any more about Winkerburg than he'd known after the last time he'd talked to him, which was next to nothing. It was some day.

Balzic pulled into his driveway and lumbered up the steps, feeling as though his calves had turned to wet sand. The pummeling he'd taken and the wine he'd drunk were also doing a polka on his back and neck. His head ached in many places on the right side. His ear felt like an abscessed tooth. He was wondering and bitching why the aspirins hadn't kicked in. It had to have been at least forty-five minutes since he'd taken them in Muscotti's.

Before he could get his key in the front door lock, Ruth pulled the door open and her eyes went wide. "Oh, Mar. Oh, baby, what happened, here, give me that bag, what happened, what happened?"

"I didn't know what kind of tea you wanted, I didn't know whether you wanted regular or herbal so I bought both. I also got rye and sourdough. They both felt real good, you know? That real good crust and that spongy feel, you know?"

"Mario, my god, what happened to your ear? And your face? What happened?"

"I need to sit down. And I need to get these clothes off. This suit's history, I think. Shirt too. When I tell ya what happened, huh? You ain't gonna believe it. I don't believe it. You know how everybody says all we need is more cops on the streets and that's how we're gonna put a stop to all the crime, huh? All the street crime? How many people you heard say that in the last ten, fifteen years, huh?"

"Here, let me take your coat off, come on, you can tell me, you can keep talkin', but you gotta take this coat off. My god it's stuck to your shirt."

"Yeah. Well, Ruthie, baby, I was right there between 'em. Right smack between 'em. The guy was in front of me, the woman was behind me, and I couldn't do a thing about it. Wham! Over my shoulder she comes, I just catch a flash of somethin' comin' around, and before I can make a move she catches him right behind his ear with this ashtray, it got a dog on it. Yeah. Big ugly ashtray, copper-colored, with a big black and white dog on it, she's holdin' it by the dog's legs, that much I can see, and she opens up his head like it's a can of salmon. So whatta ya think I do, huh? I think she's gonna whack me next, so I grab hold of her arm in two places and I bring it down over my knee, she lets go of the ashtray, and snappo! There goes the arm. Then, ta-ta! Her sister jumps me from behind, just climbs right up on my back and starts beatin' the hell outta me and tries to bite my ear off."

"Oh god, Mar. Oh god." Ruth sagged and shook her head and threw his coat on the floor. "C'mon, Mar. You need to get a bath, a good, hot bath. Go on back. Take your clothes off, I'll run the tub, get you some wine. D'you take anything? Aspirins or anything? Huh?"

"Yeah, I took three of 'em. They haven't kicked in for some reason. Bath sounds really good. No shit, Ruthie, you're the best."

"Yeah yeah, just go in the bedroom and take your clothes off. What're you supposed to do about your ear? Anything? Can you get it wet? You supposed to keep it dry, or what?"

"I didn't even ask 'em."

"That's okay," she said from in the bathroom, running the tub. "I'll call the emergency room. Is that who took care of it? Is that where you went?"

"Yeah. But that was this afternoon. Musta been two, two-thirty when I was in there. I doubt those people are still workin'."

She stuck her head around the door frame. "This happened at two-thirty?"

"No, nah. More like eleven-thirty this mornin'. It took me until—never mind. It's too confusing. Really. It was a mess."

"It is not a mess," she said. "It is a message. It is a message, Mar. And the message is Q-U-I-T! Quit! God, Mar, what if this nut would've been after you? What if she decided your head was closer? Huh? This is it, Mar. I'm telling you, *this* is it!"

Balzic didn't argue. He struggled and shrugged and tugged his way out of his clothes and sat on the bed and waited until she said the tub was ready. By the time he'd eased himself into the tub and slid down until the water was lapping over his shoulders, she was back carrying a sturdy jelly jar full of white wine. He took it, looking at her with all the gratitude and love he could summon up. "You're the best, Ruthie. The goddamn best. I love you. Thank you."

She leaned forward from the waist and said, "Don't thank me. Don't tell me I'm the best. Don't tell me you love me. Just quit."

There was nothing more he could say. He raised the glass to her in a salute. Then he rose up a little and drank some and then settled back and closed his eyes and let the hot water and cold wine do their work.

The investigation by the state attorney general's office and the state bar association was conducted as quietly as any Balzic had ever seen. It was so quiet, he didn't know it was going on until a woman identifying herself as a special investigator for the state bar association called him the first Tuesday in October to say she was coming to interview him that afternoon, she hoped that would be all right. Balzic guessed it had to be all right.

When she arrived, she was wearing red-rimmed glasses and had her hair done up in a bun, but she was very somber and sober and wore no makeup. She didn't look to be old enough to have graduated from college, let alone law school; she didn't look as old as Balzic's younger daughter. Before Balzic invited her to have a seat, she showed him her ID and a letter from the bar association stating in general terms the subject of their inquiry. Her ID said her name was Janet Blahovec. The letter said the subject of the inquiry was the president judge of the Conemaugh County Court of Common Pleas, Milan G. Vrbanic, Esq.

Though it was the first week of October it was almost as hot as it had been in August. Blahovec was sweating on her upper lip and forehead and she kept pushing a lock of hair out of her eyes until she became annoyed with it and apologized and said she had to be excused for a moment. When she came back to his office, all her hair was in place.

She tested the batteries in her tape recorder. Then she unzipped a flat vinyl case and referred to a legal tablet inside it before she asked every question. She never showed any emotion, not even a raised brow, when she questioned him. She just made some notation on the tablet after every answer. She particularly wanted Balzic to explain about when he first learned of the SWERT and when he discovered that members of his department were involved and what he did when he learned of their involvement.

"I suspended them."

"There was more than one?"

"Two."

"What was the result of their suspension? Was there a civil service hearing?"

"Yes there was."

"What was the determination of those hearings?"

"Well there was only one hearing for just the one officer. Metikosh. The other one, Yesho, took a job with another PD. In Florida. Tampa. So he dropped his request for a hearing."

"What was the determination of the hearing for, uh, what was his name?"

"Metikosh. I'm sure you can get a copy of the hearing if you want it. Probably wouldn't even take a subpoena, but don't take my word for that, 'cause I'm sure not talkin' for the civil service guys—or the FOP either. Anyway, he was reinstated. With back pay. He wound up with an official letter of reprimand. In other words, they said his heart was in the right place but he shoulda known better."

"Did you object to their determination? Have you appealed it, for example?"

Balzic shook his head. "No, nah. What would be the point? I just wanted to get it over with. I didn't want the guy on bread and water or anything. I think he made a bad move, that's all. He didn't hurt anybody. And I certainly didn't have any evidence that he stole anything."

"All right. Now tell me about Judge Vrbanic. When did you learn of his involvement?"

Balzic sighed deeply. "As a matter of fact, I still don't know whether he was involved. All I'm goin' on is, uh, my surmisin' and speculatin'. I mean, I know all the people were claimin' they were duly authorized, all the SWERT people, and that means to me they had to be sworn in by somebody who had the power to swear 'em. But I never talked to him about it. And I certainly never conducted an investigation to establish that. Or has anybody in my department conducted an investigation to establish that. Not as far as he was concerned, him specifically I mean."

"So what you're saying is you have no proof that Judge Vrbanic was directly involved."

"No. Right. Yes. But listen. All I was concerned about was there was a buncha guys dressed up in camo clothes and they were carryin' automatic weapons. And they were doin' this in my jurisdiction. And I was told by the district attorney that there was not a goddamn thing I could do about it. Far as he was concerned, this was nothin' but a difference of opinion over who had more authority in this city, me or him. I said *I* was the chief law enforcement officer in this city, and he said *he* was the chief law enforcement officer in this county which meant he was authorized over me to do what he was doin'. Least that was his opinion. And I told him—or maybe I didn't and maybe I just think I told him or maybe I just wish I told him—I told him I thought the president judge was the chief law enforcement officer, so it just sorta went round and round like that."

"So, again, Chief Balzic, just to clarify for the record, what you're saying is you have no proof that President Judge Vrbanic participated directly in the organization and perpetuation of a so-called SWERT in Conemaugh County, Pennsylvania. Is that correct?"

"Yes, ma'am, that's correct."

The young woman turned off her tape recorder, zipped up her vinyl case, and put both into a cloth attaché case. "Okay, Chief. I'll get this tape transcribed, and get three copies to you within the week. You will have to get them notarized and signed, and I would appreciate it very much if you'd get them back to me A-S-A-P." She held out her card. "Send them to this address. My phone number's on the bottom if you have any questions. Thanks for your cooperation. Good-bye."

And then she was gone. She had not even introduced herself by name.

When the investigator for the attorney general's office showed up a week later, he was wearing a gray, lightweight wool suit with fine red stripes through it and a pewter-colored silk shirt and a red silk polka-dot tie. He was graying above his ears and on his temples and he gave Balzic an extra-firm handshake. He introduced himself as J. Ellsworth Raney, Esquire. He actually said the word *Esquire*.

Balzic had to ask to see his ID.

J. Ellsworth Raney looked annoyed. He got his ID case out of the inside pocket of his fine wool coat and sniffed while Balzic examined it.

"How long you been with the AG?"

"Just a year or so. Before that I was with the bureau."

"Bureau? ATF?"

"No," Raney said, looking around the office stiffly.

"Well you said 'bureau,' I just thought, you know, Bureau of Alcohol, Tobacco and Firearms—"

Raney was starting to look appalled. "Federal Bureau of Investigation." It took him a long time to say it. His chin rose higher with each syllable. He finished with a smile of self-satisfaction.

"Oh. Well, there's so many goddamn bureaus around these days, you know, somebody says 'bureau' you don't know what you're dealin' with anymore. Farm Bureau, Bureau of Employment Security, All State, State Farm, you don't know whether you're dealin' with the government or an insurance company—not 'til you ask."

"Right," Raney said, sniffing. "Chief Blazic—"

"Balzic. B-A-L, not B-L-A. Balzic, not Blazic."

"Right. So, uh, I suppose you're aware why I'm here?"

"Not yet I'm not."

"Surely you've heard of the allegations of impropriety in regard to the, uh, paramilitary organization that was formed here on the county level?"

"I don't know anything until somebody tells me somethin', you know?"

Raney sniffed again. "Well that's the nature of my mission. To discover what you know or knew about that."

"Well if that's what you're here for, I can save us both a lotta time. All I got is suspicions and speculations and surmises. I'm gonna tell you the same thing I told the female from the state bar association was in here last week. I didn't do any investigation of Judge Milan Vrbanic. I didn't order anybody to do any investigation of him. I didn't have the time or the manpower, but even if I did, how far do you think I would've gotten, huh? Can you imagine me, sittin' here, tryin' to dig the dirt on the president judge of this county? Huh? I was so goddamn ignorant, I had people in my own department signed up in that SWERT thing, and I didn't know it 'til I read it in the paper. I was so ignorant, I didn't know 'til I read it in the paper that they were usin' equipment—and I still don't know which equipment—that was stolen outta my property room. The department's property room, not mine."

"So then, if I understand you correctly," Raney said, "what you're saying is that you have no direct knowledge of Judge Vrbanic's participation or involvement, no proof, in other words. You yourself, I mean."

"I thought I just said that. Didn't I just say that?"

"Yes, you did. I'm merely clarifying this for myself."

"Uh-ha. Speakin' of clarifyin' things, you got a tape recorder on you somewhere?"

"No. Why do you ask?"

"'Cause you ain't writin' anything down, I figure you gotta have a recorder on you somewhere. I never could get used to those things myself. I mean I know they got the kind that you don't even have to touch 'em or anything, you know? They start whenever somebody starts talkin'."

"Science is marvelous, yes," Raney said. "But to satisfy your curiosity, no, I do not have a tape recorder. I have an excellent memory."

Balzic let out a sigh and leaned forward until he had his left elbow on his desk. "Uh, excuse me, but I'd like to see your ID again and also, uh, I wanna see the name and phone number of your supervisor."

"I beg your pardon?" Raney drew back in his chair.

"You heard me. I wanna see your ID again and I want your boss's name and phone number. I mean, you walk in off the street and you try to tell me you're workin' for the attorney general of fucking Pennsylvania and you're conducting an investigation into charges of impropriety of the president judge of this county and you're tellin' me you're not keepin' records of this? Do I look like an asshole to you? Huh? C'mon, lemme see that fuckin' ID again. This conversation ain't goin' nowhere 'til I know—if this is on the square, Jesus Christ, this is the way you guys interview people? Huh? C'mon, c'mon, your ID and your boss's name and number."

Raney stood up slowly, stretching his chin upward like a great bird. "Chief Blazic, perhaps we can have this conversation at another time—when you are perhaps less defensive. Though from what I've already learned about you, from where I stand so to speak, you have much to be defensive about. But here's my card." Raney produced a business card from a slot in his ID case and dropped it on Balzic's desk. "Whenever you're satisfied that I'm who I say I am, give me a call. I'm staying at the Holiday Inn just off the New Stanton Exchange of the turnpike. Their number's on the back. They'll certainly relay any message you might have. Good-bye."

"It's Balzic goddammit."

"Well. Who would know if not you?"

CRANKS AND SHADOWS 257

"Aw get outta here. You didn't come here to investigate anything. You came in here to jag people off. If this is the way it's gonna go, I know what's gonna happen. Nothin'. Nothin's gonna happen."

Raney smiled and shrugged slightly, as though fearful that too much movement would wrinkle his suit. "Whatever happens or does not happen, Chief, uh, Balzic? Is that it? Did I get it right that time?"

"Stop jaggin' me off, okay? Just stop."

"Whatever happens or doesn't happen will not be because of anything you have done, Chief, I can assure you of that. Though I can't say that whatever happens won't be because of what you have not done. Good-bye."

Yeah, right, Balzic thought after Raney left, fuck you very much. These fuckers are trying to turn this around on me. These bastards are gonna try and say it all happened 'cause I was on a snoozeroo, like if I wasn't takin' a nap it wouldn't've happened? Oh man. Oh man oh man oh man. Jesus . . .

Balzic never heard from J. Ellsworth Raney, Esquire, again. He did receive three copies of his interview with Janet Blahovec, and, as she'd requested, he signed them in front of a notary and sent them back to her, after he'd made a copy for himself. That was the last he heard from her too.

He ran into Mo Valcanas the week before the election just as Valcanas was heading into Muscotti's. It was a bright, crisp fall day, temperature in the low sixties, almost no wind, but the sun was slanting low so that Balzic had to shield his eyes with his hand in order to see Valcanas.

"Hey, Greek, if you got no objection, let's go down the SOI."

"You wanna go to the Sons of Italy? Why? I didn't even know they were open this time of day. I thought they were only open on Sundays and holidays."

"They're open. It won't take long. I don't wanna talk in here," Balzic said, nodding toward Muscotti's.

Valcanas shrugged and nodded for Balzic to lead the way.

Inside the SOI, Balzic paid for his draft beer and Valcanas's gin on the rocks and headed for a table far from the bar. There were only two other persons there, two old men playing checkers and talking in Italian, a dialect Balzic could not begin to understand.

Valcanas drank half his gin and shrugged, the corners of his mouth turning down. "So?"

"So what I wanna know is, what's the word you're gettin' about Vrbanic? Anything? I haven't heard a goddamn thing from anybody."

"If this is what you wanted to talk about, I could've told you on the street—or in Muscotti's. I don't know anything. Haven't heard a word."

"Did you talk to anybody from the state bar? Or from the AG's office?"

"I talked to a woman named Blahovec. And to some pompous jerk from the AG's office."

"Raney? J. Ellsworth Raney, Esquire. You know, that was the first time in my life I ever talked to a shyster who actually used that word when he introduced himself. Esquire."

"Comes from a different world, Mario, that's all. Different world."

"Yeah? Where's that? I mean I knew he was from someplace I never been. What the hell was that accent he had?"

"He was from up around Boston. Some places up there, they sound like you don't know whether they're American or British. Haven't you ever heard George Plimpton talk on TV?"

"Who? Oh, that guy that, uh, the one that's always tryin' to play sports, the guy that wrote that book with the Detroit Lions, yeah, yeah, I remember, the guy that tried to play quarterback, I can't remember the name of the book. Yeah. Yeah, that Raney's accent was exactly like that guy's. Plimpton? Is that his name?"

Valcanas nodded. "I met a lot of those people when I was at Dartmouth. It was like we came from different planets."

"Yeah. Well that Raney fuck was from a different planet. You talked to him, huh?"

Valcanas nodded and tossed back the rest of his gin. He

went to the bar and got a refill and came back. "I would've got you another beer but you haven't even touched that one."

Balzic dismissed the thought of another beer with a small wave. "What's gonna happen, Panagios? What's gonna happen?"

"About Vrbanic? What? What're you asking about?"

"Yeah, Vrbanic. And the election. Whatta you think?"

"Well, Vrbanic's not up for a retention vote."

"Yeah yeah I know that. I mean whatta you think's gonna happen with the AG?"

"Nothing probably. I don't know. Maybe Vrbanic'll have to go to Harrisburg and explain himself to a bunch of his cronies. More likely he'll have to go there and get shitface with them while they tell him corny jokes about all the stupid people they put in jail. I don't know what's gonna happen, Mario. I suspect nothing—nothing for public consumption anyway."

"Don't you think anything you said is going to make any difference—to anybody?"

Valcanas sighed and shook his head. "Look. I didn't have anything on Vrbanic, any more than you did. I just said that if anybody wanted to get ambitious and do a little nosin' around, they'd find that a judge had lent himself to a very dubious operation, one that somebody oughta look at. Very carefully. But when this guy Raney showed up, I knew, or let's say I had very strong suspicions that what's gonna happen is Vrbanic is gonna get told to very quietly separate himself from these goofballs and to cover his tracks. I mean, what's anybody gonna do? Walk into court and slap a warrant on him? Put him in leg irons? Maybe if this was TV, a movie of the week, it might happen. But it's not gonna happen around here. Christ, a judge in this state'd have to get caught in bed with a goat before anybody'd even tell him he couldn't hear trials while he was awaiting his own trial—and there'd have to be photographic evidence and plenty of it. I mean, when that reporter got fired from the *Gazette*—what was his name?"

"Hussler."

"Yeah, him. After he got canned, they just stopped writin' anything about it, the SWERT, the helicopter, the county people involved, I mean, did you ever see a story die as fast as that one? I've seen stories die, but not that suddenly. For a couple of weeks it's all over the paper, and then nothin'. Bang, dead, stop. And the Pittsburgh papers and TV, hell, they never touched it after that. All we've been gettin' ever since is about how Eddie Sitko's gonna resign, he's not gonna resign, his worshippers are gonna resign, they're not gonna resign, we're gonna have a paid department, we're not gonna have a paid department, what the hell. It's a *fait accompli* anyway."

"It's a what?"

"An accomplished fact."

"What is?"

"The election. Angelo Bellotti's gonna be mayor again and Joe Radio's gonna be on Council again. They're in and Strohn and Richards're out. And Sitko and his clique are gonna do whatever they want whenever they want. And the only people who're gonna be upset are the cranks and shadows. Everybody else is gonna be screamin' to get in on the party. Tell you the truth, it's gonna look a lot like Italy about sixty, seventy years ago."

"That's what Dom said. That's what he tried to tell me one night, maybe I didn't wanna hear it, or maybe I'm too dense, but I still don't know what the hell he was talkin' about. Now you're sayin' the same thing."

"Well what's the Democratic Party around here anyway but a rubber stamp for a coupla guys who never run for election? You ever see Householder's name on a ballot? Not you I mean. You've never even seen a ballot, have you? Except the ones that they print in the *Gazette*?"

Balzic shook his head no.

"Well, you ever see Dunne runnin' for anything? Hell, Dunne and Householder are both registered Republicans. And the only election Sitko ever runs in is that sham the firemen put on every coupla years to reelect him—unanimously. And as long as the IRS keeps sayin' their precious Conemaugh Foundation is exempt from all taxes? They get whatever they want, whenever they want it, and who's to say otherwise. 'Cause they have the magic rep. 'They get things done.' Ask anybody around here. You know it as well as I do. 'They get things done.' That's what everybody says. Well, shit, who couldn't—if you had that much money and didn't have to pay any goddamn taxes yourself? That's the part that pisses me off. Between their goddamn foundation and their goddamn investments in municipal bonds, they live off the rest of us saps, they enjoy all the privileges, and they don't pay for anything the rest of us have to pay for.

"Shit, listen to me. I'm turnin' into a sour grape. C'mon, I can't sit here. The jukebox here is lousy. Dom's isn't much better, but at least he's got some Duke Ellington and some good blues. You still playin' the harp?"

"I'm gonna be playin' it a lot I think. I think I'm gonna get calluses on my lips. And I still sound like shit. Still sound like an old white dog tryin' to learn a new black trick. Maybe white people were never 'sposed to play the blues."

"That's why white people invented hillbilly music," Valcanas said, leading Balzic back out in the slanting sunlight. "Am I ever gonna hear you play? You can't be that bad."

"Only if I get real real drunk. But when I get even a little bit drunk I can't play at all. Two beers and it's just blaghhh."

A week before the election, Balzic walked into the duty room to find Sgt. Vic Stramsky holding up a copy of the *Rocksburg Gazette* folded to a story on the front page. The headline said, "Failan Disbands SWERT." "What the hell's this," Balzic said, whistling softly.

"Looks like somebody turned up the heat," Stramsky said.

"By The Rocksburg Gazette," Balzic read. "District Attorney Howard Failan disbanded Conemaugh County's Special Weapons and Emergency Response Team yesterday and abolished the special assistant detective positions that gave police powers to civilian members of the team.

"The DA said, after meeting privately with county commissioners for more than two hours, that 'we will not activate the SWERT.

"'After much discussion it was agreed the liability implications presented by the composition of the team could not be overcome.' He praised the dedication and selflessness of the original 24 participants.

"The announcement came on the heels of reports that special investigations have for some weeks been under way by both the state attorney general and by the state bar association into the team, which originally included two Rocksburg police officers, one county corrections officer, a medical doctor, and 14 members of the Rocksburg Volunteer Fire Department, among others.

"None of the civilians connected to the team had received the basic law enforcement training mandated by state law.

"The decision to disband the team, Failan explained, came after he and the commissioners debated the liability implications of mobilizing a unit comprised primarily of untrained civilians.

"Failan repeated earlier statements to this paper that he had not been aware of the roles the firemen played while conducting maneuvers to prepare for hostage situations, jail escapes, manhunts, and incidents of terrorism.

"John Theodore, chief of county detectives, reportedly had apprised Failan that the unit was necessary only to aid and assist searches for bodies and evidence in homicide cases. Theodore could not be reached for comment.

"Failan declined to say how those duties had grown beyond what he says he understood them to be at the outset. He said yesterday's decision would have no affect on the VFD's bloodhound handlers and they would remain involved in any search operation supervised by the county detectives bureau.

"Failan hastened to add that any question of liability in regard to the bloodhound handlers had been resolved and that his office had secured insurance coverage for them and would continue that coverage absent funding by local municipalities, who have long refused to pay for it.

"The DA, however, was less forthcoming about the matter of volunteer firemen in the city continuing to carry deputy sheriff's shields and IDs that give them the same countywide powers as county detectives.

"Failan said he has been unable to discuss the matter with

Sheriff Markle 'because the sheriff has been campaigning hard and it's tough to locate him.' Markle has also refused to talk to reporters, contending that he is too involved in his reelection campaign and the daily business of running his department.

"'Until further notice,' Failan concluded, 'the SWERT will only provide assistance in searches, and the civilian members will not be armed.'"

Balzic screwed up his face happily at Stramsky and said, "Well what the hell you think of this, huh?"

"I think some people had a hard time fittin' their old underwear over their new asses this morning, is what I think," Stramsky said.

"You know, sometimes lawyers piss me off so bad," Balzic said, "I mean sometimes I even look at Mo Valcanas who has been my paisan for life, and I say to him, you know, 'How could you? You, of all people, how could you be a lawyer?' But then somethin' like this happens, and it turns out the only thing that brings these idiots back to earth is the fear of bein' sued. People can get all indignant and self-righteous and moralistic as hell and nothin' happens. But let some sonofabitch remind these numbnuts they can be sued? And they don't have insurance? Shit, they go right to their knees every time."

Stramsky shook his head and then nodded and smiled. "Maybe that's what cops oughta say—you know, instead of stop or I'll shoot? Huh, maybe we oughta be sayin', Stop or I'll sue."

"That's funny, Vic. I'll have to remember that."

"Oh. There's somethin' else you oughta read. Back about the next to the last page. On the right. Julie Richards got an ad in there. Doubt if it's gonna do her any good, but she's still in there pitchin'."

Under the word "ADVERTISEMENT," Balzic found this:

To the taxpayers of Rocksburg: I have been asked repeatedly by many of you how I could question the integrity and honesty of the volunteer firemen when they do so much for us. I've said it to each of you individually when you called or stopped me on the street, and now, with the election coming soon, I want to say it again to all of you. I am not questioning their acts of bravery, their long hours of training, their quick responses to our calls for their protection and assistance. What I am questioning is their accountability.

Just because past city administrations allowed the VFD to operate without any accountability does not make it right, legally or morally. You pay taxes to us to operate this city as efficiently and as economically as we can to make this a better place for you to live. Whenever we do something wrong, legally or morally, or even if we look like we have done something wrong, you have every right to question us. Nobody can stop you from questioning us. That is your right as a citizen.

But when I was elected to Council, I learned that nobody was allowed to question the VFD, not privately or publicly. We, the Council, your representatives, were supposed to make a budget that included maintenance of all the fire halls, including labor and supplies, but the only finances we were supposed to know about was the money coming from the Foreign Fire Insurance Fund. That money comes from a two percent tax on fire insurance premiums that are written by insurance companies which are incorporated outside Pennsylvania. We were told that money existed, but we were never allowed to see exactly how much it was. All we were told was that the amount our VFD receives is based on some formula involving population and the market value of our real estate.

The fire chief says that anybody can call the state and receive copies of the audits of this money and that the audits are on record in City Hall. The most recent audits I have been able to find in City Hall are at least eight years old. The fire chief has called me a liar and says those audits are up-to-date and available to anybody.

But those audits, wherever they are, don't address the issue of how the VFD has managed to accumulate more than a million dollars in government securities, corporate bonds, stocks, money market accounts, and certificates of deposit with one brokerage house and more than a half million dollars in similar investments with another brokerage house. And that was from the last available audit of the Rocksburg Firemen's Relief Association, which is six years old.

The VFD says they need this money to supplement the rebates

from the Foreign Fire Insurance Fund. First, they refuse to tell us—you and me—how much money they've received from the state, and second, they won't tell us—you and me—how much money they receive from bingos, raffles, lotteries, and solicitations, not to mention hall rentals and bar receipts in all their social clubs, which operate seven days a week.

All the VFD will say is that they need this money to purchase and maintain their equipment and to pay death, relief and disability benefits, legal fees, and flowers for deceased members. Nobody—least of all me—wants to deprive the VFD of any money they lawfully need to do these very necessary and commendable things. All I have been saying from the start is that if the VFD has more than a million and a half dollars invested with two brokerage firms, they certainly have enough money to pay for the maintenance of their own buildings.

We have the third highest unemployment rate for a third-class city in the entire state. Many of our residents, citizens, taxpayers, your neighbors, are living on fixed incomes. Some of our citizens are stuck between one state agency that has a lien on their house and other state agencies that refuse to give them relief from real estate taxes. If they—if you—can be forced to assume that burden, the least the VFD can do is open their books to us—your representatives—so that we can budget expenditures fairly. That's what I have asked since I was elected, and if I am reelected that is what I will continue to ask. Because it is right. Because it is fair. Because no matter how brave the volunteer firemen are, no matter how many times they risk themselves to put out our fires, to pump out our basements, to rescue us in traffic accidents, they still have to pay their share just like the rest of us. Thank you.

Paid For By Supporters of Councilwoman Julie Richards.

Balzic shrugged. "Nice try. She got about as much chance of gettin' reelected as I have of makin' a record with Sonny Boy Williamson. And he's been dead for, uh, god knows how long."

"Sonny Boy who?"

"You never heard of him. Well actually there were two of 'em."

"Two of who?"

"Two Sonny Boys. Two blues guys, they both said they

were Sonny Boy Williamson. Don't ask me why, I don't know. Don't know why they never got it straightened out either. Probably both too stubborn. Tell ya the truth, I never have heard a record made by the one. I have a couple records by the other one. He made a buncha great tunes. He was a great harp player. Not technically, you know. Technically, lotsa kids, they can play rings around him now. But he had that, that growl, man, it came up from the bottoms of his toes. Gives me goose bumps."

"Mario, I don't know what in the hell you're talkin' about."

"Don't matter. I'm just talkin'. How's the party comin'? You guys out promotin' your asses off or what?"

"Well, Rascoli sure is. And I am. I don't know about Royer. Haven't talked to him about it for a coupla days. But he'll come through. Always has. You're comin', right?"

"Am I comin'? To your retirement party? Are you shittin' me? I'll be there. Bet on it. Ruthie too."

On election day, Balzic walked from his office to Hose Company Number One on Main Street, the Rocksburg Volunteer Fire Department's headquarters and largest garage. It was where they kept their biggest pieces of equipment: ladder trucks, light trucks, smoke ventilators. The social club on the second floor, which was level with the city's parking lot in the rear of the building, also served as the city's most central polling place.

Fire Chief Eddie Sitko was already greeting voters out in the parking lot with a handshake and pat on the back and handing out cards that bore the names of the candidates of the Democratic Party. A half dozen volunteer firemen were gathered around him, peeling off at the approach of every new voter to hand out fingernail files, combs, ballpoint pens, and buttons reminding all that Angelo Bellotti was a write-in candidate for mayor and that Joe Radosich was a write-in candidate for councilman.

Balzic was immediately confronted by one of the volunteer firemen who was trying with his sincerest smile to thrust a comb and a button into Balzic's hands when Sitko called out, "Hey. Don't be givin' him that stuff. He ain't gonna vote."

The campaign smile on the fireman's face dissolved into a genuinely sincere blush, and he retreated at once, trying to put a couple of his buddies between himself and Sitko.

"What're you doin' here, Balzic? You ain't registered."

Balzic shrugged. "I need a new comb. I need to watch you in action. You gonna tell me you ain't gonna give me a comb?"

Sitko smiled and shook his head and spat a long stream of tobacco juice on the macadam between them. "You're gonna watch me? You think you're gonna learn somethin', huh? Mario, you could watch me here for a month you wouldn't learn anything. And you ain't gettin' no fuckin' comb either."

"Maybe I don't have to learn anything. Maybe I know everything I need to know right now."

Sitko threw back his head and laughed. Then, still grinning broadly, he shook his head and approached Balzic until he was less than a step away and said softly, "You don't know nothin'. You might think you know somethin' but you don't. You don't know shit from shoe polish. Never did, never goin' to."

"Pretty sure of yourself, huh?"

"Never been more fuckin' sure of myself in my whole life. This one's in the bag. But if you wanna watch, you're welcome. I can't stop ya. You can even do like those TV fuckers, you know, how they do their exit poll? Ain't that what the fuck they call it? Where they wait till it's over and then they stick a microphone in somebody's face and say, real intelligent like, 'So who'd ya vote for?' You could do one of them all by yourself. You got a little notebook, right? Need a pen? Hell, if you really wanna keep score I can let you have a pen that says vote for Joe Radio."

"No, thanks. I don't need to keep score. I know how it's gonna come out. Same as you."

"Bet your Eye-talian ass," Sitko said, still grinning broadly.

"Think you got it covered, huh, Eddie?"

"Mario, I told you, I never had it covered so fuckin' good

in my whole life. It's in real pretty red shiny paper, and it's got a red velvet bow, and it's got gold sparklies all over it. And by the middle of next week? When we get all the absentee ballots counted? Hoo, boy, we're gonna fuckin' rip the cover off, and we're gonna throw a party like nobody in this town has ever seen in their miserable fuckin' lives. 'Cause you know why, Mario? Huh? You know why? 'Cause the people here love us. Yeah. We're the greatest fuckin' thing since sliced bread come back after World War Number Two. And you, my ol' buddy, my ol' pal? Your ass is gonna be suckin' wind. I won't have to look at you anymore. Oh, they'll probably let you hang on till the first of the year. Hell, the new mayor and the new Council might even throw you a retirement party. Wouldn't surprise me a bit. But come next year, Mario, your ass will be retired. As in retired retired retired. It's time anyway. You're an old dog, Mario. I know you're sixty-five. You shoulda give it up ten years ago, when you first had the chance."

"And exactly what difference would that have made to you?"

Sitko shrugged and spit another long stream of tobacco juice on the macadam near Balzic's feet. His face broke into a large grin. "Probably none at all. Probably wouldn'ta meant a hill of fuckin' beans. What kinda beans you Eye-talians like? Garbanzos?"

"I'm only half Italian, Eddie. Other half's hunky just like you."

"Wrong there, buddy boy. That hunky part ain't half of me. That hunky part I been losin' for years and years. It gets smaller every year. I keep sheddin' it like a bad skin. I'm mostly what I need to be now. Mostly what I am is a Householder. Huh? Huh?" Sitko gave a wink and a nod and came close enough to nudge Balzic with his shoulder. "If it wasn't such a goddamn hassle, I'd go to court and get my name changed, you know that, Mario? But what the fuck. I got that ol' name recognition factor with Sitko, you know? Everybody knows me by that name. Doncha think? Huh?"

"Oh they know you by that name, Eddie, there's no doubt

about that. I just don't think more than half a dozen people know you for who you really are."

"Oh right, yeah. And you think you do, huh? Shit. Double shit. Double dogshit dried up in the sun and turned white. What I am, Balzic, is what I have always been. A volunteer fireman. A public spirit. Dedicated to servin' my fellowman. That's what I learned from my old man. 'Cause he was a good one too. He knew how to put out the fires, boy, don't you think he didn't. But the rest of it I got from my mother. She had more brains in her little finger'n my old man had in his whole goddamn body, 'cept when it come to puttin' out fires. But everything else? I learned everything else from my mother, may she rest in heaven with all the other great people who ever lived. She taught me how you do what you gotta do. And that's who I am."

"She the one taught you how to use the IRS Code? Huh? Or was that your uncle?"

"Details, Balzic, details," Sitko whooped and hollered. "It don't matter where I learned the details. What I learned from my mother was how only stupid people think you gotta have money in a pile somewhere. She taught me when I was a little goddamn kid, money ain't no fuckin' good unless it spends, Balzic. She told me once, shit, she told me ten thousand times. Money in a fuckin' mattress—which is where my old man kept it like all the other hunkies—money in a mattress, that's for dumb-ass hunkies don't know any better. Money don't have no-body's name on it 'cept dead politicians. But money don't have your name on it. And it don't care whose hand it's in when it's buyin' somethin'! My mother drummed that into me, every time she caught me peekin' at my old man reachin' in the mat-tress and pullin' out a coupla pieces of cheese. My Uncle Orville is the one showed me the details, that's all he did. Him and Dunne. They showed me how the IRS lets ya do it. But it was my mother's brainwork put the idea in my head when I was nothin' but a shit-ass snot-nose kid."

"Well, Eddie, I guess she'd be proud."

"Bet your Eye-talian ass she would." He looked around

furtively and said, "You know, if you wasn't such a fuckin' hardhead, who knows? Huh?"

"Who knows what?"

"You know what I mean. But no. You had to be a fuckin' hardhead. Your head's made out of the finest Eye-talian marble. Whatta they call that, cabrera, carrera? Whatta they call that?"

"Carrara. All *a*'s, no *e*'s."

"Yeah, whatever. Whatta you gonna wind up with, huh? A grand a month pension, huh? And Medicare? And Social Security?"

"My house is paid for. I won't starve."

"Yeah, well you're used to eatin' that fuckin' pasta anyway."

"What can I say. I'm a peasant at heart."

Sitko started to turn away, but stopped. "Yeah. That's right. That's exactly what you are."

"Rather be a peasant than a three-dollar bill who's been robbin' from peasants all his life."

Sitko turned back and poked Balzic in the chest. "Hey you. You listen to me. You and your buddy boy Strohn and his girlfriend, what's-her-face, that Richards cunt, you can run your mouth motors 'til hell turns into orange Popsicles, but what I do is legal. There ain't a lawyer in the U.S. Justice Department or in the Internal Revenue Service can say otherwise, 'cause what you don't know is how hard they been tryin' for the last four years. I know what that cunt did. She sicced 'em on me. They been over my tax records like I was Al Capone. But they ain't found nothin' yet and they ain't gonna find nothin'. Ever. You know why? 'Cause Lyman Dunne got the finest tax lawyers in this country on his payroll. They know that fuckin' Section 501 of the fuckin' IRS Code frontwards, backwards, upside fuck-ing down. And no stink-ing, fuck-ing accountant in Philadelphia or Washington District of fuck-ing Columbia been able to say otherwise yet. And they ain't goin' to neither. 'Cause we're doin' what the law says, Balzic. That's what you can't get through your fuckin' head. Right fuck-ing down to the fuck-ing letter. And you and Strohn and that Richards cunt can all go fuck yourself in a big, sweaty pile and it ain't gonna change any fuck-ing thing. See ya around, Balzic. Have a nice fuck-ing day. Have a nice fuck-ing retirement."

"You lost your SWERT, Eddie. Failan shut you down, remember? IRS ain't the only ones lookin' at you."

"Don't believe everything you read in the paper, Balzic."

"It's the only paper in town. I have to. What choice do I have."

"There's all kindsa news, Balzic, you gonna tell me now you don't know that? There's the kind that says somethin' happened. There's the kind that says it didn't happen that way. Then there's the kind that says it never happened at all. There's all kindsa news. Lyman Dunne's been tellin' me somethin' for years and years. He says, 'Freedom of the press belongs to the guy that owns it.' So maybe the SWERT don't exist anymore. But just remember where you read that. And just remember you ain't read a word about it since. And a little birdie tells me you ain't goin' to either. See ya around, Balzic."

Balzic buried his hands in his raincoat pockets and watched Sitko hustle up to an old woman as she was struggling to get out of her rusted Chevy. She had an aluminum cane, and Sitko helped her out and led her by the elbow inside the Hose Company Social Club where the automatic voting machines were. Sitko kept commending her on her spirit and courage and citizenship; she told him that she hadn't missed an election in fifty years and she couldn't wait to vote for Angelo Bellotti because he was the best mayor Rocksburg ever had. She didn't like this Strohn fella, she said. He was just all the time runnin' down the firemen, she said, and that just wasn't right. It just wasn't right.

Two days after Christmas, at 5:35 in the evening, Balzic drove into the municipal parking lot outside Hose Company Number One and parked his cruiser in a slot farthest from the door to the firemen's social club, as though parking that far away would somehow prevent him from going inside. He stepped out into the frigid night air and the cold stung his ankles because he was wearing his thinnest black socks.

He tried to tug and shove and pull the trousers of his

rented tuxedo down, but it didn't work. The instant he let go of the cloth of each leg, the trousers rode back up again. The pants were two inches too short, and that's all there was to it. All he had to do to escape the cold was walk fast to get inside; that would have been easy to do except that he was almost sick to his stomach knowing where he was about to go and that he was already five minutes late before he'd even stepped out of the cruiser.

"Aw fuck it," he said under his breath and put his head down and jammed his hands into his raincoat pockets and buried his chin in his collar and trudged off toward the door to the social club as though he were walking through drifts of snow. There wasn't any snow. The macadam was clear except for candy and chewing gum wrappers and cigarette butts and cellophane and frozen chewing gum and bird droppings. An empty potato chip bag, partly stuck under a tire, crackled and rattled in the nippy breeze like static on a radio.

Balzic's teeth were chattering by the time he got to the front door, and with his chin still buried against his chest he almost collided with someone backing out of the social club door with an armload of trays.

"Hey. Watch where you're goin', do you mind? Huh?"

"Sorry sorry," Balzic said, and then stopped abruptly as the person turned and he saw who it was. "Oh god. You mean they actually hired you to cater this mess?"

Julie Richards stepped back with a start and then shook her head and laughed. "Oh! Mr. Balzic. It's you. I was gettin' ready to punch somebody. Well. What can I say? All I did was make the food and bring it here and set it up. I'm done. I don't have to go in there and sit down with those creeps and pretend like I'm enjoyin' it. I don't even have to stay around to serve it. I'm payin' somebody to do that."

"Uh, just between you and me, they pay you for this?"

"Half. Oh yeah. I wouldn't do it without gettin' half up front. I told 'em no way. And I cashed the check, believe me, like ten minutes after it hit my hand. I know they're gonna stiff me for the rest, but, hey, they're not the only ones know how to use the IRS. Besides, if I know they're gonna stiff me, and they know they're gonna stiff me, I can't afford to turn 'em down. 'Cause the way I figure it, it would've hurt me a lot worse for it to get around that I didn't want their business. I mean, I'm gonna get a lotta pleasure tellin' people they stiffed me. Believe me I am. I'm gonna work this for a long time. They're never gonna hear the end of it. Which makes me wonder how smart they really are. Don't you think they would've thought of that?"

"Well, they probably figure it's worth it to see you carryin' the food in."

"Like I'm their servant you mean?"

Balzic shrugged and nodded. "Just their little reminder that you gotta work for a livin'. And if they're gonna stiff you, like what're you gonna do about it, you know?"

"Well what exactly do you think they got waitin' in there for you?"

Balzic shrugged again. "You better get goin'. It's freezin' out here. Hey. Soon as the speeches are over, I'm gone. I'll sit down with 'em, I'll eat with 'em—I'll eat it 'cause you made it—and I'll say thanks for the watch, but then I'm gone. That's when the real party starts. And I hope you worked a lot harder on the food down there."

"Well after you eat down there, you can tell me how hard I worked. I'll wanna know, believe me. I think you're gonna like it. Hope so. Hope you hired a good band, 'cause after we get cleaned up, I'm gonna be dancin'. Gotta go. See you later."

He watched her lug her trays up to her panel truck and balance them against the side until she slid open the door and put them in and then get in and drive away. Then he turned and faced the door again and said to himself, "Come on, come on, suck it up, you gotta do it." He pulled open the door and forced himself to go inside.

He was struck immediately by the laughter: loud, raunchy, full of confidence. He shimmied out of his raincoat and hung it on one of the mangled hangers in the coatroom just inside the door. He stretched his neck and felt around the collar to make sure the black bow tie was still straight and then he smoothed the coat of the tux. He wished the goddamn pants

were longer. If there was one thing about clothes he couldn't
stand it was the sight of a grown man wearing pants that were
too short; he looked like he was wearing somebody's hand-me-
downs.

"He's here," somebody said in a mock whisper as the
laughter tailed off.

"It's about fuckin' time," Sitko roared, his face red and
sweaty, tie askew, collar open. He was the only one of them not
wearing a tux. Orville Householder, his spine so twisted with
age and arthritis that his neck and head craned forward like a
large scavenging bird, turned from the hips and squinted
through the smoke of his cigar at Balzic. "So he is," Householder said. "Our guest of honor."

Balzic straightened his shoulders and sucked in his gut.
He raised his chin, quickened his pace, and extended his hand,
shaking hands first with Householder and then with the others
in turn: former and soon-to-be-mayor-again Angelo Bellotti,
Councilman Egidio Figulli and soon-to-be councilman Joe Radosich, *Rocksburg Gazette* publisher Lyman Dunne, and, finally,
Sitko.

There was no one else, not even the other members of
Council. Balzic didn't know who else he'd expected to be there,
but that no one else was there caused his breathing to become
shallower. He was mentally kicking himself for coming, for ac-
cepting the invitation, because with each passing second he was
feeling more sure that the point of this dinner was to have some
fun at his expense. Royer, Stramsky, and Rascoli had all received invitations at the same time Balzic had, and they came
to him about whether they would attend. They agreed without
reservation that this party was being arranged just to needle
Balzic and they refused to show up and told him he was crazy
for even thinking about showing up. Now, as he looked around
this room big enough to seat a couple of hundred bingo play-
ers, Balzic wished, with all his heart, that he'd listened to
Royer, Stramsky, and Rascoli, and had sent his regrets as they
had. The only argument in favor of showing up—the only one
Balzic could remember—was that if he didn't show up, then
Householder and Sitko and the rest of them would do some-

thing to screw up the party Royer, Stramsky, and Rascoli were planning for themselves and Balzic at the SOI. Even that argument seemed feeble now.

"So what's your pleasure, Mario, huh?" Sitko said. He couldn't seem to stop grinning. "Beer, whiskey? How's about a little shooter to start the evening off, huh?"

"No thanks, Eddie. Too cold for beer and I don't drink whiskey anymore."

"You shittin' me or what? You don't drink whiskey? Christ, we got some of the best Irish whiskey ever made. We got Bushmills, we got Jameson, we got Jameson 1780 for crissake, we got Black Bush and you ain't gonna drink any?"

Balzic shook his head no.

"What a fuckin' doozy you are, no shit."

"So, uh, Mario," Bellotti said, clearing his throat and stepping in front of Sitko. "Where are the rest of them? Huh?"

"Rest of who?"

"The other officers. You know, Stramsky and Royer and Rascoli."

Balzic shook his head and shrugged. "I don't know. I thought they said they told you they couldn't make it."

"They might've told you they told us they weren't gonna fuckin' show up, but they didn't tell us."

"Edward?" Householder said.

"Well they didn't tell me is all I know."

"Eddie, please," Bellotti said, turning and holding up one hand in front of Sitko. He turned back to Balzic. "They're coming, right?"

Balzic shrugged. "I just told you what I know. I don't know anything else."

"Fucker told 'em not to come," Sitko said. "Didn't I tell ya that's what the fuck he'd do, huh? Youse wouldn't listen to me."

Householder shuffled up to Sitko's side and whispered something to him. Sitko flushed and turned and walked quickly to the bar and banged his shot glass down and pointed to it. A bartender Balzic didn't recognize filled Sitko's glass.

Balzic turned back to Bellotti. "You didn't do that, did

you, Mario? Huh? You wouldn't do that. I've never known you to be a petty person. You're a gentleman."

"Angelo, you know as well as I do I have no control over those guys. They retired. December first, I believe, was the effective date of their retirement. I have had no control over them since then. You're not exactly the mayor yet, but you were mayor long enough to know what I'm talkin' about. But in answer to your question, no. I did not tell them not to come."

"I think we should get started," Householder said, his voice cracking and creaking. He shuffled toward the single table set up across the back of the room near the bar. A buffet serving line was set up on another table at a right angle to that table. Two women in white jackets with chef's hats and aprons waited at each end of the buffet nearest the bar.

Balzic couldn't help noticing as Householder inched toward the table where they were going to eat that the trousers of Householder's tux came right to the line on his shoe where the heel began.

"He's lyin'," Sitko grumbled under his breath, but loud enough for everybody to hear. "Bigger'n shit."

Householder stopped his shuffle and turned from the hips and glared at Sitko. "I'm not going to tell you again," he said.

"Yeah yeah right," Sitko muttered.

"Edward? I mean it."

Sitko tried for a moment to outglare his uncle, but he couldn't bring it off.

Balzic had to admit that this little show between the decrepit Householder and his robust nephew might be enough to save the evening. Balzic had known from the moment he'd accepted the invitation that he'd have to find pleasure wherever he could in the hour or so he'd planned to stay, but he'd never imagined he would get to witness Eddie Sitko being disciplined like a child. That was worth almost all the rest of Balzic's growing discomfort. As he was directed by Bellotti to the seat just to the right of the center of the dining table, Balzic's stomach was churning so much he wondered whether he should even pretend to try to eat. He didn't want to ruin the rest of the night, no matter how much these men were going to try to ruin it for him.

After they'd all taken their seats, Balzic saw that there were indeed three other chairs and place settings as though these men had never doubted that their invitation would be refused. He was wondering, just as Lyman Dunne stood and tapped on a glass with a spoon, if Royer, Stramsky, and Rascoli had really mailed their regrets.

Balzic had never been this close to Dunne before. Not many people had. Dunne was notorious for his preoccupation with security and his own privacy. His automobiles—and he reputedly had a half a dozen, various models of Mercedes, Ferraris, Maseratis—all had the kind of windows that you couldn't see into. It was rumored that his newspaper building, inside and out, was covered by almost as many surveillance cameras as the county jail, despite the fact that Dunne was known to rarely spend more than a few hours in the building in any given week.

Balzic's idea was that if you really wanted to travel incognito, you'd do what any self-respecting undercover cop would do: you'd dress like a sparrow and you'd drive a starling of a car, a gray Chevy or a tan Ford, or a pale blue Dodge with four doors and two weeks' worth of road dirt. You wouldn't drive a car that was practically screaming, like a blue jay, hey, look over here, look over here! I got so much money I drive this car, redder than any cardinal you ever saw, but don't you dare think you recognize me, 'cause I'm richer than you ever thought about bein' and I just want you to envy me but I sure don't want you comin' near me. Would Dunne think like that? Balzic thought. Nah. Who the hell knows how he thinks.

Dunne had been talking for almost a minute before his words broke through into Balzic's consciousness. From the first sound Dunne uttered, Balzic didn't want to believe what he was hearing. Dunne was standing there, tall, with his silvery-blond hair and in a tux that looked like it had been painted on him, and was telling the oldest joke about cops that had ever been told.

". . . so when Officer Derzepelski found himself on Pennsylvania Avenue with this corpse at his feet, he did the only thing he could do. He dragged the corpse around the corner to Main Street because he knew when it came time to fill out his report that he couldn't spell Pennsylvania."

The rush of adrenaline fired through Balzic so that he never heard the laughter. He didn't know whether he heard anything for the next ten seconds or not. He could see Dunne laughing, he could see Sitko laughing. He could see all of them laughing. But he couldn't hear any of them laughing. The pulses in front of his ears were slamming and banging like drums.

He stood up carefully so as not to disturb anything and started walking slowly toward the front door, berating himself at every step for his pigheadedness about believing that it had been the right thing to do, the courteous thing to do, the courageous thing to do, to come here.

They were laughing and calling after him. "What's wrong with him?" Dunne said, and it sounded to Balzic as though the man was actually sincere, that he had no idea what kind of joke he'd just told. Oh bullshit, Balzic thought. Forget that. He knows exactly what kind of joke he told.

Then Eddie Sitko was in front of him. Sitko's face was split with laughter and red and sweaty and he had his hands on Balzic's arms.

"What the fuck's wrong with you, you can't take a joke? Huh? Where you goin' anyway, ya fuck? Huh? You didn't even get your watch yet."

"Get your hands off me."

"Hey, that joke was about a Polack cop, whatta you gettin' so pissed off about? You ain't a Polack."

"Don't give me that Polack shit. That joke was about cops. You bastards think you can tell a joke about a cop and it's okay because you make him a Polack? It ain't okay. It wasn't okay the first time some smart-mouth fuck told the joke—like about a thousand years ago. That's the oldest fuckin' joke anybody ever tells about cops and I ain't gonna sit here and listen to it. And I ain't gonna tell you again, get your fuckin' hands off me."

"Ouuu, ouuu, what'sa matter, Balzic, huh? C'mon, c'mon, you can tell me. I'm your ol' buddy, remember? We go way back, Muddio, huh? We go back, you and me, since forever, Muddio. Huh?"

"You so drunk you don't know I ain't drunk? Huh? Get your fuckin' hands off me, I'm not gonna tell ya again."

Balzic could feel them gathering behind him. He'd never heard them coming, his pulses were still hammering in his ears and his heart was jumping and his breaths were coming in bursts, but he knew they were there.

He jerked his arms free from Sitko's grip and stepped around him. Sitko staggered and caught Balzic's arm, as much to keep from losing his balance as to stop Balzic. Balzic jerked that arm free and found himself facing all of them except for Householder, who was shuffling toward them but had covered only half the distance from the table to where they were standing now outside the coatroom.

Balzic felt like he was choking. He was desperately trying to slow his breathing. He tried to speak several times. Sitko started to mimic him, to mock his sounds.

Finally Balzic blurted it out. "You won," he said, nodding his head so many times in succession that he got dizzy. "You won. But that ain't enough. You gotta rub my face in it. I come here . . . I come here 'cause . . . 'cause I don't want anybody to say I didn't . . . that I didn't have the courtesy to show up after . . . after I said I would. Or that I didn't have the guts. But I'll be goddamned if I'm gonna sit here and listen to that joke."

"My god, man, it's just a joke," Dunne said, smiling and looking around at the others. "Where's your sense of humor? If we lose our sense of humor, where are we? Someone said once, man is the only animal that laughs. We have to laugh, Chief. That's all I was trying to do, make everybody laugh, so what's the problem?"

Balzic thought that if there was ever any truth to the idea that somebody's blood could be boiling, he was certain his was. He thought his body was going to explode. He felt his mouth working but no words were coming out for what seemed to him a lifetime. He knew it was only seconds but it seemed to go on and on and on. Then he heard himself talking again.

"You used me. You used me and people like me, cops, other cops, Polish, Italian, what difference does it make, all we are to you is white niggers, that's all we are. You use us to enforce your laws for ya. To protect you. To protect your property. Then when you're done with me, with us, you tell me jokes to my face about how stupid we are? And then you wanna know where's my sense of humor? And you think I'm gonna sit here and laugh? What? What? Was that supposed to be some kinda icebreaker, huh? Make me feel comfortable? Make me feel like I'm one of the boys, huh?

"In a pig's ass I'm one of the boys. I found out about six months ago just how big a schnook I was for you guys. A detective, a guy with a high school education, he explains to me how you guys work it, how you use the IRS, how you don't pay for nothin'! You don't pay no fuckin' taxes! You got the game rigged."

"You sayin' I don't pay taxes?" Figulli said, stepping forward, his lower jaw jutting out. "You lost your mind, Balzic. You're crazier'n shit."

"You? Ha! Figulli, you're as big a schnook as I am. You too, Angelo. Radio. You think these guys are your buddies? Huh? These three? You think they're your pals? They're usin' you just like they used me. Like they use everybody! They're rakin' the game. All they need you for is to make sure everybody pays taxes. That's all you are. You're their tax collectors. You sweep the streets, you pay the cops, me. But these guys don't pay taxes! They get what they want—whenever they want it—and they use that to dodge taxes—'cause the fuckin' IRS says it's okay! You don't believe me, try readin' Section 501 of the IRS Code, you'll see what I'm talkin' about."

"I think the festivities have come to a conclusion," Householder said, shuffling by Balzic on his way to get his coat. He made a great show of reaching into his pocket and dropping something on the floor with a resounding clatter.

Balzic looked down in spite of himself. He was sure he knew what it was, but he couldn't bring himself to not look.

He was right. It was a gold pocket watch. Balzic bent over and picked it up. On the back was printed: "Mario Balzic. Fidelis Ad Urnam."

"How's your Latin, Chief?" Lyman Dunne said, smiling.

"Doesn't matter," Householder said from in the coatroom. "Doesn't apply anymore anyway."

"*Fidelis* is faithful, I know that much," Balzic said, going into the coatroom to get his own coat. He bumped into Householder and knocked him back a step. "Excuse me," Balzic said. "You all right?"

Householder scowled at him and huffed, "Course I'm all right. Watch where you're going. I knew this wasn't going to be amusing. I knew you wouldn't play along. A little knowledge is a dangerous thing, Chief. You ever heard that? It's not nearly as dangerous as a little power. That's what you had. And a little power gives people like you all kinds of ideas, doesn't it? About who you are and what you can do? Nothing but presumptions, believe me. Nothing but presumptions. And now, of course, you don't even have those anymore. Now all you've got is a watch. Broken, I hope. At least I hope it wasn't made by the Japanese. Good night."

"Good night, Mr. Householder," Balzic said. "Thanks for the watch."

"Go to hell," Householder said out of the side of his mouth.

"Nossir. Where I'm goin' is to a party." For the first time since he was sitting at the table, listening to Lyman Dunne retell that rotten old chestnut, Balzic felt his heart slowing down.

When he looked back at Householder, it appeared to him that Householder was already putting the whole thing out of his mind, that the last ten minutes had been nothing but an annoying trifle in his day, not even as irritating as discovering that he'd nicked himself shaving. Householder hadn't shuffled two yards from Balzic, and yet Balzic knew from that shuffle, from that hunched-over gait like a tall, spindly bird, that Householder was already moving on, in his mind if not in his body, to something else he might find amusing.

Balzic grabbed his raincoat and left without another word,

without another look back. He had the watch in hand and kept repeating to himself, "*Fidelis ad urnam, fidelis ad urnam*. Got to ask Valcanas what the hell that means."

He knew better than to try to find a parking space near the Sons of Italy, so he left his cruiser in the lot by Hose Company Number One. It was only a couple of blocks to the SOI and he needed the walk to breathe, to suck in the stinging cold air, to make his body deal with something besides fury and fear. *Fidelis ad urnam,* he kept thinking, what the hell is *fidelis ad urnam*? Well, if Mo Valcanas wasn't there, or if he was too drunk to remember, then Father Marrazzo would know. Somebody would know. Hell, Ruth took Latin in high school, maybe she'll remember something. *Fidelis* is faithful, that's what it is, it's faithful. Marine Corps motto is *Semper fidelis,* always faithful, hell, I got the *fidelis* part. Wait a minute. If those bastards were gonna give me a watch with Latin printed on it . . . those sonsabitches. It was another fuckin' joke, another chance to ask me if I don't get it, another way to make me look stupid. Doesn't matter faithful to what. Those sonsabitches . . .

He could hear the giddy rumblings of the party half a block away, the sound spilling toward him through the icy air. He picked up his pace. People were coming from every direction, from both sides of the street, some he recognized by name, others by face alone, most he'd never seen before. There seemed to be lots of greens and reds around their faces, scarves and ties, and a woman turning into the alcove of the SOI just ahead of him wore a bright red coat, and he felt something lifting in him. She was fat and had a wart on her cheek, but when she saw Balzic she smiled at him and he thought he was going to cry.

God I'm such an emotional geek. I see a woman's coat and she smiles at me and it's all I can do to stop the tear motors from turnin' on.

He slid and shuffled and sidestepped through and around people near and in the coatroom, some of them shaking his hand, others patting him on the back, on the arm, some he knew, most he did not. The music was loud, but it was a recording, and it was so noisy he barely recognized the song as being "White Christmas." He hoped nothing had gone wrong about hiring a band, he hoped they hadn't had to resort to hiring a disc jockey. He finally got out of his raincoat, but, looking at the pile of coats on the table in the center of the coatroom, he knew he'd be going home with somebody else's coat. What the hell, he thought, and threw his coat on the pile.

He was stopped three times before he got out of the coatroom by people who wanted to shake hands, and four more times before he got to the bar. He kept scanning the crowd for Ruth, for Marie or Emily, for Valcanas, for Stramsky, Royer, and Rascoli and their wives, but he couldn't move more than a step or two before somebody was stopping him and telling him how they were going to miss him and Rocksburg wouldn't be the same without him, and he heard himself repeating, "Hey, I'm just retirin', you know? I'm not croakin' out."

"Yeah, yeah, you'll get your pension, you'll sell the house, you'll be in Florida the end of January."

When he finally got to the bar and squeezed between two women, one of them squealed at him and punched him in the arm. "Muddio, you sweet thing, gimme a kiss, c'mon, c'mon, plant one on me," said the one on his right with her face scrunched up in a pucker and her eyes closed. He didn't recognize anything about her until she opened her eyes and said, "Well! How long do I have to wait?" Then he saw something familiar about her, but he didn't know what it was and he certainly couldn't put a name with the face.

"Oh, hey, yeah, it's you, uh—"

"Oh brother—'yeah, it's you, ugggh.' What, the cat got your brain or somethin'? Mary Rose Cibik for cryin' out loud, you don't remember me? If you don't remember me I'm gonna kill ya." She threw back her head and stuck out her tongue and growled a giggle. "In high school, remember? After the football games, huh?" She jabbed her thick elbow into his side.

"Hey, Mary Rose, I don't wanna say nothin', but you don't look the same as you looked then." He was lying; he couldn't remember what she'd looked like then.

"Well that's 'cause you're lookin' at my face, honey buns."

"Sorry, but your face is all I can see." He cleared his throat and looked around. "Man, sure are a lotta people here."

"Yeah," the woman on his left said. "I was just tellin' Mary Rose, I was just sayin', if they let one more person in here, nobody's gonna be able to pee without gettin' somebody else wet."

"So, Muddio," Mary Rose said, "so I used to weigh about fifty pounds less, give or take ten pounds, so? So use your imagination. Christ, don't you got any imagination? Huh?" She struggled to lean around him and said to the woman on Balzic's left, "God, my lips used to get blisters and he can't even remember."

"He can't remember what?" Ruth said, from somewhere near Balzic's right shoulder. She was grinning and her eyes were indecent with mischief.

"Mary Rose, this is my wife. Ruth, this is Mary Rose Cibik. Apparently we went to high school together and apparently she got a better memory than I do—for certain events."

"For certain events?" Mary Rose squirmed around to try to get a look at Ruth. She gave up with a wave and said over her shoulder, "This chooch used to give me hickeys the size of quarters. Honey, I hope he got a better memory for what he did with you than what he did with me."

"What else did he do?" Ruth said, her eyes growing more mischievous.

"You don't really wanna know that, Ruth, do ya? Huh? Where's Mo? You seen Mo? Where's Marie? Where's Emily? They come with you? How'd you get here? They bring you?"

"Hey, Mrs. B.," Mary Rose said, giggling in the back of her throat again, "I don't think your old man wants to talk about what else did he do, whatta you think, huh?"

"I think you're right."

"Hey, there's Mo. Where you sittin', huh? You got a table?"

"Of course we have a table. We're up front, you know? You and I are among the guests of honor, remember?"

"Memory's the first thing to go, honey, better get used to

it," Mary Rose said. "My old man can't find the bathroom. Every morning's an adventure, believe me."

"Well real nice talkin' to you, Mary Rose," Balzic said, patting her on the shoulder and turning and trying to sidle away from them. He'd caught sight of Mo Valcanas at the other end of the bar, but he was momentarily trapped by two old men shouting into each other's ear.

"Oh bullshit it was real nice talkin' to me," Mary Rose said, laughing until she was shaking. When Ruth squeezed in next to her, she said, "So tell me. What kinda guy he turn out to be?"

"You first," Ruth said. "You tell me what else he did and I'll tell you how he turned out."

Balzic was cringing and wincing and shaking his head no no no, don't be askin' questions like that, but Ruth was having too much fun teasing him, so he pinned his arms to his sides and shouldered between the two old men and into the crowd in the general direction of Valcanas.

The going was better near the dance floor; it was easier to walk through the dancers than through the crowd three deep near the bar.

The air was heavy with smoke, the music was thumping with something that now sounded like Elvis Presley, Balzic wasn't sure because mostly all he heard was the bass. He was sweating by the time he got to Valcanas's side. It was only when he was within two or three steps of Valcanas that Balzic saw his daughters seated at the bar in front of and on either side of Valcanas. As he pushed toward them, Valcanas backed away and let Balzic snuggle between his daughters. He hugged and kissed them both. "Hey, I'm really glad to see you two, I really am. Really glad you could make it."

"My god, Daddy, did you think for a second we wouldn't?"

"You think we'd miss this?" Marie said. "The only time I think there were ever more people in this place was after Grandma died."

"Don't remind me," Balzic said, his eyes instantly filling up. He couldn't remember a time in his life when he'd gone through more different emotions in a shorter time than in the last fifteen minutes.

He struggled to reach around behind him and caught Valcanas's sleeve and followed it down until he reached his hand and then shook it. "Glad you're here, Greek. Thanks for comin'."

"For ten bucks? You kiddin'? Open bar and buffet? The Polka Brothers? This may be the party bargain of the decade."

"The Polka Brothers?" Balzic said, giggling goofily. "That's a joke, right? You're jaggin' me."

"Uh-uh. I'm just tellin' you what Stramsky told me."

"Those lyin' bastards. They told me—Stramsky swore to me they were gonna get Chismo Charles and the Mystic Knights of the Sea, Robbie Klein and those guys. Those lyin' bastards. I shoulda never let Stramsky do it, that bastard. I knew I shoulda done it myself. Man, I'da got Glenn Pavone. Maybe even Kenny Blake. I knew I shoulda done it."

"Done what, Daddy?" Emily said.

"Hired the band, sweet pea. Never trust a Polack to hire a band. The Polka Brothers, Cheezus Kee-rist."

"What?" Emily shouted. "I can't hear you."

"I can't hear you either," Balzic shouted back. "Ain't it great?"

"Hey Mario, where's your glass?" somebody was shouting at him from behind the bar.

"Don't have one," he shouted back. "Gimme one. Put some good stuff in it." He shuffled and squirmed around and found himself separated from Valcanas by a short person who was struggling to get to the bar. Balzic shouted over the short person's head, "Hey, Panagios, how's your Latin?"

"How's my what?"

"Your Latin, your Latin. You remember any Latin?"

Valcanas shrugged, or started to. He had his glass of gin hoisted almost to ear level and he managed to stop the shrug at its highest point in order to stop spilling more gin on himself. A few drops did slosh on his lapel. He eased his shoulders back down. "You wanna know something in Latin?"

"Yeah. What's *fidelis ad urnam* mean?"

"*Fidelis* what? *Fidelis ad* what?" He was cupping his free hand behind his ear.

"*Urnam. Ur-nam. Fi-de-lis ad ur-nam.*"

"Oh. That's 'faithful unto the urn.'"

"Faithful unto the what?"

"Unto the urn."

"What the hell's that mean?"

"Means faithful to the end. Faithful until you die. Until your ashes go into the urn."

"I knew it," Balzic said to himself. Valcanas asked him what he'd said, but Balzic shouted, "Nothing, nothing. Where's Stramsky? Royer? You know?"

Valcanas nodded in the general direction of the wall opposite the bar. "That's where you're supposed to sit. Maybe they're there."

Balzic told his daughters where he was going and tried to make his way back across the dance floor to see if he could spot Stramsky or Royer or Rascoli. At every step, somebody was trying to shake his hand or pat him on the back or the shoulders, old women were trying to kiss him, somebody put a glass full of coppery-colored liquid in his hand, which he gave to somebody else after he'd smelled that it was bourbon, and he'd almost made it across the dance floor before Ruth caught up with him. "Mary Rose Cibik, huh?" she said after she'd pulled his ear down to the level of her mouth.

He snorted. "Oh, c'mon. I don't know her from Barbara Bush."

"Oh yeah? She said she has pictures. If you don't dance with me, I'm gonna go back and ask her to show 'em to me."

"Oh Ruthie, that's low. That really is. To get me to dance?"

"Hey, what I figure is, by the time our kids get married we'll both be in wheelchairs, so it's now or never, big boy." She slid her left hand around his waist and slipped her right into his left before he could flee. He had no place to run anyway. The dance floor was shoulder-to-shoulder with so many people filled with so much congeniality and holiday cheer that the only way Balzic could've blasted out of there was with a tear-gas grenade. "This is about as painless as it's ever gonna get," she shouted into his neck.

He sighed and said to the top of her head, "What the hell. Go 'head. You lead."

"Mario, for god's sake, all you have to do is stand here. All the rest of these people'll do the work for ya."

"Hey there's Stramsky. I gotta talk to him."

"Oh nothin' doin', you're not gettin' off that easy. You wanna talk to him, you call him over here. Now that I got ya, you're stickin' with me, big boy."

"STRAMSKY! STRAMMMM-SKEEEE!"

Stramsky worked his way through the crowd, drinks aloft in both hands. His face was sweaty, flushed with excitement.

"Hey, Mario, is this a party or what?" he shouted.

"Yeah yeah yeah, never mind. You told me you were gonna get Chismo Charles and the Mystic Knights of the Sea. What's this crap about the Polka Brothers?"

"I tried to get them guys. I tried to get who you wanted. I did, no shit. Excuse me, Ruth. But I couldn't get 'em. Hey, the Polka Brothers know some blues. No shit. Excuse me, Ruth. Yeah. They been practicin'. Honest."

"'The Polka Brothers know some blues,' is that what you said? You lyin' bastard, you're gettin' a commission, ain't ya? Tell the truth."

"Nah-uh. Mario, my cousins ain't the Polka Brothers any-more. They ain't even *in* the Polka Brothers. I'm not gettin' nothing outta this. These guys tonight? There ain't an original Polka Brother in the band, no shit. Excuse me, Ruth. My cousins sold 'em the name and everything. Sold 'em their truck, everything. Sold 'em all their old bowlin' shirts too." Stramsky thought that was hilarious. Before Balzic could say another word, Stramsky wriggled his shoulders around and, drinks still aloft, disappeared into the crowd.

"That lyin' bastard," Balzic said.

"What? I can't hear you."

"Never mind. Are we still dancin'?"

"Yes."

He leaned down close to her ear and said, "The only way

your grin could get any bigger would be with surgical instruments. You think you got me, but I don't even know what we're dancin' to. I can't hear nothin'. What're we dancin' to?"

"Who cares?" She buried her cheek into his neck again.

Suddenly somebody turned up the volume; suddenly the music was recognizable.

"Jesus Christ, that's Jerry Vale," Balzic said. "That's 'Two Purple Shadows in the Snow' for crissake."

A grizzled, wizened man with a green tie with little red reindeer all over it pulled his face away from his dancing partner's cheek and, grinning up at Balzic, said, "Ain't it wonderful. Them old songs? Huh?"

"Yeah," Balzic said, trying to grin back. "It's wonderful. This is the only place in town where you can still hear stuff like that."

"What?" the man and the woman both said.

Balzic put on his best smile and said, "I hate Jerry Vale. I especially hate 'Two Purple Shadows in the Snow.'"

"Oh so do we," the woman said.

Balzic felt sharp pain on his instep. "Man, this is murder out here. Somebody's got their heel dug into my foot."

"Me. I'm the somebody," Ruth said. "These people—"

"What?"

She pulled his head down and put her mouth against his ear. "That's me standin' on your foot."

"What? What're you doin' that for?"

"'Cause you're bein' a smart-ass. I don't even want to know how it went at the other place, but these people here aren't the same people who were up there. So you stop bein' a smart-ass right now."

"I wasn't bein' a smart-ass—"

"Baloney. You put that phony smile on and then you say you hate Jerry Vale? 'Cause you know they can't hear you? That's bein' a smart-ass. Quit it. Right now. These people're havin' a good time. And they want you to have a good time. And so do I. So knock it off. I'm serious, Mar."

"Okay okay. You can get off my foot now, Jesus."

"Testing," someone said over the PA system after Jerry

Vale's voice growled down. "Testing, one two, testing. The food is now bein' served. The buffet is open. Go on both sides of the table. The food lines are now open. Please go on both sides of the table. Hey, Joe, you think they heard me? I can never tell when there's this many people . . ."

"We heard you, we heard you!" dozens of people shouted back.

"Okay okay," the speaker said. "Would youse all let the honored guests go first, please? That would be, uh, Chief and Mrs. Mario Balzic—"

There came much applause and cheering. It went on so long that Balzic was embarrassed and started waving his hands downward, thinking that would make them stop. They ignored him.

"Okay, okay," the person at the microphone said, "if younz don't hold it down, I mean, I know there's lots of friends and relatives here, but everybody got friends and relatives here, you know what I'm sayin'? So if younz could just wait until I said who was all the honored guests—oh what the hell, everybody knows who they are. The honored guests know who you are, they know who they are, right? Just go to the front of the line right now, that's all. Huh? Oh wait. What? He wants me to announce it? Hey, I didn't apply for this job, you know? Cut me a break here. What? He says I gotta announce it. Okay, okay, I'll announce it."

The speaker cleared his throat. Balzic still couldn't see who it was.

"So the honored guests are—I already done the Balzics, right? Okay. So, in alphabetical order—no, it ain't gonna be in alphabetical order. So after Chief and Mrs. Balzic comes Sgt. and Mrs. Vic Stramsky"—another round of applause and cheering—"yeah, okay, hold it down, hold it down. And then we have Sgt. and Mrs. William Rascoli"—wild cheering and stomping of feet from Rascoli's many relatives—"and this is what I'm 'sposed to announce here, so listen up. Last but not least, Sgt. and Mrs. Joseph Royanawicz."

There was a nervous smattering of applause and a couple

of wild and wildly inappropriate cheers, people cheering before they knew what they were cheering about.

"Uh, that's what it says here, folks, uh, ladies and gentlemen, the guy you all know by the name Joe Royer wants you to all know that he has picked this night, this time, to, lemme see here, I wrote this down here so I wouldn't screw it up, uh, that's the problem. It's my writin', no wonder I can't read it. Okay okay, here we go, uh, he picked this night to, ah! Here it is. Sergeant Joseph Royer, the man younz all know by that name, he picked this time, when he is with all his family and friends, to reclaim the name his father changed because other people made him ashamed of what he was. He hopes younz will all join with him in celebrating the occasion of his second baptism. That's what it says, folks. So whatta you say? Let's hear it for—"

The rest of what he said was lost because the hall erupted, most of the people applauding and shouting their approval, but many other were applauding politely, and others, brows raising, lips pursing, were silent. More than a few people were shaking their heads and muttering.

Balzic felt himself going goggle-eyed as he looked down at Ruth. "I've known that sonofabitch for thirty years. Longer. He never said a word about it."

"I think it's great," Ruth said. "Took a lotta guts, that's all I can say. A lotta guts. C'mon, let's get in line, I'm starvin'."

When they reached the beginning of the buffet table, Stramsky squeezed in beside Balzic and said, "See, Mario, that's why I had to get the Polka Brothers. You understand? Huh?"

"Yeah yeah—whatta am I sayin' yeah for? I don't understand. How long you known about this?"

"That he was goin' back to the family name? Long time. We been talkin' about it a long time. Couple years. He didn't wanna just go in the courthouse and get it changed, you know. He wanted to make an announcement. I said, hey, what better place? So there ya are. Oh, but one thing I wanna tell ya."

"Yeah? What?"

Stramsky leaned closer still. "Watch out for Rascoli. He's half shitface already and he's kissin' everybody. He kissed me three times already, the last time right on the lips. So, hey, don't say I didn't warn ya."

"I'm warned," Balzic said, throwing back his head and laughing. "I'm warned."

"Watch out for Ruthie. He stuck his tongue halfway down my wife's throat, I'm tellin' ya. Oh, and one more thing, Mario."

"Yeah, what's that?"

"Before I get shitface myself, I just wanna tell ya. I'm glad I know ya. I'm proud I served with ya. I'll never forget ya." Stramsky dropped his head and reached up suddenly and wiped his nose with the sleeve of his tux.

Balzic threw the only arm he could get free around Stramsky's shoulder. "Hey, Vic, I'm glad I know you too. The same goes for me. Everything you said. I mean it . . ." Balzic had to turn away. When he turned back he said, "What the hell, you gotta wipe your nose with your tux. It's so goddamn crowded in here you can't get your hand in your pocket to get your hanky."

It took them five minutes to get through the buffet. There were three different kinds of pasta, penne, rigatoni, and cheese tortellini, and three different sauces, marinara with basil, marinara Bolognese, and Alfredo; halupki stuffed with pork and beef in tomato sauce and halupki stuffed with rice and mushrooms in sauerkraut with crushed tomatoes; four kinds of pirogis, potato, potato and cheese, prune, and sauerkraut; tossed salad with several different olive oils and vinegars and three prepared dressings; and Italian, sourdough, and black rye bread. Near the end of the table were bowls filled with a half dozen different kinds of olives surrounded by platters of thin cuts of salami, prosciutto, and cappicola. At the very end of the table were three heaping platters of kolbassis, each made by a different local butcher, as announced by a little card behind each platter.

Julie Richards was waiting at the end of the line. She beamed as Balzic congratulated her on the spread. "Better'n roast beef and baked potatoes with sour cream and chives, huh?"

"I don't understand," Balzic said.

"Didn't you eat up at the other place?"

Balzic shook his head. "Never got past the first joke."

"Well that's what they're havin'. Real original, huh? Hey, that's what they ordered. Myself, I think this is a lot more interesting."

"You make all the pirogis too?" Ruth said.

"Oh god no. I ordered eight hundred, two hundred of each, god-oh-mighty, no. The ladies at the Polish White Eagles make 'em. All I make is the sauces, everything else I get from my subcontractors. But Stramsky's gonna be upset 'cause he said be sure to have halushky and I couldn't get anybody to make it."

"You had them. I got one of each, see?" Balzic said.

"No no, not halupki. Halushky. Potato dumplings. Course it depends on who you talk to. Some people say 'haluski' and they mean cabbage and noodles, and some people say that and they mean potato dumplings and if you're not careful you can get into a lotta trouble with how people say the different words—especially if you're not Polish or Russian or Slovak. First time I heard about 'halushky' I got it mixed up with cabbage and mashed potatoes, and I said, oh, that's colcannon, that's Irish. Man, did I get into trouble with that. But everybody thinks theirs is the best. I'll get ten stories tonight about how I shoulda made the pirogis and nobody'll say boo about my sauces."

As they were walking to their table, Balzic asked Ruth, "Did you hear all that? I lost her after the Irish thing."

"I heard her. It was interesting. I'm glad I asked. People always think they're so different. But we're all so much alike. What's the difference, really, between pirogi and ravioli?"

"What's the difference between pirogi and ravioli, is that what you said?" Royer's eyes were bulging. "Are you nuts?" Royer—Royanawicz—and his wife were sitting down beside Ruth.

"We're all alike, huh?" Balzic said to Ruth. He put his plate down and stepped back around Ruth to shake hands with Royer—Royanawicz.

"Ruthie says what's the difference between pirogi and ravioli, is that what she said?" Royanawicz said, brushing aside Balzic's hand and embracing him. When he pulled away, his eyes were full of tears. So were Balzic's.

"She tryin' to say we're all alike? Huh? Is that what she's tryin' to say? Forget it. Lemme tell you somethin'. Ruth? You listenin'? The difference between pirogi and ravioli is the difference between Royer and Royanawicz. You think it isn't? Huh? Listen. I got three sisters. All of 'em married. They changed their names a long time ago. That's what women do, right? Or they used to anyway, you never know these days. So two of 'em, the youngest ones, they haven't said a word to me since I told 'em what I was gonna do about gettin' our dad's name back. So I look like the same guy, right? Pirogi looks like a ravioli, right? Try tellin' that to my sisters. Oh-oh, watch yourself, here comes Ras."

"What?" Before Balzic could escape, Rascoli had spun him around and was crushing him in a hug and kissing him on the lips.

"Muddio, Muddio, paisan, I love you, you know that? Huh? I love you." Rascoli's eyes were far, far away behind a veil of wine and tears. "I shoulda told you what was goin' on, no shit, I know I shoulda told you, that Yesho, that stupid prick, I trieda tell him don't do that stupid shit, commandoes, fuckin' 'round with Sitko and them jerks, you think he would listen to me? Huh? No, uh-uh, he wouldn't listen to me, but I shoulda tol' you anyway. I love you, Muddio, I'm real sorry I didn't tell you, Muddio—Roooou-theee! Cheee-zus Christ, you're be-ouuu-ti-ful, you way too good-lookin' for this guy, lemme gi' you kiss, c'mon, c'mon, stand up, Ruth-eee. Man, Muddio, you lucky somnavabitch, she's way too good-lookin' for you. She needs a guy, you know, like me, full-blooded 'talian like me, you know? All due respeck, Muddio, you ain't got the true 'talian, uh, what's the word . . . what's the word. Oh. Genes! Tha's what I'm tryin' say. Genes. You ain't got 'em. Whooo-eee'm I drunk. Where's the can? I needa pee. Bad."

Rascoli swung around and swooped and swerved and swirled his way to the men's room.

"Least he knows where that is," Balzic said. "Man. How long's he been partyin'?"

"Oh hell," Royanawicz said, "he was lit up yesterday morning. He was drunk when I called him yesterday."

Balzic shook his head and sat down, anxious to eat. "He's been drunk since yesterday and I still haven't had anything to drink yet."

"Well here, take this wine. Gerry don't like it. It's too sour for her, she likes somethin' a little sweeter. Riunite, Lambrusco, somethin' like that."

"Riunite makes Lambrusco, hon," Gerry said. "Ruth, hiya doin'? I haven't seen you since last summer, my god."

"Hey I don't wanna take your wine—what is it?" Balzic took a sip of the white wine Royanawicz had handed him behind Ruth's head. "Oh, man, you don't like this? This is great. Great chardonnay. Wonder who sprung for this?"

"Yeah, when was it? Fourth of July, I'll bet. FOP picnic, must've been," Ruth said. "So how're you holdin' up with the new name? Geez, I was just thinking of all the things you'd have to do, the phone company, the post office, the DMV, the banks, credit cards—that's not simple."

"Oh believe me, that part's easy," Gerry said. "It's his sisters that're makin' it hard. My maiden name was Krevochuko, so it's no big deal for me. Anyway, I always knew he was a Polack, he couldn't fool me. I mean, I was a little confused with the Episcopalian business right at the start, but I told him, hey, kids? We have kids, they're Catholic, forget this Episcopalian stuff. So we didn't have any kids anyway. So? So what? If it makes him happy?" She shrugged until her shoulders made her many-layered earrings jingle. "And you're wrong, Joseph. Ruth's right. Raviolis're nothin' but dago pirogies. Excuse my language, Ruth. Just don't try to tell his sisters that."

Jerry Vale's voice growled up again and picked up "Two Purple Shadows in the Snow" where it had been interrupted for the food announcement. Balzic dropped his silverware, threw down his napkin, and stood.

"Where you goin'?" Ruth said.

"Hey, I'm not gonna listen to that, I'm trying to eat here."

"Forget about it, Mario," Royanawicz said. "I saw Dom Muscotti pumpin' about ten bucks in the jukebox. He was so excited, he was goin' 'Ouu, boy, Jerry Vale, Dean Martin, Bing Crosby.' We're gonna get a bellyful of 'White Christmas' and 'Easter Parade,' believe me."

"Well I already got a bellyful of 'Two Purple Shadows in the Snow.'"

"Mar, sit down, please? I want to hear about Joe's name."

"You wanna hear about his name? I thought we already heard about his name," Balzic said, making faces about the music, mimicking the words before he sat again.

"What about my name?"

"Oh god, Ruth, don't get him started."

"Well, lots of people changed their names after they got here, but I don't think I ever heard of anybody changing back, especially not their kids. Did you, Mar?"

"First faithful unto the urn, then 'Two Purple Shadows in the Snow.' Man. What did you say? Huh?"

"So why'd you do it? I mean, what gave you the idea?"

"Man are these halupkis good. You guys try 'em yet?" Royanawicz said. "You serious? You really wanna know about my name?"

"You'll be sorry," Gerry said. "These halupkis *are* good. I like the ones made in sauerkraut better. I don't eat much red meat anymore, gotta watch my cholesterol."

"Well it started when my mother was dyin', in the hospital, you know. One day we just happened to all be there together, all my sisters. Gerry was there too, but my brothers-in-law, they weren't there. So my mother starts tellin' us about how it was when she married our dad. So everybody's thinkin', you know, she's just reminiscin', you know, or maybe she's out of her head, who knows? And the next thing she's sayin' is, like, I'm goin' holy Christ, what is this?! She goes, 'Our name's not really Royer.' And I'm the only one payin' attention. And she just blew my head apart with this incredible story about how my father got sick and tired of takin' all this crap about bein' a stupid Polack, you know, the dumb hunky syndrome, so he's walkin' down the street one day and he looks up at this sign on this building, right on Main Street, and that's how we got our name. From Royer's department store. The one that closed about twenty years ago? Sign's still on the building. So, I'm lookin' at her and I'm goin', 'Whoa, wait a second. You tellin' me our name isn't Royer?' And she goes, 'Yes, right, that's right. Our name is not Royer.' So I go, 'So when'd this happen?' And she goes, 'Before any of youse were born.' And I go, 'So what's our name?' You know, I'm goin' crazy, I'm thinkin' all my life my name's Royer, my father came over here from England. So when she tells me what our name really is, when she said Royanawicz, honest to god, it was like somebody kicked me in my chest, 'cause all I could think of was all the dumb Polack jokes I told in my life. I almost passed out, yeah. Almost fainted. I looked around at my sisters, two of 'em didn't even hear her, and the other one, Mary Frances, she's goin', 'Oh, she doesn't know what she's talkin' about, she's delirious or somethin'.' Then my mother nods off, you know. Which she was doin' then, awake, asleep, you know, she'd nod off right in the middle of sayin' somethin'. I didn't get anything more out of her until the next day. And she tells me the same thing all over again. She tells me check immigration and the Army and the union. So after she died, that's what I did. But I wasn't even sure when he came over. We're talkin' turn of the century here."

Balzic leaned close to Ruth and said, "I hope you're gettin' all this, 'cause I'm only hearin' about every other word."

"I can hear him, I can. I'm gettin' it all. It's some story, believe me. So, Joe, go 'head."

"Oh god, it was like he's obsessed, you know?" Gerry said, leaning forward to talk around her husband. "Every day he's off, weekends, my god, we're on the trail. I'm thinkin', one day I'm gonna look at him, he's gonna have ears hangin' down to here, you know, and his nose is gonna be black and wet and I'm gonna be married to a bloodhound."

"Hey, lemme tell you, Ruth, honest to god, it was the first real police work I did in about fifteen years. It was exciting. We were in D.C. goin' through the Laborers International Union archives, we were in Immigration, then we were in the military archives in Harrisburg—my father was in World War One, you know? Hey, we tracked him down every place. And every place, it was there. Joseph Royanawicz, immigration, union, Army. Born 1890 in Czestochowa, Poland, came here in 1908, joined the Laborers in 1910, enlisted in the Army in 1917, discharged 1918, married 1919 in—get this, St. Stanislaus Church in Pittsburgh. This guy who later on turns into a goddamn Episcopalian, he gets married in a Polish Catholic church in Pittsburgh. We go there, and there it is, bigger'n hell, right in the records in the cellar. Joseph Royanawicz marries Mary Stepanowski on August the first 1919. Then along comes three daughters, boom boom boom, 1921, 1924, 1928, and on June third 1930 Joseph Royer Junior is born to Joseph Royer Senior and Mary—get this now—Mary Stephans—not Stepanowski—Stephans, Mary Stephans Royer in Conemaugh General Hospital. I'm the first one in my family born in a hospital. That's the names on my birth certificate. I never paid attention to that before. All it says on my sisters' birth certificates is 'Mary S.,' no maiden name for her, for my mother. 'Cause they were all born at home. Can you believe it? I'm tellin' you, it just blew my mind. My father's name isn't Royer and my mother's name isn't Stephans. And she tells us this a week before she dies. You talk about a mystery, huh? Man."

"You still gettin' all this, huh? I still can't hear him."

"I'm gettin' it, Mar, I am. So, your sisters are really upset?"

"Hey, Ruth," Gerry said, leaning forward again. "Some other time, okay? Honest to god, it's too depressing."

"Man, who made this kolbassi?" Balzic said. "Before the night's over, don't lemme forget, I gotta find out who made this. There's no gristle in it, absolutely none, it's beautiful."

Somebody tapped Balzic on the shoulder. It was Angie Rascoli. "Mario, you seen Bill?"

"Last I saw him he was headin' for the can. You want me to go find him?"

"No no, that's all right. I'll get his brother, Freddie. Hi ya doin', Mario? Who's sittin' here, can I sit down?"

"Nobody's sittin' there, sit down, sit down."

"God, Mario, he's been drinkin' ever since he quit. He's drunk every day. What am I gonna do? I knew it was gonna be hard, but Jesus, I didn't think it was gonna be drink, drink, drink, all day, all night. He says it's just wine, what am I gettin' so excited about? He's been drunk twice today. He was drunk this mornin' and he slept all afternoon and now he's drunk again. I never saw him drink like this before. What am I 'sposed to do, Mario? You gotta tell me something to do, I don't know what to do. He can't live—nobody can live if they keep on drinkin' like this. Can they? You tell me, I don't know."

"Well look. The first thing we gotta do is make sure he's okay. So where's his brother? I'll go find him, and then we make sure Ras's okay, maybe get him outta here—"

"No no no, Mario, you don't have to do anything now. Please. Sit. Eat, eat. I'll get Freddie, it'll be okay. We'll get him. I just want you to tell me what to do from here on. I mean where do I go? Jesus, do I go to Alcoholics Anonymous or what? Do I take him to a doctor, what do I do?"

"Listen, Ang, I can hardly hear ya, I can hardly hear myself, so I don't think this is the place to be talkin' about this. But I'll tell you what. Lemme think about it, talk to some people, and I'll call ya, okay? If I don't call you tomorrow, then the day after for sure, okay?"

She patted him on the arm and stood. "Thanks, Mario, really, I mean it."

"You need any help or anything, just give me a wave, or holler, okay?"

"What was that about?" Ruth said. "She looked awful."

"Oh man, I don't know. Ras's really juicin', from what she says. She's scared, she don't know what to do. She wants me to tell her. What am I gonna tell her? I said I'd call her. So far, this retirement thing's been a real roller coaster, man. So hey. We havin' any fun yet?"

"Well the food's great. And Royer's story is great, I mean it. It's some story. Think about it, Mar. Think about wakin' up one day and findin' out everything you thought about what your name was and where you were descended from wasn't true?"

"Well there's a lotta that goin' around these days."

"What? What're you talkin' about? You know somebody else this happened to?"

"Nah. No one person, no. It's just that ever since—man, this kolbassi's good—it's just that ever since Rugs Carlucci told me how the rich pricks use the IRS Code to dodge taxes and I found out how Householder and Dunne and Sitko and guys like them set up these foundations to get whatever they want, I been thinkin' that everything I ever knew about this country, about who protects who and why and how, is—to say the least—not what I think it is—or was. I'm glad I'm gettin' out, baby cakes, I really am. 'Cause I don't think I could do it anymore, I really don't. 'Cause if you think it's somethin' 'cause Royer ain't Royer anymore, believe me, Rocksburg's not Rocksburg anymore, not from where I sit. And the part that gets me is, it's all legal. Everything Householder and Dunne and Sitko and guys like that, everything they do is all strictly legal. I mean, once the IRS gives 'em their blessing for an exemption from taxes, hey, they're home free. It's us saps, us schnooks that pay the taxes. And us schnooks—me, guys like me—we protect the bastards. We spend our whole life protectin' 'em—them, their property, everything. And then? Then they invite you to a retirement party and they insult the shit outta you with the oldest dumb cop joke in the world. Honest to god. I couldn't believe that bastard Dunne was tellin' that joke. And then he gives me a lecture about what happened to my sense of humor."

"Dunne told a joke? What joke?"

"Ah forget about it. Some other time maybe. Right now, I need wine. We need wine. Somebody needs to get us about a case over here or somethin'. I'm gonna go see about that. Be right back."

Getting to the bar was easy, now that most people were lining up to get to the buffet. He found his daughters and Valcanas still seated where they'd been, and he told them about the food, especially the kolbassi. "Some real artists at work there," he said.

One of the half dozen bartenders—none of whom Balzic knew—approached at his beckoning and listened as he asked for wine.

"Hey, Tony," the bartender said over his shoulder, "didn't you put no wine on the front table. Mr. Muscotti told us keep wine on the front table. Didn't you do it? Oh man, he's gonna be so pissed—hey, right away, Chief, I'm sorry. Go sit down, we'll take care of it. I'm real sorry."

Balzic shrugged. "Relax, relax, it's no big deal. We just need some wine over there."

"So when do the speeches start?" Valcanas said.

"You're asking the wrong guy. Stramsky promoted the whole thing, so whatever he set up. I don't know about you, but I really hope there's not a lotta speechifyin'. Lookin' at the size of that food line, it's gonna be at least a half hour before anybody says anything. Listen, you guys all right, huh? If you are, I'm goin' back and finish eatin'."

"We're fine, Daddy," Marie said. "Mr. Valcanas is tellin' us things."

"About a certain police chief?" Emily said, making a face and sticking out her tongue.

"About his dark side?" Marie said, making an even bigger face.

"Dark side, yeah, right. Catch you later."

He was almost back to the table when he caught sight of Rascoli being helped out of the men's room with his arms wrapped around the shoulders of two men who bore him a strong familial resemblance. He was singing something unintelligible and shaking his head.

Balzic caught up with them just outside the coatroom door.

"You guys need any help?"

"Nah, uh-uh, we're okay," said the older of the two. "Billy just needs to go lay down someplace, that's all. We're all right."

"Hey, Muddio," Rascoli said, eyes rolling, "'ese two guys? I never seen 'em before . . . tryin'a kidnap me . . . no shit."

"Nobody asks me nothin'," said the younger, "but I think some guys ain't 'sposed to retire, and I think he's one of 'em. Been drunk every day since he quit. Every day I stop by the house, he's swacko. Why'd you make him retire, huh? He's still young."

"Wait a minute," Balzic said. "I didn't make anybody do anything. I was ordered to lay people off. These guys volunteered to retire. I don't know where you got this story that I made 'em do anything, but it's bullshit and you can stop sayin' it right now."

"Don't pay no 'tention to him, Muddio . . . Muddddd-eeee-ooo. Paisannnnn. He's a kid . . . don't know nothin' . . . noth-eeeeng."

"Was he wearin' a coat? Huh? What kinda coat was he wearin'?"

"Aw the hell with the coat, we ain't gonna find his coat in here. C'mon, let's get outta here, get him home. Where's Angie? You seen her? Hey, Balzic, you see his wife, tell her we took him home. I don't know where the hell she went, she was right behind us."

"I'll tell her, I'll tell her. Was she drivin'?"

The older brother looked at the younger. "Was she drivin'? Lou?"

"Whatta you askin' me for? Since when you wanna know what I know, huh?"

"Aw stop cryin', ya little shit, or I'm gonna smack you one. Was she drivin' or not, yes or no, and don't gimme no shit."

"Hey. Go fuck yourself. You take him home, I don't have to listen to this shit." The younger brother pulled himself free from supporting his brother, who immediately sagged and went to one knee and began to sing, "When da moon . . . hits your eye . . . like a big-a pizza pie . . . dat's ah-moh-rayyyyyy."

"Hey! Louie! You little shit, where you goin'? I can't do this by myself—"

"You shoulda thought of that before. Fuck you. I got better things to do than this bullshit." He thumbed his nose at his older brother and disappeared out the coatroom door.

Balzic reached down and tried to haul Rascoli up by his other arm, saying, "C'mon, Ras, get up, Ras, you gotta give us a little push-up here, you weigh too much to just stay down there."

"Two . . . pur-pull sha-dozzze . . . in da snow," Rascoli sang.

"Hey, Ras, you don't stop singin' that song right now, I'm

gonna throw some coats on ya and let you sleep it off right here."

"Hey, uh, Balzic, you mind? Huh? If you ain't gonna help me then just get outta here, okay?"

"I'll help ya, I'll help ya. I just hate that song, that's all. Come on, Ras! You gotta push up on your leg there, c'mon, get your foot under ya."

Rascoli struggled to his feet with Balzic and his brother's help and then turned to his brother and kissed him and then turned to Balzic and kissed him. "I love youse guys . . . no shit. But don't get pissed at Louie. Just a kid. Where we goin'? Goin' a party, huh? Retire . . . retire party."

"C'mon, Bill. One foot in front of the other, c'mon. And stop with that shit about Louie's a kid. He's forty-four for crissake."

"I always wondered what it would be like to have brothers," Balzic said, trying to keep his balance under Rascoli's wobbling weight. "Listenin' to you guys, I'm thinkin' I didn't miss anything."

"Believe me," the other brother said, "between these two, it's a wonder I ain't nuts."

"You the middle one? Huh? What's your name? How come I never met you before?"

"I'm Fred. 'Cause I ain't lived around here for thirty years. Watchit, there's a step down, Bill."

They made it to the sidewalk finally. The icy air stung Balzic's nostrils. People were still coming, trying to get around them to get in. Some of them hesitated to ponder the scene, others to greet Balzic. Bill Rascoli shivered suddenly and seemed to straighten up, taking several deep breaths. Balzic knew it was just the air.

"So what're we gonna do now, huh?" Fred Rascoli said. "My car's least two blocks from here. How 'bout you stay here with him and I'll go get the car, whatta you say?"

"Hold it," Balzic said, spotting a black-and-white coming around the corner. "You got him? Hold him." He stepped out into the street and waved and motioned for the cruiser to approach.

Officer Harry Lynch was behind the wheel. He rolled down the window and grinned up at Balzic. "Well if it ain't the party boy himself. So what's happening, Mario, huh? Too much party for ya or what?"

"Too much for Ras. How 'bout takin' him home, makin' sure he gets inside, gets into bed, you know. His brother'll go with you."

"Did he throw up yet? Huh? 'Cause if he didn't, he better save it till he gets home. I got three more hours to go, and I ain't gonna spend even five seconds cleanin' up party puke."

"C'mon, Harry, for crissake. If he throws up, just get another vehicle, what the fuck."

"They're all out, that's what the fuck. They're all on the road. So if he blows oats I'm gonna have to clean it up—"

"'Blows oats'? What the hell's that mean?"

"Yeah. Blows oats. That's what my kid says when people puke. He says they're blowing oats. Don't ask me, what do I know. C'mon, get him in here. Here, I got some bags under the seat—if nobody took 'em. At least stick a bag under his face. Who's that with him?"

"His brother. Fred."

Balzic went back to the sidewalk where the Rascoli brothers were arguing about their younger brother. Balzic introduced Lynch to Fred Rascoli and then got out of the way while the two of them labored to get Bill Rascoli into the backseat. Lynch rummaged around under the front seat and came out with a bunch of wadded-up plastic grocery bags.

"Here," Lynch said, separating the bags and handing one to Fred Rascoli. "Keep this under his chin. He starts heavin', make sure he does it in there, you hear? I'm not jokin'. He misses the bag, you're cleanin' it up, not me, you hear?"

"Yeah I hear, I hear."

"So, Mario, this thing still gonna be goin' on when I get off, huh? Whatta you think?"

"Hey, nobody's even made a speech yet. The band's not set up either. It'll still be goin' on. Hey, thanks, Harry."

"For what?"

"For takin' Ras home."

Lynch snorted. "He's the third one tonight already. I been lucky so far. But I know I'm pushin' my luck. These grocery bags? I'm tellin' ya, they're the best thing I ever thought of this time of year. Save ya a ton of grief. I'll see ya later. Just save some party for me, okay?"

"There's plenty, believe me." Balzic waved and watched them drive off, Bill Rascoli singing incoherently, his head nodding from side to side in the backseat.

Balzic went back inside in time to hear somebody tapping insistently on a glass. At the head table, Father Marrazzo was standing behind a podium that had not been there when Balzic left to assist with Rascoli. The priest was alternately speaking into a dead microphone and holding a tumbler aloft and tapping it with a spoon. He spotted Balzic and motioned for him to reclaim his seat.

The priest wasn't having much luck getting everybody to quiet down. He kept speaking into the dead microphone and then looking around to see if anybody was trying to get it to work. In the meantime, he kept tapping on the glass. After about a minute of tapping, he turned and shrugged at Balzic and then shouted until veins were bulging in his neck, "OUR FATHER WHO ART IN HEAVEN . . ."

The crowd fell immediately into an edgy silence.

Marrazzo smiled triumphantly and said into the microphone, which came live at that moment, "That's for all the people who think prayer has no power. Believe me, ladies and gentlemen, when six little words can get this many people to stop talking—that's power."

The silence softened as a wave of relieved laughter swept over the room.

"So, while I have your attention," the priest went on, "let me say first that I am here not as pastor of St. Malachy Parish, but as honorary chairman and master of ceremonies of this dinner. Let me also say that for those of you still eating and for those who're still in line, if you have food in front of you or when you get it in front of you, eat, for heaven's sake. Over the years I've learned there's no good time to interrupt a meal when food is served buffet style, so if you have something to say you'd better say it when you're ready because nobody else is. So, please, eat, eat. Just don't talk.

"We're gathered here tonight to celebrate four men, four men whose years of police service taken together stagger the imagination. A hundred and twenty-five years of service. A hundred and twenty-five years! I won't bore you with flowery praise about their dedication, their loyalty, their unselfishness, their decency, their honor, their bravery—"

Stramsky jumped to his feet and folded his hands in prayer and called out, "Oh please, Father, bore us, bore us!"

"Victor," Marrazzo said, shaking his finger at Stramsky, "you promised. You promised I would get all the laughs."

Stramsky shrugged amidst the howls of laughter and bowed toward the priest and turned up his palms as though to say, It's all yours.

The priest waited until the room was silent again and then, with his straightest face, said, "Ladies and gentlemen, I assure you, never in the history of police work was there a plea bargain to equal my bargaining with that man over who would get the laughs. But seriously, ladies and gentlemen . . ."

The hall exploded with laughter. Stramsky threw back his head and laughed so hard he lost his balance and nearly fell over backward in his chair. The priest, beaming, turned to Balzic and nodded many times, brows raised, as though to say, Well, pretty good so far, eh?

As the crowd fell silent again, Marrazzo looked around and grew pensive. "I'm going to be very serious now, ladies and gentlemen. Despite Sergeant Stramsky's pleas for me to bore him with praise, I assure you that nothing I could say here tonight would, or could, equal the respect, admiration, and affection shown by the people of Rocksburg when word began to spread that there was to be this celebration in honor of these men's retirement from active duty. So let me begin."

Marrazzo reached into his pocket and brought out a small sheet of paper. He adjusted his glasses and said, "First, the Sons of Italy donated this hall, they waived their rental fee—don't applaud, please. This list is not very long but I implore you to wait until I've finished. Thank you.

"Every bottle of wine, every bottle of whiskey, every keg of beer, every can of soft drinks, every cup of coffee, every morsel of food on that glorious buffet was paid for by the citizens of Rocksburg. And they did it with the proceeds from spaghetti dinners, pirogi sales, cake sales, raffles, and bingos. And Julie Richards, who arranged the preparation of this feast, refused to accept payment for her labor.

"To the men we celebrate tonight, to Mario Balzic, to Victor Stramsky, to William Rascoli, to Joseph Royanawicz, there is nothing I could say now that could ever match this remarkable outpouring of feelings you, the people of Rocksburg, demonstrated, over and over again, as you gave your money, your labor, your time so these four gentlemen would have a night to remember as long as they live. And to ensure that we all have a record of this generous goodwill, the Emory Printing Company has graciously agreed to publish a book containing the names and the contribution of every person, company, business, church, or fraternal organization who gave their support to make this celebration possible. And Emory Printing has promised to sell the book, when it becomes available, at a price necessary only to cover the cost of materials.

"So, guests of honor, I am convinced that when you see the number of names in this book, when it's eventually assembled, you will be astounded, as I was, by the depth and breadth of the esteem in which you are held by this community, and I think even Sergeant Stramsky will see that there was no need for me to bore you with my praise.

"I wish now to offer a toast. Please stand and join me in raising your glasses and your hearts. To Chief Mario Balzic, to Sgt. Victor Stramsky, to Sgt. William Rascoli, to Sgt. Joseph Royanawicz, you were there when we needed you. Wherever you go, the gratitude of the people of Rocksburg goes with you."

The crowd rose amid shouts of "Here, here" and joined the toast.

Balzic had to bite his lower lip to keep from sobbing. He squeezed Ruth's shoulders so hard she squirmed around and looked up at him. Before she could say anything, he bent down and kissed her. When they pulled apart, they were both crying. "Better enjoy this, Mar. 'Cause the hard part's just starting."

"I know," he said. "I know." But he knew that he didn't.

Father Marrazzo cleared his throat and waited until everybody sat back down. "When we were making plans for this celebration, many people came to the committee and to me to ask if they could speak here tonight, to tell some story, some anecdote, some personal recollection about how one of these men touched their lives in some way. Seriously. I was amazed by the number of people who wanted to do this. Getting people to speak in public—well, somebody said once that it's easier to get men to charge a machine-gun nest than it is to get them to stand up and say a few words in public. Thirty-seven people! Honestly, thirty-seven people wanted to speak here tonight. The people on the committee were at a loss. They didn't know what to do. I remember somebody saying that's more people than when they give away the Oscars in Hollywood— and we all know how long that show lasts every year.

"So the hardest part of the committee's work, really, the very hardest work, was deciding who we would let speak. And because nobody wanted to offend anybody by having to notify them that they wouldn't be allowed to speak, because there just wasn't enough time, what it came down to was, what was finally decided, was to let one person speak for them all. So we let the thirty-seven people vote. We said, pick one person, one person you think best represents you to say what you would want to be said—and somebody who understands the virtue of brevity.

"Ladies and gentlemen, I give you the overwhelming choice of the thirty-seven people who wanted to speak. I give you the mayor of Rocksburg, Mr. Kenneth Strohn."

Immediately, there erupted applause and cheering and loud whistling from people who jumped to their feet and then found themselves standing shoulder-to-shoulder with people equally vehement with their boos, groans, and catcalls.

Strohn, who had not been seated at the front table, appeared at the podium from somewhere on the opposite side of the room. He looked around the room, smiling faintly, waiting with hands in the coat pockets of his navy-blue suit. He made no effort to silence the crowd, instead turning to Balzic and Royanawicz and Stramsky in turn and giving each a thumbs-up sign. At last, the crowd tired of trying to outdo each other in expressing their emotions about the outgoing mayor; they resumed their seats, and, except for the occasional clattering of dinnerware and glasses, the room was quiet.

"Guests of honor, ladies and gentleman, Father Marrazzo," the mayor began. He spoke extemporaneously; he had no notes.

"We're here tonight to honor and celebrate the careers of four police officers. Before I became mayor eight years ago, I have to confess to you now, I was almost pathetically ignorant about the true nature of police work. I'm sorry to say that I was, like too many people in our society, far too greatly influenced by the entertainment industry about just what police work involved. I believed what I'd seen in movie theaters and on television. I believed about the police what I had been led to believe by an industry that is far more interested in getting your leisure dollars than it is in presenting any accurate portrayal of what police work actually involves.

"To give you one illustration of my greatest ignorance about the police, I confess, I was, like many people in our society, convinced that plea bargaining with criminals was not only unnecessary but that it had totally corrupted our judicial system. I remember watching the first plea bargain I ever saw with horror. I was literally horrified, as I watched and listened to what went on. Chief Balzic was one of the police officers directly involved in that plea bargain, as was an assistant United States attorney, and I remember the great pains both of them took trying to make me understand what I was seeing, and hearing. What I eventually came to understand was that one of the great myths perpetrated by the entertainment industry—that crimes are solved—is just that. A myth. What I started to learn that night was that plea bargains are the cornerstone, the heart and soul, of justice in our society. Because—and this is the lesson taught to me by Chief Balzic not once but many times over the years—the simple fact is that without corroborating evidence from a participant in a crime, a crime is almost impossible to prosecute. Oh it happens every now and then; I'm not going to say it never happens. But, in most cases, the only way the courts will ever hear corroborating evidence is because one of the participants in a crime has been offered a reduced sentence in return for his guilty plea and for his testimony against the other participants. And that's what is known as a plea bargain. And, ladies and gentlemen, what I learned from Chief Balzic over the years is that without plea bargains, our judicial system would collapse. That's not a very dramatic story, I know. But it was the most important lesson in civics I ever learned.

"As many of you know, I'm in the insurance business, have been all my life. I wouldn't dare to guess how much money I've helped to distribute in damage claims, for loss of life, loss of property, injury, pain, suffering. But until I became mayor, I had never seen an automobile accident. Incredible as that sounds, I'd never seen one. Don't ask me how I'd managed to avoid that in my life, but I had. Within two months on the job as mayor, I saw my first auto accident. I'm certainly not going to ruin your dinner now by telling you what I saw. What I do want to say is that, while I watched Sgt. Vic Stramsky take charge of that terrible scene that night, it was driven home to me just how much we expect from our police officers every day.

"A day or so later, Sergeant Stramsky told me that he'd been fighting to control his emotions just as hard as I had, but you would never have known it to watch him taking charge of the whole scene, everybody, firemen, ambulance personnel, witnesses, relatives, notifying the next of kin. And he did it after his shift was over; he'd been on his way home; he'd already put in a day's work. Like me, he'd come upon that traffic accident just because he happened to be driving on that street. He put in another twelve hours—after he'd already put in eight—and he was back on duty the next day at the time he was supposed to be back on duty.

"Stramsky didn't even get a letter of commendation for that. When I approached Chief Balzic to ask whether Stramsky should get a letter of commendation, the chief looked at me, and said—I'll never forget this—he said, 'What for? He was only doing what he was supposed to do.'

"It was Sgt. Joe Royer—Royanawicz—while he was also

off duty, who showed me another misconception I had about police work. I happened to be driving through the Flats one day about a month after I'd seen Stramsky in action at that accident, and I came upon Royer and two women who were punching and kicking and screaming at each other in the middle of Washington Street. I learned later that they were mother and daughter. Mother and daughter. Both of them were covered with blood. They had been fighting in their apartment and the neighbors called the police and Royer responded because he was going home and he happened to be the closest officer to the scene and when he arrived they had moved out onto the street.

"Ladies and gentlemen, I give you my word, that was one of the most violent fights I've ever seen in my life—no John Wayne, no Clint Eastwood, no dope dealers, no Hell's Angels, no Mafia. It was a mother and her daughter, and it was incredibly violent. It was awful, and there was Royer trying to get it stopped. And he did. Don't ask me how he did, I can't tell you. But the next day in the paper, I couldn't find any mention of it. Not a word. When I asked Royer about it, he just shrugged and laughed. He said that neither the mother nor the daughter wanted to press charges, so as far as he was concerned that was the end of it. But for about one minute—because it was over that fast—for about one minute I gained a vastly different perspective of what police officers routinely contend with every day. Routinely contend with. That, ladies and gentlemen, is the most charged statement I can make tonight. It was and is the most disconcerting thing I learned about police work in all my years as mayor.

"Before I became mayor I had no idea that police officers routinely contend with situations in the streets every day that require their immediate judgment and action. But unlike judges, juries, appeals court judges, and ultimately supreme court judges on both the state and federal level, police officers don't get a chance to debate for days and weeks about those situations. They don't get a chance to disagree about what should have been done or what they might have done. They have to do something. Right now. Decisions from the appellant courts come down two, three, four, five, six years after the fact, decisions where the votes are two to one, three to two, five to four on how a police officer should have acted, on what he should have done or not done, on what he should have said and when he should have said it. We, you, me, all of us, we expect our police officers to know the right thing to do—and to do it without hesitation. We expect them to leave their homes every day and to protect us and our property and to do so with the clarity of mind and precision of thought that we do not expect from a justice of the Supreme Court of the United States. We give the justices of our highest courts the luxury of debating the issues and the time to carry on the debate. Their clerks research the law for them. But we, you and me, we not only expect our police officers to be wiser, shrewder, more intelligent, more knowledgeable about the nuances of the law, ladies and gentlemen, we require it! We demand that our police officers know as much law as a high court judge—but we never send them to law school. We demand that our police officers carry out their duties without hesitation when they are confronted by situations of such extreme confusion in the midst of extreme violence that not even Solomon himself could untangle them. And yet, some of these situations are so commonplace, so routine, so ordinary they do not even attract passing attention from our local newspaper.

"After that fight between the mother and her daughter, I searched the paper the next day and discovered that no one at the paper thought that fight was worthy of three paragraphs, not even on the last page of the paper. I'm not criticizing the people at the paper. What I am saying is that what confronted Royer in the middle of Washington Street that day was so routine, so ordinary, so commonplace, that nobody at the paper thought it was newsworthy. But as sure as I'm standing here, I tell you that if Sergeant Royer had not been there, one of those two women, mother or daughter, would have killed the other. Their rage, their fury, their contempt for each other at that moment was palpable.

"Royer didn't get a letter of commendation for that either. Same reason, said Chief Balzic. 'What for? He was only doing what he gets paid to do.'

"And now I'd like to tell you what I learned from Sgt.

William Rascoli. It was an altogether different kind of lesson. Rascoli and I both happened to be in the emergency room of Conemaugh General for different reasons when a man was brought in by Mutual Aid Ambulance. The back of his head was covered with dried blood, there was a bruise over his whole upper back, and he was babbling as though the head wound had destroyed his ability to speak. He had no identification. He'd been found wandering in his pajama bottoms in an alley in the Flats near the old elementary school there. Rascoli took it upon himself, on his own time, to find out that the man had apparently had a stroke while he was shaving, fell backwards against his bathtub, and then after he'd regained consciousness had managed to get out of his apartment. If Rascoli had not done that work, on his own time mind you, that man's relatives, who lived in another state, might never have known what had happened to him, and the state, us, you and me, might have had to assume responsibility for that man's care. That never made the paper either. And Rascoli never received a letter of commendation, but if it hadn't been for his work, his intelligence, and his perseverance, the story would have had a far different end.

"Well, ladies and gentlemen, that's just a little of what I learned from these men and that's just a very little of what they faced, these four policemen, in their long years of service. And for that service, we are all grateful. It is my happy task now to speak for the people of this city, the people Father Marrazzo spoke about so eloquently moments ago. It is my happy task to say to these four officers that the people of Rocksburg believe you have all earned some rest and relaxation, and that they have furthermore put their money where their mouths are. In addition to the generosity Father Marrazzo has already spoken of, I now have the great pleasure to tell you four gentlemen that the citizens of Rocksburg have collected enough money to send you all on a six-day, five-night vacation with all expenses paid for two to the destination of your choice—as long as it's in Clearwater Beach, Florida, as long as it's in the off-season, as long as you fly USAir, and as long as you stay at the Sand Key Radisson Hotel."

Great gasps of joyful surprise and excited laughter rumbled

over the room. Then the crowd rose and began to applaud, and they applauded and cheered and whistled for nearly a minute.

Strohn waved his hands downward until he finally got them to stop and sit down again.

"Father Marrazzo wanted me to be sure to say that all the details of these vacations including a full accounting will be in the book published by Emory Printing, and that these vacations would not have been possible without the expertise and hard work of Mike Valenti of Valenti Travel Agency. So from the people of Rocksburg to you, Chief Balzic, and to you, Sergeants Stramsky, Royanawicz, and Rascoli, happy vacation. You've earned it. Thank you all."

Before anybody else could react, Stramsky jumped to his feet and bellowed, "Thank you! Thank you very much! I'm speakin' for all my friends here when I say we thank you all very much. We'll never forget this! Never! But now . . . now, it's time to do the happiest dancin' there is, 'cause we're gonna pol-kaaaaaa! We're gonna polka until the sun comes up or our legs fall off, whichever comes first!"

And with that, the Polka Brothers' drummer counted out four beats on his sticks and the band, accordion, clarinet, bass, drums, and a singer, began to play and sing:

"Roll out the barrel,
We'll have a barrel of fun.
Roll out the barrel,
We'll have the blues on the run."

Balzic shook his head and groaned to Ruth, "Would you listen to what Stramsky thinks is the Polka Brothers know some blues. Do you believe it?"

"Oh quit your bellyachin' and let's do it," she said, pulling him out onto the floor. "There'll never be another night like this one. Not for us. So just do it. Just dance!"

And they did. Until the sun came up.